GLASS FLOWER

GLASS FLOWER

DAVID PROCACCINO

atmosphere press

Published by Atmosphere Press

Cover design by Kevin Stone

davidprocaccino.com

atmospherepress.com

For my children

1

Is That All There Is?

That song, that weird blonde singing from the transistor of Malory's brain. He can't get her out of his head, can't get Honey out of his head. Stupid pop tunes. They blow out Malory's eardrums. Pop, pop, and he hears only bass. War sucks away the treble, and blood makes sideburns down his cheeks, curving to his lips, salty like the sea. The helicopter's cabin flashes, whirligig sparks, orange and yellow explosions.

Operation Arc Light? Crazy to think that. No B-52s in Cambodia. Crazy, and yet. Something just hit him. A tearing. Not good. This is the moment you're supposed to feel different, right? Everything should pass before your eyes, but Malory thinks of songs, damned songs, always jingling on AM Stereo 99. *More MUUU-sick, Double-You Eye Be Gee, Filladelpheeahh!*

Eight thousand, eight hundred miles away, records are spinning, just like Malory. Remember the dead air when the overnight DJ had to pee and go smoke dope? The station played battle songs on the Fourth of July. A week later, Maria and Honey waved goodbye to him at midnight, still ninety degrees on the tarmac. Strange that both of them were there. Vietnam had come for its due, remember? *Mine eyes have seen the glory,* and falling through, he sees the jungle canopy, the Huey's belly ripped away. *He's got the whole world in his hands; he's got the whole wide world in his hands.*

He's got Scotty's leg, part of it, in his hands, or maybe a piece of loin or chuck. The copilot's dead, and George is grabbing the cyclic, but when is recess, and when's the rain going to stop? The rotor bisects the cockpit, and a thousandth of a second later, George. Now THIS is the way to fly, top-down, like the Tropical Turquoise '64 ½ Mustang sailing down Barker's Mill Road in Glenwyth, Pennsylvania. *Hey, Dad! Look at my somersaults. Look!* Ruthie. She was always so happy. Not always. Not when Malory was leaving.

Never again. This is his final departure. Now it's just him and the trees. How can their leaves be so green? Shouldn't they call it Agent Green? Army stupidity, spray the trees to expose NVA, but the leaves aren't disappearing. They're so bright that he can drink them and live forever. No one can kill Malory. Red and green, midnight Mass, nineteen-forty-something, mother and son alone in the pew, so nervous he could wet his pants. She brought him downstairs after Communion to spare him another humiliation. Hadn't they had enough already? She looked old even then, her face already caving. *Don't worry, Jimmy. I didn't forget. The shotgun's right there, right there under the tree.* A twelve-gauge for a boy. She knew where he was headed.

Malory wants Ruthie to do another somersault. It's all so green! And then that sinking feeling comes up his throat. Soon he'll be part of the jungle, the trees, the trees, all his life he's been searching for trees such as these. First layer, second layer, boughs ramming the leftovers of the cabin. It's his own private forest, along with glass and bone for Christmas ornaments. But who needs a garden when you can have a tree in your own skull?

Everything spins like a waning world, and then the Huey can't somersault anymore. Malory rests upside down. His left arm stings, but thank God he writes thank-you notes with his right. He wipes his eyes and sees, because they still work, that it's just a mild burn. The arm's still there, good, because he throws with his left, always ambivalent, and what good's a father who can't play baseball if Maria gives him a son? Malory's legs, those oaks that got him into Penn when Sister Michael Frederick nearly flunked him in physics because his father dumped her in 1935 when she still dreamed of men, his legs are still there. He can move them, and he doesn't see any bone, at least not his own. He still has his gun, the M1911, another Christmas gift but from the Frankford Arsenal. Everything works, and it's almost like the Huey burst its guts to accommodate sightseeing. How many people visit Cambodia like this?

Malory unbuckles the harness. He flips down, turns himself right side up, and falls to the heaving jungle floor. His arm's fine but not his flank. His vaporized uniform has burned off the skin beneath, now crusty like an overdone pizza. His crackled dermis doesn't hurt, at least not yet, but it smells, maybe like ruined leather. Then he smells something else: Jet Propellant 4. It's like the kerosene that kept Malory and his mother from freezing to death in Lehighton, at least when she could pay the fuel dealer. He loved that sweet odor because it meant comfort. It meant life, but what does it mean now?

He runs, then thinks: *They're coming, but which they?* Malory spent every summer before the war dipped in Pennsylvania humidity, but those days were a mere preview. Water fills his lungs, and *Raindrops Keep Fallin' On My Head.* But where's the pitter-patter? Come to think of it, there's no sound at all, and even the bass is gone. He wipes his cheeks and traces the blood to his ears.

How will he hear them? Malory never could listen, even when both of his eardrums were intact. When he was just a psychiatrist, he loved all those voices, the accents of Philadelphia, Lehighton, and Swedesboro speaking fear, lust, anger, and loneliness. Now he hears the pumping of his carotid arteries, not much longer probably.

Malory finds a rock. It's a crappy foxhole, but then he sees a tangle of brush, and he cuts it, a lot of it. His blood dapples the harvest like abstract art, a picture titled *Dying Dog*, but if they get that close to notice, he's Charlie's regardless. Still, survival is a reflex. So, he covers himself with rubber tree branches. And he waits. Nothing. Longer. Something. Vietnamese. The staccato phrases are distinct and growing more so, despite the wreckage of his tympanic membranes. It's like the entire NVA has come for Malory.

He has his sidearm's muzzle pressed like a teddy bear to his chest, and the safety's off. No one will know when Malory pulls the trigger. Well, almost no one. If that fails, there's always his knife. But then Sister Michael Frederick stands aloft, and why did the sisters always have male names? She lectures into the ether about the seven deadly sins, and Malory wants to tell her that angels never visited Cambodia. She has always been the embodiment of pain. She nearly ruined his life with that C- in physics. Now she's standing there in the jungle, in full habit, the most feared sister at Our Lady of Precious Blood. That was the school's name, no joke. She refereed cross-country meets, whistle and rosary tangled on her cloistered neck. *Eloi, eloi, lama sabachthani.* Screw that. He lifts the gun and waits. He sees one NVA coming into view, AK-47 hanging limp at his side. The man's looking at a small something, a map maybe. Bad idea. Wait, it's a boy.

This was all Malory's choice. He didn't have to be here. He could have joined the Coast Guard, Maria's wish. Damned Santoni. He was the one who had to be impressed, and Malory will impress, with the gold star in Maria's window as Santoni passes by on the way to the Glenwyth Cricket Club. And Honey? Damned Honey.

It isn't the whole NVA, just one. Malory shakes himself. This is no dream. It's just Cain and Abel; quite real Abel is, smiling even. *Like To Get To Know You.* Easy. Unseen, from the rear, Malory will push him down and stab his back through the left, fifth intercostal space, just like he learned at Fort Sam.

The Huey explodes, and the boy turns to look, AK-47 still slung at his side. He can't be more than seventeen, acne instead of stubble, Ruthie's prom date in a better world. Malory lunges, knocks him down, and rams the knife into the boy's heart, popping the balloon. Then Malory grabs the boy's slender neck, squeezing, squeezing, blood spurting from the blackness behind crooked teeth.

Something falls from the boy's pack. When Malory's done, and it's all over, it's not all over because the thing's a photograph, a black-and-white girl. Malory picks it up, and she doesn't even look like one of them. She looks like Maria.

And then, done with remembering, Malory sees that he is strangling Maria, and she's suffocating. His trembling hands spring from her neck, and Maria heaves, gasping. This is Mrs. Malory, Doctor Malory actually, if it hadn't been for their daughter Ruthie.

Malory's not dreaming. In fact, Maria's punching and kicking him, Sicilian blood in her eyes. He can't say anything. The words are gone. Everything hurts. Then, after a pause, she takes her nails and abrades the part of his abdomen where he used to have no skin. She wants him to remember. Then her head slumps back onto the pillow, and she's crying. After a long time, when he no longer wants to vomit from pain and shame, when he is only numb, he places his hand on her belly, thinking he might feel a kick, but she casts his arm aside and rises. She's already briefed the Santonis about maybe needing the other guest room if the bed proved too tight for her pregnant form, and there she goes.

Alone, Malory wipes the sweat from his face. He walks out the front door and down the lane to the dock. The dinghy is there, and he gets in. Rowing out to the middle of Barnstable Harbor, he takes it all in, from the Sandy Neck lighthouse to the Pilgrim Monument, the sad glow of another day rising from the east.

Malory knows it's all over, and only the thought of ingratitude to his hosts keeps him from drowning.

2

Cotton-mouthed, maybe even still drunk, Dr. James Ashe Malory considers his wife. Somehow Maria sleeps, the already wilting heat gumming her obsidian hair. It's always crowded across the edges of her forehead in that Mediterranean way, like all that hair might take over her face at any moment if she wasn't careful. It was one of the first things that Jim ever noticed about her.

Following the unknown logic of a vanished night, husband and wife have returned to their marital bed. Maria may have even found time to read. *The Man in the Gray Flannel Suit* lies next to her, the twenty-five-cent paperback's spine split down the middle, making two tablets. Reading is all she does anymore, like she's studying for a class on the twentieth-century novel. When Jim touches the pages, they feel damp. Tears?

Sweat. In the strange wake of Hurricane Agnes, a Bermuda high has settled over the East Coast, making Barnstable County as hot as Philadelphia. So much for a vacation. Jim stares at the bedroom window and between its curtains sees his mentor, Dr. Edward Santoni, watering tomato plants from a Campbell's can. The man's head swims in bluish-green, the harbor opening up beyond him. His double-breasted, pinstriped suit from the endless rounds at the Philadelphia State Hospital is gone. Instead, the senior psychiatrist wears a pair of olive trousers and a ribbed tank top. It's 10:00 a.m., and he sips red wine. He's late for his watering.

Maria stirs. Jim lies on the bed and puts his head next to hers. Her eyes flash open and then slide shut. Naked below a maternity camisole, she has gained little weight. She's a full sixteen years older than when she had Ruthie. There was inexorability to that pregnancy, as if nothing could have interrupted the girl's entry into the world, but now Maria's body seems undecided. He notices that tiny wrinkles have appeared around her mouth. Her eyes dart beneath fluttering eyelids.

A half-hour later when he returns from the outdoor shower, already perspiring, Maria smokes a cigarette. She shouldn't do that, he's told her, but habit overwhelms knowledge. Besides, her nerves need calming. Why else would she have married a psychiatrist?

She's also dressed, tidied, and opened the curtains. When he comes to her, she slides away and sits in the room's solitary chair, so small it must have been meant for a child. She will not look at him, but he can see that her Qiana shirtdress places a paisley sun above her navel, above their child. Blue, wavy beams emanate from the dress's core, and a single braid snakes down to her chest.

She looks at the wallpaper, but her head's turn accentuates the tears. "Maybe I should move out," she says. He wants to say that he'll move out, but then there's Ruthie.

She turns back to this madman of a husband, filleting him with her eyes. This reassures him. Anger, he understands.

"You need help," she says.

He moves toward her. "It's over."

"Over? Ever since you've been back, you've acted like it's no big deal, like you've returned from a night at the bowling alley." She's right. There've been no yellow ribbons.

He responds silently. Then, he repeats, pronounces really, "It's over."

"It'll never be over if you can't even admit that it *was.*" Maria puts her head in her hands. "How are you going to help our boy?"

"How do you know it's a boy?"

"How do you know it isn't?" she snaps, and there she is, seventeen years younger, on that freshman-year, blind-date disaster, October 1955. She was a steel reed, looking more like a boy than the buxom German girls he had known in Lehighton. She was different, all right. Those were the plump days of Mamie Eisenhower, when Roger Williams topped the charts with *Autumn Leaves* and Indochina was so irrelevant it had been left to the French. That night, his worst problem was trying to change a flat on a '41 Dodge while Maria Sedara hovered over him, arms folded, like one of the Precious Blood nuns minus the habit.

In those college days before hippies, there was no braid. Instead, she wore her jet-black hair in an elfin bob. It was the "mature" cut that the seventeen-year-old had adopted for her valedictorian speech at the John W. Hallahan Catholic Girls' High School. He can still see her in that tight, pea-green sweater with the ruby elephant brooch above her breast. Despite the all-American costume, Maria resembled an imported food not stocked at most supermarkets. Like the animal in her jeweled pin, she never forgot anything, and she called things as she saw them. Her beauty was brutal, kind and impatient at the same time.

The Luxury Liner—the Dodge's name sounded absurd even then—sat marooned in the narrows of a Saturday night, South Philadelphia intersection. Cars honked, and greasers screamed: *What a yooz doin'?* He inspected the jack and saw that it was bent. Should have known. He borrowed the car from Woody Dixon, whose life was too charmed to have to change tires. The Dodge was

Woody's backup car, used only for emergencies and then with reluctance. When that boy from Glenwyth, a blueblood through and through, drove down Woodland Avenue, it was in his Mercedes gull wing, with his steady, Louisa "Honey" Sharpe, at his side. Miss Sharpe, three years Maria's senior, was Miss Sedara's roommate for a semester at their sorority and the architect of the blind date.

The jack's not going to work, he told Maria.

How do you know it isn't? she shot back. Back then, there were 750 American military advisers in-country. The newspapers still called it Viet Nam, two words, not yet enough blood to stick them together.

"You're right," he says, trying to remember that he should always say that. "It could be a boy."

"It could be." Then, "You could have killed me."

He says nothing.

So Maria gets up, puts on her glasses, stares at him like a vice principal, and goes to the dresser mirror, where she stabs her lips with red.

"I had my own dream," she says. "You were a toreador, but not in Spain. It was Franklin Field, but it wasn't. The seats went miles into the sky, and they were filled with millions of people screaming." She twirls her braid, fingers moving up toward the roots.

"Was there a bull?" he asks.

"Oh, yeah, and it was bleeding." She removes her glasses and slides them into their embroidered sleeve.

He wants to stroke her back and hands, and again feel the girl Maria, palms sweaty even in the cold of an October night. Despite the heat, a muslin scarf now hides her neck. He touches the cloth, wants to pull it off to see the crude outline of his fingers or maybe just a vague redness.

She turns and walks off, saying, "We have to go."

Ten minutes later, they sit with Ed and Natalie Santoni on their slate patio. Even the butter is sweating.

"McGovern? Are they daft?" Natalie holds the rolled newspaper as if about to beat a naughty dog. Santoni's wife is a Democrat but a pragmatist. She's also English, at least formerly. She met her husband during their war when Santoni was stationed in a Sussex manor-turned-interrogation center. During his service, he took tea daily and suffered his only wound in a lawn tennis match.

"McGovern's for 'amnesty, abortion, and acid,'" Maria says.

Santoni frowns. "He flew thirty-five missions. I'm not saying you vote for him, but you can't say that he opposes the war because he's a coward." Maria wanted Jim to join the Coast Guard, and her father, with help from his longtime friend, a South Philadelphia Congressman, had given Jim the chance. He would have been stationed in the city at the foot of Washington Avenue, but then Santoni got involved.

"Nixon will make McGovern look stupid," Maria says, "and make himself look stupid in the process. That's the thing about Nixon. He always does that."

Santoni sips his wine and lights a cigar. It's Cuban, like the embargo never happened. Natalie and her husband used to vacation in Batista's Havana.

"Nixon may be a lot of things," Santoni says, "but he's not stupid."

"It's all relative," Jim adds. "The Democratic National Committee is so dumb it can't even figure out how to lock its own offices. Did you see that in the paper? Anyway, Eagleton will sink McGovern. Who wants a VP who's had ECT?"

Turns out McGovern's boy, Thomas Francis Eagleton, had electroconvulsive therapy or, to the uninitiated, shock treatment. Most people think it's for lunatics only, but while a resident, Jim delivered it to prom queens and bank presidents and everyone in between. It's not just for the insane, but do you really want someone who's had five hundred volts pass through his skull to have his finger on the Bomb?

"Nixon won't need Eagleton's medical chart to win," Santoni says. "He'll pardon Calley before the election."

William Laws Calley. Jim hadn't thought about him in a while. Where was the lieutenant? Leavenworth? Jim had been to Son Tinh after the fact and had heard all about the My Lai murders, although they weren't exactly printed in *Stars and Stripes*. The question was obvious: Why were twenty-two deaths worse than all the others, worse than Scotty's? The answer was clear. There was a right and a wrong way to kill, and if you ever got confused, well, the people who killed correctly would make you an example.

Natalie snatches her husband's cigar from the ashtray and presses it to the patio's slate with the ball of her sandal, like the Virgin Mary stepping on a snake. "Is that strictly necessary?" Natalie asks. "She's pregnant!"

Maria blushes and rifles through her purse monogrammed MSM. She pushes her cigarettes from view and turns to her husband. "Cigars are the least of my worries."

Santoni asks, "Are you two going to go for a swim before you leave?" There's a private beach at the end of the private lane where the Santonis built their house.

"I don't think so," Maria says. "We need to get back by ten to relieve my parents. I don't like them driving at night back to New Jersey."

"You should have brought Ruthie," Natalie says. "She's a gem."

"This was supposed to be our romantic weekend away," Maria says.

Jim considers the Mustang, top still down from last night's drive to Woods Hole. As if buffed with steel wool, the car sits scratched and pathetic in the Cape Cod sun. He was supposed to have a Corvette by now, a convertible, if he was lucky. Growing up,

Jim could no more imagine having a nice car than he could remember when his mother's hair wasn't white and thin, with a bald spot for a crown. There were Packards, Cadillacs, and even Pierce-Arrows in the Lehighton of his youth. But for Ruth Malory, an automobile could never be more than a broken-down piece of crap that took you from a shitty apartment to a shittier job. Jim's father had liked cars, and that said it all.

Santoni asks Jim, "When are you in the office?"

"Tomorrow." Tomorrow. God.

"The answering service called me this morning, and there's a referral. A Harvard kid, some kind of psychotic break, drugs maybe. Father's a bigwig, a cabinet member or lieutenant governor or something." Since Jim has known him, Santoni has been psychiatrist to the stars, charging a hundred dollars an hour, the high fee an undeniable proof of value. Santoni's Italianate nub was no deterrent and may have made him even more beguiling to his mostly Episcopalian patrons, who imagined that psychiatrists had to be at least a little exotic. But not too exotic. That's where Santoni's English wife came in.

Ed downs the rest of his wine. "Maybe you could see him, if you can fit him in."

"That's a good one," Jim says, looking at his wife, the woman he can't support.

"Funds are not an issue," Santoni continues. "It doesn't sound all that interesting, and he's probably not a good psychoanalytic case, not that you're looking for that." Santoni's distaste for ten-year psychotherapies has alienated many in the field and brought him closer to others who find Sigmund Freud a best-forgotten relic.

"I could fit him in," Jim says.

"Here's his number." Ready for the moment, Santoni produces a card.

"Glenwyth?" It's the Pennsylvania town that touches West Philadelphia and shares nothing with it but a border. The Santonis have made it to Glenwyth, and so have the Malorys, just barely.

"Old Glenwyth," Ed says, "and I mean very old Glenwyth."

"So, what's the story?" Jim asks, eyeing Maria and knowing she wonders how they'll pay for their next gallon of milk.

"He was doing a prayer dance or something on the seventeenth hole of the Glenwyth Golf Club. Spent a month at the Institute and then was discharged to his parents' TV room. There's only one catch. Parents say he won't leave the house. You'd have to, at least at first, do house calls. It's quite a house. Also, the parents are in Bermuda. Their attorney was the one who called."

Bermuda. Jim will never get there. But he never thought he'd get to Vietnam either. He remembers the rubber plantation workers and their families, lined up in the hundreds, waiting for smallpox vaccinations and dental extractions. In his Medcap unit, psychiatrists were dentists, and nurses were dermatologists. Something was better than nothing, the logic went, and so the medical staff took anything. The Huey sits nearby, blade still turning. Which one of your patients would blow your legs off? You never could tell. Neither could you tell if your Huey would make it back to base or find its end under the canopy of a Cambodian forest.

"They'll pay for the travel time, so you basically get two sessions," Santoni explains.

"But I can be anywhere in Glenwyth in under five minutes," Jim says, seeing an ethical trap, another of Santoni's tests.

"They said they'd pay for two sessions, so take the two sessions. They want someone good, and they know the kid's tough."

Maria taps her husband on the shoulder. "Take the two sessions."

"I would agree," Natalie says.

"Think of it like this," Santoni says. "They can pay you or pay it to Uncle Sam. These folks are in the seventy percent bracket, and your fees are tax deductible."

"What's the name?"

"Quinton Graves. As in the Howell-Graves Saw Company, the great-grandfather maybe. I have one in the garage. I'm sure you do too."

Maria gets up from the table, her brunch dishes in hand.

"No, you don't," Natalie says. "You have a long drive."

"Anything else I should know?" Jim asks, sweat already soaking his shirt.

"Just take it easy. It's not like you're back in Vietnam."

~

Jim and Maria make it to New Bedford with the convertible top down. Then the horizon darkens, and the skies pour. He fastens the top, but rain has puddled on the blue vinyl seats, mixing the cabin's air with water. Maria twists her braid, cars pass, and only the thwack of the wipers and the blot of rainwater on the top keeps Jim from edging off the road into sleep.

She says, after an ocean of silence, "I'm going to reapply."

"To what?"

"To medical school!" He should have just yes-deared.

"You mean now?"

"I know it sounds crazy." She turns to the window. The green enormity of Connecticut has begun, far too long to avoid an argument. "My mother could babysit when I'm on the wards." Somehow caught in the sensory brambles of her pregnancy, she winces and squirms beneath her seatbelt, unbuckling it.

"What are you doing?" Jim asks, remembering the twelve-dollar surcharge for the seatbelt. It was, according to the salesman, an optional but essential new safety feature for the intern and his "beautiful wife and daughter."

"It's just too damned tight." She closes her eyes and grits her teeth. "You know, I may still be enrolled."

She was then Maria Sedara Malory, Class of '64 at the Woman's Medical College. They wouldn't take her at Penn when they admitted her husband. Where's her file now? Maybe swimming in a flooded basement or fallen behind a chipped radiator. She made it through the first two years, the basic sciences, with honors, but when she faced her first clinical rotation—general surgery—and the dreaded internship that would follow, she left on a Friday and never returned. Her departure just happened, like the folding of that 1962 summer into fall, and then everything was different.

That autumn, Maria walked Ruthie to and from kindergarten at the Glenwyth Elementary School, and after the final bell, they went to the park for hours, merry-go-rounding and drawing mazes in the sand. It was as if Maria were still a medical student but now on her child-rearing rotation. Facing the forced labor of his own future internship, Jim wasn't disappointed by her choice. Instead of coming home to a sleep-deprived co-resident and a neglected daughter, he found a warm dinner and a beautiful wife in capri pants and curls. All in a house paid for, $12,500 in cash, by her father, the butcher from South Philadelphia.

Her parents had always supported Maria, with both love and money, and when she revealed her decision to quit, they were unstirred. Jim had expected apoplectic phone calls and unintelligible Italian between Maria and her parents. Yes, she could speak it in a pinch. Maria was their only child, after all, and Jim would always be an outsider, not a fleck of Sicily within him. If she had grown unhappy about dropping out, he hadn't noticed. But he doesn't notice much anymore.

"Dr. Muller-Lyer liked me," Maria says, recalling her dean with the Austrian accent, a sort of aged, feminized Captain von Trapp.

"She begged me not to go."

"She might be retired."

"She's not a day over sixty-five."

Sixty-five? Ten years ago, the woman looked more like eighty, like she might have served in the Austro-Hungarian medical corps. The mummified administrator was incensed when she heard the news about Maria, even making an emergency house call to the Malorys' bungalow to re-enroll her star student, by force if necessary. Maria, however, had conveniently managed to be absent, retreating to what was then her parents' weekend place in Swedesboro, New Jersey. Now they live there full time.

"Would your courses still count? And who's going to pay the tuition?"

"My parents, of course, like everything else. Why are you always so negative? You're always such a pessimist." And so ungrateful, she might add. Maria prevented him from flunking physics in college, like he almost had in high school.

"It's just, why didn't you decide before—"

"Before what!" Again flashes the fury of Mount Etna, hidden at the fondue parties and Civic Association meetings. Jim looks at her now-unbuckled seatbelt and gently puffed stomach. "You can't blame me," she says. "I had other things on my mind."

As a physician, Maria could not have hoped to have more than a single child and be taken seriously, especially by her few female colleagues, themselves mostly childless. At age five, Ruthie was already precocious, facile with anecdotes and insights, the desired guest at adult dinner parties. She wasn't always easy, and sometimes gloom welled in her eyes for no reason at all, but she was smart. She was supposed to be enough, but when Maria withdrew from Woman's Medical, there were soon grand plans for a quintet of Ruthies, each more fabulous than the next.

So, with the Cuban Missile Crisis, the fall of 1962 also brought a bonanza of lovemaking, with nothing in the end to show for it. After a year, they both knew there was a problem. Undeterred, Maria read infertility textbooks, queried the experts, and made hundreds of note cards detailing her body temperatures and cervical fluid viscosities, checked by the hour. Her zeal soon collapsed to uncertainty, hope to desperation. *Did you have the mumps? Was there a masturbation problem?* She peppered him with questions, and his semen, collected in Styrofoam cups, was analyzed. In the end, she learned that a peculiar pH abnormality, easily remedied, killed his sperm before they could reach their target. It was almost funny, and by December 1971, Maria was pregnant.

"Why do you even need to be a doctor?" he asks, posing the question more to himself. "It's not like we need the money."

"We need the money. How many patients do you have?"

"A good number," he says.

"Okay, then what if something happened to you?"

"Like what?"

"Like last night," she says.

Wildness smolders in her eyes, a chaos that has always scared him. She bites the cuticle of her right forefinger, and a drop of blood falls to her shirtdress, getting lost in paisley.

"Then why'd you quit?" he asks. She's never offered a plausible explanation. "You would have made it."

"It was just too bright." She pulls off the scarf. Her unmarked skin has forgotten the trauma, and she will probably outlive him anyway. "It was like staring into the sun. When I was cutting cadavers, that was one thing, but when I thought about the real living, dying people, I couldn't do it." There was also the general pall of her anxiety that summer. Maria had been checking locks, making lists, and re-, re-, re-reading paragraphs, the last an especially bad habit for a medical student.

He looks down at his lap and sees Scotty's leg extending from the armrest to the gearshift. "They're still living and dying," Jim says.

"But I'm not scared anymore. Maybe—"

"What?"

"Maybe if I went back and did psychiatry, we could practice together." Maria's smile bursts open and then constricts with caution. She studies her husband, observant as she has always been, waiting for his reaction.

For his part, he daydreams a combination medical practice-*salumeria,* roped soppressata dangling above their heads. He can't blame her. It was her model from the first butcher shop at 22nd and Tasker: mother at the register, father in the back with the knife, and Maria darting in front of the counter, up-selling customers to sirloin when they came for chuck.

"We could," he says. Could. Not strong enough. Across the Mustang's vinyl bench, she's bawling, eyeliner spreading across her face. "What did I say?"

"Nothing." She blows her nose, already clogged with snot. "You didn't have to say anything. I feel sick."

Maria looks to the side of the highway, searching for a place where she might tell him to pull off, but there are no exits.

"You're like a ghost," she says. "Being with you is like grabbing at the air."

He considers this and wonders if she might vomit all over his car, the very same that she washed and pedicured when he was in Vietnam.

"Come on. Let's discuss it."

"No. I know what you think. I'm going to take a nap and wake up in front of our crummy house."

"But you're sick. I'll pull over."

"Throwing up won't help."

Maria grabs a pillow from the backseat, places it between her frame and the passenger door, and dons an eyeshade. She's snoring in minutes. The whir of the tires and thwack of rain on the convertible top makes him want to sleep alongside her. So he pinches himself to stay awake.

She will leave him—maybe not today, maybe not in a year, but she will. She would have already if it weren't for Ruthie. When he came back with a Purple Heart, Maria granted him a grace period for another baby, which will make it even worse when she realizes finally, conclusively, that he really is made of air.

He could crash the Mustang just like Scotty crashed the Huey, but Jim thinks of Ruthie drifting away, and his stomach clenches like one hand squeezing another. Like Washington fleeing Boston, summer of 1776, Jim faces humiliations to the south, but Hessian bivouacs have been replaced by Howard Johnsons. The Connecticut Turnpike makes him feel like nothing more than a fast-sliding bug. If he could claim that he left himself on the Cambodian border, everything would be understandable. The invalid would be excused, the narrative completed, but the war revealed more about Jim than it destroyed.

Using one hand to hold the steering wheel, Jim reaches with the other for Maria. Finding her abdomen, he feels kicking. Maybe he won't leave. Maybe she won't either. As East Lyme turns to Old Saybrook, and West Haven to Milford, Jim finds himself back in West Philadelphia in that red-letter year of 1955. Surrounded by a sea of thin black ties, Maria was one of two women in that hundred-person organic chemistry class, as out of place as the Thai exchange student they used to see on the Woodland Avenue trolley. Jim seemed so sure of himself then, almost obnoxious, his hand darting up like the bell in a hammer-swinging contest.

He hadn't thought much when Maria switched with another student to become his laboratory partner, allowing the two of them three hours together every Thursday afternoon. Decaffeinating coffee beans and making chloroform: These were cheap dates. He talked, and she listened—and listened. Boy, did he talk. When Jim told her that he intended to become a psychiatrist, she almost burst into laughter, and he knows now that she must have worried about her financial future with him.

By the time they had mastered the Diels-Alder Reaction, and the winter displays were up at Wanamaker's, the path was clear. He was a virgin, she was not. When it happened, she wasn't trying to get pregnant. She was most definitely trying *not* to get pregnant, but the word from Dr. Pietrolongo came along with her fall grades—all A's, perfect. Unbelieving in the obstetrician's office, Jim insisted there had to be a mistake. Later, on the way out, he tripped on the man's brownstone stoop and fell into the slushy gutter of South Broad Street.

They were betrothed within the week, his mother's filigree engagement ring with its puny stone offered from bended knee. Pleased by Jim's quivering pilgrimage to Swedesboro, her father enjoyed the affair, as if he were watching a stage drama as plausible as any other. A cancelation at Palumbo's allowed a small ceremony the week after New Year's, and after three days in Atlantic City, Jim found himself in Maria's girlhood bed, another stuffed animal added to her collection.

Ruthie came in August 1956, and the five of them lived in that three-bedroom row house on Roseberry Street through graduation. He got along well with Maria's mother because he intuited Carmela's domestic domination and devoured her *cannoli.* His doing what needed to be done brought him close enough to Maria's father. Angelo and his son-in-law would shoot together in Swedesboro, which, in the last days before the Commodore Barry Bridge, seemed less New Jersey than North Dakota.

The Sedaras considered Jim and Maria children with their own child, and so it was acceptable that they behaved as such. Carmela raised Ruthie during the day, and Jim and his wife filled in as auxiliaries at night between laboratory practicals and calculus problem sets. Maria was usually up anyway. She was a poor sleeper even then. The infant was colicky, like something in her was tuned too tight, but in time, Ruthie commenced the ballistic progress that continued to the present. Initially, Maria suspected that her mother's parenting of the child, assumed to be better than Maria's, somehow engineered Ruthie's achievements. Yet the more she thought about it, the new mother understood and proclaimed that it was genetics and luck. Maria and Jim's best parts fused in Ruthie, but it could have gone the other way.

Jim lowers the driver's window, and a river of humidity flows in. The rain has stopped, and the mile markers have changed. They've almost made it to Port Chester, New York, still in one piece after interminable Connecticut. Looking down at the Byram River, he knows that Ruthie should have come. There would have been fewer arguments. It's always been the three of them, except when he went away. They used to sleep together in that Roseberry Street double bed, surrounded by Maria's girlhood doll collection looking down at the new husband and wife with their own real baby. He was always worried that he would roll over and smother Ruthie, but Maria, nervous as she was about everything, never seemed to care. She wore white gloves in those days and so, as a child, did Ruthie. It was all so much cleaner back then, but white gloves would look strange with the psychedelicized fashions of today.

And now Maria wants to go back to medical school? It's hard enough for a woman to get in the first time and so much more so for a dropout to return. The original departure had been impulsive, and so, readmitted, why wouldn't she leave again, especially with a new infant? The previous flight had come after a random request from Ruthie that her father bake her cupcakes for a school party. The appeal hadn't itself been the trigger for Maria's quitting. He would later learn that what Maria couldn't stand was the usual and customary way her husband acquiesced and mixed the batter. Work and motherhood—there was no longer any point in trying to have both. She would just be a plain old mom, like Jackie Kennedy and all of Maria's friends who really did wear pillbox hats in those days. There was one problem. In 1972, hats were out, and bell bottoms were in, but how would the outcome be any different?

In a sort of petition, he says to her, "I love you."

She jerks awake and yawns. "Enough to choke the life out of me?"

Jim should explain, tell her about the other combat veterans who have strangled their own wives. He could ask for forgiveness, but there is only the strum of the Mustang's tires on the New England Thruway. Any minute now, the Ford may break down and leave them stranded, but if his marriage and car are doomed, there's still his daughter.

"It wasn't you," he says.

"Then who was it? I know, you can't tell me," she says, arousing. "You'll never tell me."

"I'm worried about Ruthie."

"And you change the subject. She's a straight-A student, she never gets in trouble—"

"That's not what I mean." He wants to say that for all her promise, Ruthie is just like him; that part of him wanted to go on those Medcap missions to Cambodia; that he's no different from William Laws Calley; that he can see that same hunger in his daughter; that he killed a man.

"Forget it," he says.

"Fine. Forget it, or maybe you can talk to the great Dr. Santoni when his majesty returns to Oakmont." Maria's talking about the Santonis' main residence, a prolix Tudor on two level acres that has a name and seems bigger with each of Jim's visits.

"I suppose."

"Or you can save the money you pay him to discuss me and all your problems, and pay me instead."

"You'd make a good psychiatrist," Jim says.

"Hardly. You'd actually talk to a good psychiatrist."

In the fall of 1956, with the five of them wedged into that house on Roseberry Street, there were similar comments. When Maria returned from classes to see her baby at night, she felt every bit the teen mom that she almost was. She was only nineteen, mortifying for a girl with a head on her shoulders. Not used to the neighborhood where she had spent her life packed like an anchovy, Jim kept running, getting stares and honks as he jogged through South Philadelphia, nearly mowed down more than once. He knew what she must have been thinking. *This guy's not coming back.* Jim's father had left. Why wouldn't he?

"One day, I'm going to buy you the finest mansion in Glenwyth," Jim says.

She looks out the window. "I'd live under a bridge if I could have you back."

There's no use explaining. Maria wouldn't get it. Jim isn't even sure that he gets it. Since his return, everything has been duller, muted somehow. Sometimes he wonders if any of it really happened. The more pressing question of everyday life remains. How do you seek wealth and your own personal Oakmont when desire has been burned away like the skin around your guts, and there's nothing real outside of that jungle? Hunger was as necessary to ordinary life as oxygen, and Jim might as well be on the moon.

Still, there had been moments when the haze cleared. Like in SFO when he was an hour stateside and a long-haired freak shouted *Baby killer!* Still in uniform, Jim flattened the hippie with a left hook. A nearby policeman smiled and walked away, whistling *It's Nice To Go Trav'ling.* Five free drinks and six hours later, having crossed the country that he killed for, Jim heard the stewardess say—or at least he thought she said—*Welcome to Philadelphia. Set your watches back a hundred years.*

He stares at the road but sees the following morning's schedule—the vacancies, no-shows, and failed interpretations. He would have been better off tossing beef sides in one of his father-in-law's plants. Angelo asked him to join the business a decade ago, to become a vice president, and Jim reacted then as he might have to a demented syphilitic at Byberry.

"This kid, Quinton Graves, how am I supposed to fix him?" And the shattered bones, always the bones. "I want to help him."

"Then listen," Maria says. "They always tell you if you listen."

"But what do I say?" he blurts. "I used to be able to talk about anything. I actually believed what I said, and they did too."

"Jimmy, you make me want to throw you against a wall sometimes, but I've never stopped believing in you. Maybe that's my problem." Maria nuzzles into him, and he puts his arm around her. He'll never understand her, and maybe that's the secret of anything that lasts.

He turns on the radio—*1010 on your radio dial. Damage from Hurricane Agnes now conservatively estimated at two-point-nine billion dollars and a mother of seven found dead in her Soundview apartment, but at least nine percent of New Yorkers rate the administration of Mayor Lindsay as "good," according to a new Gallup poll. Five minutes outbound both decks at the GW, fifteen at the Lincoln, but avoid the Holland, where it'll take you up to an hour.*

The car passes over the George Washington Bridge, the Hudson glowing in the swollen sun. What if the GW collapsed? It's the same question every time he crosses. Somewhere, his new patient sits ensconced in his mansion, high above Glenwyth's own river, waiting, maybe a gun at his chest, kill or be killed.

They pull over at the first Esso on US 46. While he pumps 98 octane, Maria forces down the top, vinyl creasing.

"Easy!" he says.

She looks at the Mustang and, kissing her fingertips, massages the top. "In my next life, I'm going to come back as a car."

Sweat pools on Jim's neck. When did it get so hot again? Back in the driver's seat, he turns on the radio and cranks it up above the buffeting wind. *"Hi ho hey, chew your little troubles away…."* He turns the dial. "*….I'd like to buy the world a Coke….*" He turns it again. *"I regard this long and sickening involvement of the United States in this conflict in Southeast Asia as the most immoral act in our national history …. Why is it that this killing must continue? Brought to you by the McGovern for President Committee."* Can't wait until this stupid election is over. *"Song sung blue…."* What the hell is happening with today's music? *"Reaching out to find a way to make tomorrow a brighter day, making dreams reality, more than ever Nixon now for you and me …. He's made a difference. He showed us how. Nixon now, Nixon now, Nixon…."*

Somewhere around Hightstown, the top back up, Maria dozes again, snoring even louder. She doesn't even startle when Jim follows her into sleep and the Mustang nearly slides into the metal of the Burlington-Bristol Bridge. *Psychiatrist, Vietnam veteran, dies in car crash with pregnant wife, orphaning teen daughter, only grandchild of one-time South Philadelphia butcher.* He jumps to attention, flips the radio on, and turns up the volume. *"You're my dream come true, the answer to, everything little sweet thing the whole night through. It's Wibbage Philadelphia on nine nine O, Wibbage on your radio, WIBG Philadelphia."* He hasn't heard that jingle in a while, maybe ten years. Maybe radio stations also have flashbacks.

Turning onto Barker's Mill Road thirty minutes later, Jim sidles the Mustang against the granite curb like he's putting a baby in a crib. He kicks the parking brake, and Maria startles. Although it's past ten, the temperature seems at least fifteen degrees warmer than it was two hours earlier. The bungalow's windows are thrown open, and every light is afire. He can't argue. Angelo and Carmela have been paying the electric bill for more than a decade. Like the Series 75 Cadillac in the driveway, they can afford it. Even on the front sidewalk, he hears Mary Tyler Moore taking a nothing day and suddenly making it all seem worthwhile.

Through the porch window, Ruthie and her grandparents squint at the twelve-inch, black-and-white Sylvania that has become the family joke. His parents-in-law purchased one of the first color sets in South Philadelphia, Maria never tires of telling him. She checks the front door and, finding it locked, rings the bell, sounding the tri-tone melody of their lives.

"They're home," Carmela sings, the cadence of Palermo fresh in her voice.

Four hours later, Ruthie sits up in bed and confronts a picture of her younger self and parents: Memorial Day, Glenwyth Park, 1968. She used to love that celebration because, during it, she could actually believe that her town was a place where friendly neighbors spoke to each other, and she didn't feel lost in a world of cut yards, hissing streetlights, and hidden conversations. In the picture, she holds a rainbow lollipop and wears a pink party dress with a pleated skirt almost perpendicular to her stomach. Ridiculous, but that's how Ruthie used to be dressed and more so when her father went away, with all the endless trips to the Girls' Department at Wanamaker's. She was like a movable mannequin set up for a crowd.

In the photograph, the eleven-year-old stands between and beneath her parents, her growth spurt not yet arrived. They look worried. There were a lot of concerned glances that year and a lot of photographs. Before her husband went away, Maria was obsessed with documenting the most insignificant occurrences, but the girl can't remember the last time she saw her mother grab the Polaroid.

Ruthie takes the silver-framed image and, flicking on her reading light, studies it. Her father looked different then, more than just four years younger. What was different now? When he came back from Vietnam, he didn't appear any worse for wear, and it wasn't like he killed anyone, anyway. But what if he had? Well, he hadn't. He spent his days at a desk in an air-conditioned office talking to soldiers who wanted to run. Still, in the photograph, he seems unlike the man who just pulled in a few hours ago.

She gets the strangest of thoughts. What if her father actually died in Vietnam, and the man who returned was an impostor? There was a movie like that with Gregory Peck and Ingrid Bergman. They played psychiatrists, one real and one fake, kind of like her parents. She should see that picture again sometime. Maybe she should demand to see her father's dog tags. Didn't she ask once, and he told her that he threw them out? Anyway, the idea's nuts, completely out there, but she's been having a lot of strange thoughts recently. She's always seen connections where others haven't, and her teachers have praised her for that, called it brilliance, but when does thinking differently become thinking wrongly?

Ruthie herself has been a fake for as long as she can remember. People think she's happy, but she's not, never has been really. The thing is, no one has ever known or—with the A's and good behavior—thought to ask. There's no reason for her unhappiness. Her parents don't beat her, and they don't much scream at her. There's always been a distance between them that anyone can see, but that's like most of the parents in Glenwyth. Anyway, her parents, real or not, are so messed up that Ruthie's had no choice but to appear normal.

It's after 2:00 a.m., and she hasn't slept more than ten minutes the whole night. Maybe that's the problem, maybe why everything's so dull and unhappy. Just like her mother, Ruthie has never been a great sleeper. Her auburn hair feels like greasy rope, and the sheets are a puddle. She went right to bed after her parents' arrival, too early for getting up at noon. Yesterday, she would have slept even later but for the whine of her grandfather mowing her parents' lawn. He had to get it right for their return. The grass had grown a foot since the last cut, the supercharged yield of the hurricane.

If only it would rain tonight. It's so damned hot. Why can't her parents have air conditioning? Eliza has it at her house. Maybe Ruthie could go up there and bang on the Dixons' door. The most frustrating thing is that Ruthie's grandparents could buy a hundred air conditioners and give one to their granddaughter. Her grandparents are well-off, maybe even rich, but her grandfather wears work clothes and her grandmother cheap house dresses.

They save rather than spend, and that allows Grandpop to give her ten-dollar bills when they visit, sometimes twenties. Angelo tells her to tell no one. So she deposits them in a coffee can in a shoebox in her closet, trying to be extra safe, and maybe there's even enough to buy her own air conditioner. He's told her something else and sworn her to secrecy. He has drilled seven compartments into the foundation of the Swedesboro house and in each placed gold coins. If you were to hear such a story, you'd think it was just that—a story. But Ruthie has seen the coins, the frizzle-haired lady with her sunbeams on the front and the fat eagle on the back. Angelo's told her that it's not legal to own gold coins, although this seems odd since they say *United States of America Twenty Dollars*, right on the front. Sometimes, when things have been bad, she imagines running away and begging her grandfather for the treasure, her fare to another country.

In Swedesboro, she is never denied, but when her grandparents come to Glenwyth, they become crossing guards. She's been allowed to walk the block into town, but her friends have been off-limits. Her parents have not demanded or even suggested such restrictions, but Grandpop and Nonna believe that only prostitutes and criminals go out at night. This from the grandfather with the illegal gold. So Ruthie and her grandfather have watched a lot of television—*Columbo, Mannix, Owen Marshall,* just to name the law enforcement programming—while her grandmother has ironed in her wide nightgown. It's been a revelation how many unwashed sheets and bath towels her parents have accumulated.

Her grandparents aren't bothered by the heat. They've looked comfortable the entire weekend, like they finally found their ideal climate. Even today, with its high of ninety-nine, eighty-seven percent humidity, Grandpop wore a long-sleeved work shirt and khaki pants, and Nonna spent the afternoon tending the chard she planted in the Malorys' disappointment of a garden right after Hurricane Agnes. That was after the three of them attended nine-thirty Mass at St. John's. Her parents never make her go, except on Christmas and Easter, even though the church is only a block away. Nonna had said, "You remind your mother to water my plants tomorrow!" Those were Nonna's plants, and this was her house. Maybe Ruthie's grandparents like it hot, but she wonders if her brain might melt.

She could try to draw, she's always been good at that, but it's a million degrees. She has opened the two windows in her bedroom, but there's no wind, and the fan blows hot air. She turns it off and walks to the window facing their neighbors, the Althouses. They're ancient, and the husband uses a ventilator to assist his breathing at night. She can just hear it in her bedroom, a gentle whishing.

Through the other window, she sees the deserted street. Not a car passes. But it must be cooler out there. It must be.

She puts on her happy face T-shirt and a wrinkled tennis skirt. Ruthie looks around the room, and her dolls tell her not to go. But why does she even have dolls anymore, like she's six years old or something? After removing the screen from her window, she climbs through it. The grass is dry beneath her feet, the water from last month's hurricane boiled away.

She walks around to the other side of the house and sees that her parents' light is off. The street where she has lived since she was four has become a long harbor, its ships in for the night. She steps by her parents' window down the two concrete paths to the open garage and withdraws her Schwinn. An unopened Coke can sits in the handlebar basket. When she is out of earshot, she rips off the pull tab, warm sugar fizzing forward, and flicks the seal into the Althouses' liriope. A car passes in the distance on Wingohocking, but she has Barker's Mill to herself and sails across Athens without even a look. The crickets of memory are everywhere.

A minute later, Ruthie leans her bike against the retaining wall that keeps the Glenwyth Pharmacy and its lime rickeys from cascading into the street, and walks into the middle of the intersection that centers Glenwyth. She takes the Coke can, now empty, and throws it into the air.

She looks up Barker's Mill, then Athens, and there's nothing in all four directions. Lying down in the middle of the crossing, she makes an X with her limbs. She'll hear any cars coming. She scissors for what seems like an afternoon, and there's nothing. She springs up, caffeinated, and mounts her bike. In the A&P parking lot, she figure-eights, but the lights make it easier to be spotted. She knows where she'll go.

She pedals up Athens and, maneuvering her bike around the chained entryway, turns down the driveway that leads to the playground where she grew up—Glenwyth Park. She pumps past the merry-go-round and the sandbox and finds the swings. They are remote from the playground's other attractions, as if designed to isolate a single girl while her friends laughed on the jungle gym. Some of the swings have seats that dangle uselessly from single chains. She finds a functional swing, gets on, and pushes, gaining momentum first with her legs, and then with the thrust of her body. The arc widens. She used to fear that the swing's quarter-circle would become a circumference, and she would spin around the axis, free of gravity, forever.

She swings until exhausted and jumps down to the grass, freshly mowed like her own yard but too low for this heat. The turf will brown in a week, but tonight it feels like carpet. There are no stars, not even moonlight, just lightning bugs, greenish-yellow, here but for an instant. Is her father finally sleeping? Sometimes he gets up in the darkness, and his walking out of the house awakens her. When she was younger, she thought his remoteness temporary, but maybe it was a prelude to his actual departure. At least she's been sent a replacement, fake as he might be. There were other girls she met at the 1969 Fort Dix Christmas party whose fathers never came back at all.

The air is cooler now, even refreshing, with its temperature seemingly equivalent to her body's. Her parents might be checking for her in her room, but then again, when has that ever happened? They trust her, and they always will. After all, she is, her parents have said, a good girl.

"C'mere."

When Ruthie first hears it, she thinks she might have fallen asleep. But she's not dreaming. The bicycle lying next to her still has the same white, plastic woven basket with the ridiculous daisy on its front.

"Yeah, that's right," someone whispers. "You."

She rolls over. It's a male voice, but then again, it's muffled. There's no one, just a tangle of vines, obstructed and lurid.

"I'm right here," he says. She jumps to her feet and must be facing him, although she can see nothing. "That's right. Over here."

She could say something, but what? "I've been watching you for a while. I won't hurt you," the stranger says. "I promise." She could scream, but he's at least thirty feet away in the bushes. She could run, but the bike is right at her feet.

Ruthie raises the bicycle and straddles its frame.

"You can go," he says. "I won't stop you. But do you really want to? You don't, do you? Come in here with me."

"Who are you?" she asks.

"You know."

"I'm not kidding. Who are you?"

"Who are *you?*" he replies. When she says nothing, he says, "I'll never leave you."

"Do you—do you know me?"

A pause. "Yes."

She launches the bike, nearly falling, and pounds the pedals, ripping the gears down to first, and then back to fifth. She turns around. Is he following? Running? Just missing the metal post at the edge of the park's driveway, Ruthie careens back onto Athens and, in seconds, takes the left to Barker's Mill. At her house, she drops the bicycle in the front yard. She will think of an excuse later. Tearing open the window, she vaults inside and slams it shut, locking it. Ruthie sits at attention until dawn, cold despite the oven of her room, when she hears her father banging around and showering. Then she falls asleep and dreams.

3

A few hours later, Jim twists the "play" knob of his new answering machine, which will mostly be used for cancelations and second thoughts.

"This is Nilso. I'll be at a VECU committee meeting when you get to VA on Wednesday, and so I want you to be aware of the new SPAMC protocol we're developing, specifically with regard to but notwithstanding—" Click. Delete. Major Donald Nilso, USA Ret., is Jim's boss at the Veterans Administration Medical Center in Philadelphia, or VA, the word "the" sometimes eliminated by insiders, as if to maximize government efficiency. A man who talks in Central Office acronyms, Nilso decides which patients leave the psychiatric ward and which remain.

"Dr. Malory, this is the Medical School Library. You have several overdue books, with a total current fine of a dollar thirty-five. To avoid a negative report to the Dean's Subcommittee on Library Management, please—" Delete. Next.

"It's Honey. We couldn't get out of Stone Harbor until this morning, and so I'm sorry we missed Eliza's 9:00 a.m." So that's why she never showed up. "We could do Wednesday at three, although that's not the best either, and I absolutely promise that she will be there next Monday. I appreciate your understanding." This means that Honey appreciates that he will not charge her, even though she has all the money in the world. "Also, I was wondering if you could call me in one or two Hycodans, or maybe a week's worth, if it's not a bother. Dr. Santoni is away. Oh, the Glenwyth Pharmacy, that would be fine. Also, we'd love to have you and Maria over for tennis and dinner this Saturday if you can swing it. Also, if you don't mind, Santoni writes me Quaalude for sleep, and—" Delete. Next.

"Oh, this is Honey again. Sorry. When you do see Eliza, I want you to talk to her about her diet. She's going to turn into a big fat pig if she's not careful." Delete. No more, thank God, and if Jim prescribed methaqualone to someone who drank as much as Honey and also took painkillers, Santoni would never let him hear the end of it. But Ed, who gets free Eagles tickets from the Quaalude rep at Rorer, does whatever the hell he wants and gets away with it.

Jim turns the machine off and surveys his scheduling book. Like loose front teeth, the day's appointments have all fallen away, leaving a deeply rooted canine—his 3:00 p.m. with Quinton Graves at Sycamore Lodge. That's the family estate, originally on a hundred acres but now on twelve. Jim has seen the mansion before in a book of old Glenwyth, two pantalooned girls sitting beneath a razor-sharp gable, mother and father standing next to a carriage and its quarter horse. The house looked old even when it was built, presiding not over trees but acres of farms. The neighborhood was young then, with few of the snuff barons and iron kings who would later become the place's neighbors.

Jim's office on Athens Road near the center of town was built around then as well, the original post office he believes, but the mail has been processed elsewhere for at least eighty years. Whatever else has come between, the landlord couldn't much remember when, two Christmases ago, Jim signed the lease using a check from his in-laws. 949 Athens Road maintains its mercantile roots, with two large picture windows in the front, the golden haze of a stenciled "Dry Goods" still visible to the observant passerby. To provide the necessary anonymity, Maria made bamboo blinds for the waiting room. Now only slices of people can be seen from the sidewalk and even from the front porch. Anyway, there are few pedestrians on Athens, the Porsches and Mercedes drifting by.

An overly large waiting room and a forgotten kitchen—now storage closet—exhaust the first floor. A stairway bends to the second, which comprises an unused bedroom facing the road and a larger sitting room in the back. Jim works there in shabbiness, overlooking the stubbed yard where a vegetable garden must have supplemented the postmaster's wages and fed his struggling family. Could these parents have squeezed more than a single child into such quarters, or was the family just a three-cent stamp? The second floor's front room must have been the child's bedroom. One afternoon, with nothing to do, Jim peeled off wallpaper in the front room and found pencil drawings of flowers, horses, and carriages.

The backyard blazes with weeds. The summer and fourteen trillion gallons of water from Hurricane Agnes have created a jungle in Pennsylvania. A cemetery looms above and behind the yard, tiny stones of some Protestant sect, and next to it, the Odd Fellows Hall. Odd Fellows? In Lehighton, those were the drunks and beggars who lurked in Municipal Park, not more than a single social rung beneath Jim and his mother. The two of them were the rarest of things in those days, fatherless and husbandless. Jim had known his father, at least for a few years. A veteran of World War I, the salesman from Philadelphia had guarded Cape May, at Camp

Wissahickon to be precise, and had acted, Jim's mother said, like he was John J. Pershing. She was blind when she saw him and deaf when he spoke, and Mr. and Mrs. James C. Malory had the biggest wedding the Asa Packer Hotel had seen in all of 1936.

In the beginning, the three of them lived in a sprawling house not far from the hotel, but cirrhosis killed Jim's father not four years later. When he died, a swollen, yellow pincushion of a man, Ruth Malory would not let her son come to the hospital. Then there were debts, lots of them. Mrs. Malory repaid the last in 1957 when Jim was a junior, and there was no life insurance. So the Malorys fled Mauch Chunk and made it one station down the Lehigh Valley Railroad, to Lehighton.

Probably half the Valley's shareholders lived in Glenwyth and attended St. Christopher's, the Episcopalian church visible from Jim's window. It's on the road to Sycamore Lodge. Rich people have always lived here along with a few servants. He can't see Quinton's house, but Jim knows from the topography that it is there, looking down at his office. The best houses for the richest people were always built on hills, higher than everybody else.

He enters his empty waiting room, and even the magazines look absent. Locking the front door, he walks to the intersection of Athens and Barker's Mill. The sky is stunned, colorless and cloudless. A shade less stifling than it was on Sunday, the heat still grinds, making Glenwyth a part of the Deep South, no one in a rush. On its corner, the Wayside Inn stands hard by the road, and the Glenwyth Luncheonette sits idle. It's too hot for a hoagie. Further down, the Glenwyth Pharmacy and the A&P look unchanged from when Jim, Maria, and Ruthie arrived a decade ago from South Philadelphia.

Glenwyth has always been a mystery to him. Some houses have porches, but few of these display people now or ever. Jim knows the Althouses, but his other neighbors are like actors in movies seen only in previews. There's a township commissioner, a barrel-chested life insurance salesman, and a middle-aged stockbroker with a watch fob. He met these three at a Civic Association meeting five years ago to protest the creation of a westbound entrance to the Schuylkill Expressway. It was odd that these men would fight the modification of an interstate already burned across the river-front and offering only eastbound access, but they were all locals, with the concurrent belief that a flawed present always was superior to a changed future. So it seemed, and so Jim stayed quiet.

When he returned from Vietnam in December 1970, he wanted no celebrations. Some of the older men, veterans, would stop him at the A&P to promote the Legion Post. Somehow they knew all about him, but patients were shy to suspicious when they learned of his past. They eyed him like he might remove his prosthetic leg and shock the little children. That all his limbs remained was irrelevant.

It's a quarter past one, another fragment of another empty hour. He could walk to Sycamore Lodge for the three o'clock appointment, arriving early, but the trek would slick him with sweat. Maria was supposed to drop off the Mustang at the office by two-thirty. Instead, he'll surprise her.

As he walks up the sidewalk a few minutes later, Jim sees a police officer stepping onto the street. The man tips his hat. Maria sits in the living room, staring at their shaved log coffee table. The normally squawking television has silenced, the black and white turned to a dull, vacant green. She pushes her cigarette into the ashtray.

"You shouldn't do that," he says.

"You shouldn't do a lot of things."

"Let's start again. How are you?"

"Great, like I'm back in South Philadelphia." He studies her. "The Althouses were robbed," she explains. "Apparently in broad daylight while they were at the hospital visiting his sister. Nothing was taken, but someone was in their house. The door was wide open when they got back."

Jim notices that a yard-long crack has formed in the plaster above Maria's head. "The old guy probably forgot to lock it," he says. "He's probably worked up about McGovern."

Maria straightens up and presses her maternity skirt, steadying herself. "How was your morning?"

"Good. I got the new answering machine set up, and I got four messages in fifteen minutes."

"Did you call about the water heater?" Maria asks.

"Sorry."

"I guess you're busy."

"Well, not exactly. Eliza canceled. I mean, she no-showed, and then Honey canceled for her three hours later. I'm sure Honey expects not to be charged. Don't you love it?"

"Some people never change," Maria says. "It's like that time she made me pick up her mink stole from storage—"

"—and made you pay," Jim says, completing his wife's sentence, and maybe that's good enough for a good marriage. He can still see The Ladies Shoppe on Walnut Street, the extra "pe" added for class. It's now demolished like so much else in the West Philadelphia of his memory. Did coeds once wear furs? When Miss Sharpe and Miss Sedara were roommates for a semester, they were the oddest of odd couples, but in the sixteen years since, their paths have been weirdly parallel. Honey, after all, found the bungalow for Maria and then acquired her own house a half-mile away.

"Just be glad you're not Eliza's mother," he says.

Maria frowns. She could have been a nun, with her broad shoulders and sudden sternness, maybe even a mother superior like Sister Michael Frederick.

"It's a bit strange that you're still treating Eliza," she says. "She and Ruthie have become a lot closer since the end of school."

"I didn't want to see her, if you remember. Honey called you, and then you told me to do the first session for free, like her mink stole."

Jim shouldn't be criticizing handouts, considering how everything in the room has been purchased directly or indirectly by Angelo and Carmela. At least he did a combat tour, although Medcap wasn't supposed to involve fighting. The best that Woody Dixon—Eliza's father and Honey's husband—could do was to serve in the Naval Reserves as a financial analyst.

"I never told you to see her," Maria says.

"Okay. I'll terminate."

"You don't need to be so black and white."

"I'll terminate," he says, but he knows what she's thinking, because he's thinking the same thing. She remembers that check in his hand after the initial evaluation, one of his first after opening his practice. During supervision, Santoni had thought it a bit unusual that Jim was treating the daughter of his wife's friend and college roommate, but Honey said nothing of it. Or maybe she thought that with Dr. Malory, she would have an easier time getting her daughter's therapist to spill the beans.

"How much more do you have to do with her?" Maria asks.

"A lot." Eliza was the kind of patient for whom therapy seemed as necessary as breathing. "She's still smoking like a chimney, for one thing."

"Marijuana cigarettes?"

"No, Lucky Strikes. Of course, marijuana." He should also tell Maria about the psilocybin and LSD that drift through Glenwyth like psychedelic fallout.

"I can't believe it," she says, pursing her lips like J. Edgar Hoover, ready to take on the narcotics trade. "Have you told Honey?"

"I can't do that, and as far as I can tell, she doesn't do it in school." Doesn't she? He's never thought to ask. "She just smokes the stuff in her bedroom and listens to Pink Floyd."

"Pink who?"

He rolls his eyes. "Forget it."

"You know they don't provide the best example over there," Maria says, stating the obvious. The two couples have had many boozy dinners since 1955, with another loaded in the chamber. Afterward, the Malorys will stumble back to their bungalow, and the Dixons will speed away drunk in their Porsche, hoping to avoid the Glenwyth Police before reaching their glass and silver box of a house perched on its own Rock of Gibraltar.

"Girls don't drink beer anymore," Jim says. "It makes them fat." When Eliza started treatment with Jim, she was 135 pounds. Last week she was 105. When he told her this, a sly grin spread across her face. She was, after all, aiming for 101, and that was where she would stop. Or so she said.

"What about Ruthie?" Maria asks, as if her husband will solve the mysteries of the universe. Her pupils have widened, and her voice is taut. She gets up and paces the parlor, looking a bit like Carmela, without the house coat and with ankles not yet as sturdy.

What about Ruthie? How is he supposed to know? Instead, he says, "She doesn't do any of that stuff. She's much too practical. She's already studying for the College Boards."

"I hope you're right."

"Of course I'm right," he says.

"So what are you doing for Eliza?"

"We're talking about some of the things that she's been through in the past." Maria stares at him, an inquiring mind wanting to know. "I can't tell you any more than that."

"But you always tell me."

It's true. In his letters, he told her everything about his patients in Vietnam, the ones who could never sleep again, the ones who loved every minute, and the ones who strangled their wives at night.

"This is different," Jim says. "Her mother's your best friend. Hey, has Pietrolongo checked your thyroid? Let's get some air in here." He opens the locked windows facing the street, three of them for the house's three inhabitants.

"You're going to make it hotter," Maria says, "and she's not my best friend. She doesn't even like me, and if she does, it's probably because she always can remind herself that she's thinner than me."

"She's not thinner than you, I mean, not thinner when you're not pregnant."

Maria clears her throat. "How much do we have in the checking account?"

"Why?"

"I bounced a check."

"I don't know," he says, drooping.

"I'll call my parents."

Call her parents so they can write another check to plug another hole. When Jim was growing up in Lehighton, the town's medical men, Heinz and Trexler, drove Plymouths and Studebakers. They were often paid in turnips or not at all, and didn't seem to care, at least when Ruth Malory took her son for checkups. The doctors' children weren't special, either. In the summer of 1954, Jeannie Trexler sold tickets alongside Jim at the Embassy Theater in that stainless-steel booth that resembled a gas chamber.

That wasn't even twenty years ago, but in 1972 Glenwyth, the doctors who've made it, which is everyone except Malory, act like bankers. Santoni and his peers drive XK-Es, SLs, and DeVilles. They wouldn't talk to Ed if he were a concrete contractor like his father Salvatore, but this was the age of the medical profession, from which even psychiatry, the runt of the litter, profited.

"I'm doing my best," Jim says.

"You should have made Honey pay for the missed session."

"Why are we talking about Honey?"

"You brought her up."

Jim is silent for a while. Honey must be back from Stone Harbor and just around the corner.

He asks, "Do you think we might—"

"You need to stop thinking about Mister Dister."

"But you said Pietrolongo said we could."

"He was being theoretical. You'd have to shower again, and there's no hot water."

"Even better," he says. "Where's Ruthie?"

"I dropped her off at Sunny Lane. She swims until at least three," Maria says, looking immediately regretful. "Your best friend Honey is picking them up."

"They belong to a stupid pool, when they have the Atlantic Ocean."

"We should probably join," Maria says. "Do you want me to ask my parents?"

"I want you to go into the bedroom, without your parents."

"And when I fall over laughing, you can get what you want?"

"I want you. You're the best-looking woman I ever went out with."

"I'm the only woman you ever went out with."

After more persuasion, back and forth, yes, no, maybe, Maria yields, obstetric catastrophe be damned, and Jim loses interest. Conflicted by something he can't see, he sits soft and dumbfounded on the bedspread until she instructs him, another physics problem to be solved. After much coaxing, he finds himself staring at the back of her head, a piston moving in low gear. He sees another ratty paperback on her bedstead, this time *Waiting for*

Winter, and all he can think of is the Dixons' house on the hill. He could tell Maria about the Dixons. The plot's better than any John O'Hara, but Jim couldn't tell the whole story. *Just too bright, like staring into the sun.*

And how does Ruthie fit into the narrative? Eliza might not be an advisable friend, but is there really a duty to warn? If so, warn who? Ruthie, Maria, Honey, the headmistress of Miss Stroud's School for Girls? Maybe Jim should dial Santoni on the bedstead phone and seek his counsel. The master always offers answers, just as he grows his tomato plants and steers people from the Coast Guard to Cambodia.

After a few minutes and some damp fireworks, Maria yawns. Then she flops onto her back on the far side of the bed. Jim showers, puts on his bathrobe, opens the blinds, and sees a neighbor he can't even name watering her lawn in the distance.

"Just make sure Ruthie's safe," Maria slurs. "And set my alarm for three. What do you want tonight?"

"We could go out."

"Are you sure? We spent a lot in Massachusetts." Only they didn't. Aside from gas, tolls, and hamburgers at rest stops, Ed and Natalie covered everything until the final night's dinner at Woods Hole. When that bill came, each of the four diners understood Jim's need to pay and the humiliation if he didn't. But maybe his picking up the four movie tickets for that weird Swedish film where one of the sisters cuts her vagina with broken glass and rubs the blood on her face, maybe that was too much.

"It's just money," Jim says.

"Right. Just money. Anyway, you've slept better since we've been home, none of the tossing and turning. When I wake up, I watch you. You know, so—"

"Let's just go to the Wayside," he says.

Not even looking at him, she replies, "Why don't you just screw whatever you have to do this afternoon and stay here with me? We could stay in this bed forever. Remember when we used to dream about that? Remember, on Roseberry Street?"

"I should be home by six, and you don't have to watch me."

"Okay," she says. He kisses her hand, and Maria rubs his leg backhandedly, blindly. Then she tightens just enough for Jim to see. "Make sure you lock the door."

Ruthie and Eliza lounge in parallel. They've moved their chaises up the hill from the pool so that the splashing of toddlers dominating the Sunny Lane Swim Club softens to a din. Chlorine makes Ruthie's lungs ache.

She has known Eliza since Glenwyth Elementary, but in second grade, Eliza transferred to Stroud's. She hated it from the beginning, forced each day to adopt the bland habit of a maroon jumper. She was placed in the classroom for the mediocre students present in every private school. That was ridiculous. Even in second grade, there was nothing average about Eliza.

The two stayed in touch, if somewhat less frequently, and their distance allowed Ruthie to appreciate Eliza not with the dullness of everyday acquaintance but as an object of a growing—if not altogether pleasant—fascination. It wasn't that Ruthie worried, at least not at first. But as the years passed, Eliza thickened and broadened, soon binging and purging Reese's Peanut Butter Cups and whatever else they sold at the Glenwyth Pharmacy. At Eliza's insistence, Ruthie took an oath not to tell anyone and, in doing so, understood real friendship. The cutting came in middle school, and still Ruthie said nothing, not that anyone would have listened. Ruthie's father was in Vietnam by then, and that was all that Maria could think about. When Ruthie would go over to Eliza's house,

Mrs. Dixon was always talking about furniture, walking around the house with a wine glass in her hand. She also wanted to know all the news about Dr. Malory, which seemed odd, but Ruthie figured that maybe she felt bad because her own husband should have gone over and didn't.

According to Eliza, cutting and vomiting were challenging at first, but then easier and finally natural, as if they were always meant to be. The scars were visible if you knew where to look. But no one looked, and so the problem grew for two years until it burst like a pimple one Sunday morning when Eliza was found shivering in a tub of salmon-colored water, a disassembled safety razor resting at her side. So Mrs. Dixon called Dr. Malory, back a few months from Vietnam.

When her grandfather offered to pay Ruthie's tuition to Stroud's for tenth grade, she was less than eager to transfer. Her father didn't care one way or the other. He had gone to high school in a place where they had a week's vacation after Thanksgiving so kids could shoot deer. How he had gotten into Penn was anyone's guess. But Maria wanted her daughter in Stroud's and wanted it bad. When Ruthie objected and linked her reluctance to Eliza, whose problems were now well known, Maria made the point that the girls would be in separate grades. Ruthie would start in tenth while Eliza would be in ninth. They wouldn't see much of each other.

So Ruthie entered Stroud's, abandoning the jeans and halter tops that were by then the standard public high school outfit. From last September to a month ago, five days a week, she wore a maroon kilt, a white blouse, and a blazer. Thank God it was summer. Although Eliza had been friendly from orientation week, it was only in the spring that she drew Ruthie into her circle.

"This club is all kindergarteners," Eliza says, her hair blonde like her mother's and still naturally so.

"I know," Ruthie says. Down the hill, a small boy bounces a multicolored beach ball off the heads of other children.

"We should go to New York this weekend. You want to?"

"I don't think my parents would go for it," Ruthie says.

"It'd be great, you and me. We can get the train right in Athens." Eliza picks up an amber bottle of baby oil and rubs a handful over her bony skin. "Forget about the Saint-Tropez tan. This has iodine."

Her eyes hidden by sunglasses, Ruthie studies the knobs and tubes of her friend's body. Was she this thin when they showered together after tennis this spring? That was three months ago.

"If you're on board," Eliza says, "Honey can't say no." Ruthie's friend doesn't use the terms "my mom" or "my mother." The woman is simply "Honey."

"Which means she trusts one of us."

"Oh, she trusts me, all right—to screw everything up." Eliza removes her sunglasses and squints. "Finally, the sun."

"You can still tan even when it's behind the clouds."

"Okay, Honey. Thanks for the tip."

"Sorry," Ruthie says, feeling like a governor to a machine always spinning out of control.

"What are you sorry about? This place is so stupid we can't help but say stupid things. I can't believe that we're spending the best years of our lives in Glenwyth. Nothing ever happens here. Now, if we went to New York—"

"Maybe we could go without telling them," Ruthie says.

A grin comes over Eliza's face. "Is that Ruthie Malory talking? H-E-double hockey sticks!"

"I don't tell them everything I do."

"Really? Like what?"

"Doesn't matter."

"You're lying."

Right, like when Ruthie stole from the lunch line at Stroud's, snatched her father's psychiatric notes on Eliza from his briefcase and read them, and talked to that weirdo in the bushes. Like when her father came back from Vietnam and she took his pistol before giving it back when he thought it was stolen. The next day, he went right to the police and gave them the gun, telling his wife and daughter that the war was over.

Ruthie says to Eliza, "What if I told you there's a guy—"

"I wouldn't believe you. What's his name?"

"Why does it matter?"

"I guess it doesn't, because all men are shits anyway, and boys are worse. But if there is a guy, I would forget about all that romance crap."

Eliza tells her psychiatrist the same things, but he brushes it aside, dispensing chestnuts like *You haven't met the right fella* and *Your time is going to come.* Eliza has told this much to Ruthie many times.

But what would her father say if Ruthie told him about the man in the park and how part of her wanted to stay and hear what else he had to say? Her father would probably serve up the same crap he tells Eliza, and, by the way, does he actually think all that garbage is true? Maybe he just says such stuff for the fifty dollars an hour, and besides, who wants a pessimistic psychiatrist? Or maybe he's so optimistic that he's convinced by his own nonsense, which would be even more pathetic.

"Everything I know, I know from Honey," Eliza says. "She doesn't believe in romance. She doesn't even believe in sex. My parents sleep in separate bedrooms. I bet the woman hasn't had sex since Burtie."

"What does my father say to that?"

"He squirms a lot. You want to smoke?"

Ruthie feels a tugging in her stomach. "I hate tobacco," she says.

"C'mere." Eliza gets up and walks over to the chain-link fence that separates Sunny Lane from its neighbor, a wooded expanse marked with a rusted green township sign saying, "Land Under Development." Vandals have gouged a hole in the metal, and beyond it runs a path. "Come on."

Her shoulder blades like miniature angel wings, Eliza disappears into the woods. Ruthie can hear her friend's voice trailing off. "'I shall not seek nor will I accept the nomination of my party for President of the United States.'"

Ruthie gets up, walks to the fence, and looks behind her down the hill. The boy with the ball has disappeared. Already the crowd thins, another day wasted. The sun has retreated again, and this all seems like a pretty bad idea.

She nevertheless follows through the torn wire and then between vines and stalks to a small clearing where her guide sits by a doused campfire. The ashes look new since the last storm. Reaching into her bikini top, Eliza produces a small plastic bag filled with green flakes and rolling papers.

Ruthie's eyes widen. "How'd you find this place?"

"You don't think people come here to swim? This is the best part of Sunny Lane." Eliza lines the marijuana on a paper, rolls it, and then licks the edge, sealing the deal.

"Where did you get that?"

"Let's just say that a friend in need is a friend indeed."

"We better go back."

"C'mon. It's straight from Humboldt County," Eliza says.

"Where's that?"

"Colorado. Your parents are probably smoking the same stuff."

"My parents don't do that."

"They did it when they were over with my parents once." A pause. "I'm pretty sure of it." Anything is possible in that house on the hill, and yet it seems doubtful. Ruthie's parents are so square they play records by the McGuire Sisters. That being said, her father drinks more and more these days. Before he left for Vietnam, there was never much liquor around, but now he boozes every night, two, three, or more. It's a good thing he gave away that gun.

Eliza lights the joint, inhales, and blows three smoke rings across Ruthie's face. "My dad taught me how to do that," she says. "He is the best-est daddy in the whole world!"

The odor is green and sweet, not quite ripe, and like nothing Ruthie has ever smelled.

"Don't worry. It's not like it's hair-o-wine or anything," Eliza says, doing her best jive.

Maybe Eliza's right, and anyway, what's the big difference between a puff or two and all those drinks? Ruthie's own mother smokes cigarettes, even though she's pregnant.

With that, twenty minutes later, after some instruction and violent coughing, Ruthie lies flat in the dirt, looking up through the trees toward the haze of a half-expired Pennsylvania summer. The whir of the expressway grows with the approach of rush hour. Things make more sense now but also are frightening, and Ruthie wonders if she's being watched.

Eliza has brought her black transistor radio from the chaises and planted it next to the forgotten fire. *Just My Imagination* comes on, and the world suddenly makes sense. When it's done, Ruthie wants to listen to that song again and again, but WDAS (the girls have tuned to Philly's rhythm & blues station) cuts to commercials. Her parents still like WIBG, but that's for old people.

Meanwhile, Eliza overflows. "Can you believe that? I mean, can you fucking believe that?"

"That's sad," Ruthie says.

"Yahhh....Yahhh...." A mist of detached regret and cannabinoid insight has issued from Eliza's mouth. Between tokes, she has anatomized the failure of her parents' marriage and their respective shortcomings. Honey and Woody are both alcoholics but have come to that destination via different routes. It's only a matter of time before the Dixons will divorce. Eliza's sure of it. It would have happened already if it weren't for her brother Jimmy, the one who can't talk.

"I saw my mother vomit when I was five," Eliza explains. "She told me she ate a bad clam. I can't blame her, though. My father always called her fat, that mother-trucker."

"My father's not so great either," Ruthie says. "It's like he's not all there, like he's in a trance, and my mother—"

"At least she loves him. You can see it on her face."

"Maybe, but if that's love, why does anyone get married? It's like she's always running after him."

"No, he talks about her at least once a session. He'll never leave in a million years." Eliza mists briefly, ridiculously, and then comes the waterfall. "I wish someone loved me."

With the unremarkable becoming threatening, the tragic has become absurd. Ruthie laughs out loud.

"What?" Eliza asks, annoyed. No reply, and so she lunges. "WHAT?"

Ruthie must stop herself. This is so embarrassing and cruel. "You? Everyone loves you. You're, like, the most popular girl at Stroud's."

"They're not real friends." Eliza tries to wipe her eyes with the thin straps of her bikini top. "Damn it!"

"What are you doing?" Ruthie asks.

"I'm upset."

"Don't be." Ruthie stands up, staggers, steadies, and hugs her friend.

"So I was right. You just hang out with me because I'm popular."

"You are popular, and you're also Cocoa Puffs, but in a good way."

"You're beautiful," Eliza says, and Ruthie's not sure how to respond. "I mean like a sister. I wish you were my sister. I always wanted a sister. What if we were? Wouldn't that be great if we were twin sisters? We could do an ad for Doublemint Gum."

"We don't have to be sisters. We can be best friends."

"You wouldn't want me," Eliza says and turns away. "I'm just bad."

"You're not."

"I am. Honey's right." Eliza peels down the front of her plaid bikini bottom and displays a series of red cuts, variously scabbed, marking the northern boundary of her pubic hair. She has carved a word in block letters on her skin: "FAT."

Ruthie feels like she might faint.

"What? Are you surprised?" Eliza asks. "This is where they cut you when you deliver twins. You can ask Honey."

"You said you stopped doing that. You told me that."

"Well, I didn't."

"You have to stop. Promise!"

"It's that or this." Eliza holds up the joint and sucks in another drag. "And I can't stop vomiting. I tell your father that everything is A-okay, but I have to clean myself out."

"Why don't you tell him the truth?"

"He wouldn't get it, but it's not his fault. Nobody understands unless you've been there."

"He's been there. He's seriously messed up." Even if her father hasn't been replaced, he was never there to begin with, and if he was always like this, that would be even worse.

"I made you sad," Eliza says, touching Ruthie's face.

"Me? No." But Ruthie cries and thinks less now about her father than that peeper in Glenwyth Park. Having carved her own skin, maybe Eliza could understand wanting to jump into the bushes. "I'm fine," Ruthie says. "I am. You have to tell him."

"I may," Eliza says. "But only so he doesn't blame himself when I'm dead."

She takes the end of the still-lit joint and presses it between her fingers, wincing. Then she studies the red spots on her thumb and forefinger and smiles. "I feel better already," Eliza says, turning back toward the pool. "Honey's probably looking all over for us, and she knows it here like the back of her hand from her riding days." Eliza snickers. "This is where she used to hunt."

~

The driveway for Sycamore Lodge begins at two sandstone pillars and an adjacent gatehouse twice the size of the Malorys' house. Jim has noticed similar entrances throughout Glenwyth and its nearby towns, but in most cases, the sentinel structures have been sold off, the paths turned into public roads. There's nothing public here. The gatehouse seems unoccupied, its windows shut despite the heat, and there's no car in its gravel parking spot. Jim guides the Mustang up the driveway toward the main house, passing stands of beech and oak, dense without interruption. At the top of the hill, the drive straightens for a direct approach to the mansion, lined on both sides with old, peeling sycamores. A 1967 black-on-black Corvette convertible, top down, stands nearby in the white-pebbled courtyard. Jim slips the Mustang abreast, like a poor cousin come to visit, and gets out.

With little effort, he can see downtown Philadelphia. Looking back at the house, Jim notes an octagonal porch, a sharp gable with a pent roof below, and a sextet of chimneys. He took an architecture course as a gut back in 1956 and never thought it would come in handy. Honey was in that class. They sat next to each other in the lectures, and eyebrows were never raised. Jim still remembers the professor's lingo and now observes louvered shutters, ochre brick, oriel windows, and stone quoins. One of the recessed windows beneath the steep central gable catches Jim's eye. He sees a face in the glass.

There's no doorbell, just a large iron knocker. Jim bangs it. No answer. He pulls out the letter delivered to his office this morning by courier from Tower, Tilney & Webb, 146 South Broad Street, Philadelphia, Penna. There's no zip code, as if the firm has turned its nose at new-fangled innovations.

Dear Dr. Malory:

You will no doubt be surprised to see this communication, especially on the letterhead of our attorneys, but our stay in Bermuda has necessitated the intermediary of counsel, grateful as we are for its Telex facilities. We wish that we could be present to participate in Quinton's care, but he has strictly forbidden it, saying that he will refuse all treatment if we return. As you will see, Mr. Evans watches over the house, and we have been in contact with him frequently to ensure that Quinton has not engaged in any dangerous behavior since his release from the Institute. Here is what we know.

Until very recently, there was nothing to elicit any serious concern. Quinton was always a studious boy and very sensitive. He was solitary, though, reading fantasy novels and building model airplanes, and had few friends at White's. In middle school there, he was bullied, harshly. This was a great source of stress, that is, how we dealt with it, and we might not have dealt with it effectively. Quinton never knew how to talk to others all that well, and I suppose we didn't know how to teach him.

He would talk—a lot—but about things people didn't understand or didn't care about. His IQ was tested around that time at

167. He never seemed to understand social graces, and so it was that he was harassed at White's. In ninth grade, he left for Exeter. He didn't study, we're sure of that, but he did well nevertheless. Although he was no longer bullied, he was thoroughly ignored.

We were terribly pleased when he was admitted to Harvard, and when he went off to Cambridge, we had high hopes. Although he passed his courses in the fall, there were isolated reports of odd behavior: taking showers with his clothes on, wandering in ethnic neighborhoods, and even inviting miscreants to my husband's gunning cottage on Sandy Neck. Over the telephone he would rant about his "plans," the museum, and his flowers, always his flowers, whatever that meant.

The term ended in May, and only by our intercession with multiple professors did he pass. This particularly enraged him. We were still in town then, and when Quinton returned, it was clear that he had changed. He would not leave the house as far as we could see, but then after we left, we learned that he would depart at odd times and go to unknown locations. I believe you know the rest.

I hope that you can persuade him to let us return. We do so want to help but are willing to wait patiently here until you feel it is time. We appreciate your coming to the house, and enclosed is a retainer check for $2,000, renewable as necessary from Mr. Evans' account. We value the word of Dr. Santoni, and he said that you are the—

Jim beholds the enclosed check. He's never seen a draft so large. When he separated from the Army and got his DD-214, he received a payment somewhere near a thousand, some sort of VA benefit, but this seems far more than twice as much.

The door opens. Jim stuffs the check into his pocket, like he's been caught with a piece of pornography. The letter falls to the ground, and a gray-haired man with a chiseled jaw stands at the threshold. Gone is the livery; Mr. Evans wears a three-piece suit.

"I'm Dr. Malory."

"Thank you for coming," Evans says, his British accent all but lost. He picks up the letter and hands it to Jim. "Quinton is not well. Would you please follow me?"

The men walk into the foyer, and Jim gazes up through three floors of open-well stairs, black oak covering the walls. "Let me take you to—"

A silver tray crashes to the ground, a foot from the butler. Its plates shatter. A bearded man-boy with hair longer than George Harrison's sings a falsetto arpeggio and slides down the banister.

Quinton Graves wears briefs tie-dyed the colors of a rainbow. For an instant, he stands in front of Jim. The vestiges of a mannered greeting remain, but only for a moment. Then he hops through the open doorway like a rabbit. Jim hears him scream, "Get in the car! I want to show you something!"

Get in the car? A house call, conducted in a drawing room, might be an accepted psychiatric practice, but a car call? Jim's never heard of that, and he can't imagine his colleagues would approve. He reaches into his pocket, as if the commotion might have dislodged the check. He could make some excuse, come back at another time, and march right up to the Provident Bank on Athens with the deposit. The teller would look at him strangely, delicately summoning the manager to ensure that a fraud was not in process, but the two thousand dollars would clear by the weekend.

One year, Jim's mother made thirty-three dollars and nineteen cents a week at a box factory, and that was after driving an hour each way over the mountain to Shavertown on bald tires ready to burst. Some nights Jim wondered if the '32 Chrysler would go off into an Appalachian ravine. Around then, she learned to pull her own teeth if the pain was bad, but she sent Jim to the dentist and spent a full ten dollars on that gun for Christmas.

"Get in the car!" Quinton orders.

Once, twice a year, Jim's maternal grandparents would forget the defiance that their oldest child had displayed in marrying that charlatan. They would summon their disinherited daughter and her son up the hill to the big house for dinner. When it was over, the two of them would leave with nothing except the understanding that Jim's very existence was unforgivable.

The engine jerks and rumbles.

"Get in!" and Jim obeys. "It's a 427. You've got to have 103 octane to run it right."

With Evans standing on the front step, the tires yell, and the car rockets across the straightaway. Careening down the hill, the Sting Ray fishtails and bounces onto Wingohocking in the wrong lane. The absence of cars coming the other way means, at least for this moment, that they stay alive. Heading eastbound toward the city, Quinton shifts into fourth gear. They're already going sixty. "Get out of the way, you cocksuckers!" He passes four cars across the double yellow lines and through the curves.

"Quinton!" Jim is ignored. When they hit Sorrel Lane, which empties onto the expressway, Quinton faces a quandary.

"Do we take the Schuylkill? Do we?" The green river glistens in the sun, like the Mekong used to do. "I can't stand traffic, and this goddamned road was jammed the day it was built." Jim wants to provide a detailed answer that might address the question and keep them breathing, but the wind makes it impossible. "I think we chance it."

The car hits seventy on the downhill of Sorrel Lane. After a slight pause for the on-ramp, they skid onto the interstate. Within a minute, the car squeals to one hundred twenty, mid-afternoon July, little traffic.

"Where should we go?" Quinton asks. "We can be anywhere in forty-five minutes at this speed, and I remembered my American Express card!" He produces the green plate from his underwear and offers the card for Jim's inspection. "Should we go to the Harvard Club? Do you think they'll throw me out?"

"Slow down!" Jim pleads. To think of it: surviving Vietnam to die in your dream car, the kind you've been waiting for your whole, poor, on-the-county life.

"Give me one good reason why."

Jim points to the gas gauge: E for Empty.

Quinton sees the fuel's reclining needle and burns with rage. Searching for an appropriately profane expletive and finding nothing, he deflates and says, "We'll have to go to the Arco on Athens. They always have 103!" He rips the car off the road at Pencoyd, returns to the westbound expressway, and then exits at Glenwyth. Instead of Sorrel Lane, he makes the right onto River Road at fifty, rolling the roadster but for divine grace.

They are not alone. After the turn, a policeman, hidden behind the railroad bridge, lights his flashers. Seeing the pursuer, Quinton presses the gas, and the engine strains higher. But the surge is brief. The 427 coughs, burps, gasps, and then groans to silence and coasting stillness. The cruiser pulls up, and Jim can see through the rearview mirror that the officer has emerged, hand on his gun. There are fissures in the macadam. In last month's hurricane, River Road sat beneath three feet of water.

While the patrolman ambles to the Sting Ray, Quinton prepares to bolt. But Jim braces Quinton's leg and says, "He will shoot you."

The officer now stands on the driver's side. "May I see your license, sir? And where are your clothes?"

"I left them at home," Quinton says. "I figured I just needed the American Express card. You know, don't leave home without it?"

He reaches for the door handle.

"Don't get out of the car." The policeman walks back to his Dodge Polara and then returns after what seems an hour. "You were going fifty-seven in a twenty-five-mile-per-hour zone, and I think that's being kind."

Quinton laughs. "Is that worse than 114 in a fifty-mile-per-hour zone?"

"You a wise guy? You want me to impound the car?" The officer studies the passenger, sitting quietly and staring face forward, like he's seen him before. "Captain Malory?" The psychiatrist doesn't know what to say. "It's Michael Lord. You don't remember, do you?"

"I'm sorry," Jim says, reddening.

"The trees? Remember that thing about the trees? I still think of that. I was the guy from Swampoodle, well, used to be, until it turned. I was at the Eighth Field Hospital."

And so Jim remembers. He did psychiatric evaluations for six months at Nha Trang at the beginning of his tour. They were no big deal, not dangerous. Maybe Vietnam wasn't going to be so bad after all. After a bullet had grazed his spine, Private Lord had been terrified to go back to his unit, obsessed with returning home. In this particular case, Captain Malory had restated the words of his cross-country coach, Sister Michael Frederick: *Jimmy, don't run to the finish line. Run to the next and only the next tree.* In this way, with one's goal hidden from view, getting there became easier. It had worked for Lord, if throwing yourself back toward annihilation could be considered working.

"It's good to see you," Jim says, noting Lord's limbs, all present and functional. "You got out."

"Yup, and they can't draft you twice. You live around here?"

"Right in town. You?"

"Pencoyd Hills. It's a little place. The township makes you live here, to be on the force, but the schools are good. This guy's a friend of yours?"

Quinton ruminates on the teak steering wheel.

"In a manner of speaking."

"You better ask him to slow down," says Lord, his mouth in Quinton's face like a sergeant's. "And put some clothes on. We've had multiple reports of a black Corvette convertible ripping up the road. I suppose I could bring him in right now. Should I do that, Dr. Malory?"

"I think he's got the message." The driver says nothing. "Quinton?"

Still nothing.

"I'd keep an eye on this one," Lord says, tearing a citation from his pad. "You need a ride, Doc?

Eying Quinton and imagining what hell might break loose with the three of them in the squad car, Jim says, "I think we're going to walk."

"All right. I'll take care of the towing. And kid, next time, you might want to check the gas gauge."

Lord is hardly back at his patrol car when Quinton gets out and walks down River Road. Don't follow. Let him go. Get into the squad car and ride back to the office, the safe, easy choice. Return the check and forget this ever happened. It's so obvious and so impossible. The problem, as usual, is Santoni, just like when Jim wanted to join the Coast Guard. Ed said the words again and again: *Only through crisis can we become who we are meant to be.* So spoke the man who spent his war in the Sussex countryside playing tennis. But Jim didn't have to be persuaded then or now. The lurid fascination of what lay ahead was more than enough.

He offers his seersucker blazer to Quinton, and Maria's words ring in Jim's ears: *They always tell you if you listen.* And so the patient begins. Quinton came to Harvard Yard, and the rich New

Yorkers treated him with disdain, this irrelevant Philadelphian no matter how much money he had. "Fucking people from the Upper East Side, thinking everyone else is lucky for a pot to piss in!" His narration jumps to and fro like a skipping record. On a lark, he had taken Spanish at White's and then at Exeter. "It was so easy, like I already knew it." He had no desire to attend college, whether Harvard or Shippensburg, but he wanted to get away from his parents. So he went to Harvard. He was able to bluff his way through the first term, and the only thing that captured his attention was a course called "The Natives of the Sierra Madre."

When Jim arrived at Penn, he could have no more imagined taking a course on the Indigenous peoples of South America than he could have envisioned sitting naked in front of the Ben Franklin statue at College Hall. Penn was meant for getting into medical school so he could get a job and money, for himself and his mother.

But people like Quinton saw things differently. He was looking for something beyond his next meal, and over Christmas break, he joined his professor for a field study in Nayarit. What he saw there changed his life. He resolved that he would study anthropology, with a specific focus on Native American culture. His parents were "supportive," but only because they considered his academic program as useless as any other major that he might choose before taking up a respectable career.

"They wanted me to join Brown Brothers or some other nonsense like that," he says, pretending to fasten a necktie and squeeze it around his throat. "No, thank you." In the second term, though, he couldn't avoid the core curriculum: biology, mathematics, and the dubiously titled Moral Reasoning.

"From Harvard, moral reasoning, now that's a good one," he says. "Whether it's with the Nazis or Dow Chemical, Harvard is always on the right side of history."

By spring Quinton's interest in the Indigenous Americas was

all-consuming. Cutting class and flunking tests, he spent most of his time on Cape Cod searching the dunes for artifacts. His interest had expanded beyond the peoples of Mexico to those of North America.

Jim wants to interrupt, but the hike up Sorrel Lane, cars whizzing by, has winded him. He needs to start running again, despite the pain.

"Can we take a break?" Jim asks, pickled in sweat.

"If we walk, I talk. Even better, let's run."

"I'm out of shape, Quinton."

"No, you're not," he says, and takes off.

Jim tries to follow. After a minute, maybe two, he feels the skin of his abdomen catching fire and stops. Quinton makes it maybe four hundred yards ahead before turning back to the panting man no longer young.

"I used to be a runner," Jim says.

"Let me guess. Penn State."

"Penn."

"Really."

"I was in St. A's," Jim says, pausing. "For a semester."

"Wow. I guess you can't read a book by its cover, but I suppose my parents wouldn't have hired you if you weren't somehow Ivy League."

"Why did they hire me, Quinton?"

"I have no idea."

"You were in the hospital, right? They found you dancing on a putting green."

"That was living my life to the fullest. Let me carry you, and then I can run." He bends and tries to lift his doctor.

"Don't do that," Jim says, wincing. "I know you're depressed."

"No."

"Anxious?" Jim sounds like a textbook for psychiatric interns.

"No. Why would I be?"

"Do you want to commit suicide?"

"I want to live. I want to take it all in. It's wonderful!"

"How about your thoughts? Do they race? Do you have grandiose ideas?"

"Not at all. My ideas make perfect sense, and I know they're right."

While the two walk back, past acre lots and three-car garages, Jim sees the diagnosis and relaxes. Quinton has textbook mania. Doctor and patient can meet three times a week for the next year to talk about Huichol art while the real work is done by 900 milligrams of lithium twice a day. In the end, Jim will look brilliant while his patient's illness evaporates like a puddle of fetid water. Maybe he should prescribe lithium to Eliza and Honey as well, and they can share their pills.

"We're almost back," Quinton says. "Should we go for a swim?"

Preposterously, the psychiatrist replies, "Yes." Minutes later, they tread water in the Graves' pool. Mosaic tile forms the floor and walls, and gargoyles spit water in all directions. Some of the stone creatures sit removed on a tarp, engaged in demonic conversation.

"We're restoring the pool," Quinton says. "You have any kids?"

"That's an odd question."

"Well, how are you supposed to help me, assuming I need help, if you don't have any kids yourself?"

"I have a daughter."

"Right," Quinton says, smiling. "Not a toddler."

"No."

"So you had her when you were young, you and your wife?"

"Yes."

"What's her name, your wife's?"

"Maria."

"I love that name. Whenever I see a Maria, it's like she has the whole world inside her because she gives birth to God."

"I never thought of it that way," Jim says, his diagnosis settling on a single word: wacko. "Have you had any medical illnesses or hospitalizations?"

"Of course not."

"Allergies?"

"No. Anything else, Herr Doktor Professor?"

"Not really. I'd like to start you on lithium carbonate tonight, 900 milligrams twice a day. What do you say?"

"Absolutely not." Quinton splashes Jim with water. "There's nothing wrong with me."

"But your mind is racing," Jim says. "You're doing things that are dangerous."

"Dangerous? That's a question of perspective."

"You're going to kill yourself or someone else. It's just a matter of time."

Quinton laughs. "We were taking a joyride in my L88. It's called hot-rodding, and all the 'yon teenagers' do it. Go down to River Road on a Friday night, although I wouldn't bring that car. The kids will think you're a Mustang Sally."

"See?"

"What?"

"You're talking non-stop," Jim says.

"And I'll keep talking. I can think, I mean really think, for the first time in my life. It's like the cobwebs have cleared, and I can see things for how they truly are. It's like the Huichol! They get it! Do my parents get it, with this barn and their bond coupons and their never having done anything in their lives? What the fuck? They can't handle the truth. Ashes to ashes, dust to dust. Render unto Caesar what's Caesar's, and unto God what's God's! Can you dig it?"

Jim reads the pool's sundial: 5:30. That means a half-hour to return to Maria and Ruthie, thirty minutes to look normal by forgetting another piece of the trauma that is his life. Lord was right there, offering an out just like that congressman who was going to get Jim into the Coast Guard. And yet there's some part of Quinton as inescapable as the burning Huey beneath the rubber trees.

The patient repeats, "Can you dig it?"

Jim doesn't know what to say. Instead, he gets out of the pool.

"Why do you walk like that?" Quinton asks. "It's like a limp, but not exactly."

"I walk like that because it hurts."

"Why?"

"I was burned."

"Dropped coffee on your trousers?"

"My helicopter was shot down in Cambodia."

Quinton springs from the water and directs Jim to a poolside table. "Did anyone else live?"

"Nope."

"Just you?"

"Just me."

The young man's mind races. "How bad was it?"

Jim presents the crinkled wrapper of his abdominal skin.

"There's a graft," Jim says, "but you can tell. The nerves are all messed up."

"Did they have to cut it off, you know?"

"No. The burn stopped three inches north and four inches west." The doctors told him that, no joke. Jim should stop right there, but the Mississippi of his mind floods forward.

"You should have been dead, but you're not," Quinton says.

"It was luck. Maybe I was wearing my seatbelt. I don't know. I blacked out, and I woke up in the Second Surgical. I had all my limbs, I could walk. I wasn't maimed, at least not after the graft. I couldn't hear, but they fixed that. I live with it."

"You're so flat about the whole thing," Quinton says. "It's like you don't even believe you're alive." Before Jim can respond, the patient closes his eyes, face tightening, and opens them again. "You were meant to live. It's a sign. You're a healer." A pause. "As long as you're not a liar. Are you a fucking liar?"

"No. It's all true."

"Then I might take the medication. I might, but it's much more important that I take you. You're the only one who can understand me," Quinton says, and Jim almost believes him.

They continue for a while, setting appointments and talking cars. Back in his clothes, wet again with curdled sweat, Jim calls the prescription into the pharmacy from the house phone. Then, escaping to the Mustang, he flips on WIBG and drives home while Joey Reynolds shuts up and plays *(Last Night) I Didn't Get To Sleep At All.* Jim looks in his rearview mirror, half-wondering if Quinton is running after him.

When Jim pulls up to the house, his thoughts on Marilyn McCoo, he fails to see that Ruthie, rocking on one of the porch's chairs, has been staring at him from the moment he turned onto their street.

Passing her on the porch, he puts his hand on her shoulder and says, "What's wrong?"

Her eyes are bloodshot, like she's been crying.

"What?" he asks again.

"Nothing."

"What?"

She says, "I'm not sure I like you."

4

Jim studies the three medical students who have been rounding with him for the past two hours and wonders if he was ever this annoying. There's Rod, already a surgical intern in his own mind. He's asked more than once if the students will get a chance to view a lobotomy and, if so, whether he can assist. Kent, with sideburns that have overtaken his jaw, keeps saying "groovy." *The patient complained of auditory hallucinations and then killed his wife. Groovy!* Then there's Sloane, a globe of a man just released from the laboratory who has referred four times already today to "my research." Is he the one who keeps farting?

They've just concluded afternoon rounds on the VA inpatient psychiatric service.

Jim spends the overnight from Wednesday afternoons to Thursday mornings there to get major medical insurance, dental, and a fraction of a weekly salary, in case the office on Athens remains empty and Angelo and Carmela stop paying the electric bill. Having convinced Jim to join the Army, Santoni has also compelled him to teach medical students, for free. The former could be justified as patriotism, but agreeing to the latter has been insanity. The paid part of the job doesn't begin until 5:00 p.m. when the students leave. Then Jim evaluates walk-in patients in the emergency room, performs consults on the medical floors, and generally tries to prevent psychiatric catastrophes.

In its inestimable wisdom, the federal government carved the VA from the ancient Penrose Cemetery so that funereal obelisks are visible from each cafeteria window. Penrose is a necropolis, echoing for blocks westward from Woodland Avenue to the river, which makes the hospital building look like a crematorium. It's the same street where Jim, Honey, and Maria used to spend their time a few blocks away. Strange how life took him to Cambodia and then plopped him right back in West Philadelphia. The hospital is only twenty years old, but already a gray pall oozes from its bricks. Designed without air conditioning, the VA retains a terminal stickiness throughout the year. The marble floors are dirty, and strange smells hide in corners.

"Dr. Malory," Nurse Tucker says with the twang of South Carolina, "how are you today?"

"Aldyce, it's like you always say: They can hurt you, but they can't turn back the clock. How are you?"

"Fair to partly cloudy." Like many of the nurses at the VA, she's black and has served in-country, explaining her equanimity at thrown breakfast trays and on-unit suicides. Her hair is straightened, and a starched white cap sits on top. "Dr. Santoni's in the conference room."

"Thanks." Jim turns toward a door with a faux brass plaque marked "Doctors," but before he can enter, a small man in the customary brown scrubs of the unit inserts himself in front of the knob.

"Doc," the man says, "I gotta show you something. I got this sore on the front of my head." The man points to wrinkled but otherwise intact skin.

"Yes, Mr. Vassaluzzo. I remember that."

"I'm really worried about it."

"I understand."

"How about you take a look? You can give me some cream or an ointment. Do you think I'll need surgery? Or maybe get me an X-ray." Rod angles closer for an inspection and, seeing nothing, turns away in boredom. Leaning against the wall, Sloane peruses *The American Journal of Gastroenterology.*

"I know what you believe," Jim says, "but sometimes our fears make us see things not as they really are."

"Doc," Vassaluzzo says, "I hate to tell you, but you've got the same problem."

"All right then. Can I do anything else for you?"

"I need surgery!"

"Not today."

"Maybe a blood test?"

"We'll consider it."

"Thanks, Doc. You're the best." The man scurries back to the TV room where a group of veterans watches Mike Douglas and Mayor Frank Rizzo watching a hula hoop demonstration. TV was so different before Jim went away. Mary Tyler Moore was a repressed, black-and-white housewife in New Rochelle, and now she's an unmarried Minneapolis news writer in color.

The conference room is an inflated closet with boxes stacked to the ceiling. At a metal table, Santoni sits next to a tall man with a face lined and blank. He must be the patient for today's examination, imported from the outpatient clinic. Unlike the unit's inmates, he wears a blue blazer, khakis, and a pinpoint white Oxford.

"Gentlemen, this is Mr. David Black. Mr. Black, this is Dr. Malory and our medical students. May they listen?"

"Why the hell not?" Black says, a wire coiled under tension. His black hair, gray at the edges, stands up like he's been shocked.

Santoni straightens his legal pad and starts to write. "Okay. Nilso told me that you've had a number of symptoms related to your time in Vietnam."

"I have nightmares. Pretty much every night."

"What are they about?"

"You wouldn't want to know."

Santoni turns to Jim and the students. "You'll note the avoidance."

"I don't avoid it," the man says.

Santoni moves his chair closer to Black. "There's no need to get upset. It's totally normal. You shouldn't be ashamed. You were a pilot?"

He nods.

"What was your rank?"

"Well, originally, I was a captain in the Air Force, late '50s. I was at Ramstein, pretty boring, never saw any combat of course. Then I flew commercial."

"Why'd you stop?"

"I got my fill of stewardesses."

Sloane laughs out loud, and Rod punches him in the leg.

"So you got tired of flying Jello salesmen to business meetings in Miami?" Santoni says, no one laughing. "What happened next?"

"After the Gulf of Tonkin, I wanted to get back in, but they said there was no room in the Air Force. So I joined the Army as a chief warrant officer. Dustoff. Right, you've never heard of it. It was MEDEVAC." Kent's brow furrows in confusion. "We were rescuing the injured."

"How many missions?" Santoni asks.

"I have no idea. I did two tours."

"Were you shot down?"

"Twice."

"Where?"

Black laughs. "You want coordinates?"

A loudspeaker in the ceiling blasts static, and the patient jumps. After the noise clears, an anesthetized female voice says, "Your attention, please. This is an announcement. Please join us in the Multipurpose Room this evening at 1930 for ice cream and cookies courtesy of the Perkiomen Valley Chapter of the Daughters of the American Revolution, followed by a showing of *Son of Lassie* starring Peter Lawford and June Lockhart. All veterans and their families are invited to view this exciting story of love and war in Nazi-occupied Norway. You won't want to miss it. Thank you." Silence.

Santoni eyes his subject. "You jumped."

"It's fine," Black says.

Turning to the students, Santoni says, "Note the increased startle response." To Black, "So, you've had several episodes of trauma."

"Of course. I flew MEDEVAC. I saw everything."

"The wounded?"

"And the dead. Sometimes even medics and doctors." Black pauses. "You know." And everyone does know. Bored just a moment ago, the students are now rapt. They know the war is ending, but the draft is still in place, including the Berry Plan, the Doctor's Draft. One bad evaluation or a reprimand from the dean might still send Sloane, Rod, or Kent where Black and Malory have been.

"I don't think it would be helpful to discuss the trauma specifically," Santoni says. "But if you could discuss its effects."

Sweat pooling around the elastics of his underwear, Jim looks at the boxes perched behind his head, tilting towers ready to tumble down. Uncle Sam started a war that could never be won and built a hospital in Philadelphia without central air conditioning.

"The nightmares are the worst," Black says. "Sometimes you

wake up, and you don't know where you are. You think you're in-country, maybe you're dead. Other times, I can reach out and touch one of those kumquat trees you see over there. Then I'm pulling in the hoist with the load litter."

"What's the feeling you get in those moments?" Santoni asks. "Horror?"

"More like numbness."

What a stupid question, and of course Santoni wouldn't know. He spent his war drinking gin and tonics. The numbness doesn't go away, Jim knows that. Last summer, there was a Dodge Dart crumpled against a tree on Athens. Minutes earlier, it had ejected its passenger, something between a ragdoll and a missile, onto the gravel. She was a teenage girl, both femurs sticking out of her legs like hockey sticks. Jim tried to resuscitate her, mouth to mouth. When it was over, and the ambulance removed the body, he drove home, parked the Mustang in the garage, and smoked a cigarette in the dark.

Santoni continues, "Are you married?"

"Was. Twenty-three years."

"I'm sorry."

"She wasn't."

"Children?"

"Two, but they're grown and gone."

"Where is—"

"She's gone back to her sister in Easton," Black says.

Like Maria fleeing to Swedesboro in 1969 when Jim got his orders. There was such pain then, but how does he feel nothing now? After his overnights, he drives back to Glenwyth on the expressway, the same road where Quinton nearly killed him. At home, he finds Maria sitting in her maternity nightgown with a pot of hot coffee and a plate of muffins, like nothing even happened. She came back, even if he didn't.

"What do you do with your time, workwise?" Santoni asks.

"After I got out—"

"Which was when?"

"'69. I didn't want to fly anymore, you know, fat businessmen to Miami. So I started doing pools, swimming pools."

"An interesting choice."

"A buddy from the Army took me in when I got back and basically gave me a franchise for five hundred bucks. It was easy. Everybody wants one, and you only work for half the year. It's good money too. Given what I make, I probably shouldn't be coming to VA."

"You mentioned that you got out in '69," Santoni says.

"August thirteenth. Would have been the twelfth, but the C130 took enemy fire on the way out, and we lost an engine. So I had to stay another day in paradise with all the REMFS." Black smiles. "Sorry. Rear echelon motherfuckers."

Santoni asks, "How do your nightmares compare to when you first got out?"

"They weren't bad back then. Then they found the remains of Billy in May '71. He went down in '68 and was MIA. He was my roommate in flight school, and then he was in my unit, doing Dustoff. I had to do advanced flight school over again for three months, even though I had been an Air Force officer. Typical Army bullshit."

"So what's the worst part?"

"You have to ask me that?" The patient looks down at the floor's stained carpet and then out the window. The cemetery slopes across the view, stones everywhere. "You ever go to Bartram's Garden?"

"No."

"It's right down the river, 54th Street."

"I've heard of it," Santoni says. "It's a house and park of some kind."

"Yeah, it's beautiful. Well, kind of. It's surrounded by sewers and factories and abandoned cars and a housing project and all this garbage, so I guess it's not that great. But when you get there, and you go inside, you're free from all that. You can imagine the city when it was just farms and cows and milkmaids."

"That sounds restful," Santoni says.

"I go there a lot, and when I'm there, it's like none of this ever happened. Of course, it did, but I can pretend it didn't. And then it's all okay, even if it isn't."

Jim and his wife went there with Ruthie when they all lived in South Philadelphia. The stone farmhouse was closed at the time, and the family spent their drizzly afternoon wandering through the decayed grounds. The place was known for its ginkgo trees, the same species that survived the atomic blast of Hiroshima.

Santoni says, "It sounds like a wonderful spot. Do you think you'll get back there?"

"Very soon indeed," Black says.

"Well, I want to thank you for your time. I've spoken with Nurse Tucker, and she'll take you off the unit to the lobby."

"Thanks, Doc." Black gets up slowly and limps out of the room. He walks like the villagers lined up for vaccinations, tilting on their prosthetic limbs of dried bamboo and metal pipe. Then he's gone, silence in his wake.

After a minute, the senior psychiatrist asks, "So what's the differential diagnosis?" When no one replies, Santoni elaborates. "Mr. Black presents a classic case of traumatic neurosis. It's textbook really: nightmares, flashbacks, dissociation, and even increased activation of the sympathetic nervous system. Did you see him jump?" This makes Ed smile, a bit of clinical amusement. "If you didn't have his file, you might have thought that he lost the left leg below the knee. Or maybe it was saved by some surgical hero leaving low function and chronic pain, which might be even worse."

"Which is it?" Jim asks.

"Surgical hero, but the leg was probably the only reason he got out, probably forced out. This kind of guy wouldn't have left on his own."

Sloane looks queasy. His limbs are important, thank you very much.

Santoni studies the medical students. "Which would you rather lose: a limb or your mind?"

No one answers. So Sloane says, "What's the cause? I mean, at the brain level."

To the psychoanalysts, Santoni elaborates, the trauma brings the patient back to infantile fantasies of murder and mayhem, but this theory never made sense to Jim. The patients he treated in Vietnam with traumatic neurosis never wanted to kill their fathers or seduce their mothers. The problem was more straightforward, even obvious. Soldiers, having suffered traumas, relived those traumas in infinite recurrence.

Jim explains this, and Kent asks, "Why do they relive it?"

"Is it a form of muscle memory?" Rod asks.

Neither of the psychiatrists has an answer, not even Jim, with his constant companionship of bone and blood, fire and burns. The discussion saunters on, and the students, having learned nothing, wonder whether obscurities like hypercalcemia or neurosyphilis might be the real cause of Mr. Black's symptoms.

"He looks normal," Rod says.

Sloane says, "When he's sitting down, you can't even tell."

Jim's gaze wanders away. Other than being a bit thin, Eliza looks normal—can't tell with her either. Same thing with Honey. How many times has he wanted to ask Ruthie about Eliza and her mother? Ruthie must have an opinion, she always does, but how does he find it? Emboldened by the breakthrough with Quinton, Jim wanted to ask Ruthie on Monday night when the three of them dined at the Wayside. That was before the day's check was even cashed. She seemed preoccupied, as if facing an imminent chemistry test, but more than that. She was angry, like her father was somehow to blame for the way that the world was.

In contrast, Eliza was more focused and energetic in this morning's session than Jim can ever remember her being. She was analyzing him, like she was waiting for the moment to ask a long-anticipated question. She wasn't supposed to come to the office until the following Monday, but yesterday Honey changed her mind and insisted that Jim see the girl this week. There was the usual talk about her mother's drinking and her father's infidelities, but Eliza spent most of the time relating how grateful she was for Ruthie. Eliza was still cutting, yes. She was sorry that she never told him that, but she had never really thought about how it affected other people. This was awkward, but Jim's relief at the honesty washed away any concern that his daughter might be so much a part of her friend's case. Eliza even invited her mother and the family's caboose child, Burtie, to join them at the end. Honey never leaves the boy. She could well afford a babysitter, but for her, the kid is an amulet always to be worn.

5:00 p.m. drifts by, and Santoni leaves the students with Jim. Without the presence of the senior psychiatrist, the one grading them, they reveal what they're really thinking, that they don't give a crap about Mr. Black. No matter how fascinating the discussion, the psychiatry rotation is meant to be a vacation, not like surgery or internal medicine. Plans have been made, in the laboratory, at Smokey Joe's, or with a nurse in the call room. No one cares about psychiatry, and the attending physicians stupid enough to have fallen into the specialty couldn't do anything else anyway. That's what Rod, Kent, and Sloane—sounding more like a law firm than medical students—must be thinking.

A few minutes after Jim excuses the students, the ceiling speaker jumps to life. "Dr. Malory, paging Dr. Malory. Please call the emergency room. Urgent page for Dr. Malory. Thank you."

An overhead page means that normal attempts at communication have failed. Jim checks his belt. No pager. Damn. He must have left that plastic ingot of a thing in the call room. Not good. Nilso, Jim's boss, covers the ER on Wednesday afternoons but meets with administrators from 3:00 to 5:00 p.m. to discuss topics ranging from in-hospital entertainment programming to the color science of psychiatric interior design. Today, Nilso proposed painting the emergency room a peculiar shade of pink, contending that it would lead to fewer outbursts and staff attacks.

The speaker squawks again. "Dr. Malory, please call the emergency room immediately. This is a Code White, repeat Code White."

The voice sounds panicked, unusual for the VA where, unable to be fired, most approach their jobs with indifference. In his initial VA training session, a pale reflection of Medical Basic at Fort Sam Houston, Jim promised to uphold the Constitution and not commit insurrection, but what the hell is Code White?

"You need some help?" Santoni asks.

"Oh, hi. I guess I'll find out."

"When you have a moment, I mean, not now, I want to know about Quinton."

The mania, the kidnapping, the delusional folkloric fascinations, where to begin?

"He started lithium on Monday night," Jim says, looking at the overhead speaker. "He's like the kid who sits alone at the dance, getting angrier and angrier. Hey, how about breakfast tomorrow at seven?"

Santoni shakes his head. "Have to be in Harrisburg to meet

with the Governor's Task Force on Neurotic Wives. Shapp wants to make it harder to commit them. Can you come to Oakmont on Saturday afternoon for supervision?"

"Sorry. We're going to Glenwyth Cricket for tennis and a few G&Ts."

"The Dixons?"

"How'd you guess?"

"I've been meaning to talk with you about that. It's a sticky situation with Honey." Santoni reflects on his words. "You know, that's a pretty good one, sticky with—"

"We didn't invite ourselves."

"No, I guess not, but you throw in Eliza." He doesn't mention the scotch, vintage port, and yellow, green, and blue liqueurs that will follow when the two couples return at the end of the evening to the Dixons' metallic shell of a house.

"I want to talk about Ruthie," Jim says.

"What's wrong?"

"I don't know. She looks down."

"Well, it's a good thing she has a psychiatrist for a father. We'll have lunch next week before rounds. You better get down there before they call Nilso."

They part, and knowing he should go directly to the ER, Jim instead enters his call room, the last chamber before "Mechanical" at the end of Four East. At times Jim has seen the VA's EOD (another federally funded acronym for Engineer on Duty) pass into that room to adjust a flywheel or oil a sprocket. With the door open, the whining grind of the VA's internal organs sparks Jim to attention. Even with the door closed, the continuous vibration thrums, the workings of a world that few know.

Jim's cell is a former hospital room, a general's suite really, with a private bathroom and a window overlooking the cemetery. But tonight, yesterday's sheets sit unchanged, and the room's heat is stultifying. Even in July, the VA makes warmth, hidden radiators banging through the night, unstoppable, while crazy brains, wrecked by war, steam. Many nights, the emergency room is bare, and Jim remains in bed. But noises in the wall murder his sleep.

He picks up the pager. How many pages has he missed? None, other than four from the ER. He clips the pager to his belt. Even in the call room, an overhead speaker shouts, "Dr. Malory…."

When he enters the emergency room, two police officers stand over Nurse Tucker, collapsed on a gurney. They are joined by the ER doctor who holds vials of just-drawn blood. Tucker hyperventilates, and the heart monitor shows a rapid pulse. Her white cap bobs up and down like a starched buoy.

"What happened?" Jim asks. The VA's emergency room is a barn where curtains separate the stalls, and the other patients mostly look at Tucker.

"She came saying she was having chest pain," says the ER doctor.

Jim leans above his nurse. "What's wrong?"

"That man from the floor, I got talking to him, and he said he was going to kill himself, and I knew he was going to do it. I think he's already done it. What'd you all do to him?"

"How'd he get out?" Jim asks.

"While I was trying to figure out what to do," Aldyce says, "he slipped right out the door with those medical students. They should flunk! I should have called the police, but he was gone, and then I couldn't breathe."

The ER doctor shears an electrocardiogram from the machine. "You're not having a heart attack," he says. "It's probably anxiety, but we'll have the blood gas back in a second."

Defenestration, strangulation, dismemberment by elevated train—is Black's neck already broken, his body burned like a Buddhist monk's? He didn't seem depressed, but neither does Jim.

Anyway, depression isn't what kills. Suicide takes energy, something the sad don't have. It also takes isolation, agitation, hopelessness, and doctors being too stupid to ask.

An orderly arrives with a scrap of paper and presents it to the ER doc. "The gas is good," he says.

"Aldyce," Jim says, "It's anxiety. Your heart's fine."

"Not for long," she says.

Black could be anywhere in Philadelphia, but where? If you were committing suicide and saying farewell to the world, what would you want for your last portion of reality? When Jim was growing up, the *Lehighton Times* used to print the final meals when there were executions. *The prisoner had chocolate milk, two cheeseburgers, French fries, and a bowl of maraschino cherries.* There was always some odd detail, as if the prisoner were speaking in a culinary code.

The nurse sits up now, breathing more slowly. "I should have asked him where he was going!"

"Did you see him go toward the front or the back entrance of the unit?" Jim asks.

"The back." The hospital's parking lot, the trolley, cabs, and, further on, the El, all are accessed from the front. The back entrance, seldom used, empties onto Vintage Avenue, which leads nowhere except to Gray's Lane, which intersects with 54th Street at Bartram's Garden.

Jim picks up the phone and dials Nilso's extension. It rings multiple times before the supervisor picks up. "Hello?" He's annoyed.

"Dr. Nilso, a patient just went AWOL. He's suicidal. He's one of your—"

"Listen, I'm in a committee meeting right now with nursing and social work and the Third Assistant Director, along with the Second Undersecretary, who's come up from Washington. You should contact the psychiatrist on call."

"That's me."

"Malory? Oh, right. Okay, good. Well, deal with that, and then you should come up to this meeting. We're talking about process redesign for the VECU, and I think—"

"I gotta go." Jim slams the phone down with an expletive, then wonders if Nilso heard him.

Jim sees an officer he knows, Corporal Cedillo, and doesn't have to explain. "Cover me," Jim shouts to the ER doc, not waiting to hear if he will.

A blink later, Cedillo and Malory, in a VA Police car, have driven over an abandoned railroad cut and turned onto the cracked parking lot of Bartram's Garden. It's vacant save a 1959 white-on-white Eldorado convertible. They pull up to it, and Cedillo gets out. He walks to the chrome rear bumper and, producing his pocket notebook, copies the plate number—6Y7 separated from 204 by a cracked Liberty Bell, with the motto Pennsylvania Bicentennial State '76.

"You sure this is his?" Cedillo asks. "Who'd want to kill himself with a car like this?"

"It's him. I'll bet you a nickel," Jim says. Ruth Malory used to bet nickels.

"I'm going to radio in the plate. How well do you know this guy?"

"Not before today."

Cedillo looks down at the crumbling asphalt. "I don't know, Doc. Tucker was pretty shaken. What do you say we have a look-see together? This guy may be mental."

Jim runs his hand along the rear bumper and the conical taillights, sharp enough to wound. "I don't know. Two people may scare him off." He checks the door handle. Unlocked. "Can you believe this? Like he wants it to be stolen."

"Maybe he doesn't need it anymore," Cedillo says.

"I'm going to go myself."

"No. I know where you've been, and you don't deserve to be shot by some sorry-ass wingnut and drowned in the Schuylkill."

"How crazy can this guy be?" Jim asks. "His '59 is mint."

"It is a fine car. I almost bought one in my dreams."

"She made you get the Vista Cruiser, right?"

"Nah, we compromised. I got a '67 Thunderbird. It's no '66, but it's not bad." Cedillo looks down at the ground. "He could be armed. I'm calling for backup."

"No. That'll be the end."

"Then let me watch your back, at least."

"All right."

A stone barn stands on one side of the parking lot, the manor house on the other, and the garden tilts down to the river. No trace of Black. City Hall squats in the distance, capped with its statue of William Penn, who looks to be holding his reproductive member when seen from the right direction. This was a joke that Jim learned freshman year in his semester of fraternity life before he had to drop out and move in with the Sedaras. He shouldn't be remembering such nonsense now, but all he could think about in Vietnam was the WIBG Top 99.

A quiescent factory lurks to the left, painted letters vertically monogramming its smokestack: ELS-N PT A. Jim's mind fills in the missing letters: FELS-NAPTHA. That was the special soap that could prevent poison ivy. When he was eleven, he got it so badly that sores covered the inside of his mouth and below his tonsils. His mother always had Fels-Naptha around after that, but at a quarter a bar, it wasn't to be used as an everyday soap. If only the rest of life's terrors could be as easily removed, like the product's wrapping proclaimed, *within 30 minutes of exposure.*

Still no Black. Maybe he's not even here. Maybe the car's a

plant, and he's taken a train to Easton to kill himself and his wife. But the trains don't go to Easton anymore, just like they don't go to Lehighton.

The same year that Woody Dixon told him about William Penn's penis, Jim was invited to dinner at a rowhome, a quarter the size of the Sedaras', on a treeless side street not far from here. That would have been his last actual date before meeting Maria. The girl worked in the cafeteria at Houston Hall, and he was desperate and lonely. She was Dianne something, Italian, like a preview of the main attraction. Seventeen years ago, on the night of that date, he would have passed the same smokestack coughing fumes, still breathing, not yet dead. The girl's father worked there, and there were stacks of Fels-Naptha bars in the bathroom. Dianne DeLassini. That was her name. The neighborhood then must have been a clutch of working factories, lights ablaze on a Saturday evening at the beginning of the second shift, alive with clanking. Now, there's only the distant whoosh of the expressway carrying people never knowing that this place exists.

He scans the sloping garden, its remaining specimens surrounded by collapsed trees and rusted fences. No sign of Black. Then Jim understands. Before there were guns, knives, and cyanide, there was water, the same stuff in swimming pools. He runs to the river's edge, a rainbow of bobbing plastic bottles, tires, and oily foam. There he sees Black strapping barbell weights to his legs with electrical extension cords.

"Mr. Black?" The patient doesn't look over and instead continues with his anchoring. "Do you remember me from this afternoon?"

"Sure."

"What are you doing?" Jim asks, and Black glares. "Alright, but there's an officer up in the parking lot."

"Fine. He can shoot me. Death by cop."

Jim grabs Black's arm. "Are you carrying?"

"Do you think if I was and wanted to shoot you, you'd be able to ask? Besides, I was just at VA. You can't carry a firearm at a federal facility, regardless of state licensure. 18 USC Section 930."

"It could have been in your car."

Black pulls an M1911 from his pants and drops it to the muddy riverbank. "Why are you so shocked?" Jim picks up the weapon. "So shoot me," Black says. "It'll be easier than this."

The gun feels familiar, like Jim's arm is complete again.

"How about, how about—" Jim says, stepping back, emptying the chamber and putting the bullets in his pocket, but not finishing the sentence. Then he's panting, and blood pumps through his carotids, like he's just run the mile in high school. "How about we take a break and come back to this later?"

"No. There won't be any later." Black glances at the farmhouse up the hill and sees Cedillo leaning against its porch. "You'll commit me."

"I won't," Jim says inexplicably.

"What do you mean? Hey, you don't look so good."

"I'm fine, and what would it do, anyway? You'll be right back here after you get out, and I'll be somewhere else."

Black stops his preparations. "Aren't you worried you'll get sued or reprimanded or court-martialed?" Jim tries to respond, but nothing comes out. He finds a dry spot away from the bank and sits. "Doc, don't get offended, but you look like you're the one who should be in the hospital."

"The only person who saves a patient is the patient," Jim says, steadying himself, his strength returning. "It may seem bad now, but what do you know about how you'll feel in the future, and what about the guys in your unit? What are they going to say when they hear about Chief Warrant Officer Black jumping into the Schuylkill with weights on his legs? And then what are they going to do, in the Hudson, the Columbia, or the goddamned Nesquehoning?"

"You're from Carbon."

"Born and raised," Jim says.

"I used to hunt up there."

"And you can again, or you can give up. But what about your brothers in VA nursing homes, tubes in their cocks, the guys who used to be hot-rodding and picking up girls at the drive-in and listening to the Beach Boys before this whole nightmare? Do you want to tell them that you fucking threw in the towel?"

Black softens almost into sadness. "You're not going to commit me?"

"Do you think if I wanted to, you would have had the chance to ask that question?"

Black unwraps the weights, one by one, and stacks them. Then he genuflects, bowing his head in his right hand. Jim should summon Cedillo now. That's one of Santoni's rules: *If you've got it sold, get out of the room.*

"Can I ask you a question?" the psychiatrist nevertheless says, bowing next to his patient.

"Yeah."

"What the hell were you doing?"

Black says nothing, then, "You wouldn't understand. You weren't there."

"I was. Nha Trang and Cambodia."

Black tinges with embarrassment. "Okay. So you know. Every day, every minute of every day, I'm there, Captain. From Fort Mother-Rucker to Cam Rahn to Camp Holloway, back to McCord, and everything in between, from Fucking New Guy to short-timer. But see, I never was a short-timer, because I never left. I meant what I said about the kumquats. I'm still there, and I can't take it. Every time I put in a pool, I'm digging a grave. It's easier to just end.... I know it's weak. So I'm weak."

A freight train lumbers across a railroad bridge over the river.

"Tell me about Billy," Jim says.

Black shrugs. "We were at Camp Holloway, late '68, we were both FNGs. He was from Flyheads, New York, or some piece-of-crap burg like that. He always loved aviation, built model biplanes and all that. We were both in flight school at Rucker, but we didn't know each other. We only met at Holloway. One night we're sitting in the GP medium tent that we slept in, mosquito nets and everything, and he says he knows he's going to die."

"That's crazy," Jim says, knowing it isn't.

"He wasn't there a month, and I could have saved him."

"How?"

"I could have convinced him that he wasn't going to die—and then he wouldn't have." Black is right; things were different in Vietnam. Think you would die, and you did. Think you would live, and, well, maybe.

By the time of Jim's tour, his mother, thank God, was already dead. His brothers and sisters had never been born, his cousins were unknown, and his father was just as absent as he had been by the time of Jim's fifth birthday. It would have been easy to drift away and be pulverized into pink mist like so many others. That's what it looked like when you stepped on a landmine, but Glenwyth and everybody in it kept him alive. When Jim couldn't remember the town, he thought of the Mustang and how he had always wanted to drive it top down in a snowstorm.

"You can't make someone believe," Jim says. "It has to come from somewhere else, from God or whatever. And how are you even going to try with all this?" Jim sizes up the beehive of weights. "How are you going to save the next Billy if you can't save yourself? You feel the guilt, but what good does that do? You survived. He didn't. You have to make something good of it."

"Are you really not going to commit me?" Black asks.

"I said no, but you need help."

"Where?"

"The outpatient clinic. You see Nilso."

"Him? No, thank you. You treat outpatients?"

"Me? Sure, but I'm just here one night a week," Jim says. "During the day, I don't even work in the city, and anyway, I'm not supposed to recruit people from the VA. In fact, there's a direct order."

"Where's your office?"

"Glenwyth."

"I live in Glenwyth, near the Cricket Club," Black says. "How much a session?"

"But it's not covered as a VA benefit. You'd have to pay."

"So. How much?"

"Fifty," Jim says, dodging the word "dollars" and wondering if he sounds like a desperate merchant on Thong Nhut Boulevard.

"I'll pay for ten years with a single pool."

"I could get fired if they find out."

"Nobody's going to know," Black says. "I'll cancel my next appointment with Nilso and disappear like any other vet he doesn't give a shit about. You think he'll notice?"

"I could see you tomorrow at nine," Jim says, not missing a beat. He has Quinton in the afternoon, but the morning's planner is a sea of lined white.

"You got it, and I pay in cash." Black stands and looks up the hill toward Cedillo. "Wing abreast?"

"You go first, and I'll follow. He'll be a lot calmer if we leave all this junk."

Black glances at his assembly of weights. "Well, I'm sure some street kid who lifts will find it and think it's his lucky day." Jim picks up the M1911, and they walk back.

In the parking lot, Cedillo asks, "Everything okay?"

"Doc calmed me down." Soon the patient and Cedillo are talking about their tours, two players on Uncle Sam's basketball team. After more pleasantries, Black pulls out his keys, but Cedillo intercedes before Black can open the Eldorado's door.

"You made quite a mess back there," the officer says.

"I know."

"Tucker is a tough one," Jim adds. "I haven't seen much get to her. She did two tours at the 67th Evacuation." Jim hands Cedillo the gun and bullets.

"Very nice," the officer says, checking the slide and ejecting the magazine. "This is as clean as your car. Listen, Doc. How about you take the Polara, and we'll take the Caddy?"

"Right," Jim says, "and Nilso will accuse me of misusing federal property. I'll ride with Mr. Black."

"That's generally not considered a good idea," Cedillo says.

"He's cool. He's going to give me a good deal on a pool. Listen. Thanks for everything."

Shaking his head at the stupidity of officers like Dr. Malory, Cedillo departs in the government-issued Dodge, and the two men are left with the Eldorado. "Does this thing have a power top?" Jim asks.

"I guess you've never driven a '59." Black gets in, twists the key in the ignition, the engine hums, and the top glides down, hidden in a minute beneath a matching tonneau cover, everything white.

Jim opens the passenger door and sinks into the leather pillow of a seat. Even next to a man who, less than twenty minutes ago, was prepared to drown himself, the psychiatrist wants to sleep. Riding in an automobile has sedated him ever since he got back, but it wasn't always like that. Freshened by serial coffees, he drove fourteen hours straight with Ruthie, Maria, and her parents to the Twine Ball Museum in Darwin, Minnesota. There, and at the Lincoln Home and the Indianapolis Motor Speedway, the Sedaras looked like refugees from some foreign land. That was 1963, when Kennedy was still alive and Maria was content with *Mastering the Art of French Cooking*.

He dreads what awaits him back at the VA because the summer nights are always the most difficult. The heat keeps the patients away from Dr. Nilso in the afternoon. When the broil breaks around 10:00 p.m., deep into Jim's shift, they start coming and sometimes come through to the next morning when the cycle begins again.

Black steers the Eldorado through the deindustrialized streets, graffiti covering the sides of buildings clean just a few years before. Trash sits on sidewalks, and the porches of the rowhomes are mostly bare. Now there are steel grates on storefronts, St. Andrew's crosses bolting them in for the night, but behind the storm doors with their carriage logos, people eat dinner and watch Walter Cronkite, just like in Glenwyth.

"Where should I drop you off?" Black asks a while later. He's been whistling for the past several minutes, everything right with the world. The afternoon seems like an unannounced tornado, deadly but marked afterward by blue sky. They turn onto Woodland Avenue, and the VA hunches above the road's shoulder.

"You can pull around in the front circle."

Black maneuvers the car to a stop in front of the guard house, upon which is posted: 18 USC SECTION 930—FOR YOUR SAFETY: No knives, guns, or weapons allowed in this facility.

"I'll see you tomorrow," Black says. "And I'm safe."

"All right. It's 949 Athens, on the other side from the bank."

"Convenient. I may have to sell another pool." And there Black is, in a hundred kitchens, presenting blueprints to anxious parents and joyful children, predicting years of summer fun and omitting the possibility that this one might be his last. "Oh. Here. You can shred it." It's a sealed envelope with a single word for an address—

WHY.

The Eldorado curves out of the driveway and disappears behind construction in the urban renewal zone that the university has become. Unable to move the campus to Valley Forge and abandon Philadelphia like everyone else is doing, the trustees have been blasting away the surrounding neighborhood, trying to make a suburb in the city and expel the undesirables. The crumbling campus that Jim and Maria knew, with its trolleys, gas stations, shoeshine boys, and twenty-cent hamburger stands, has become as remote as Ben Franklin.

Finding a bench inside the flower grotto that surrounds the VA's monument to its unknown soldier, Jim opens the envelope.

July 5, 1972

To Susan, Eddie, and Dotty,

I've written this letter many times, and each time, I'm struck by its cowardice. I know that I should be focusing on the three of you and how this will affect you. In fact, that thought has kept me going since I got back. I know that your pain should be enough to keep me going, but it isn't. There were so many men I tried to help, and although I did help some, there were far too many that I failed. I'm a FAILURE, and if I remained, I would fail to help you when you most needed it, sooner or later, and that I couldn't bear.

Please know that I have always loved you very much. I just can't take the pain. There's nothing you or anyone else could have done. You'll think that there was—if only we had, he had, if only—and you'll be wrong.

I believe that Jesus will forgive me, and I know that I will see you all again in the next life.

One final thing. Please don't sell the Eldorado for cheap. They'll never make another.

Davey

After the crash, scourged with pain, Jim thought about writing his own letter, but then he remembered his dead mother and the black spaces in her mouth behind her jealously protected front teeth. With those wobbly shards, she had held on for dear life, and what would Sister Michael Frederick have said? His mother was dead, but nuns lived forever.

Jim folds the letter in quarters and places it in his shirt pocket. Soon, Black will be easing the Eldorado into his garage and walking into his empty house, Dotty in Easton, Susan and Eddie wherever. There, he will confront the silence and find it comforting or maddening or, just maybe, reason enough to blow his brains out with one of his ten other handguns.

Sweaty and cold at the same time, Jim returns to the ER and gives the all-clear because it is all clear, at least for now, until Nilso or Cedillo bangs on the call-room door to deliver the bad news about Black. Or maybe Jim's getting ahead of himself. Maybe everything will turn out all right.

When he scans the chalkboard where new admits are logged, he sees a gift from heaven. Not a single psychiatric patient has arrived since the transfer of duties, which means there are no new evaluations to complete. Nurse Tucker is gone, discharged and sent home with sick leave. The staff's attention has turned to a patient vomiting blood, who, presently unable to speak, will become Nilso's problem in the morning. The chief will see his patient between meetings, discussing the man's alcoholism but never forgetting the importance of the SPAMC protocol, whatever the hell that is.

It's 7:45 p.m. There's no cafeteria in the VA, but because of a loophole in federal law, staff members are issued patient food trays when available. Jim takes the elevator to the basement and, before entering the dispensing room, dons a hairnet and paper booties. Inside, he stands for several minutes until a man comes to him and says, before Jim can even ask, "Doc, we only got purées tonight."

"I'll take it." After signing a form in triplicate with a chained ballpoint pen, Jim receives a food tray. Translucent plastic lids cover the plastic dishes to keep the meal warm. He peeks at a cup of pea soup, a side of apple sauce, and the main course, puréed pork chops with mashed potatoes. He has stowed ketchup and mustard upstairs under the optimistic belief that Heinz's and French's can make anything palatable.

Inside the call room, he turns on the TV, perched at the ceiling, and sits down with his tray and condiments. The sound comes on, and then the picture, arising from a shimmying dot. It settles into the image of Flip Wilson, dressed in plaid with a golden bowtie, standing before his own name in giant white letters. The phone rings.

"Hello?" Jim asks.

"Is this the psychiatrist on call?"

"Yes."

"What's your name?"

"Dr. Malory. How can I help?"

"Doc, I have a very serious issue going on down here."

"I don't mean to interrupt you," Jim says, "but what's your name?"

"Bob."

"Bob?"

"Just Bob." The man sounds like he's from South Philadelphia, like a character from Jim's days on Roseberry Street. "As I was saying, I have this issue here in my apartment. I've been a very good tenant all these years, never said a mean word to nobody, but my neighbor has been watching me, and this Monday when I went out to come to VA," here the caller cuts his volume and whispers, "he broke into our apartment and installed security cameras, and he's watching us, me and my daughter. Now, I don't want to do anything crazy, Doc, but I can't take this invasion of my privacy. I just can't do it. Here's the other thing. He's going to rape my daughter. I know it, and I'm the only thing protecting her."

"How old is she?"

"Almost sixteen."

"I could call the police," Jim says, imagining the girl in her Catholic school blouse and saddle shoes, probably attending Hallahan just like Maria, if the daughter is even real. But Bob has moved on to other subjects, explaining how the neighbor is calling Bob a "homosexual." There's nothing that Jim can do but listen, and then, without anything being resolved, Bob turns off like a light switch and hangs up.

The calls continue for the next three hours, dribs and drabs, a brain-damaged sample of fifty years of American war. Meanwhile, Flip greets and dismisses both Joan Rivers and Redd Foxx, and then gives way to James Garner, the peace-loving, cycle-riding lawman of Nichols, Arizona. With Garner a parody of his former, durable self, the show is destined for cancelation. Then comes an overripe Dean Martin singing about everybody loving somebody sometime in a song that predated the Summer of Love and now survives it.

Jim is tiring but nevertheless speaks with a grandmother who reports that her "grandchild" has threatened to shoot the extended family; a veteran who says that his doctor was going to prescribe him more Valium but went away before having the chance to do so and, "So can you write a few extra prescriptions, Doc?" and a social worker from another VA who wants to transfer a patient to Philadelphia, with a scheduled arrival at 0330. There are no open beds on the inpatient unit. Even if there were, Jim could do nothing. Nilso has decreed that inter-hospital transfers will only be accepted between 0830 and 1630 and then only when approved by himself. On this single point, Jim—not wanting to be awakened—and his boss agree.

When the phone quiets, he calls the ER and asks about any pending consultations. None. With each minute that passes in a shift, the chance of being forced to evaluate another patient falls, with a semi-exponential reduction during the overnight hours, spiking a bit before 8:00 a.m. when his tour concludes. As the threat of more patients becomes hazy, its hard outline fading, Jim sees a vista of uninterrupted sleep, if Mechanical can just shut up and a breeze can present itself.

Shifts with no requested evaluations are no-hitters. The much rarer ones with no evaluations, as well as no calls from the floor or ER, and no orders to be placed, are perfect games. Although there's now no possibility of the latter, Jim might still get a no-hitter because his interaction with Black wasn't a true evaluation. The psychiatrist wrote nothing down, although he probably should have. As the night deepens, the man seems more like a passing phantom, with no more chance of reappearing than the Phillies have of winning the World Series.

Jim dons his scrubs-as-pajamas, lowers the TV volume, and lies on the bed. The mattress is about three inches too short for his frame, which means that he has to sleep diagonally like the rein forcing beam of a door.

It's only eight miles as the crow flies to Barker's Mill, but tonight Jim might as well be in another galaxy. Still, he picks up the phone, dials, and says, "Hi."

"Hi to you," Maria says. "How's your night?"

"I'm still alive. I'm telling you, you should think twice about this medical stuff. Can I talk to Ruthie?"

"She's out."

"Where?"

"I don't know. Probably Eliza's."

"Kind of late," Jim says, "but I guess it's summer. What are you doing?"

"Me? Just reading."

"Yeah, that's what I'm going to do. You know, maybe we should go away again, just you and me."

"We just got back," Maria says, "and we can't ask my parents again."

"So Ruthie can watch herself. We could go down to Atlantic City, like when we got married. You remember it?"

"How could I forget?" Mr. and Mrs. James Malory spent their frigid honeymoon riding the tilt-a-whirl at the Steel Pier. Cloaked and bundled, they did it over and over again, for free in fact after the ride operator heard their story. "Crazy thing is," Maria says, "I actually liked it."

"I wish it was January," he says. "It's a hundred degrees in here tonight."

"Well, try to get some sleep, and hopefully, things stay quiet."

"Yeah. Hey, you remember that song?"

"Which one? All you ever do is think about songs."

"Our Winter Love. You remember?"

"That came out about a hundred years ago. You've got to stop living in the past."

"Listen, I'm sorry."

"For what?" Maria says, and Jim understands that she knows exactly for what.

"I don't know. I should have made things easier for you, right from the beginning."

She yawns. "And where would the excitement have been in that? Go to sleep."

"All right."

"And don't eat breakfast in the morning before you get home. I'm going to fatten you up if it's the last thing I do," she says, and hangs up.

Muffins, coffee, and Maria: only ten hours to go. Maybe everything will work out in the end. Jim places two *American Journal of Psychiatry* issues at his bedside, but he falls asleep, forgetting to take the Quaalude 300s that he, like Honey, gets from Santoni.

When Jim half-rouses an hour later, the Star-Spangled Banner has already played. The television screen has reverted to its test pattern, the feathered Indian head surveying a mandala of circles, crosses, and grids. When he sinks back into sleep, he stares at that first TV, the Sedaras' on Roseberry Street. He took third shift, giving Ruthie bottle after bottle of formula, all she did was eat, and he stared at the pattern for hours, nothing on, thinking himself as much a memory as that Indian.

Soon Jim finds himself in an ancient stone amphitheater, the creation of the Romans. He stands on the orange clay of the stadium floor, ringed by two concentric chalk circles. Flowers dot the ground, perhaps thrown from above, but by whom? He's alone until he turns and sees a bull standing behind him, forty feet away. It is massive, and it bleeds, red dripping into the dust. Spears stick out of its rump, and it snarls, stomping and kicking back its cloven hoofs. Then it charges, and now the seats are filled with screaming spectators. He dances, jumps, and does midair somersaults. He's no mere matador but a superhero. Denied its prey, the bull fumes.

The dance continues, with the toreador ever more exhausted, and the bull more infuriated, no end in sight. Until there is. Ready to rush him for another parry, the bull instead jumps over the wooden barricade into the crowded stands, goring spectators, their blood flooding into the stadium and rising to the level of his neck. And that's when he sees Ruthie sitting in the top row, unconcerned above the madness, like it's no big deal.

The phone rings. "Lo?" Jim answers.

"VA operator. I have a call for you."

"Yeah." Jim has the phone to his left ear, now the better one. He lies motionless in the darkness, still not completely awake.

"I'm looking for the doctor," the caller says.

The voice is familiar, pulling Jim toward alertness.

"Yeah, that's me."

"Doc, I was thinking. What do you do with someone who has no conscience? You try to make a human connection with him, but there's something so wrong with the guy that all your care and affection enable him and make him more evil. What do you do with a guy like that? See, if you make him better, and he does something really wrong, then it'd be your fault, right?"

Jim knows the voice, but maybe he doesn't. Maybe it's just some crazy Marine who has lost the ability to sleep and hates everyone who hasn't, including the poor fool on call at the VA.

"Umm....is this an emergency? Are you looking for someone in particular?"

"No, but you are the doctor on call, right? I mean, you're being paid to speak to veterans, right? I mean, it's not like you're sleeping when you're supposed to be working, right?"

Annoyance tugs at Jim. "What do you say you call your doctor in the morning?"

After a long pause where the psychiatrist thinks that the connection must have died, the caller says, his voice more muffled now, "Sure. I'll do that. You get some rest, Dr. Malory. You've got a long day ahead of you tomorrow."

The early morning passes in silence. When Jim awakens after seven, he has forgotten the dream and remembers only the strange caller who knew his name and wanted something other than drugs.

5

"So who's next?" Woody asks.

He is beaming, fluorescent in his tennis whites. The stockbroker has just defeated the psychiatrist, 6-1, 6-love. They've been playing on grass, an unforgiving surface for the uninitiated outsider. It's Saturday afternoon, and this could go on for hours.

"I'm done," Jim says, joining Maria and Honey on the courtside patio.

Woody follows and finds the Manhattan that he's been sipping between games. Other club champions may drink water or orange juice, but he prefers something with a bit more kick.

"You know that exercise is good up to the confinement," Woody says to his wife, using the term without irony.

"Oh, really?" Honey says. "Thanks for the obstetric advice, Dr. Dixon."

"I wouldn't be surprised," says Maria, who, unlike Honey, has come dressed to play. "Probably increases placental circulation."

"You needn't go back to medical school," Honey says. "You already sound like a doctor."

Maria offers Jim just the slightest snicker. Turning back to Honey, she says, "And you sound like an architect."

Honey smiles. "Still have that edge. That's why we're best friends."

Ignoring his wife, as he usually does, Woody has returned to the court to practice his serves. "No more delaying tactics."

Honey raises her finger to her husband. "You'll try to make sure that she doesn't deliver the baby in the doubles alley?"

"You should be thinking of your husband," Woody fires back. "I'll be lucky if she lets me out alive."

"We'll play a set. No more," Maria says, her belly mostly concealed by the conical folds of her maternity tennis top.

"You were very good. I still remember," Woody says. Maria played freshman year, before she had to give it up along with the glee club and her sorority to move back to South Philadelphia.

"And I still am," she says, "for a girl who learned to play on courts with chain-link nets." When Maria rises to join her ex-roommate's husband on the court, Jim stands with her, thinking she will look back at him and bid him farewell, an Amazonian going off to war. But she forgets him amidst the more important matter of her opponent. "First in!" she shouts.

When Jim sits down, Honey pulls her chair toward his, but something invisible catches, and she winces.

"Are you all right?" Jim asks.

"I will be." She pulls a small, brocaded tin from the pocket of her white bell bottoms and, with the lightness of a bird wing, swallows two more Hycodans. Honey never wears shorts. "God bless the bright young minds of the pharmaceutical industry. I'm sure they'd hire you if things don't work out with your practice," she says.

The pill case lies carelessly open on the glass table. There are at least thirty tablets remaining.

"Don't you look like I've contracted the pneumonic plague," she adds.

"But I only called in a half-dozen."

"Well, the rest are from Dr. Santoni, of course. Oh, all right. I forgot that they were in another purse. I'm just being honest."

"I think you should see a pain specialist."

"Why, when I have the best two psychiatrists in the land? Anyway, all physical pain begins with the emotions," Honey says, reviewing her all-American husband. Then she jolts, grinds her teeth, and frowns. "Just give me a minute, just a minute." She tightens further and grins with agony. "All right, all right, ahhh. Just need to make sure nobody notices. That's what mother always said."

"Where is it?" Jim asks.

"The usual place, which is everywhere. When I was a girl, you know, afterward, it was just in my leg, but then it gradually took over the rest of my body. What do you say? Should they have just cut it off? I could have gotten used to it, I'm sure, but how you would have gawked at my peg leg. Remember the song? *Will You Still Love Me Tomorrow?*" She smiles, and the pain seizes her again, screwing her eyelids shut. "Let's just sit here and watch that fool play tennis with the woman I could never be."

Jim touches his abdomen and senses his own band of burning, gnawing, and itching. Some days, his mid-section feels flush with scampering spiders, and on others, wrapped in ice. These are the aftereffects of the burn. Today, his sensory spirits have hummed quietly, offering little torment, but almost in sympathy with Honey's pain, his skin raises its voice, preparing to scream. He jerks toward the table, the pills sitting before him. He's tried Hycodan before, with little success.

Honey sits petrified in a stoic attempt to silence her body's rage. In this noble pose of suffering, Jim can more easily think of her by her more extended, formal name: Louisa Honoria Sharpe Dixon. How she became Honey, he has no idea, but it has been so since Woody introduced her in 1955. With blonde hair exploding like Brigitte Bardot's, tamed ineffectually by one of Eliza's headbands, Honey has shed her pearls-and-gloves cocoon of the Eisenhower Era. Now, surrounded by the white- and blue-haired women of the Glenwyth Cricket Club, some not ten years her senior, Honey resembles a turned-on, tuned-in, and dropped-out refugee from an Ibiza beach.

He tries to talk, but she raises her hand, stopping him, stopping the universe. She has been practicing this skill since eighth grade when, riding for Stroud's, she was thrown against the bleachers at the Devon Horse Show and fell like a cracked egg into the mud. She has told Jim this origin story, here and there, from one perspective or another, in bits and pieces, for the past seventeen years.

Bacteria invaded the girl's broken femur, and within days of being admitted to the Children's Hospital, she was awash with fever. Soon there were hushed discussions about the future of her leg. With her father on business in Los Angeles (with his lover) and her mother intoxicated, Honey was in effect, at age thirteen, her own agent. One of the hospital's pediatric infectious disease men suggested a novel antibiotic, rarely before used and rumored to kill as many patients as it cured. Despite intravenous administration, the medication did nothing except ruin the majority of her accessible veins.

Jim glances at Honey, her eyes still closed. He studies her wrists and sees the bizarre varicosities of her damaged veins, even now visible beneath her skin, a signature of the past. He was always an easy stick, the nurses at the Second Surgical told him. They gave him whatever they needed to shut him up. In the early days, right after the evacuation, when his pain was intolerable, he was always talking about Honey. They must have thought she was his wife, and he would never believe them when they reassured him that the infected burns were on his abdomen and not his leg, and that they couldn't very well cut him in half, now could they.

They could, and they were going to cut off Honey's leg, above the knee it would have been, the worst, but when the final surgical preparations were being made, the child demanded that her antibiotic dosage be increased and agreed that a three-inch steel valve be installed in her chest to receive whatever dose of the medication was necessary to kill whatever was inside her. Worshipping no God to speak of, she prayed to the void, just like Jim had done, and after two weeks, the infection receded. After a month, the battle was won, sort of. Longer-term side effects were a different story. Along with her leg, Honey's pain remained, as she was told it might, and grew. So began her first romance, with painkillers. After the crash and the skin graft, Jim had developed the same love, but it faded because he came to understand that opiates would do nothing for the twisting and grinding that now engirdled his waist most hours of most days. The doctors told him in Vietnam that burns created a special kind of pain that would never go away.

But morphine was Honey's friend, and between injections, she dreamed. Her room at the Children's Hospital overlooked, distantly, the significant architecture of Rittenhouse Square, and in those desperate days of her illness, the vista was her escape. Months later, she could recount every building in her sight, and she grew curious about the different styles that had been used to create the environment—Georgian, Victorian, Renaissance Revival, and the Beaux-Arts. When she returned in a wheelchair to Stroud's, the equestrian girl was gone. Now she read about cathedrals and Le Corbusier, eating croissants and eclairs. Two years later, she had gained forty pounds and the ashamed compulsion to lose that weight and more. She would not only return to her former self. She would become a better version, without the sports. After that, by whatever means necessary, she avoided being the person whom others called plump, full-bodied, broad, excessive, overweight, fat, or simply disgusting. She was on it.

Honey was not an actual architect, but in her twenties, she created her own shrine on a five-acre plot above Wingohocking, the land a wedding gift from her parents. Although the Bauhaus Style was becoming common in places like New Canaan, it remained unknown near Philadelphia. Yet from the time of the housewarming gathering in 1962, she knew that she had created a beautiful thing, and this gave her pleasure. She saw the dwelling as a testament not to her brilliance or taste but to her control, and she loved having the Malorys over.

"Do you miss the house where you grew up?" Jim asks.

"Now that brings a smile," she says, eyes still closed. "Out with the old, in with the new."

Honey had grown up in circumstances opposite Jim's. Her family had been the last occupants of an ancient farm granted to her forefathers by William Penn himself. By the early fifties, it sat between shopping centers and apartment buildings sprouting on City Avenue, Philadelphia's border with Glenwyth. The tiny rooms, outdated fixtures, and low ceilings seemed overhung with the past. So Honey wasn't disappointed when she left for the College for Women and her parents sold the property to a developer who obliterated it for office buildings, a hotel, more apartment houses, and another shopping mall. A parking lot now covers her girlhood swimming pond.

"Why do you ask?" she says.

"Santoni says that if you think of something random, the pain goes away."

"You shouldn't listen to everything that man says. Anyway, that place makes me think of my father, which makes the pain worse. But," she says, brightening, "nothing that Charles Pfizer and G.D. Searle can't fix."

Jim wants to ask her more about the forgotten farmhouse, pushed away so that she might appear the image of modern, free-style perfection. Whatever chaos she might feel inside, her flaxen hair, tanned face, and winnowed body convey not the failure of control, but its success.

"It'll get better," he says.

"For now, but it'll be back. It always comes back, but suppose I had more children? The pain was always better during my pregnancies. Do you think I should?"

Jim is unsure of what to say. Despite evidence to the contrary, he always thought of Honey, unlike Maria, as never wanting more than a single child. Her version of Philip Johnson's Glass House was, after all, child-proofed, in that it was designed to be inhospitable to anyone who did anything but sit and calmly read The Classics on designer sofas.

Although she admitted to anyone who would ask that she never enjoyed children, Honey had quite a brood. A few minutes after her twin Jimmy, Eliza had emerged from the womb screaming and had not stopped. From the beginning, Honey had wanted to trade her in for a quieter model. Like a change in barometric pressure, the girl's cries made her mother's leg throb. In some ways, Eliza was Woody. She was always forgetting things, taking the easy way out, not paying attention, turning in tests too early, and never seeming to connect A to B. There was no ultimate consequence to this; she would have enough money to live comfortably forever, even if she never worked, moved to The Barclay, and subsisted on room service. But Honey had dreams for her daughter, just as she had for her husband in the early years.

With Eliza, there had been shimmers of talent at Glenwyth Elementary. Throughout lower school at Stroud's, however, she became more average in all respects except her anger. The girl looked to have everything and acted as if she had nothing. The infractions began quietly and then grew louder, culminating in her visits to Dr. Malory. And yet the last session was different because it contained something completely unpredictable: hope.

Nothing was predictable with Honey and her kin. When Jim was over in Vietnam, and when everyone had concluded that Honey's reproductive life was over, she had Burtie. When Jim heard the news in one of Maria's letters, he was perplexed. He would have rather expected Nixon to visit Zhou Enlai for a state dinner than Honey to have another baby with Woody, but both had happened.

"I'm pooped," Maria says, suddenly looming above her husband and Honey.

Woody asks Jim, "Are you recovered? I'd like to groom you for the member-guest round-robin. Game?" Jim never played tennis before his move to Glenwyth. There, at the public courts in the center of town, he tried to learn and become a proper suburban gentleman, slapping the ball at the backboard while Ruthie played on the swings. His efforts, though, have been no match for Woody's muscle memory of his own childhood on the same grass.

"I could be," Jim says, wondering what Woody thought about Honey's scars the first time he saw them.

"Maria can sit this one out," Honey says.

Without discussion, the men obey and proceed to the court. Jim wins the first point with a fortuitous ace but then drops the next four to lose the initial game, establishing a pattern for the rest of the set. The ladies look out across the grass court to the green wasteland of the club's great lawn. It's so wide and barren of anything but tonsured grass and tennis courts that the curvature of the earth seems visible. The Cricket Club's sandstone clubhouse sits on one side of the field. On the other, a row of still-living Dutch elms, immune to the blight, stands next to a private lane that leads to more hidden drives and paper roads where many of the club's members live. With storms having passed through earlier, the sky bleeds blue to the horizon, where another cumulonimbus forms.

"Can you feel the kicking?" Honey asks.

"Just this month, it started," Maria says.

"It's wonderful, isn't it?"

"It doesn't exactly feel wonderful at 2:00 a.m."

"At least it's not twins." Honey shouts to Jim, "Don't give up!" The set continues, the psychiatrist falling further and further behind.

A few minutes later, Honey says, "I'm angry at Eliza."

"What's the matter?"

"She's just—" Words fail the mother, the enormity of it all overwhelming. "We got her course list for next year, and she's signed up with all the dumb girls. No honors anything. Don't get me wrong. They're at Stroud's, and so I know that nothing's easy, but still."

Maria picks up her tennis racket and places the head into a trapezoidal wooden storage frame. "Mark my words," she says, tightening the brace. "Eliza will be fine."

"I wish she was more like Ruthie."

"Well." There's a pause. "Ruthie's not perfect, you can be sure, and as far as courses, I'm not sure what she's taking. Some kind of math and English, as well as French, I suppose. Not sure about honors."

Honey scowls. "She has nothing to worry about. I expect she's a shoo-in at any Ivy she chooses."

"Maybe," Maria says.

"Where else would she go?"

"Maybe she won't even go to college."

"What?" Honey groans, like she's witnessed the beheading of a small animal. "Now you sound like my husband. You don't want her to be average, do you?"

"I want her to be happy."

"I suppose that's her choice, but what do you do? Just sit back and do nothing?"

"It's not the end of the world if Eliza doesn't take calculus in high school," Maria says. "She's a great kid. With Ruthie, we never pushed her to excel and—"

"And she's done just that," Honey interrupts, fumbling for a cigarette. "Well, you're lucky, as usual. It's just hard. I was never like Eliza, but my father was just like Woody."

"She's a smart girl," Maria says, lighting her cigarette on the tip of Honey's. "She'll be fine."

Between foot faults and netted balls, Jim smells the tobacco, hears the name Eliza, and loses the little concentration he has left. He stares at them. Honey and Maria are talking, and this makes him nervous because anything they discuss might somehow involve him. Eliza. He can imagine where the conversation is heading, Honey criticizing the girl and Maria suggesting tolerance. But as Mr. Sedara told his son-in-law when he came hat-in-hand, having impregnated the man's daughter and seeking advice, *Wise men don't need it, and fools won't take it.*

And like that, the skies in Jim's mind clear. He wishes that he could toss his racket, run from the Cricket Club, and summon Eliza for an emergency session on Athens Road. How has he missed it? In Eliza, Honey expects another catastrophe, another case of osteomyelitis. There had been no warning then. Why would there be any now? Had Eliza been less intelligent, less sensitive, or less obsessive, the girl might have ignored her mother's not-so-hidden censure. Instead, its brackish water seeped through her, rising to higher levels of consciousness until she herself shared the blame.

A ball sails around Jim's racket. "What are you doing?" Woody shouts. "You're not even trying."

It's so obvious. Eliza hates her mother and then hates herself for the hatred. So the cycle continues with greater waves of emotional pain, reduced if only temporarily by sex, drug use, and self-mutilation. By sickening herself, Eliza might get her mother to care, and if she doesn't, so what? Being abused is better than being ignored.

Taking the net, Jim finds the ball and wallops it toward Woody's head.

The all-American dodges and returns the ball to the backcourt to win another game, saying, "Now that's the play I've been waiting for!"

Jim wants to stop and write it all down, but Woody will not take no for an answer, and the Bataan Death March to the locker room continues.

Around that time, Honey asks Maria, "Do you think I'm too hard on her?"

"You are fairly demanding."

"So I should be like Woody, getting drunk in the garage and frittering away his father's money?"

"There's a middle ground."

"You of all people know that I'm not a middle-ground kind of person," Honey says, looking down. "She just bugs me, I don't know, even the smallest things. Like her hair. She has beautiful hair, but she won't wash it, and so it's string cheese. None of the boys she knows seem to notice, but that's just the point. If she took care of herself, she wouldn't be with reprobates like Quinton Graves."

Maria's hands tremble. "I think I'm ready to play again," she calls out.

"Not yet," Woody returns, after a backhand.

"And then there's her appetite," Honey continues. "We've

talked about that. What? Don't act like the cat's got your tongue."

"You need to be more Italian," Maria says, gesticulating. "We have curves. Tell me about this Quinton boy."

"Oh, no, no, no. I don't want to ruin our evening. He's absolutely dreadful."

"I see."

"No. You don't."

"Well, how's Burtie?"

"A breeze, of course, as usual. He couldn't be more different from the other two." After a pause, "With Jimmy and all of his problems, I should have sent Eliza to boarding school." Honey drops her cigarette butt to the ground and screws it into the perfect grass. "I want to get her away from that Quinton. Another great Main Line dynasty gone bad."

Maria ignores this. "Did I tell you? I called the dean this week, and she said that I could return as a third-year medical student."

Jim steps from the court just in time to hear his wife's fabrication. She's done nothing and talked to no one.

"That was quick," Maria says.

"And relatively painful," her husband adds.

"What time's the table?" Honey asks.

"Six," says Woody.

"Then we should wrap up this bloodbath," Honey says, standing up when her husband sits down.

"But what about my drink?" Woody asks.

"Maria and I will meet you at five-of on the porch," Honey says.

And with that, the women drift away to the ladies' locker room, leaving the men in mild confusion, unsure if the bad things they've done and the good things they haven't will remain unspoken.

Ruthie slides the embroidered oven mitts over her fingers, grabs the pan from the range, and drops it on a wire trivet. She and Eliza stand in socks because shoes aren't allowed inside. Mrs. Dixon doesn't like dirt.

Stuck at the Dixons' while their parents play tennis and get smashed, the two girls hesitate to light up. So they bake. Eliza had wanted to use the Betty Crocker mix sitting in her cabinet, but Ruthie insisted that if they were going to make "hash brownies," they were going to do it right with whole milk, eggs, and Belgian cocoa. A week ago, Ruthie had never smoked marijuana, but since then, when she's smoked it, her odd thoughts about her father and everything else have seemed a bit more unremarkable, the sadness more bearable.

While Ruthie cuts the confection into sixteen squares, Eliza walks to the hi-fi and sifts through the shelf of records. Bailey, the Dixons' Labrador, lies unconscious on his circular bed.

"My parents have the worst musical taste, all this easy-listening stuff. Look at this: *Lisbon at Twilight.* Who's George Melachrino?" Eliza examines another album, a green-colored LP displaying a black-and-white photograph. "Brasil '66 isn't bad. Wait. I'm going to get something from my room, but you have to make sure to remind me to put it back. Woody gets pissed when I use his turntable."

A moment later, Eliza returns with an aqua-blue LP sleeve that, on close examination, displays a disembodied ear. "This one's good," she says, lifting the needle and bouncing it with a boom onto the platter. "This is my favorite band and the best album of 1971 if you ask me, especially on the B-side." The record starts with nothing but the single tweet of a whistle or maybe a bird. Then it repeats, blending into the plucks of a reverbed electric guitar, echoing, organizing the song's first plaintive melody, then collapsing into the refrain, repeating twice, before the entrance of the vocal, something about an albatross hanging motionlessly.

"This is good," Ruthie says, downing a brownie, then another. "And this music."

"Pink Floyd is always good," Eliza says.

"I don't feel bad. I'm sure our parents are getting hammered right now."

"*C'est vrai.* You ever hear of Syd Barrett?"

"No," Ruthie says.

"He had to leave the band. He went crazy."

The two girls, sitting opposite each other on the living room's two Mies van der Rohe sofas, fall silent. Between them, a brick fireplace, dead for the summer, dominates the room, its chimney rising through the ceiling next to two clerestory windows. Although not even high yet, Ruthie wants to consume the song, especially when it drops any pop pretensions and devolves into *music concrete*. She has never heard anything this incredible before.

Everything has been so strange since the peeper in the bushes, but her life also proceeds with a new kind of logic, a river carrying her forward. Two years ago, she would fall asleep wondering whether this was the night her father would be killed. While he was in Vietnam, she was still in public school. She remembers her class making care packages, and a recurrent nightmare was returning from school to find the soldier delivering the bad news to her sobbing mother.

When he returned, she thought it would be the best day of her life, but it was just another day. She's never understood why, but now it's making sense. It's not so much that the real Captain Mallory didn't return, but rather that he's always been a phony. That would explain a lot, and maybe that's why she's been so angry lately. After all, how could she not hate an impostor, a fake like herself? Ruthie has felt herself to be unreal, although that's not new. Weird as it is, she's had the feeling for as long as she can remember, but it's stronger and, for the first time, natural. Anything is possible now, as the edges of objects soften and concepts, previously tough and rigid, flow together.

The song is over, and Eliza flips the record. The A-side begins with the sound of bellowing winds and then the echoing of a banging bass guitar, hitting the same note over and over again, smashing into Ruthie's brain. She has a headache now and is having difficulty aligning her binocular vision into one image.

"Do you think I could lie down?" she asks.

"Sure. You're staying in Burtie's room tonight. I'll get you towels." But Eliza does nothing, already having forgotten the request.

After the first song, the album presents a more comforting melody, and Ruthie feels reintegrated, but only partly. Her parents are a mile away, and she is suddenly so stoned she can barely speak. Unconcerned, Eliza studies a book pulled from her parents' shelf.

"What are you reading?" Ruthie sees the title: *Modern Man in Search of a Soul.*

"I don't know. Someone probably gave it to my mom. She's never read it, I'm sure. She doesn't have a soul, and she doesn't read anything except *Architectural Digest.*"

Ruthie now understands how brilliant it is to title a magazine *Digest.* You read it and in this way, absorb the material presented inside, just as you would digest a piece of cake.

"That's so amazing," Ruthie says. "I have to see that magazine."

Eliza finds a stack of them on a side table and hands them to Ruthie, who flips through. "So cool," she says and a moment later tosses them onto the parquet floor. Ruthie walks toward the living room's floor-to-ceiling windows. The curtains, a foamy material threaded with silver filament, are drawn. Ruthie pulls them open and says, "This view is incredible!" From the Dixons' house, one of the highest points in Glenwyth, one can see the village and many,

many trees. Sycamore Lodge stands on an adjacent hill. What's remarkable, however, is how few people being seen can see the Dixons. Sitting back from the cliff's edge, their house is invisible to everyone except invited guests and hang gliders.

Up until now, Ruthie thought of the Dixons' home as isolated. It was like Mrs. Dixon—and yes, everyone knew that Eliza's mom had made the plans—was trying to set up a safe house that would never be located. That was sad, but now it doesn't matter because Ruthie understands there's no escaping anything. Everything is connected everywhere.

"It's like a jungle out there," she says, pressing her face against the glass, chilled by the churning motor of the Dixons' central air conditioner, a new invention that Ruthie otherwise has seen only in movie theaters. She should have come to the Dixons last Sunday night when she was greased with sweat. Here, the moisture is on the other side of the glass, tiny beads and rivulets driven by an unknown hand. "And I want another brownie."

"I'd hold off on that," Eliza says. "You've had like four. It doesn't hit you right away."

"They're so good."

"You have to appear somewhat normal when our parents get back."

But there's a new normal. In the water arrayed on the living room windows, Ruthie sees a complete world that was previously hidden from her. If nobody understands her—not Eliza, not even Ruthie's parents—maybe it's because she's stolen all the understanding for herself. Even the grains and globules of water across the plate glass now make sense. She could tell the world about this secret knowledge, but they'd laugh at her. Her mind has always been like a 78-rpm record in a 33-rpm world, and so she's mostly stayed silent, unable to accept that everyone else doesn't see what she sees. They just think she's smart and remark to themselves about how she keeps it all together, but they don't see how she's bored by everything except the thoughts flying through her brain.

When that psycho was about to jump from the bushes, she was terrified, and she ran for her life. All the same, part of her wanted to be pulled in to see what she would find. If she hadn't been interested, she would never have left her bedroom, and she also would have never allowed herself into the gravitational field of Spencer Elizabeth Dixon.

"Helloooo!" Eliza says. "Can you hear me, Miss Malory?" She stands over Ruthie like a doctor trying to pull a patient from a coma.

"I'm done," Ruthie says, rubbing her abdomen, "but we can't exactly leave them in the refrigerator for your mom and dad."

Eliza shakes her head. "Honey doesn't eat, and when she does, she sticks to narcotics. Oh! We could give them to the woodland creatures."

"Good idea," Ruthie says, but not before gobbling another brownie, leaving only four squares for five acres of squirrels. Eliza slides open the glass door, and the two walk out onto the patio. They sit facing each other on the retaining wall, the flagstone beneath their feet still warm from the day's heat. They take turns breaking apart the brownies, hurling the bits down toward the creek along the road.

Then Eliza reaches into her pocket and pulls out a pack of Marlboros. "You want one?" A few passing cars can be heard distantly, but otherwise, the two girls are alone in silence, blocked from the highway's drone by the surrounding hills.

"Sure," Ruthie says, grabbing the lighter that sits between them. It's a stainless-steel Zippo, engraved with two crossed rifles and below that an eagle. It bears the words "US Army," which is strange, even now, in this wavy world.

Eliza lights Ruthie's cigarette, and they squint through the smoke. "Where'd you get this?"

Eliza whitens. "I don't know."

"I thought your father was in the Navy."

"Yeah, the Navy." Eliza throws another brownie bit off the cliff. "Or maybe the French Foreign Legion. I really am stoned."

Ruthie stares at the lighter. "My dad was in the Army."

"Yeah, I know. I've heard it about three thousand times."

"Who's Quinton Graves?"

"Why?"

"He's one of my dad's patients," Ruthie says. "He went to White's."

"So?"

"I read his file. I figured maybe you knew him. You know everybody else."

"Never heard of him. Did you read my file?"

"No."

Eliza sizes up her friend. "Maybe you're not such a good girl after all," she says, "and by the way, I don't actually want to know what your father wrote about me."

"It's great not having any neighbors," Ruthie says.

"Sometimes. It can be creepy too. You could be strangled up here, and no one would hear you scream." Eliza blows a smoke ring over the cliff. "Honey likes it that way. No one she cares about can hear all her crazy-ass ranting day and night."

"I don't like your mother," Ruthie says.

"Me neither," Eliza returns, "but the good news is that she'll probably kill herself before I get the chance." They both cackle.

When the laughter stops, words are harder to find. Ruthie feels guilty for saying such a thing, even with Eliza's approval and nastier comment, but Mrs. Dixon has always seemed a bit too interested in Ruthie, like the woman in the gingerbread house. To hear Mrs. Dixon speak to Ruthie, you'd think she thought the girl was a

Nobel Prize winner. And who would seek out for her daughter's psychiatrist the father of the girl's best friend? They are best friends, aren't they?

"How old were you when you first cut?" Ruthie asks.

"Nine," Eliza says.

Nine? When Ruthie was that old, she wanted only her dolls and to watch *Wee Willie Webber's Colorful Cartoon Club*, weekday afternoons at 3:30 p.m. on Channel 17.

"What was so bad back then?"

Eliza lights another cigarette. "I wanted to die when I was eight."

"Why?"

"No matter how bad things get, there's always one thing you can control."

"What?" Ruthie asks.

"I don't want to talk about it." As Eliza eats one of the remaining brownies, Ruthie imagines her friend, in the maroon tunic of Stroud's Lower School, lying silently on the driveway behind the Porsche, waiting for Mr. or Mrs. Dixon to put the car into reverse.

"I'm not feeling so good," Ruthie says. "I need to lie down." This time, Eliza gets it. The two go inside, and she leads Ruthie to Burtie's room. Mrs. Dixon has deposited him at a babysitter's for the night to avoid, when the Dixons returned, the unpleasant interaction of children and Blue Hawaiians. Good thing he's not around. The kid always stares at Ruthie, like he's possessed or reading her mind or something. The room has floor-to-ceiling windows, and a low-slung bed sinks into green shag carpet.

"You okay?" Eliza asks.

"It's so sad. You were eight or nine."

"But don't forget, it's like dog years. A year with Honey is seven with anyone else."

"I want you to tell me what it was like."

"No, you don't. You just think you do." Eliza pulls down the cream duvet on her brother's bed, his crib recently discarded according to Mrs. Dixon's accelerated parenting schedule. Ruthie has never seen one of these coverings before, being used to the mismatched sheets and polyester blankets in the Malorys' linen closet. Like the bidet in the master bathroom, everything made of stone, wood, cloth, glass, and metal has been carefully planned at the Dixons.

Ruthie lies down and is tucked under the comforter by her friend, who follows her into the bed. The two girls lie next to each other, hugging, and then Eliza exits the bed and room. A moment later, Ruthie hears her best friend entering the hallway bathroom. After a few moments of quiet, the house settling into itself, Eliza's throat strains and heaves. A paroxysm of coughing follows, then silence, then the toilet's flush. The bathroom door opens, and Eliza walks out. She enters her room and falls into her bed, and it is the everyday routine of it all that makes Ruthie want to cry the most.

She remembers nothing more until she's awakened by a female cry. Eliza's? The sun remains, lowered and weakened. She must have imagined the scream. Now there's just snoring. Ruthie tries to go back to sleep, but the snoring continues. Soon she focuses on it, her sleepiness ebbing. She gets up and walks to Eliza's door.

"Do you have a Midol?" whispers Ruthie, sandpaper rubbing her brain. She hears nothing but the snoring behind the door.

Still clothed in the jeans and T-shirt (a technicolor peace symbol) that she wore an eternity ago when her parents dropped her off, Ruthie walks back to her room and stands next to the window. Nothing new here—trees and more trees, leaves from last fall in a decomposing bedspread covering the land—and then a man emerges from around the corner of the house, walking in the twilight. He wears Levis and engineer boots, a leather vest, and no shirt. A knit side bag is slung over his right shoulder to his left hip.

Jim Morrison was dead. Or maybe he wasn't. With brown hair, thick, long, and curled like a woman's, the man is about to disappear from view. Then he stops, aware that he's being watched. He turns to see Ruthie looking at him through the window and walks toward her. Soon he's standing feet from her, separated only by glass, and he's the most attractive man she's ever seen. The bedroom has a casement window, and Ruthie opens it.

"I was looking for Eliza," he says to Ruthie. She forgets her breath. "Eliza. She hasn't moved, has she?"

"Yeah. No, I mean. No. We're friends." Ruthie stiffens in the man's sad gaze, searching for assistance.

"Well, I figured that. Can you tell her I stopped by?"

"Sure, I will, or do you want me to go get her?"

"No, but tell her I found out something she'd love to know."

"You want to tell me, and I'll pass it on?"

He stares at her and smiles. "No. No, I don't think so. On second thought, just tell her I'm going to the Cape for a few days," he says before turning and disappearing into the Pennsylvania summer.

"Hey! What's your name?" Ruthie shouts into nothingness at the stranger. For all that Eliza's shared, she's said nothing about him, and this secreting makes him even more beautiful.

Ruthie knocks on Eliza's door, but there's no answer. She taps it open and sees Eliza asleep on her bed, naked, damp, supine, and snoring. The sugary sourness of vinegar hangs in the air.

Ruthie goes back to her room, thinking her visitor might have returned. He hasn't, or has he? She sees something wedged between the metal screen and the window frame. It's a small piece of white card stock perforated with gridlines. On one side of the card, tiny clown faces are blotted onto each of the small squares, and on the other, someone has scrawled a Glenwyth phone number. That wasn't there when he left, but Ruthie understands. This man is a magician.

The sun burns in blurred, dying suspension above the Cricket Club lawn.

"My father would have qualified for the 1940 Olympics if the damned thing hadn't been canceled," Honey says. She has changed from her courtside uniform of white bell bottoms to a frilly aquamarine pant suit showing far too much for Glenwyth, stares be damned. "Double Scull. He was also Commodore of the Schuylkill Navy. He was always aiming for one sort of conquest or another."

And so the dinner goes.

The topics move from Stroud's to the difficulty of finding dependable lawn care, the Democratic Convention to dividends. At dinner, like at the tennis match that preceded it, the Dixons maintain technical advantage over their guests.

"You've got a bull market that is basically unstoppable," Woody says, smelling of bay rum and salt water. "Vietnam is over, inflation is falling, employment is rising. Just look at the earnings. That's what Mr. Market does." Woody smiles like he's speaking about a wealthy next-door neighbor. Jim has never met Dow or Jones. The Malorys, or more precisely Maria, invest the shaved remainders of their weeks and months in whole life insurance and in a cigar box in a cabinet above the dishwasher.

When Jim was growing up, the market never meant anything except Haas's Grocers on Coal Street. It was there that, bearing a short list of items like powdered milk and oleo, he first encountered economics when Mr. Haas looked at him stone-faced and told him that Ruth Malory needed to pay in cash. When he returned empty-handed to this mother, he was not scolded. Instead, she brought him into town and instructed him to wait on a bench while she took care of some business in a pawnshop. After she emerged with five dollars in her fist, the two of them had dinner at the Palmerton Dutch Buffet.

"Jim," Woody says, "do you hear me about Mr. Market?"

"I think so."

"Let's make an action plan. Do you own the Nifty Fifty?"

"Not sure."

"Well," Woody says, slugging his Tom Collins and waiving a waiter for another, "if you're not sure, then the goddamned answer is, 'No, Woody, I don't own the most innovative companies that are going to dominate the American economy for the next fifty years.'"

"Like—" Jim turns to Honey for an answer, but she's a million miles away.

"Like Polaroid, Sears Roebuck, and S.S. Kresge, to name a few."

"All right," Jim says. "Maybe it's unstoppable, but stocks have been going up for a long time, and as far as inflation, I don't think it's falling."

"It's definitely not falling," Maria says. "At least not with hamburgers." The sleevelessness of her floral print dress accentuates her growing stomach and makes her look as if delivery may be imminent. "My father talks about inflation all the time, and he sells a lot of hamburgers. The cows just keep getting more expensive, and when he asks the brokers, they say that the feed is going up, the land is going up, and all that jazz."

"But look at gas," Woody says. "I just filled up the Lincoln at the Arco, and Hi-Test is at thirty-six cents a gallon. It was about thirty cents a gallon fifteen years ago. That's about a one percent increase a year. You call that inflation?"

"I guess not," Maria says. "But—"

"Where are our meals?" Honey interrupts, annoyed. Jim and Maria have dined on the Cricket Club's sandstone porch many times, guests of either the Dixons or the Santonis, and the service has always been slow. The appetizers are long gone, and the bread bowl is empty. Honey and Woody have nearly finished their third cocktails.

After summoning and castigating the club's manager for the evening's delayed service, Honey turns to Jim. "So, how's Eliza doing?"

Just like that, he's supposed to hold forth? He slugs the remainder of his whiskey and motions to the waiter for another. "How do you think she's doing, Woody?"

"She seems okay," he says. "Passed everything this year. Could have been worse." Honey rolls her eyes. "What did I say?"

"Dr. Malory meant: Do you think Eliza is happy?"

"She's an adolescent girl," Woody says. "How many of them are happy?"

"I was very happy when I was sixteen," Honey says without irony. "I had the world in front of me with endless possibilities." Having searched the table for any available food, Jim chews some peanuts and a moment later finds one stuck in his throat.

Woody turns to Maria. "Is Ruthie happy?"

"I guess she's not unhappy, but I don't know what's going on inside her. Five years ago, she would tell me everything, but since Jim got back, she's pulled away. I don't know." During his tour, Jim often considered the blessing of Maria's infertility. Two women, one grown and one nearly so, could without distraction support each other, both during the waiting and if something worse followed.

The meal's unexpected appearance ends the conversation. The waiter serves a small dish of greens—no dressing—to Honey, and clams casino to Maria. Offered cutlery more like daggers than steak knives, the two men get to work on their strips. With the demands of digestion too great for politics or money, Honey and Maria compare Cavalier King Charles spaniels and bichons. Burtie, Honey says, deserves his own dog, and Maria nods. What would the

Sedaras think if he spent seven hundred on a pooch? That's what the mutts that wandered the streets of Lehighton were called. And what about Ruth Malory, who plucked Jim's boyhood dog Butch from the Carbon County extermination facility for fifty cents?

Jim cuts his steak. Although delayed, the filet bulges magnificently and has been cooked to his exact request. He takes the first peppered bite, and the sinews dissolve under the crush of his molars. He still has them, remarkable for Army dentistry. The waiter has poured Chateau Leoville for all, including Maria. When its tannins blend with the steak's protein and fat in a flushed moment of indulgence, Jim can almost believe what Santoni tells him again and again: *You never step into the same river twice.* Maybe Vietnam is over, and maybe he just needs to own the Nifty Fifty, and everything will be all right. One can remember trauma, but, again quoting Santoni, *The memory is not the trauma.*

As is customarily done for outsiders, the two guests have been seated so that they look out over the grass and most fully experience the club's splendor. Filled two hours ago with singles and doubles players, all clad in white, the great lawn has emptied itself save a small girl in a pink jumper, another Ruthie somersaulting. In the distance, along the bank of elm trees, a man in a blue blazer walks with purpose. The twilight makes Jim squint, but he can see the peculiar lankiness even across the field. He stops chewing. It can't be. It can only be. It's David Black, as if the Schuylkill has overflowed its banks and reached the Glenwyth Cricket Club. When the walker passes out of sight behind the clay tennis courts, Jim eyes his steak and sees a mass of flesh no different than his own. "Will you excuse me?"

He is ignored in the talk of Stone Harbor and dog shows, and so he gets up. To avoid suspicion, Jim bypasses the stairs that lead from the porch to the lawn and instead exits into the club, perhaps making a bathroom visit. Finding his way through several basement passageways, he reemerges near the locker room, out of sight from the porch, and soon overtakes his patient.

"Dave!" he says.

The man turns around. "Jim."

"Nice night."

"It is." The haze has evaporated, the day's sky dissolving into cloudless purple. The psychiatrist says nothing, and then the patient says, "Oh, I get it, you thought—"

"No, not at all," Jim says, but that's exactly what he thought. Racing from the porch to the far end of the lawn, Jim knew that Dave, prevented from killing himself, turned his obsession from suicide to the person who saved him. Somehow divining his doctor's dinner plans, the patient tracked Jim down, hid the Eldorado behind the paddle tennis courts, and then walked the great lawn, spying on the psychiatrist and his party.

"This is the best time of day for a walk," Dave says, noting Jim's incredulity. "I live down the hill on Cassatt Lane. You can make a house call if you like."

"I'm having dinner."

"I understand. Did you get the letter about the capital assessment and dues increase? Inflation my ass—"

"Actually, I'm a guest," Jim says, like he used to explain when Woody carried him like a suitcase to parties after Jim had to resign from the fraternity.

"It's a great club. I don't have much in common with the members, you know, all this Main Line junk, but the grounds make it worth it. I walk them every other night. It's a third of a mile around, and I do it twelve times."

"Of course," Jim says, wilting. "I'm sorry to bother you. I was just—"

"You were just coming out of the men's locker room in the middle of a dinner party on the porch. I know, but don't worry. See, you were thinking about me. I can tell. After today, you know that you can do it."

The two men had so connected in the first official session that Dave stayed for an additional fifty minutes, and if only it was that easy. Maybe Jim could do this. The psychiatrist and his deep-pocketed patient agreed to meet near daily, both knowing that the diagnosis from the VA was correct. When Dave joined the Army after discarding his captain position in the Air Force, he had planned to be a flight instructor, sharing the pearls of combat aircraft operation learned in a previous war. There was no hotheaded desire to get the Medal of Honor or to prove himself worthy to some long-forgotten superior. Dave wasn't even looking for adventure, but wars press on like freight trains. In the blink of an eye, he found himself departing Clark Air Force Base for Vietnam.

"It's not me," Jim says. "It's you. You can do it."

Elevated and emboldened by the first session's success, Jim got the idea to make Dave an experiment. They would together test the theory that a patient could be desensitized to trauma by re-exposure to it. The insight wasn't originally Jim's. By chance, he had attended a lecture in 1967 given by a South African psychiatrist and former army medical officer visiting Penn Med. The doctor observed that cats could get used to fearful stimuli if exposed gradually and repeatedly. He replicated the technique in humans and called it systematic desensitization. The lecture was sparsely attended, its ideas dismissed, but they stuck with Jim.

At today's session, the patient listed his traumas. There were seventeen, all from his two tours in Vietnam. He had been in Korea as well, but that conflict was absent from the list. Following the precepts of systematic desensitization, Jim directed Dave to rank the traumas, and together, doctor and patient practiced a series of relaxation techniques. In the next session, scheduled for Monday, Dave would in Jim's presence start to narrate and record the traumas on a reel-to-reel in the office on Athens. Using another player at his house, the patient would listen to the taped recitations and, in this way, become inured to their tragedies.

"Have you felt better?" Jim asks.

"That's a relative question, but yes, relatively."

"Good." Jim gazes back toward the porch at Honey and Maria. "I should be going."

"I hope you got the oysters."

"Not at six dollars a dozen. I'm from Lehighton."

"Maybe we can have a session here sometime," Dave says. "Then they'll really be surprised they let me in."

"It's nicer than Bartram's Garden."

"There's only one thing, Doc. Suppose we go through all this, and I stop getting anxious. That doesn't change anything. All the terrible stuff still happened. Or suppose your plan makes me worse?"

Jim eyes his patient for a second, almost angry at the man for ruining the moment.

"Okay," Jim says, "think of it like this. What happened will always be sad, but in the same way that a movie is sad. You feel it, but you can step out and get some popcorn or go to the bathroom or kiss your girlfriend. Your life goes on."

"But what if the bulb is blown?"

"No one is ruined," Jim says.

"You're an optimistic one, I'll give you that, but I guess you'd jump off the top of VA if you didn't think like that."

"I have more immediate problems," Jim says, "like how I get back to that damned dinner party without anyone noticing."

"I'd let them notice. The truth always comes out in the end anyway."

"People lie all the time," Jim says, "and sometimes they never get caught."

Dave eyes Jim and says, "I think we may need the next session to teach you about the way the world really works. Until then, go through the locker room, and I'll keep walking in the other direction, back behind the tennis courts. From the porch, they'll never know we talked." Dave disappears behind a wall of arborvitae.

At the table, Jim finds that a silver dome has been placed over his steak. To no avail; it has cooled into roast beef. The ladies are gone.

"Sorry about that, Woody."

"You didn't miss much. Of course, they had to go to the powder room just after you left. Probably planning a *coup d'etat* at the Parents Association."

Jim considers a rejoinder but decides against it. There's no point. With the accouterments of children and wives stripped away, the psychiatrist has more in common with Haile Selassie than with his dinner host.

"You think Eliza's doing okay?" Jim finally asks.

"All things considered. She is her mother's daughter. Even with all the servants, things weren't so great back in the old days at the old Sharpe farm, if you know what I mean. You met Honey's mother, didn't you? Three generations of private school tuition for three crazy women. I wonder if the alumnae newsletter would be interested."

By the time Jim came to know Honey, Mr. Sharpe was living mostly in California and Mrs. Sharpe at the Metropole, a Philadelphia hotel long past its prime. When Jim met the woman at her fifty-fifth birthday party, their single encounter, she was already a gray apparition with a string of pearls and a swollen abdomen, still drinking over her thin, mannered lips.

"I suppose Stroud's was a lot cheaper in the Depression," Jim says.

"But just as effective in preparing girls for life," Woody says with a wink.

The two men are greeted by a waitress pushing a dessert cart. She's sixteen, maybe seventeen, with a shock of curly red hair tamed into a bun with a wooden stick. She might be one of Ruthie and Eliza's friends, one of those other girls hiding in the shadows.

Woody grins at Jim and then says to the girl, "This looks good."

"Yes, tonight we have tunnel of fudge cake, bananas Foster, and—"

"Thank you very much," Woody says, losing interest in the confections. Glenwyth Cricket bars the children of its members from working at the club, and Jim can tell with even a sentence that the waitress takes the Philadelphia & Western trolley from somewhere in the city.

"How do you remember all those items?" Woody asks. "I haven't seen you around here before."

"I'm new," she says, straightening her shoulders.

"For the summer?"

She nods. "I'm going to Penn in the fall."

"Wow! Scholarship, huh? We went there. I was '56, and my friend here, what were you, doctor?"

"'59," Jim says, looking down and away.

"You play much tennis?" Woody wonders.

"I mess around," the waitress says.

"Mess around. Bet it's more than that. Where'd you go to high school?"

"Hallahan—"

"Oh, we know it," Woody says. Turning to Jim, "What are the chances?" Then back to his new friend, "You're going to play at Penn?"

"No, I'm not that good."

"I was all-Ivy in '56," he says. "We almost won that year. We were playing Yale and—"

"You were playing Yale, and what happened?" Honey asks, with the greatest of interest. She has returned, along with Maria, two bees swarming the sweets. "We all want to know," continues Honey, smiling first at the waitress, who steps back, and then at her husband.

"I suppose I've told the story before," he says.

"But you haven't, husband, not that I can remember. I'll have a sherry," Honey says, dismissing the scholarship student. Then to Maria, "My mother would never be without her sherry."

The waitress drifts away to the bar.

"I haven't seen her around," Honey says. "She's very well-spoken. Maybe that's the problem with Eliza. Maybe she needs a proper job. What does her psychiatrist think?"

Before Jim can say anything, Maria turns to her husband. "I've told Honey all about medical school."

"Isn't it wonderful?" Jim says, trying to sound enthusiastic.

"But who's going to take care of the baby?" Honey asks. The question has been frequently posed. Women seem less bashful about it than men, always wishing to gloat about childcare conundrums.

"My mother," Maria says.

"We're moving back to Roseberry Street," Jim adds.

"Very funny," his wife says. "We have a guest bedroom for my parents. They're very modest people."

"They could always help you get a bigger place," Honey says. "There's a beautiful colonial for sale on Athens, a flag lot too, for privacy. Jim could even walk to work."

"We're not moving," Maria says.

"I always loved your mother," Honey says, "but she's not getting any younger. If she changes her mind, I could be your nanny."

Maria involuntarily looks at her husband and then back at her ex-roommate. "That's very kind."

The girl with the sweets returns. While Honey glares at Woody, the waitress says, "May I offer you ladies one of our delicious desserts?"

Around ten, the girls awaken from their stupor. Still high, they make Jiffy Pop and watch Doris Day turn from boring housewife to Madison Avenue detergent spokeswoman, only to have her husband insist that she resume life as a dutiful doctor's wife. She agrees, but not before transforming the family swimming pool into a giant soapy bathtub. Ruthie saw this movie when she was younger but never realized it was so brilliant, the detergent suds meant to wash away those crazy, feminist ideas. Continuing the medical-man theme, the Late Show turns serious. Rock Hudson accidentally kills the town doctor and then blinds his widow, Jane Wyman, a woman who in real life was married to Ronald Reagan, the guy who made LSD illegal. Eliza says this to Ruthie before falling asleep again. But Hudson meets a mysterious painter, who inspires the playboy to become a skilled neurosurgeon, and later saves Wyman and, by extension, the governor of California. Ruthie wants to yell at the screen that the lives of doctors aren't nearly so dramatic.

And then, even later, the Dixons come home.

Having returned to Burtie's bed, Ruthie rouses to the sound of smashing glass and Bailey's barking. She listens silently. At first, she wonders if her parents have returned with their hosts and if a melee has somehow ensued, but there are only two voices—Mr. and Mrs. Dixon's.

"You are such a fucking loser!" Honey screams. "Why the hell did I ever marry you?"

"Honey, please," Woody says.

"And your daughter is just like you! I hate you. I hate her. And I hate our son. I hate Jimmy!" Another piece of glass shatters. Can Eliza hear all this? It seems likely. This is a modern house, with paper for walls.

"You shouldn't drink so much," her husband says.

"Me? Not drink so much? I need to drink more! Here's a knife. I want you to stab me through the heart so I can bleed out all over this wonderful living room in this wonderful house, and then you'll be happy because you'll have gotten what you always wanted! You and Eliza! You might as well get it over with. You've been doing it by degrees for twenty years!"

"Can you please just go to bed?"

"For what? To wake up to another shitty day and more pain? You're going to learn what pain is. You mark my words."

"I'm leaving," he says. A door slides, and the Porsche revs into the night.

"Where are you going, you piece of shit? You think I care? You piece of shit! You piece of…." The words collapse into sobs, just feet from Ruthie's door. Nothing happens for a minute, maybe more, except the vibration of the wood from Mrs. Dixon's heaving. Then the hidden figure walks back to the kitchen.

Ruthie wants to crack her door and peer out, but she doesn't dare, and there's no need. She can hear everything.

In the kitchen, Honey pulls the phone from the wall and spins its rotary, the mechanical crank sounding through the door and maybe through the universe. A second later, she says, "Jimmy, I mean, Dr. Malory. I can't go on. I know you won't hear this until Monday, but I need to meet with you. I have something that I have to say." And then she smashes the phone against the wall.

6

A few days later, Dave sits mute on the couch, his torso vertical and true. With his eyes closed, he may be praying. The bulky microphone aims at his mouth from the magenta glass table in the center of the office. Jim presses the record button, his scar burning, and Dave speaks.

"Okay. We've just made a drop-off at the Ninety-third Evac in Long Binh, guy with a broken leg, he'll be fine, and there's another Dustoff call. It's raining like crazy. It was always raining over there, but this is the real thing. It isn't our turn, Dustoff 20 is supposed to do it, but he's an FNG and not real good at instrument flying. So, Tommy and I go right back out. Jack is the crew chief, Rich is the medic, Bob's the gunner. The job's about forty kilometers up Highway 13." He stops.

"What's the matter?" Jim asks, pressing pause on the recorder.

"I can't do it."

"Take it slowly. You can open your eyes if you want."

They remain closed. "All right. We're heading up Highway 13, no problems. The VOR is set at 355, which should take us right into

Chon Thanh, and then the pickup site is about four clicks from there, right outside of Minh Hung. The weather's terrible, but the pickup's right near the road. Now, I have this feeling we should go back. It may be some bullshit call. So I ask Tommy to get them on the radio, and there's no answer. We're passing through Chon Thanh, and we're about two minutes away, and still nothing but static. I say to Jack that we're going back, but Tommy says let's try one more time. We do, and they confirm. Only one wounded. We've come out here for this? You can't see anything except when the lightning flashes. The rain bangs on the windshield.

"Huey is bouncing back and forth in the turbulence. I slow us down to maybe eighty-five knots. After a while, they guide us down a narrow side road, but I make a mistake. I don't know what I'm thinking. I don't turn off my lights. It's so goddamned stupid, but it's like I forget.

"Somehow, we manage to touch down in a space that's about two feet wide without destroying the rotors. They bring the guy in, and his hand is broken. Not amputated, not even crushed, not even compound-fractured. It's like a hangnail! I'm ready to lose it, completely lose it on the lieutenant, but Tommy cools me off. So we get the guy, and then we're back up. I realize what an idiot I was with the lights, and I turn them off. Should be smooth sailing from here. We can go left, or we can go right to get back to Thunder Road. We go left. We're at maybe three hundred feet, just above the trees. A lightning burst opens up, and it's like the Fourth of July for maybe five seconds, and the VC start shooting. Rounds blast through the cabin, one goes through Tommy's neck. Blood is pumping out onto the windshield, strong at first and then weaker. All hell's breaking loose. Rich and Jack and even the guy with the broken hand are doing mouth-to-mouth. There's blood all over the place, all over me." Dave pauses. "Tommy's dead by the time we get to Lai Khe."

Jim has stopped listening. "I can't do it," he says, remembering what he told Quinton. If the burn had been a few inches lower, Jim would have lost more than his mind.

"What?" Dave opens his eyes.

Jim breaks for the consulting room door. Bounding down the stairs into the waiting room, shabby and empty, he passes through the postmaster's kitchen and out into the backyard. There he falls to his knees and vomits. Again. No more. Again. More?

Dave squats next to his comrade and puts his hand on Jim's shoulder.

"I'm sorry. It must be food poisoning," says the psychiatrist. Doctors are supposed to be perfect.

Dave shakes his head. "Food poisoning, huh? And I thought you didn't order the oysters."

"I don't know, maybe—"

"You look like death. Why don't we call it a day? I'll still pay you. We could take a ride and talk." The Eldorado sits over weeds on the unkempt lawn, its triple whiteness inviting Jim in. He removes his tie, its blue now stained with orange and brown, and drops it in the dented trash can behind the building.

"No," Jim says. "We should go back upstairs. We should continue."

"In the shape you're in?"

"We have to do our work in an office."

"Who says?"

Indeed, who says? Ed always talks about the importance of maintaining limits, but he has weekly lunches with the Quaalude rep. What sense do boundaries make when Jim, even now, splits his time between Glenwyth and Cambodia?

"Let's take a ride," Dave says.

With the passenger door opened, Jim slides in. Dave follows on the driver's side, rolls the Eldorado backward, and turns out onto Athens.

"Where do you want to go?" he asks.

"I don't know."

"When's your next appointment?"

"Two."

"So I'll pay you for a triple, which means we have two and a half hours. Let's go up the country." Hearing no objection, Dave takes Athens Road toward its eponym.

"Wait," Jim says. "I forgot to lock the office."

"It's not like anyone knows you're there anyway," Dave says, and they both smile.

After several turns, the outermost houses of Athens appear. These are two-story post-war colonials, with brick and aluminum siding and little ornamentation, homes that Honey says should make architects lose their licenses. Soon these give way to grander Victorians and Queen Annes, their wood and stone turrets standing assertively. When they were still in college, Honey had taken Jim on a driving tour of her town and told him where he and Maria would want to live when they left South Philadelphia.

The two men approach the railroad, the original spine of Glenwyth's development. They pass under it as an electrified Local crosses above, steam trains once using the same tracks. Then Dave turns onto Oregon Pike.

The day Jim returned from the war, the expressway had been jammed. So Angelo and Carmela, with the Malorys in the back seat of the Cadillac, went from the airport to Glenwyth through West Philadelphia and finally on Oregon Pike. That may have been the last time that Jim was driven anywhere. Returning to Pennsylvania, he had expected to be struck by the place, to perceive its reality in a hyperacute way because of his absence, but it had been just another Tuesday afternoon in Glenwyth. Maybe he had never left—not Glenwyth, not Lehighton, and never Cambodia.

The sun warms them in the Cadillac's abundance of white. Less fanciful cars crawl nearby, devoid of urgency. The two men leave US 30 and turn into the college, entering an arboretum that extends over the hill, a small remnant of Penn's Woods. Just as mahogany and rubber trees cover Cambodia, oaks, spruces, and elms make their own jungle on the college's grounds. Some of the trees are dying, though, conquered by beetles and fungus. Jim sees their defoliated crowns. The undulating elms along Quaker Avenue, planted by the college overseers when Lincoln was newly killed, will all have to go.

They turn out of the college and pass Oakmont Avenue, with Santoni's house sitting at its summit. Then, with the help of a green light, they continue across Whitby Pike, the Oregon's sister, at a gallop. A series of back roads takes them by the neo-Georgian mansions around the Cricket Club's golf course, where Quinton went crazy, and then by residences born of the humbler architecture of hemmed expectations. The land on which these homes stand was still undeveloped after World War II, but the estates were abandoned around the time that Honey's father sold the ancestral farm. Although the Glenwyth commissioners try to obstruct development, they always give in, because it's all about money.

The driver and his passenger enter a suburbia of split-levels and backyard barbecues, but a few more turns take them onto an ancient road that passes several barns, all hard by the macadam. The Eldorado eases down a hill, and they pull off the road to a stop underneath a silent overpass.

"We're here," Dave says.

"Not exactly the country."

"But close enough." Jumping from the car, Dave climbs up a steep embankment next to the overpass, and Jim follows. They hop a chicken wire fence and then a concrete barrier. The two men now stand in the northbound lanes of a freeway without cars or paving, its concrete substratum left naked. To their right, the road extends around a curve undisturbed, but to their left, it progresses perhaps 150 yards and then dead-ends at a bedrock cliff.

Dave asks, "Wouldn't it make sense to secure the full route of your highway before you start building? Sounds like the Army must be in charge." In fact, the state highway authority's plan had been blessed by the towns along the route before construction, but then a litigious widow with a lot of money and even more love for her bees, whose apiaries still stand at the apex of the bedrock, sued to stop the road. The two men walk to the end of the concrete and lean against the rock face that defines her property line. High above them, bees buzz, and a superannuated dowager knows that she'll be dead before the bulldozers defile her front lawn.

"The road will be built," Jim says. "They always are."

"Are you feeling any better?"

"A bit."

A violent cold front came through the previous night, scrubbing away the humidity with dry Canadian air. Although warm, the day hints at the vulnerability of summer, so easy to forget in a Philadelphia July.

"I'm sorry," Jim says.

"For what?"

"Like the kids say, for the freak-out."

"There's no need. I know it happened to you, too. I mean, I know you were over there."

Jim frowns. "You're paying me, not the other way around. Which is good because I couldn't afford your fee."

"You're right. You couldn't. But if you talk about yourself, then we'll both get better, and you know the only people we can talk to are people who have been there. Because they know that nothing else is real."

No one else understands. Dave is correct about that. And

maybe no one wants to. It's true that Jim banned festivities upon his return, but if he hadn't, he knew that he would have been sitting with his wife, daughter, and in-laws, all alone with the ribbons, kazoos, and beer. The politics of the age were just part of it. The war was nebulous, and that's what drove people away. Everyone with a brain always knew that fighting communism was a complete joke. Were the NVA and Charlie going to invade California? They just wanted independence and had for a millennium. The real reason was so Uncle Sam could show the Russians that we were crazy enough to pursue guns and butter and maybe in the process drop a few H-bombs, no matter what the Gulf of Tonkin Resolution said. There were times in Cambodia when Jim had prayed for an H-bomb.

"I wasn't even supposed to go," Jim says. "The whole thing was insane when you think about it. I was thirty-two, married with a kid. Ed was still in the Reserves, Lieutenant Colonel. He told me I should join before I got drafted, but the calls were down already. It was early '68, but everyone knew we were getting out. I don't know. Maybe I was bored. College, medical school, residency, it all just blurred together. From the time I got to Philadelphia, it was like I was pulled along by some kind of machine. I was trapped, I guess. I could have done the goddamned Coast Guard."

"You had Ruthie. And Maria," Dave says. When Jim hears his family's names from another's mouth, he wonders if he should be sharing so much.

"They were always drifting away."

"Yeah." Dave lights a cigarette and offers one to Jim, who demurs.

"And then that goddamned Santoni. He told me I'd be at Fort Dix or someplace like that. I was, for a year. It was the second one that was the problem. I don't know. They gave me my orders, I was going over, and you know, you get thirty days off to tell everyone you love them and make sure that your life insurance premiums are paid. Of course, Maria was pissed. Boy, was she mad. She basically moved with Ruthie to Swedesboro until the last week, when her parents told her to get her ass back." Jim stops. "Why am I telling you this?"

"You know we didn't just meet. I mean, we did, but we didn't." Dave has a point. No alcohol, not even *Ba Muoi Ba 33,* disinhibits like the shared experience of death deferred.

"Not much happened at first," Jim says. "I was at Nha Trang doing psychiatric evaluations. My chief, Major Huddleston, knew Santoni from the class of God-knows-when, and so I guess he was covering for me, keeping me behind the ferns in the air conditioning. At six, I'd go over to the Officer's Club and get tanked and wake up covered in bites because I'd forget to sleep with the netting. I never got malaria, even though I rarely took the mefloquine. It gave me diarrhea, weird. It was like a nine-to-five job. You just happened to be in this humid, dirty, shit-can place on the other side of the planet where most people spoke two languages, neither of them English."

"And?"

"From time to time," Jim says, "a VC with a command detonator would blow up a car or a house with a Claymore, and an hour later everything would be normal again. You just had to do the job and not very well and make it to the next day, and you were good. In some ways, it was easier than being back here. You saw the people who had to be seen, but it was all the same, and then you got drunk every night. There was no reputation to uphold and no practice to build. It was just about making it through. I also did Medcap, vaccinations and physicals, dentistry, but mostly I was at Nha Trang. The guys would get analyzed and then go surfing."

"Sounds like you were living the dream," Dave says.

"It never occurred to me that Huddleston might not stick

around until the end of my tour, and one day, I came into the hospital, and a nurse tells me that he's on a C-130 back to the States. Within the month, I was on Dustoff full-time. It was like some kind of sick joke. It's like they forgot I was a psychiatrist, and suddenly I was a general medical officer but not even. It was like they ran out of medics." Dave gently punches his hand against the bedrock wall.

"Didn't you tell them you were a psychiatrist?"

"I did, but they lost my file, or at least it seemed like it. I know, it's unbelievable, but that's the way it was over there, you know. And sometimes I think that they knew exactly who I was and that they just decided to fuck me." Like everyone else. Like Jim's mother having to drive the snowy road to Shavertown, so she could pay off her dead husband's bank loan for a fifteen-year-old wedding.

"And what better way to fuck you than send you to Cambodia?" Dave says.

"Yeah. You know, May of '70 was crazy, but I'm surviving. Same with the rest of the summer. You keep thinking you're going to die, and then you don't. And then, September twenty-third." He stops. "I can't do this."

"You can," says Dave.

"You can. I can't. Let's get back in the car."

"Okay, we'll take a break." Climbing down from the stymied highway, the men get into the Eldorado, and in minutes, they exit the outermost band of the suburban galaxy. Without words, they pass occasional houses, some predating the nation, but mostly pastures and fields high with corn, ranch rail fences, and crumbling stone walls.

Jim says nothing, and neither does Dave, but they both know that the splinter must sooner or later be removed. If there were ten hours to explain the crash to Dave, there would be a million to wonder why Jim survived and the others didn't.

Luck? Chance? Sister Michael Frederick? Jim had Ruthie and Maria to get back to, but George Pisano, the crew chief, had three children and a wife not due to inherit a meatpacking business. She lives in Northeast Philadelphia, and she's even Italian, but he's never called on her. Not once. There was also Scotty and that Vietnamese ghost with the acne. He's the one that Jim dreams about, over and over.

He sweats. With the slightest provocation, he will coat the Eldorado's white leather with greenish-brown vomit.

"Pull over," he says.

"It's fine."

"Pull over!" the psychiatrist screams. Jim jumps from the slowing car, trips on the moving gravel, and throws up on the shoulder, producing more bile and acid than he could imagine from a hundred dead VC. When it's over, Jim returns to the car.

"I can't forget the kid," he says, wondering if his fear of ECT has been all wrong. Maybe three thousand milliamperes delivered to both temples three times a week for four months will let him forget.

Replying with silence, Dave restarts the Eldorado and drives toward Glenwyth. When the men have forgotten everything and nothing, Dave asks, "You want to get something to eat? You probably threw up three thousand calories."

They have drifted back to the main highway, and four hundred yards down the road, Dave spots a window-service restaurant next to a cornfield. The establishment has a caricatured statue of a rabbit prancing on its roof.

"I can't eat in this car," Jim says.

"How many times do I have to tell you? It's just a car. Here, take this." Dave hands him three brown capsules. "It's ginger. I learned it over there. You could swallow a cactus and not throw it up after these." Jim obeys, and the nausea slides away. Soon, they are parked in front of the restaurant, eating cheeseburgers and sipping root beer.

"Dave?"

"Yeah?"

"You still want to die?"

"Of course."

"What?"

"Yeah. I still want to kill myself."

"How?"

Dave's words are unbelievable, like the '64 Phillies having a six-and-a-half game lead with twelve to play and then losing the next ten and the Pennant.

"You look surprised," Dave says.

"Well, it's just that you look better."

"I looked the same a week before we met."

"You want to kill yourself?" Jim asks. "Even right now?"

"Not at this moment, but I did earlier today. I'm just being honest. Isn't that what the patient is supposed to do?"

"Yes, I guess, thank you," Jim says, not at all thankful.

"You've obviously never been suicidal yourself."

"Not exactly."

"Then how are you supposed to treat me?"

"A cardiac surgeon doesn't need a heart attack to do open heart surgery."

"No," Dave says. "You know that you can't stop someone from killing himself if he wants to do it."

"Yeah."

"You also can't convince someone that life's worth living. They have to find that out for themselves." If so, what the hell has Jim been doing since he visited the State Hospital at Wernersville when he was fifteen and decided to become a psychiatrist? It seems preposterous that a medical specialty could be built on such *terra infirma*, but maybe this is why they laughed at him at the end of the internship year when he left internal medicine. Maybe they were right. Maybe his mother was right when she said, *"But I thought you were becoming a real doctor?"*

"So we're wasting our time," Jim says.

"There you go again. I think you need a psychiatrist, and by the way, you are helping me, even now. You could have committed me, but you didn't. You trusted me, and so I trusted you. I'll wait, okay?"

"Okay, but for how long?"

"Maybe forever. I have a reason not to do it, and when I get the urge to blow my brains out, I'd have to ask myself, 'What would that crazy psychiatrist think?' And that's not the half of it. By showing me how troubled you are, and I can tell you are troubled, you've given me even more reason to wait."

Jim never learned this sort of thing in residency.

Dave continues, "It doesn't mean I don't want to do it. To change that quickly would be too easy, and that's not the way the world works. You have to be happy with postponement because it's just a matter of time until you postpone indefinitely, and I'm starting to think that you know all this and that this was your strategy all along."

If only Jim were that masterful.

"But I don't get it. Why do you need to die?" Jim asks, knowing the answer to his question.

"Isn't it obvious? I went left when I should have gone right and in the process killed my copilot."

"It could have happened to anybody, and we weren't supposed to start with that trauma."

"Forget the medical books. Anybody with half a brain could have called off the mission for a guy with a broken hand. End of story."

"You've got to forgive yourself," Jim says.

"Just like you have to forgive yourself when I jump in front of traffic because you said the wrong thing. See how easy it is?"

The gurgling of the Eldorado's engine offers the only answer.

"Then how do you live with all the uncertainty?" Jim asks.

"You either do, or you don't."

"It's kind of scary not knowing if you'll make it."

"Yeah, and anything else is just kidding yourself. But, if I had the chance to make it right again, to save someone else, that might fix me. Maybe I should enlist for a third time, but there's never going to be another war."

Jim sighs. "I have to go back. My two o'clock." He wants to cancel the rest of his schedule and crawl back to Barker's Mill Road. He can tell Maria that he's been vomiting, and he won't be lying. Then he can sleep away the afternoon. Not yet cranky from the stolen sleep that will come with her return to medicine, she'll bring dinner on a tray, and he'll watch *Laugh-In.* He needs a laugh. When Jim was in training, he thought of surgeons as soon-to-be-well-paid plumbers. Now he sees they're the lucky ones, cutting and welding, tightening and loosening. Days spent stopping leaks and increasing flow are days spent in certainty. Better yet, forget human flesh, and find a butcher's knife, a meat slicer.

The men make it back to the office by 1:45 p.m., and after handing Jim a hundred and fifty in cash, Dave departs. There are no new messages, making Jim realize that his fantasy of a packed schedule is still fantastic. Looking at his schedule book, Jim remembers that Quinton is due at 2:45, not two. Relief rushes in. The window air conditioner, consuming light and destroying heat, pumps chill and dust into the small room. Its hum silences the outside world. If not on Barker's Mill, Jim can sleep here, neutered into unconsciousness.

He sinks into the loveseat assigned to his patients. His legs hang over the armrest, and he wraps himself in a black and red afghan knit fifteen years ago by Carmela. Although the retainer's half-spent, this will be only the second time that Quinton has come to the office, despite his earlier promise to come daily. The first time last Friday, he was forty minutes late, allowing for only a ten-minute session, although Jim gave him thirty, having no subsequent patient to justify a hard stop. Maybe he won't come at all today.

A feathery calm envelops Jim. All will be right if he can just sleep. The answers are always there. For Kekule in 1865, the atoms danced, forming strings and then a snake, slithering and eating its own tail. Jim recalls little from organic chemistry except for the German who first described the structure of benzene, and Maria, always smarter, getting every problem right. He drifts into oblivion, and the people of Jim's life are aligning, not as a snake, but as the apices of a triangle, swirling and collapsing in on each other.

Then an emphatic knock pulls him back like some toxic smell from the chemistry lab. It's 2:02. It can't be Quinton, and the mail already came.

"Jim?" It's Honey, and what if he was in session? Can't she read the sign?

"Just a minute," he says.

Maybe she assumes, knowing the dubious demand for his services, that he couldn't possibly be with a patient. Or maybe she doesn't care. Or maybe she sent Eliza to such a third-rate psychiatrist because her daughter doesn't deserve any better.

He springs to attention, yanking tight his newly replaced tie and constricting his belt. There's the slightest scent of vomit. The slobber of his nap has run down his cheek. Wiping the spittle away, he opens the door. The hostess of Saturday night's horror show stands before him in a dress of pink elephants walking across a lime green field. She wears a narrow-brimmed straw hat and oversized sunglasses.

"Are you with someone?" she asks.

He wants to say yes, but he admits the obvious and adds, "Not until two-forty-five." An error; the answer will give her more time to talk. He ignored her message from the weekend, trying to avoid the story behind the sobs, but she never takes no for an answer, never has.

"Good. I have to come in. I need a session. Can I have one? A family session without patient? Your receipts sometimes say, 'Family Session with Patient.'" Perhaps this is her due after signing the check for his steak. "Please?"

He motions her in, and she pushes through, plopping into the loveseat just warmed by her daughter's psychiatrist. She removes her hat, positions it upside down on the ottoman, and drops her sunglasses into it. "I'm leaving Woody."

"What?" Jim says, his disbelief brimming a bit too excessively.

"It's over. I simply can't tolerate another minute, and it was over before it started. You know that, you of all people. We could die any minute. We should make the time we have count."

"Have you told him?"

"No, but it's been terrible since Saturday night. He knows there's a problem, but then he's always known that. He doesn't get me. He never has. You understood more about me in ten minutes than he has in twenty years." And there she is, sitting on that park bench next to Ben Franklin, leaves fallen, December '55. He had come to meet Maria and instead found Honey coatless in a powder blue suit, undaunted by the cold. Those ten minutes was the first time he really spoke to her. "Do you know that I met him in tenth grade at dancing school?"

"I'm not sure you told me that."

"That was when I could walk again," she says. "Well, he was always looking at the other girls."

"Then there's someone else?"

"Someone? There's a legion, a chippy on the exchange floor, a girl from personnel, and his clients, of course, more than one. He takes them to lunch to review their portfolios, without their husbands of course. Do you think that's right? He doesn't seem to care, and neither does the Stock Exchange."

"I'm sorry," Jim says, more resigned than surprised, but Eliza has told him everything, including the names.

"Will you hold my hand?" She closes her eyes and leans back into the folds of the loveseat.

"I'm sorry?"

"My hand," she says. "I simply need a friend, and please don't think otherwise."

Jim imagines Maria naked on their bed in self-inspection, fingers overspreading the flattened basketball of her gut.

"Honey...."

"I just need some comfort. I'm leaving my husband."

"Yes, I understand, but—"

"Fine," she says, flicking her wrist. "Maybe the problem is with men generally. Maybe I should seek out a Boston marriage." She laughs slightly and then steadies, turning serious. "Do you remember when you wanted to be a poet? I thought it was very noble. Do you still write? You never talk about it."

"You know that I don't." He had taken a single poetry class, first semester of freshman year, but words abandoned him after Maria sat him down and delivered the news at Wanamaker's Grand Crystal Tea Room.

"Well," she says, looking satisfied. "I guess we all have to give up certain things."

"Maybe you should consider marital therapy," he says, annoyance welling. "Maybe give things another chance." Jim has the singular impression that Woody sits beyond the door ready to burst in at any minute.

"Marital therapy requires a marriage," she says, and after a pause, "I'm telling Maria right after I leave here."

"Really?"

"Of course, and what's it to you? She's the smartest woman I know, and she never liked Woody. She didn't think I should have married him, but I doubt she's ever told you that. I didn't listen, of course. She told me many things. That was quite a semester when we lived together."

Jim stares at this interloping lynx, purring before the lunge.

"You know that I love Maria," Honey says. "I really do."

"Of course."

"Do you know how beside herself she was when she found out about Ruthie? I was her big sister, that was the sorority lingo, and so she came to me. She wasn't two weeks out of being a pledge, and she was afraid to talk to Carmela, although I'm not sure why. The woman seems endlessly understanding."

"She's mellowed."

"I suppose that's right, but Maria was upset like I'd never seen her. Do you know what a terrible time that was for her? No, I suppose not."

"Honey—"

"Why do you always interrupt? You sound like Burtie, and I can't imagine what your patients think. You thought it was all very simple, that you just appeared with that silly ring and made everything right, but she's never told you the full story, and I don't blame her. I mean, really, your mother's ring? Well, Maria had some crazy ideas." Honey pauses and studies her listener. She puts on her sunglasses. "I'm not trying to look like Audrey Hepburn, I assure you, but I'm getting a headache, and the light makes it worse." Jim scans his office, dim at midday. Maybe Honey does look like Audrey Hepburn.

She says, "She even had her train ticket to New York. There was a doctor, if you can call him a doctor, must not have been a block from Pennsylvania Station, not like it was even legal in New York. They should have never pulled that old station down, and to think that there's not even a Pennsylvania Railroad anymore, not even a Penn Central! We lost quite a lot of money when the Penn Central went belly-up and the bonds went for four cents on the dollar." Honey pauses and rubs her leg. "I'm sure Maria's never told you, but I sat her down and said that she would do no such thing, and she didn't. I'm not proud of a lot in my life, but I'm proud of that, and I deserve something for that, don't you think?"

He closes his eyes. "Why are you telling me this?"

"So that you never forget how little you know. You shouldn't judge me because I want to hold your hand."

"I don't judge you."

"Says the cool, calm, collected Dr. Malory. Where are you exactly? I mean right now."

"I'm here," Jim says.

"But you're not. Does anyone tell you that? You're somewhere very far away, and it's not good. Eliza has said as much."

"Here I am, talking with you, on Athens Road in Glenwyth, Pennsylvania."

"And lying through your teeth," she says. "You need to be in the moment. You should learn to meditate. I'm going to do it myself."

"That's very good, Honey, but what do you want?"

"For you to be my friend. I think I deserve as much. Is that so wrong?"

"I suppose not, but Maria—"

"Shhh," Honey says, putting a finger to her lips. "I regret I even said a word, and it's not like I'm asking you to be my Escamillo."

Jim slides his chair toward the loveseat. After the lunch at Wanamaker's, he had suspected that the cause of his impending marriage might evaporate, by chance or by more deliberate action. There was the sense that fate might somehow intervene, that the governor might issue a pardon, but he had never imagined that the chief executive reviewing his case was Honey.

"I just want someone to hold my hand," she says.

Starting tentatively, he touches her index finger, the same digit that God used to create Adam. Farther down, her palm swims in sweat, just like Maria's.

"Isn't your air conditioning working?" she snaps. "I guess it's just hot, another July in Philadelphia. This place reminds me of the farm before they demolished it. My parents thought air conditioning was only for people from Wynnefield, if you know what I mean, the people who prefer not to eat bacon. Can I have a drink? Ever drink in the office, Jimmy?"

"No," he says.

"No, I didn't think so," she says, cracking a smile. "My father always had whiskey in his office. In fact, he had a fully stocked bar. It seemed odd to me as a little girl, but as I got older, I thought it was a mark of distinction."

"I'm afraid I'm dry."

"You can't fool me," Honey says. "I bet there's a bottle of Jim Beam hidden between your files."

"You shouldn't be drinking with Hycodan and Quaaludes anyway," he says.

"I take them as needed. You know. You wrote them." Her grasp tightens, a vise upon his hand.

"I don't want to rush you but—"

"Time's up? Get out?"

"Not at all."

"But we need to discuss Eliza and how I break the news to her," Honey says. "This could push her clean over the edge, and she's not well, you know."

Not well really means *Eliza, you're stupid; Eliza, you're fat; Eliza, you're a loser.* The truth is that Honey enjoys delivering bad news to the girl.

"I'm sure you'll find a way to tell her," Jim says.

"Well, of course, but I want your professional opinion."

Instead, Jim can think only of the old Penn Station, grime upon its pink marble, awaiting its own destruction. He sees another Maria, also not yet demolished, sitting in a room shabbier than his, waiting for the doctor.

"Do you have these awkward gaps while you're talking to patients?" Honey asks.

"It's going to be challenging," Jim says. "Eliza's struggling."

"Well, of course, but how do you mean?"

"Is this off the record?" Honey turns her fingers like she's locking her lips and throwing away the key. "I think she's still cutting," he says, "and she's palling around with a guy who's pretty disturbing. I think he's selling drugs, maybe breaking and entering."

"That could describe many of her male friends. Who is he?"

"She won't say his name. I've tried."

"I could guess."

"Who?"

"I'll let her tell you. She can't keep a secret," Honey says. Distracted by forgotten train stations, illegal medical procedures, and commutations undelivered, Jim looks for an exit from this swamp of violated confidentiality and sees none. "If you fix Eliza," she continues, "you'll win the Nobel Prize."

"I'm not sure this is the right time for you to leave the marriage."

Honey scoffs. "You're wrong about that. It will be another disappointment, but not a fatal one. Eliza thinks he's a cad and that I'm cruel. She'll have to go to boarding school." She lets go of Jim's hand.

He tries to interrupt, to soften the blow, but no rebuttals come. Honey's right. With Burtie oblivious and Jimmy away, Eliza knows she's the one reason for her parents' continued cohabitation, and so her guilt has bloomed.

"It's better if she cuts her time with us both, no pun intended," Honey says. "Lawrenceville might be a stretch, but I know the admissions director. He went to White's, would you believe, and we were, well, friends."

"I don't think she's ready to leave home," Jim says. "She needs a mother."

"We all need a mother, but that's not to say that we can have one. Anyway, she'll fit right in, and maybe meet a Princeton man. This boy, have they had sex?"

"I think so."

"Which means yes, and what a shame. Do you think it's genetic?"

Jim sneezes. "Excuse me. I'm sorry, this air conditioner is filthy." He'll ignore Honey's question. "Even if Eliza's all right, you also have to consider Burtie."

"'Consider Burtie.' Listen to you. He won't know the difference. In that way, he's like Jimmy."

"I hadn't thought about him."

"No one thinks about Jimmy except me. You know that Woody always blamed me, like Jimmy was my fault. I suppose that was the beginning of the end. You know, when I named him that, it wasn't like I knew he would never speak."

"It's just a name," Jim says. "Jimmy is no less valuable than any child."

"And yes, Virginia, there is a Santa Claus. I spent every Tuesday afternoon for a year and a half with the rector at the Redeemer, but the Christian thing doesn't work. Maybe I'll turn Hindu and have a thousand more lives and ten thousand children."

"You'll need to consider custody," Jim says.

"Don't be absurd. I'll have full, of course."

"I suppose Woody could get an apartment big enough for visitation."

"Or shack up with that redhead from the Cricket Club," she says.

"But you have to anticipate that he may contest Burtie."

"You're kidding, right? He couldn't care less about Burtie because the boy is nothing like him. Anyone can see that." She's correct. The toddler shows more industry in a week than his father displays in a year. "Burtie's mine," she says, like a hen who has conceived a poult without needing a tom.

But why should Honey leave Woody now? It seems improbable that another girl with straw hair has broken the camel's back. The hat flopped on the loveseat brings everything into focus. Honey is the one having the affair, but with whom? Although a great beauty even in her thirties, Louisa Sharpe—as she will now demand to be called—presents certain difficulties overshadowing her looks. Although she's rich, is she wealthy enough to make a man forget the timeless maxim: Marry for money, and you'll earn every penny of it?

"For now, say nothing," Jim says. "See how you feel in a week. You may change your mind."

"You make fifty dollars an hour for such nonsense?" He has no reply, not even a *bon mot* to deflect her question. Jim looks at his watch, which then drives Honey's eyes to the wall clock. "I guess I should go."

"I have a patient soon."

"You know, life doesn't always work out. Sometimes you can't get what you want. Or maybe you get some of what you want, but only a glimpse of it and not what you need. That's probably worse. I don't suppose you listen to the Stones anyway. Maybe you'll write a poem about it all."

"How's your pain?" he asks.

"Same shit, different day. I wasn't always like this, you know. I wish you had known me before the accident. In third grade, I organized the girls to collect flowers for the incurables, that's what they used to be called, which made it strange when one of my classmates handed me a bouquet of pansies. This caring stuff is all fake."

"You cared about Maria," Jim says, and for no reason he can discern, he feels angrier than he has all day.

"Say hello to her for me." Honey stands and dons her hat. "And to Ruthie. They're always in my thoughts."

Jim retakes Honey's hand and pulls her back down to the couch. "What would make you happy? If there's any fairness, you do deserve that."

"Careful," she says, rescinding her palm, wagging a finger, and standing back up. "It's fraud to promise what can't be delivered. Besides, what I truly need is to get the Lincoln washed, and I think your next patient is probably here. I'll have to send an extra check with Eliza."

"Don't worry about it."

"Fairness, you said it yourself, and by the way, what did your supervisors tell you about giving away free sessions? Even I know that from *The Psychiatrist.* Do you remember that show? They should have never canceled it."

"I'll walk you down."

"As if I didn't know it by heart," she says.

The two navigate the narrow stairs into the waiting room. Quinton Graves, no longer naked but for a loincloth, sits low on the waiting room couch, his heels planted atop the magazines sprawled over the room's table. He wears a red polo shirt and seersucker shorts, utterly transformed from hippie to preppie. His hair is also short, and for a moment, Jim thinks he must be wearing a wig hiding the riotous locks underneath.

"Mrs. Dixon?" Quinton asks, almost inaudibly but still smashing to bits the first expectation of psychiatric waiting rooms: anonymity.

She stops, takes it all in, and glowers at Quinton. Then she turns to Jim with the appalling force and burn of an incendiary. It was like that in Operation Arc Light. The bombs came from the sky, and you never knew what hit you.

When she's gone, Quinton asks, "You treat Honey Dixon?"

"Let's go upstairs."

Quinton doesn't move. "I should give you a break if you've spent the last forty-five minutes with her. Hold on a minute. I'm still catching my breath. At least she can pay. Wow. She sure is a bitch, but she's not bad-looking for someone in her fifties."

"She's not in her fifties," Jim says. "And I can't talk about other patients." What the hell is he saying? She's not his patient, but if not, why did he just give her a session?

"Whatever," Quinton says. The two walk up the stairs, Jim first and his patient following. As a resident, when Jim saw psychiatrists enter their offices in front of their patients, he thought this protocol disrespectful and dangerous. Now, he follows it as well, wondering about the day when he will be shot in the back.

"So, how are you feeling?" he asks.

"Everything is slower," Quinton says. "I'm not sure I like that. I'm not getting as many ideas, and I have to go to the bathroom all the time. Also, I'm getting the shakes." He holds up his hand, and Jim can see an extra-fine tremor, a sign that Quinton's taking the lithium.

"How's your sleep?"

"I'm sleeping, which is boring. What's the longest you've ever been up?"

"Two days."

"When?"

"In college."

"You should try five," Quinton says.

"I wouldn't want to."

"It's better than LSD."

"Have you tried that?"

Quinton laughs. "You're supposed to ask how much and how recently. That's what they say in the textbooks."

"Okay. How much and how recently?"

"If you really want to know, I just took three tabs at eleven. Jeez! Can't you take a joke? You're not going to make it in this line of work unless you get a sense of humor."

"You were pretty agitated last Monday. Were you intoxicated then?"

"'Were you intoxicated?'" Quinton says in the mocking tone of an Edwardian dowager. "'Jeeves, bring around my phaeton and fetch me a cup of chamomile.'"

"Were you tripping?"

"Wow. Outta sight! Groovy man. You sound like Dick Clark. What's the big deal? We went on a drive. A very fast one, but you lived. Oh, that's another thing. I find driving while sleep-deprived intensely pleasurable."

"Until you kill yourself or someone else," Jim says.

"And since when has that happened?"

"What does it feel like when you don't fall asleep?"

"At first, you're tired, and you can't stay awake, but if you can stay in the light, that all goes away. Like maybe your clock resets or something. You start to see things darting by in your peripheral vision, like snakes, but by the time you turn your head, they're gone. Then you feel cold, no matter what the temperature."

"You like that?"

"What's not to like? All the rules of perception are broken, and normal mentation is revealed for what it truly is, a sham." Mentation—Quinton has been reading the psychiatry books.

"I guess the normal around here is pretty boring," Jim says.

"It's not so much boring as it is despicable." The insight crystallizes. For some, like Woody, wealth leads to philandering and inactivity. For Quinton, an oasis of prosperity provides an excuse to axe its date trees and drain its springs.

"Despicable is a strong word."

"Not really," Quinton says, "when you know how the privileged create and perpetuate themselves."

"I'm not sure I follow."

"They only exist because of what they consume. One guy, say my great-great-grandfather, gets an idea of how to make a better saw. So he builds a plant dumping all kinds of poisonous crap onto the land and into the water. Okay. Maybe he builds a pretty good saw, but after the first few, he doesn't make the saws himself. Other guys make them, and they live in a bunch of shitholes along the Delaware, polluted by his factory so bad that the workers' kids can't even swim. But Graves doesn't care because he builds Sycamore Lodge in Glenwyth, with a butler and ten in service. Even Howell gets screwed out of the fortune, but of course, they still keep his name on the company. Like Scrooge and Marley, even though Marley's been dead for seven years."

"Your family pays income taxes," Jim says.

He shakes his head. "They made their money a long time ago before there was an income tax, and now they just protect it and make it grow with trusts and fancy lawyers. They pay a lot less than you think, and same thing with your patient Honey Dixon."

"She's not my patient."

"Yeah, whatever. As far as I can see, you're the only one actually working. My parents don't work. They don't even control the company, which pisses me off. I should—"

"What?"

"I'm not telling you."

"You have a lot of anger."

Quinton rests his chin on the hand of his propped-up arm and closes his eyes. "No."

"No what?" Jim asks.

"Just no. If I told you how I really felt, you'd commit me."

Jim grits his teeth. He has stepped on the grenade, the patient who communicates risk and won't say more. The clock says 3:07, which means that Quinton wins the battle if he remains silent for the next twenty-eight minutes. Immediate, direct opposition will acknowledge and strengthen Quinton's resolve to silence, but the psychiatrist goes all in.

3:07:30—"Quinton, I'm just trying to help you."

3:08:20—"This is a waste of both your time and mine."

3:09:15—"You know, I could commit you."

3:10:27—pathetically—"What am I supposed to say if your parents ask me how this is going?"

3:12:20—Jim picks up the copy of *The Inquirer* that sits on his desk and then throws it to the ground.

3:13:30—"Please talk?"

With this final surrender, the tumblers click into place.

Quinton says, "You can ask me questions, if I can ask you, one for one." The psychoanalysts say personal disclosure is a bad bet with poor returns, but didn't Jim gamble with Black and throw Big Red? So Jim rolls the dice again and says, "Deal."

"I go first. Why'd you agree to see me when you can fill up your schedule with Honey Dixons talking about their tennis elbows?"

Jim says instead, "I try to help people. I'm trying to help you." It's true even now, which almost shocks Jim, like it would make more sense to want to shoot Quinton through the forehead.

The patient guffaws. “You got to be kidding me. Are you fucking serious?”

“It’s my turn,” Jim says. “What was it like for you at boarding school?”

“You have to be more specific. I could get out of that one so easily and give you nothing, but I’m going to be nice. I liked New Hampshire.”

“What was it like?”

“I mostly read comic books while the other guys fucked girls from Miss Porter’s and Ethel Walker. When I was a junior, Exeter went coed, and that was even worse.”

“So you never had a girlfriend?”

“Well, that depends on how you define girlfriend. Not up there.”

“Were you bullied?”

“That’s two questions. How do you get along with your wife?” Quinton asks.

“We’re still married.”

“What a ringing endorsement of matrimonial bliss!”

“We’ve been together almost seventeen years.”

A sliver of a smile passes over Quinton’s face. “You married early, not much older than I am now.”

“I suppose,” Jim says, clearing his throat and moving on. “Were you bullied?”

“I’m going to give you this one as a bonus,” Quinton says. “I was just ignored at Exeter. By then, it was like they realized that it was best if they didn’t mess with me. But my classmates at White’s were assholes. I should blow them all up with an ANFO bomb. See, I’m saying more than I should, and that was a joke, in case you’re thinking of calling the Glenwyth Police.”

Jim hasn’t heard the term ANFO in a while. Didn’t some crazy engineer talk of it at the Eighth Field Hospital?

"You're thinking of the University of Wisconsin at Madison," Quinton explains, seeing the puzzlement in Jim's eyes. "There was an upperclassman from White's who went there, but he wasn't blown up, unfortunately."

"Quinton—"

"What? Should I forgive? The kids at White's wanted to see the weak suffer and squirm like ants before being burned alive with a magnifying glass. And we had to go to chapel each week." The patient springs up and peers out one of the office's windows.

"What?"

"Nothing. I thought I saw something." He sits down again. "That's how the boys at White's felt good, with anger and a bit of the old ultra-violence. You ever see that film?"

Jim squirms in his chair, remembering the movie that drove Maria and him out in the middle and threw them into an argument.

"Tell me about Lehighton," Quinton says.

"It's ninety miles north and a million miles away."

"And your parents?"

"My mother worked. She was in the ILGWU." Quinton's brow wrinkles. "The International Ladies' Garment Workers' Union."

"Not a happy housewife sitting by the pool?"

"No."

"So, she was an organizer?"

"She was too far into the dirt to organize," Jim says, remembering how a union man attended her funeral, which was paid for, after an inadequate burial policy, by the Sedaras.

"And what about your father?"

"Ask me anything," Jim says. "There's not much to say."

But Quinton can't forget the wisps of Ruth Malory. "That's amazing. Your mother was in an actual union," he says, like an entomologist with a new insect.

"What did you do when you were by yourself?" Jim asks.

"I used to collect model trains, which was a good hobby for a teen loser. You're not going to believe this, but I had the complete Lehigh Valley in O Gauge, including the John Wilkes and the Black Diamond. Whatever happened to them?"

They stopped running, and Lehighton's station was pulled down. There had been only a few years that Jim, Maria, and their toddler could catch the Reading in Philadelphia, transfer at Bethlehem, and visit his mother on the squealing passenger cars of the Valley. When her kidneys failed, he had to drive up in the Mustang on the Northeast Extension.

"They all disappeared," Jim says. It was ironic that his mother's poverty and her resulting lack of dietary protein had delayed her renal failure. In the end, Jim wanted to transfer her to the University Hospital, where researchers experimented with dialysis, but she wouldn't cross the Blue Mountain, worried about the bills of Philadelphia doctors and embarrassed by the unaccountable fetor coming up from her insides. The last time he saw her, before she blew away like sand, he came alone. She seemed reluctant to speak with him, like she didn't deserve to be in the presence of her son, the physician. Her shrinking mouth was a deep, quivering, folded bowl of skin.

"I bet your mother wasn't any Honey Dixon," Quinton says. "What was her name?"

"Ruth."

"Ruth? Man. The world is a funny place, isn't it, eternally returning and all that Friedrich Nietzsche stuff?"

"I don't follow you."

"Never mind," Quinton says, closing the book.

Jim eyes his watch—3:35 even—and says, "Well, then." Relief rushes in. The subsequent schedule stands vacant, assuming no more surprise visits from Honey. The psychiatrist can stop, but if he doesn't, and if he makes the blunder of exploration in the final moments of the session, all bets are off. And yet, if Jim just said something else, took another risk, they might connect, and Quinton's anger might abate, if only for a moment.

Instead, Jim says, "We should probably conclude for today. We've covered a lot."

"But I'm not finished."

"How do you mean?"

"One day," Quinton says, "I found a way to feel better and to get rid of everything that ever hurt. There was an abandoned house, and so I set it on fire. I just sat there, and I watched it burn down. It felt so good."

"Where?"

"I'm not going to tell you, but when I did, all the pain went away. Presto! Just like that! But then it came back. So I did it again, the arson part."

Jim looks at his patient and asks, "You're serious?"

Quinton smiles. "What do you think?"

"I think you're making up a fantasy, projecting what you'd like to do."

There's another pause. "If you say so."

"Then I guess we'll talk about that next time. Tomorrow at two?"

"Sure, since my time's up on your gold pocket watch. But what about that bitch Honey Dixon and her cunt daughter? Don't you think you're in a bit too deep?"

"I guess we'll have to discuss it tomorrow," Jim says, standing up and thereby delivering the universal cue for departure.

Without objection, Quinton rises from the loveseat and walks down the stairs, exiting the building with the slam of a door. Without even leaving his chair and with the air conditioner still on, Jim hears the final word of the session, a scream really, "Motherfucker!"

He rises and goes to the window. Jim expects to see Quinton hop into the Corvette and peel away down Athens. Instead, the patient lingers in front of the office, looking to both sides like he's waiting for someone. Then Quinton gazes up and behind, directly at Jim, sarcasm clawing at the psychiatrist's eyes.

Quinton smirks, looks away, and walks across Athens. He sits on the bench in front of the pharmacy, assuming his place and role in a play. There, he stretches, relaxes, and reclines. He lights a cigarette. It's almost like he wants people to think that he has been waiting for much longer than a minute.

Jim is about to return to his desk and its paperwork when he sees Ruthie walk up and lean her bike against the bench. She sits next to her father's patient, and Quinton puts his arm around her shoulder. They kiss, a remarkable thing for a public road in Glenwyth, not to mention in clear sight of her father's office. Ruthie doesn't care. She's in love.

7

A week or two later, Maria checks the lock on the bungalow's front door for the ninth time, the beginning of another endless loop. Her fingers are bleeding. She really must stop this, both the chewing and the checking. With each repetition, she feels relieved and turns to walk to the bus, which will take her to Ike's Seafood in Athens. Yet before she can reach the end of the concrete ribbon leading from her front door, she forgets that it's locked and returns to inspect it. This transitory amnesia is odd. She seems to remember everything else in her life. So the loop continues for fifteen minutes and counting. It was like this in medical school. On tests, she couldn't stop checking her answers, often running down the clock with multiple incomplete questions. On dissections, she would identify nerves and vessels, but then, doubting herself, resume cutting until the cadaver part in question was liquefied. The weight of the rituals made even the most basic tasks unmanageable.

And she's supposed to make dinner? Friday afternoon, and she promised Jim that she would serve linguine with red clam sauce, one of his favorites. Maybe if Jim ate more and gained a few pounds, he might relax, and his scar wouldn't hurt so much. Suddenly, they have money, their own money, enough to buy real food and not feel guilty about it. Having spent few dinners at home the past three weeks, Ruthie will even join them, along with Angelo and Carmela, which seems remarkable. Ruthie's gone out more in the last three weeks than in the past three years. Maria's tried to let her daughter be, to not be another Honey Dixon having too much to say, but maybe this is the time for more mothering rather than for less. After all, the stay-at-home days are coming to an end.

Four days earlier, Maria marshaled the will to call the Woman's Medical College and ask for Dean Muller-Lyer. The secretary who answered told her that the school's leader of thirty years had retired. Maria was transferred to the new dean, Dr. Phyllis Weinberg, a professor Maria remembered from the first time around. Maria almost hung up while on hold, but the dean herself got on the phone, and the woman's wispy voice was anything but fearsome. If anything, the school's top official sounded like a patient waiting to be cared for. Of course they could meet, the dean said. So, without white gloves but with her hair sprayed to metal and squeezed into an old-fashioned black wool suit left over from Ruthie's pregnancy, Maria took the bus into Philadelphia a few days later and met with Dr. Weinberg, who now sat in a wheelchair.

The medical school dropout took a half-hour to explain her story, throwing everything in, including the husband she met freshman year of college, his time in Vietnam, her parents who didn't understand medical careers, that she never believed in herself, and that she never had to believe in herself. On and on Maria went, as if Dr. Weinberg had the day set aside for this nonsense, but the dean listened, her palsied hands clasped in her dead lap.

When Maria concluded the exhausting story of her life, the dean responded by saying that Dr. Muller-Lyer was "forgetful" and living with her "baby sister." Imagining her mentor's dementia, Maria considered her own mortality and wanted to run from the room. Without Muller-Lyer as an advocate, her readmission was doomed, but the conversation continued. Dr. Weinberg also remembered Maria; fondly, it turned out. Ten years earlier, she had scored the highest grade in the professor's immunology class, at a time when the instructor looked unafflicted and unremarkable. Maria wanted to ask about the dean's disability but didn't. Dean Weinberg left it at that, saying, "I only wish that I—" As the dean meditated on the pregnant rotundity in front of her, Maria knew what the woman meant.

The loss of a decade insignificant to someone who could no longer walk or have anything except nieces and nephews, Dr. Weinberg outlined a process for re-entry. Maria would take several proficiency tests, prove the absence of "moral turpitude," and pay a twenty-five-dollar fee. When Maria learned that pittances separated her from a resumption of her schooling, she wondered if she might deliver the baby then and there, but the dean gently ignored the applicant's not-so-hidden agitation. It pleased Dr. Weinberg that this mother of a teenager and, soon, a baby, this wife of a troubled psychiatrist in need of major psychiatric treatment himself, would again be a medical student. Weinberg's exploration of Jim's pathology surprised Maria. She obviously wasn't the only person who realized he needed help.

She imagined September 1974 as her earliest possible date of re-enrollment, but this was far too conservative. Like the loving but firm older sister Maria had wanted and never had, Dean Weinberg stated that Maria would return when the 1972 fall term began and complete her first clinical rotation in pathology. There was no *could*, and September was less than two months away. Beached whale that she was, Maria imagined that she might in theory sit and study slides of thromboses and sarcomas without too much effort. When Maria delivered, the dean said, the student would take six weeks off and then come back, depositing the child in something called a "daycare" that had been set up for children of faculty. It seemed odd and even dangerous to leave an infant with strangers, but the caregivers were trainees from the medical school's psychology department, and the place was being run as a sort of educational experiment, with weekly institutional review.

Leaving the meeting with a folder full of mimeographed forms, Maria thought she might pass out, and for a moment she forgot where she was. People outside the dean's office were staring at her, she knew that. She was a sorry sight, and she should have at least been wearing gloves to cover her bitten fingers. In mere months, she would be a witness to incised abdomens and trephined skulls. The surgeons worked their medical students, and to the female trainees went the goriest jobs. What was she thinking?

Now, a few days later, trying simply to board a bus to Athens to buy clams, she's beset with a similar amnesia. At the bus stop nearest Barker's Mill, she checks the posted schedule again and again. Then she counts the passing cars, pausing only when thirty-nine have gone by. That had been one of her good numbers since childhood. But then another car passes, ruining everything. She'll have to start again.

So she walks back to the house. Grabbing the door's brass handle, the remnant of a sturdier time, she turns it clockwise and then pushes into the house, repeatedly. Locked, locked, locked...she intones the word seventeen times, another one of her good numbers. If only the feel and sound of the dead latch pressing the strike plate were just right, she could go to the market. Each time, though, the noise and sensation are off, and Maria repeats the ritual. She's engaging it again when a black Corvette convertible screams down Barker's Mill, rattling flowerpots, distracting Maria from her mission. What a jerk. The car squeals to the right at the corner of Soapstone.

She should call the police but doesn't have the license plate. It's pointless anyway. A sympathetic officer will listen to her complaint, promise to do everything, and then forget that she even called. They still have no idea who broke into the Althouses'.

Maria returns to the knob when she notices Eliza standing nearby, the girl's thin legs straddling her ten-speed. She wears a white miniskirt and a yellow polo with huge lapels.

"Hi," Eliza says, embarrassed to catch Maria in her compulsion. "Is Ruthie around?"

"She's at the library."

"That's smart. I'm sure she's doing her summer reading. I can't believe it's August."

"How's your mom doing?" Maria asks, turning from the door. Wet spots form on the walkway, the western skies darkening.

"Busy, like always."

"I'm so sorry."

"Oh, yeah, but it's okay. It's not like I'm the first kid whose parents are splitting. My dad's already moved into Philadelphia, and Honey's redoing the kitchen. She's importing tile from Italy, which is a total pain, but she says we'll never sell the place with 1962 countertops."

"Well, I'm sure it will be beautiful when she's done." The Dixons' kitchen might have been used twenty times in the past ten years if one excludes reheating take-out and mixing drinks. "Did you help her pick them out?"

"No," Eliza says, looking down. "You know her. She always knows exactly what she wants."

For a moment, the girl looks like she'll mount her bike and disappear down Barker's Mill, but she lays it on the grass and sits on the porch steps. Maria stares at the knob, but Eliza wants to talk, maybe even needs to. "You want some chocolate chip cookies?"

Maria asks. "I made way too many."

"I don't know."

"It's going to rain. You don't want to be on Wingohocking in this, the way people drive these days. Come on." Without even fake objection, Eliza obeys. Guiding her bicycle up the porch's two steps, she leans it against the wooden railing. A black metal glider, green wicker furniture, and an outdoor dining set crowd the porch, providing enough seating for twelve.

"Do you and Dr. Malory and Ruthie spend much time out here?"

"Sure."

"What do you do?"

"We eat, we talk. I've slept out here a few times. Years ago, with Ruthie, we had her Girl Scout troop meetings here, at least in the summer."

"I never did Girl Scouts."

"I know. Honey didn't like it."

"The cookies, that's why she didn't like it," Eliza says.

"I suppose," Maria says. "You know, where I grew up, in the city, people sleep on screen porches all the time. When I was a girl, it was so hot, with all the concrete and asphalt, you couldn't stay inside."

"What was it like?"

"Like camping, only without the skunks. They were too scared to come to South Philadelphia. Let's get some cookies." Eliza follows Maria through the living room, dining room, and into the kitchen that will never be redone. Green and white asphalt squares, most of them cracked, tile the floor. Some are missing, revealing a black underside of dried, useless glue. The refrigerator resembles a safe, with a menacing, cylindrical head on top. The oven has bulbous knobs, and two circular fluorescents stack to create a ceiling light. The room's other concession to modernity is a red Formica table rimmed with ribbed steel. Someone has strewn a pattern of thin white and blue boomerangs across its surface, and a plate heaped with Tollhouse cookies stands at the table's center.

"I'm not sure Honey would approve," Maria says. "This isn't exactly *Better Homes and Gardens.*"

"No, it's great. I bet you make wonderful meals here."

"I do, when my mother comes over."

"What's your favorite?"

"Well, she makes a mean *braciola,* and I stand around watching. We even do the seven fishes." Eliza scratches her head. "It's an Italian thing."

"You get along with your mother?"

"Now, but not when I was your age," Maria says. "She was very demanding, and it was difficult to measure up, I guess you might say. Hey, I have an idea. Why don't we go out to the porch with the cookies? We can talk."

"I don't know—"

"Eliza—"

"All right."

Maria pours two large tumblers of milk and places them on a tray with the cookie plate. Eliza pulls back the kitchen door and then the front, making way. Raindrops have turned to a downpour pounding the porch's slate roof. A dog runs by and then its owner, a newspaper futilely draped over the man's head.

"You need an umbrella?" Maria shouts, but the words are lost in the aquatic din. "It's coming down," she says, eating a cookie. Thunder cracks.

"Cats and *dog,*" Eliza says.

"That's not bad," Maria laughs. "Wow. It's really coming down. You couldn't have ridden your bike in this."

"They didn't say it was going to rain on the noon news."

"They don't know anything. They said Agnes would be a heavy

rain, and then it washed out half of Pennsylvania. Are you going to have a cookie?"

"No, I don't think so."

"Eliza, what teenager doesn't like chocolate chip cookies?"

She reddens. "I was always taught to say, 'Thank you, but I've already eaten.'"

Maria sighs. "Your mother was insatiable when we were roommates. She used to hide candy under her pillow."

"I think that's the point."

"You're probably right, but what if you had just one cookie, maybe two?"

"I would eat them all."

"But what if you didn't? What if you just ate one, two, maybe even three, and then told yourself it was all right, that you weren't going to swell up and explode?"

"I could never do that."

Maria takes the girl's hand and says, "But what if you told yourself that you could?"

"It's not that easy."

"Try."

Like someone awaiting poison, Eliza takes a bite. Loosening, curious, she has another. "These are good."

"What did you expect? Hydrox?"

"My mother gets those, but only Bailey will eat them." Maria has been accosted by the Dixons' yellow Labrador on several occasions. The dog has a nervous condition only relieved when he urinates on one of the Dixons' rugs or chews through a door.

"At least Bailey's happy," Maria says. There's a spark and then a blast of thunder not a quarter-second later. "Holy moly! That was close." Eliza eats another cookie and slugs down half the glass of milk, followed by two more cookies. Then, hitting a wall, she stops and seems somewhere else.

The two are silent for a time, and then Maria asks, "Are you happy?"

"I guess as much as I deserve."

"You deserve to be more than happy," Maria says.

"Who deserves anything? Did Jimmy deserve what he got?" Maria has nothing to say to that. Eliza looks up at the porch's ceiling and its immobile fan, then to the street, and to the relentless rain. Mist encircles her eyes. "I have to go to the bathroom," she manages, getting up.

"Eliza—"

"It's fine. I promise."

Maria screws her lids shut and thinks of her husband when he was thousands of miles away in Cambodia. He wrote that he was still in Saigon at his metal desk, but she knew that he was lying. Maria had tried to keep him here in Glenwyth, and she had failed. A moment passes.

Then: "Eliza!" The mother is inside and banging on the bathroom door. "Come out here now." Silence, maybe too late. "I'll break it down if I have to."

Maria taps the door, and it pops open into Eliza's thigh. She doesn't move, and the door wasn't even locked. Inside, a sweating, kneeling shadow dangles her head above the toilet bowl. The water's been flushed. Eliza has removed her top and thrown it into the corner, rendering herself naked from the waist up save her brassiere. Cuts, some healed, some from today, ring her lower back and abdomen. There's a new scar, maybe a few weeks old: FAT.

"Tell me," Maria says. "I want to know everything."

Eliza says nothing, frozen like another piece of powder room porcelain. Maria hugs the girl, a difficult feat in the cramped space, but Eliza pulls herself behind the toilet and whispers, "Don't look at me."

"I am looking at you, and I will keep looking at you as long as I need to. You're going to stop this!"

"No," Eliza says, her voice barely audible. "I can't stop it."

Maria grabs this rag doll of a girl and pulls her upright, standing her straight. "Yes. You can."

Eliza flops onto the toilet seat, and Maria sees tears falling into grime and dust.

"I don't deserve to stop it."

"You deserve nothing else. I want this to be the last time."

"You don't know what it's like. You've never been there."

"I may not have been there, but I could tell you about all the other places I've been."

"No," Eliza says, looking right at her best friend's mother. "I don't want you to cry."

"It wouldn't be the first time. It won't be the last," Maria says and wonders how a ghost could have impregnated her twice. It won't be the last time, will it?

The two of them sit frozen until Maria says, "You know, I've always been terrible at cleaning, which I'm sure you've noticed. Now, with you sitting there, all I can think of is how bad a job I've done on this floor. What do you say we get some mops?"

Eliza coughs a brown clot of vomit. Studying the blob in her palm, she smiles at the absurdity of it all. A half-hour later, the two have made the bathroom floor spic-and-span. Next, in the Malorys' bedroom, Eliza sits on the bed with her shirt hiked up. Maria applies ointment to the wounds and wraps them in gauze with the care of a surgeon.

"I've never done this," Eliza says. "I just let them be."

"They might get infected."

"Do you think they'll scar? That's stupid. I know the answer."

"The body is an incredible thing and can take more than we ever imagined." Maria looks at Eliza. "As long as we're alive."

Back on the porch, Maria says, "I'm going to give you baking lessons. Don't worry. We'll start slowly."

"You know—" Eliza says.

"What?"

"No. It's too rude. I can't say it. You'll hate me. You'll never let me come back."

"Why?"

The girl pauses, thinking. "You've never—well, you've never starved yourself."

Maria laughs out loud. "No."

"I wish I was like that."

"It can be arranged. Pretty soon you'll be making and eating *cannoli* all day long."

"Maybe I could come here once a week and talk to you," Eliza says.

"Me? Sure, but you see Dr. Malory. Do you want to stop with him?"

"I'm not saying that. It's just—"

"I'm only a mother."

"But you're going back to medical school. You're going to be a great doctor."

"If I graduate."

"Here's a promise," Eliza says. "We'll both graduate."

"Deal."

"I wish—"

"What?"

"I wish that I could tell you something, but I can't."

"Now that's not fair. I've known you since you were born and your mother a long time before that."

"Yes, I know, but—"

"Then what?"

The mist returns, and in a flash, Eliza is bawling. "I hate myself. That's why I throw up and cut."

"But you're beautiful and smart."

"Not as much as Ruthie. It doesn't matter. I'm a horrible person, and that's why I want to die. And now it's even worse."

"Why?"

"Because of what I've done to Ruthie. It wasn't supposed to work out like this."

"I don't get it. What have you done?"

"I can't tell you. You'll tell Dr. Malory, and then he'll tell Quinton, and then—"

"Quinton? Quinton Graves? What does this have to do with him?" Eliza has silenced herself. "What do you mean? Why?"

Beyond the porch, the rain has gone as quickly as it came, and the sun pushes through thunderclouds.

Eliza sees this and jumps up. "I have to go. I'm sorry about everything."

"Wait. You have to explain. We're talking about Ruthie. What about Quinton Graves?"

Pain spreads across Eliza's face. For an instant, she looks like a refugee bearing witness to pillage and disaster, and this says more about that glass and silver box above Wingohocking than Maria has ever imagined.

"I have to go, I'm sorry. Please forgive me." In one motion, Eliza pulls her bike away from the railing, jumps on, and hops it down the stairs, fishtailing before she finds her balance and the wet macadam of Barker's Mill.

Maria follows Eliza skidding toward Athens, tracing the path of that goddamned Corvette. High above, there's no rainbow. *Forgive you for what?*

Maria returns to the house for her umbrella. There's no telling when the rain will return. Slamming the door on her way back out, she's so distracted that she leaves it unlocked, giving whatever demons she fears a free and clear right of entry.

Honey exits her Lincoln and stares at the granite steps of the Founders Building. Every Friday afternoon, she comes to this place and considers the grand stairs which flare down and out from the entryway to the parking lot. They are not handicapped accessible, odd, but then few of the parents who come to visit require such accommodations. If they did, how would they have reproduced? Also, few of the patients ever leave. She grabs hold of the copper railing, now turned green, and pulls herself up to the door. The first time had been so hard, as if crossing the threshold would make the situation real. Now it's just another entrance.

The other mothers that Honey has known over the past years have let themselves go, sartorial optimism turning to house dresses, the process aided by the winds of informality blowing through the new decade. Honey, however, has become ever more austere so that she now impersonates a costume designer's vision of a perfume company CEO. Stylish and commanding, she can coo or kill. She has pulled back her blonde hair in a bun and wears a slate gray suit. Inside, her heels tap the marble floor all the way to the visitor's desk. Mrs. Crawford has been there from Honey's first visit, one of the few with Woody, and she seems not to have moved since that time.

"Hello, Mrs. Crawford," Honey says, unclasping her black-and-white rectangular purse for a pen.

"Mrs. Dixon, how are you feeling today?"

"I'm doing well. My leg hurts a bit, but they say rain, at least up in Glenwyth."

"I hope it's not too bad," the attendant says, offering Honey a clipboard with a sheet that she signs. "I don't know about Glenwyth, but down here, it's dry as a bone."

"I can see. The flowers in front look horrible. Do you think they might let me do some watering after the visit?"

"How could they say no?"

"Maybe they can think about it. It's nice that Jimmy's been calm enough to be able to go back to the cottages."

"Indeed, it is! You know your way."

"Yes, of course. Thank you."

Honey clacks by the desk and enters a long corridor, interrupted on either side by wooden doors framed in marble, with frosted glass panes and gold lettering. The ceiling is at least twenty feet high and curves semi-circularly, making the hallway look ecclesiastical. At its end, Honey passes through two doors and stands at the top of a hill. Beyond it, twenty small brick houses make a downwardly sloping loop. She walks to the right and goes to the second house, with a carved wooden sign above its threshold—DIXON. The cottage didn't always bear this name, but the required donation was only a thousand. Now she'll have to give another thousand to change the name to SHARPE.

The stench of feces blooms inside the cottage.

"May I help you?" A woman emerges from one of the bedrooms, holding a heap of soiled linen.

"Yes, I'm here to see Jimmy Dixon. I don't believe we've met. I'd shake your hands but—" Honey smiles. "Where's Mrs. Connelly?"

"She quit. Now it's me. Mrs. Mahoney."

"It's wonderful to meet you."

"I'll bring Jimmy out. He's been very calm. I think the new medication's working. You can have a seat." The attendant nods toward the stained couch.

"Why not?" Honey says and lowers herself into the swampy cushions. This is the cottage's living room, empty save for the sofa and a television with rabbit-eared antennae. Honey knows the two pieces well. They used to be in her basement and before that in the Dutch colonial at the end of Little Lane near Glenwyth Cricket. She and Woody lived there from graduation until they built the place on Wingohocking. The family to whom they sold it hadn't stayed; too tight or maybe a job transfer. Earlier this year, Honey drove to her former home, and peering across its picket fence, she was shocked to see the living room painted orange. Things were changing in Glenwyth, but it would never be Berkeley.

The lane was indeed little, more of a driveway than anything else, with three houses on either side of the private road. She loved the sound of that, and it had seemed so safe when, in the spring of their senior year, she, Woody, and Maria drove out from West Philadelphia, and he carried her inside while Maria chuckled nearby. Honey was already admitted to the master's program in architecture at the university, but nested in her own house, she lost interest in further study. Woody was working then, and despite the nagging sense that their emotional dialogue transpired in separate languages, she was happy, maybe for the first and only time. Getting pregnant was the newlyweds' charrette, and when Honey learned it was twins, she felt sublime pleasure. The potential risks of a double pregnancy were as theoretical as nuclear fallout.

Mrs. Mahoney returns leading a large, adolescent boy by the arm, and sits him down, directing his shoulders to the sofa. Despite a face of picked scabs and a stubbly head, Jimmy is a teen idol, his facial proportions with a striking all-American symmetry. Dressed in khakis and a rep tie, he could be class president.

"I'll be in the other room," Mrs. Mahoney says from her thin lips. "If you need me."

"Thank you. Hello, Jimmy."

The boy fixes on her for a moment, but only by chance. His gaze searches the room as if trying to locate a hidden insect. Then, locking his eyes on something that only he can know, he tilts his head almost perpendicularly.

"How are you doing today?"

Nothing.

"I'm redoing the kitchen, and so I hope we can get everything right enough for a home visit. I think you'll like it."

He again says nothing but makes a strange noise, a repeated "t" sound.

"We're going to be selling it, which I know may upset you, but I'm going to get another house, and it will be wonderful."

"Tih-tih-tih-tih-tih-tih-tih-tih-tih-tih-tih-tih," he says, getting up, his energy rising.

Honey straightens her back and checks her hair, coiffured this afternoon. She has survived Woody, and she can survive this. The future is going to be better. She can and she will be happy.

Just before Jimmy was two years old, he had a fifty-word vocabulary and could speak three- and even four-word sentences. *Mommy, mommy, the tees, the tees, I love the tees.* He would say that as they sat looking up at the pin oaks and elms that loomed above that backyard on Little Lane. When she and Woody moved after college, Honey told people that it was the nicest street in Glenwyth, and it was, in those days.

Honey and Jimmy would play together in that backyard, and Eliza would sit alone, ripping the dandelions. Jimmy was her mother's favorite, Eliza knew it even then, and Honey couldn't argue. She realized that her soul was only capable of just so much love.

The words didn't disappear suddenly. The loss was so gradual that Honey didn't notice it at first. The articles disappeared, and then the verbs. Having been a delightful infant, Jimmy was now beset with tantrums. Soon there were just nouns, fewer by the week. The pediatrician was baffled—*I've never seen anything like it.* It was only after a visit to a neurologist at Children's Hospital, the same building where they almost cut off her leg, that a diagnosis was obtained. Early infantile autism, which she had never heard of. By Jimmy's fourth birthday, there was only *t, t, t, t, t, t,* and other guttural sounds, as well as head-banging and screaming. Honey researched the condition and even obtained a second opinion from Dr. Kanner at Johns Hopkins, but she went alone with Jimmy and a maid. It was then that Honey realized that Woody had not been and never would be present. She was alone, and yet she wasn't. There was also Eliza, a ghost cowering in the corners. She, too, watched the horror of her brother's disappearance, but not only his. Her mother was also fading from her. There was no choice after that but to leave Little Lane and find somewhere else to accept the new life that she had been given.

"You have something on your face," Honey says. "Let me wipe it off." Brown smears his cheek, and Honey's not surprised. For years, Jimmy has played with his own waste. When she tries to dab it with her handkerchief, he swats her hand away and jumps up in agitation, as if an insult has been delivered. He flaps his hands rhythmically and then hops onto his toes, bouncing like a pogo stick.

"I'm sorry. Please sit down. I didn't mean to make you upset." He is not, however, pacified, ripping at his tie, trying to remove it but gagging himself instead.

Mrs. Mahoney steps into the room. "Is everything all right?"

"It's fine." For the first time since Honey got out of the Lincoln, all that anger flashes. "I can handle it." Mrs. Mahoney walks back into the kitchen.

There's only one way, barring an injection, to calm Jimmy down. He veers around the room now like the insect that he was chasing. She must get behind him. If she grabs him from the front, she risks a fracture, or worse, but taking him from behind will calm him. Not yet. Not yet. She draws him to the couch, and then he lunges, falling over the arm to a prone position. She jumps on top of him and clasps her arms beneath his chest.

"Mrs. Dixon!" Mrs. Mahoney says. "That's my job."

"And that is my son!" Honey pulls him to the upright position. He sits on her lap, her suit jacket askew, hair mussed. "It's okay, Jimmy. Mommy's here." She squeezes him. Since the change, she has mollified him with firm touch. At first, he struggles, but mustering all of her strength, she feels his resistance drain away. "Mommy's here. She's always here. You see, Jimmy? Mommy's with you all the time, and soon she's going to bring you home. You'd like that? I know you can't say it, but I know that's how you feel. Mommy knows. I'll sing? Okay? Yeah. Okay." She sings:

"Hush-a-by, Don't you cry,
Go to sleep, little baby.
And when you wake, You shall have cake,
And all the pretty little ponies.
Paint and bay, sorrel and gray,
All the pretty little ponies.
So hush-a-by, Don't you cry,
Go to sleep, little baby."

Honey sings it again, and then a third time. Jimmy sleeps, the deadness of his weight crushing her. Never before has she felt as much a mother as she does at this moment. She has failed so completely in her creation and never before felt so alive.

~

Somehow, despite everything she knows of physics, Ruthie keeps the joint lit at seventy miles an hour. If she had suggested to her honors physics teacher that something like this was even possible, he would never have given her an A this spring, but the laws of the universe have been repealed. The impossible has become probable and sometimes unavoidable.

For as long as she can remember, Ruthie wanted to ride a motorcycle but was sure that she never would. Her parents call them "donor-cycles" because of the propensity of their killed riders to give up their kidneys and livers to those in need. Everything but brains because what surgeon, even if he could, would transplant the thinking parts of someone dumb enough to ride a Triumph Bonneville? At least that's what her parents tell her. Maria worries when Ruthie and her father drive around Glenwyth in the Mustang, ancient tree limbs waiting to fall down. What would she think now?

The ride exhilarates. Helmetless, Ruthie sits behind Quinton, his head also bare, her arms locked around his abdomen. They have abandoned the streets and gone to that partly built highway that runs through the towns west of Glenwyth. Anticipating its use as a drag strip, state officials have placed obstructing concrete barriers along the road's length and, in spite of themselves, have created a slalom course, turning this particular section into a not-so-secret mecca for motorcyclists from New York to Maryland.

"This is so cool!" she shouts over the growling of the cycle. The two have been riding the road for an hour without seeing a police officer. Meant to be a limited-access highway, and presently without on-ramps, the strip is not easily monitored by the pigs—Quinton's word. They pass the joint between them. Although Ruthie worries that this might impair Quinton's steering, he handles the bike like a feather.

"Yeah!" he screams. Ruthie has known Quinton for less than a month, and she already wants to marry him. He's not, well, nice, but he is brilliant and beautiful. He is also present, a knife blade seeking blood. She can take the bad with the good, given his declaration through actions that he will never drift away or dwindle with fear like her cowering parents, both humbled in their own private ways. Ruthie's previous self, stuck in a similar vise, could have never imagined such an adventure. Now it seems as lush and lovely as a magic carpet ride. It's pretty simple. He's like a book that only she can read, and the two of them have been put on this earth to be possessed by each other.

"We should go soon," she says. "I have to have dinner. My grandparents."

"Relax. We can get back in fifteen minutes." Fine. Make that twenty. Ruthie wants her parents to see Quinton pulling up to the porch on the Bonneville because she knows what they'll say. They will saddle her with their guilt, worrying that she's too young to be dating, let alone a college boy. They will do their best to push their voices into her head, thinking she won't be able to get them out. Why should they care? Maria's the one who made Ruthie take Enovid since she was thirteen, like she might get pregnant or something. There were several rough periods in the beginning, which provided a flimsy justification for birth control. Nevertheless, Maria told their shared gynecologist—that old guy from South Philadelphia with whom Ruthie's mother shared a history of weird nods and knowing winks—to write the prescription. Beyond that, the risks of men have not been addressed, which means that Ruthie technically breaks no rules while she and Quinton do their laps on the aborted highway.

"My mother—" She wants to continue, but the engine's outcry silences her words. In the past several days, a cloud has come over Maria. Throughout Ruthie's childhood, the woman has been anxious, but now she seems panicked. She's been asking Ruthie a lot of questions. *Where are you going? When will you be back? You better call me when you get there.* It's pretty unfair since Ruthie is having fun for the first time in her life. But this medical school thing could be good. Her mom won't be able to say much when she's spending her days in Philadelphia delivering babies. Besides, there's nothing to worry about, and so her mother should take it easy. And her father, well, he's off in his own world anyway.

That's okay because Ruthie can handle herself. After all, she's been handling Quinton. After the fifteenth lap, he pulls the motorcycle to the shoulder and kills the motor.

"Oh, man," he says, wiping the sweat from their foreheads with his red bandanna.

"This is a great bike."

"You like it? I'll give it to you."

"That's crazy," she says. "I don't know how to ride."

"I'll teach you."

"My parents would kill me if they saw me on this."

"Then they don't have to see you," Quinton says. "You can keep it in the stable at my house and come get it whenever you want."

"What about your parents?"

"Yeah, as long as I don't bring it to Bermuda. I know, I'll rent you a garage in Glenwyth, your very own."

"How much money do you have, anyway?"

He stares at her and grins. "You really are from South Philadelphia, aren't you?"

She blushes, stung and flattered at the same time. "I'm not going to let you give me a motorcycle."

"Money's like shit," he says. "It does nothing unless you spread it around. As far as how much I have, remember this: Whenever Honey Dixon and Helen Hope Montgomery Scott meet anyone, they think exactly what you just asked."

The mention of the name Dixon cuts at Ruthie, but it's all right. This is the way Quinton is and will be, and she better get used to it. Rich people are supposed to be stingy, but Quinton's generosity reminds Ruthie of her grandfather's. He was the man who became rich because he saw dollar bills as no more valuable than grains of sand. It was never about the money for Angelo—her mother has told her this many times—and so money flowed to him like a river.

"So, if you can't or don't want to sleep," Quinton continues, "you can get the bike out in the middle of the night and drive to the beach, as long as you pick me up first." He runs his fingers along Ruthie's hair, streaked with blonde highlights from lemon juice and last month's sun. Lighting another joint, he hands it to Ruthie.

"You really are nuts," she says.

"Not at all. I just live."

"But you have to sleep."

"No, I don't. I haven't slept in two days. You'd think it would make me slow, but I feel sharper than ever. A couple of weeks ago, someone suggested that I get more sleep. I tried it, and it was the worst thing I ever did. It was like I was back in high school, grabbing at ideas that I couldn't quite get. Now everything is clear. This doctor gave me this medicine to calm me down, but I took it for three days and then threw the rest in the Schuylkill. The fish are a lot mellower now, I guess. You just have to appear calm at certain moments, and then you can do whatever the hell you want when people aren't looking."

Ruthie takes a big drag, with smoke coming out of her nose, and she doesn't gag. She's getting better at this. Warmth and understanding flow into her. There's also fear, even paranoia, but their rumblings are distant, like before the hurricane came earlier this summer, a million years ago.

"I love you," she says.

"I love you too. Where have you been all my life?" He pulls her close, turns her around, and kisses the back of her neck.

But held in this way, she says, "You're going to forget all about me. You won't even remember my name after summer vacation."

He pauses. "You're not the prettiest, but you know that you've taken me."

And Ruthie does know, which makes it all okay.

"I'm sure there will be plenty of, umm, beautiful, rich girls waiting for you when you go back to college," she says.

"Who says I'm going back? Harvard's just like White's and Exeter, filled with a bunch of arrogant fucks even more arrogant because they suppose nobody knows it."

That Quinton might not return to college has lurked in Ruthie's mind from the beginning, but what would he do in Glenwyth or Philadelphia or even New York? He wants nothing to do with the Union League, the Porcellian, or even the Rabbit, places she'd never heard of before Quinton spoke of them.

He continues, "Maybe I'll go to the Cape and live on Sandy Neck in the lighthouse. You can come too. There's a fireplace when it gets cold."

"I have school, remember? In five weeks. And I can't drop out. My parents are not quite as enlightened as yours." But Ruthie wants to drop out, which seems both unexpected and natural. There's no point in Stroud's or any other school anymore, even though Ruthie remembers feeling the complete opposite three months earlier.

"You don't think your parents ever dropped out of anything?"

She smiles and remembers her childhood and her newly accessible mother, the one-time medical student without the white coat.

"QED," Quinton says, and kisses Ruthie on her lips. Then he grabs her bottom and moves his hand around until, with hesitation, she pushes it away.

"You have to earn it," she says.

"Gladly. You're my princess, and you can take the rest of your life to decide."

My princess? From their first meeting, Quinton has spoken archly. The effect has sometimes been humorous and sometimes just odd. But odd doesn't seem so weird anymore. These days,

Ruthie can hear her thoughts in her head like voices coming from the Althouses' backyard.

"I'm in eleventh grade, and really not even." The words leave her lips, and Ruthie already wants to smack herself. She sounds like a Mouseketeer. Here she has a rich college guy calling her a princess, and she may next blurt out that she only had her first period two years ago. So what if he's a little strange? So what if he's a lot strange? So is her grandfather with all his gold.

"Eleanor of Aquitaine was fifteen when she married Louis the Seventh," Quinton says. "And then there's Isabella of Valois. She was six and already the wife of Richard the Second. She was a widow at ten and died in childbirth at nineteen."

"How do you know all this stuff?" she asks. Quinton shuffles random historical facts like so many playing cards, the next one to be dealt a mystery. She also understands that for her to be a princess, he must be a prince, and it's as good a term for Quinton as any. He lives in a castle, has multiple carriages, has more gold than even her grandfather, and, in a way, is exiled.

"I just remember things," he says. "I always have."

"You know you're going to go back."

"Nope. College is a waste. I just can't sit there and listen and write papers and go to office hours and all that bullshit. It's just too slow."

"But if you don't go back, and you move to Sandy Neck, what are you going to do there? That would be slow, too."

"I have plans. I wish I could trust you. I'd tell you all about them."

"You can."

"No. Not yet."

She looks at the Bonneville. "If I trusted you, why can't you trust me?"

Quinton slackens. "Can I trust you?"

She wants to say yes, and a voice inside objects, however more softly than it might have in the past. She is trustworthy, maybe too much so. Consider Eliza, always cutting, burning, and purging. Ruthie has said nothing about that to anyone, not to her mother, not to Mrs. Dixon, and not to the great Dr. Malory.

"I think so," she says. "I think you can."

"Okay, then." He looks animated and even happy for a moment, until a stream of sad anger mixes in. "I've never been able to trust anybody. People are such assholes, you know?" Maybe she is his princess, or maybe just the first girl who has ever been nice to him. Ruthie puts his hand between hers and rubs it.

"I'm sorry you had to go through all that," she says, thinking about that patient file she read last month, the one she never mentioned to Quinton. "Maybe you should still be seeing your psychiatrist. I mean, I know you're better, but—"

"Never," he says.

"You might feel better."

"I said never. Why don't you go to one?"

"Hey, dummy, my dad is a psychiatrist."

"Yeah, he is, isn't he? He's quite the family man too," Quinton says.

Ruthie can't argue. Not until 1969 did Maria celebrate her marital anniversary, when her husband was "over there." Before then, it was just another day, which was natural enough. The Nussbaums, for example, never had a Christmas tree. People just did things differently. But that anniversary evening in 1969, Ruthie realized just how odd it was that her parents had never before honored the occasion, whatever its date. Then came the calculation that her birthdate was less than nine months after her parents' wedding, and whoever gets married in January, anyway? Ruthie knew that her birth had not been early. If it had been close, Maria could have lied and claimed prematurity, but Ruthie was no idiot.

Her parents had married because of her, before she was a she, which raised another question. What if her mother had decided that Ruthie should not have been at all? There was an article yesterday about this exact issue in *The Evening Bulletin.* There was some kind of case at the Supreme Court.

But Ruthie had been made after all, and what the hell were her parents thinking? Maybe it was simple. Maybe it was just that they both did the things that they were supposed to do. Her father joined the Army when he could have been in the Coast Guard. He did his duty, but did he want to, and did he want to get his girlfriend pregnant two months into college? And when she got pregnant, what did Maria think then?

"Why don't you introduce me tonight?" Quinton asks.

"Because they don't even know that I'm out with you," she says, "and that we've seen each other every day. They don't know that I've been to New York on this motorcycle without a helmet."

"We could get helmets."

"You'll meet them. Just not yet."

"All right, but I have nothing to be ashamed of. I want to marry you."

"Quinton!" Her face turns scarlet.

"I have to."

"Why? We just met."

"It's too hard to explain."

"You can try. I'll like it."

"Fine," Quinton says. "You give me hope."

"That's good, but it doesn't mean that we should get married, at least not right now."

"It's more than that. I used to have so much anger. I still have it, I guess. But I think that if we were married, it would go away. Suppose you had a part of you that wasn't so good, and then you found a way to make it better. Wouldn't you want to do that?"

"Sure."

"Well, that's how I feel with you," he says. "When we're together, I know I could be a good person. Shit, I could even manage a factory making saws and do all this crap people do around here, if you wanted me to. I could be a regular person. I could be—" here he stops, "—normal."

"But what's so great about me?"

"You're the most wonderful girl that I've ever seen."

"But not the prettiest," Ruthie says, wanting to stop the conversation right here. It reminds her of all the nights standing in front of the mirror. She has large eyes and a nice smile, but her shoulders are too wide, just like Maria's. Her hair, although auburn with bangs, is limpid, and her thighs have assumed a certain broadness that suggests how her grandmother must have looked in the twenties. Ruthie doesn't look Italian until you underexpose a photograph and her hair darkens. Then she looks like a Medici.

"But you're the smartest," he says, which is what everyone has told Ruthie since she was a child and which is not good enough.

"You'd rather be with Eliza. She's beautiful."

"She was beautiful, and no, I could have been with Eliza."

"Are you—"

Quinton sneers. "No. She's a drone in your hive. I guess I shouldn't say that since you're friends."

"Then you don't think she's attractive?"

"God, no. It's like that song—*What's The Ugliest Part Of Your Body?* It's her mind." Quinton has introduced Ruthie to Frank Zappa, a quadrophonic stereo system blasting The Mothers of Invention last night while the two of them made out.

"That's not nice," Ruthie says. "Her mother's crazy. Her mother's—"

"I can't argue there."

"Creepy. You never went out with Eliza?"

"No! Ours was," he pauses, "a business relationship." Ruthie almost wants to laugh out loud. So that's where Eliza got the dope. Ruthie has to fix Quinton. That's what she has to do. "I promise," he says.

"You know, it's bad to steal your best friend's boyfriend," she says.

"I am not now, nor was I ever."

"Then how'd you know Eliza?"

"I told you, and before that, she was just one of these people who was always around. She's like wallpaper, blood red wallpaper I mean." Quinton takes in the highway. "We probably should get back. We really should get back." Further down, two police officers have hopped the fence onto the road. To exit the highway onto a street, Ruthie and Quinton must return to the overpass where they entered, but the men in blue have blocked that end and are walking toward them. The other side of the road, however, terminates at a fence. There's one way out.

"Get on!" Quinton shouts. She obeys. He strangles the throttle, and the engine revs. "Need a hole. Need a hole!" He turns the bike toward the fence and sees a gap. "We got it."

"But we're going into someone's backyard!" she screams.

"It's a farm, and it's owned by one of the nastiest women in Pennsylvania. She also happens to be my third cousin, and she spends every summer in Maine!"

The machine pulls through the fence and then hobbles down a small hill, Ruthie's kidneys leaping into her lungs.

"Oww!" she shouts. "Easy!"

They soon find themselves in the middle of an untended apple orchard with rows of broken trees radiating out from a mansion. Passing to the back patio and then cutting around to the front courtyard, Ruthie sees a house overtaken by decay, shutters fastened or cockeyed, a tree limb through a side roof, a swimming pool filled with black water.

"She's not your cousin," Ruthie says.

"Probably is. Everyone on the Main Line is related."

They're soon on a regular road, and the police officers are nowhere to be seen. Twelve minutes later, Ruthie hops off the bike at the foot of Barker's Mill, and she's sure that her grandparents have already arrived with many questions.

When she makes the first step to the porch, the world spins. She grabs the rail for a second and closes her eyes. Life seems to be twisting, but maybe her problem isn't physical. At this moment, she has the very real feeling that when she steps into the living room, her parents and grandparents will be able to read each and every one of her thoughts. This fills her with dread, but there's a way out.

She bites the inside of her cheek hard and soon feels the warm saltiness of blood on her teeth. She feels better. Then she takes a deep breath and does her best to resemble the person she used to be.

"Limoncello?" Maria asks.

Basted with kitchen sweat, she stands above the dining room table, brandishing the bottle of yellow-green liquid that tastes like lighter fluid. If everyone gets drunk, at least they won't remember the evening's food.

Although the consumption of meat on most Fridays has been permissible for nearly a decade, Maria would no more serve steak to her parents this evening than wear a nightgown to a parent-teacher conference. So the main course has been linguine with red clam sauce, after one of her mother's recipes. The original plan was to catch the Glenwyth bus to Athens to get clams brought in this morning, but Eliza's visit relegated Maria to the seafood section of the A&P. Instead of the bulging little necks, she found only their miniaturized cousins.

Trying to reassert some element of normality, she asked Carmela to come early, hoping for culinary guidance, but the sauce was a disaster, tasting like salty metal. Sautéed, the clams became the size of pencil erasers and just as fibrous. Not even the bottle of Amarone that Jim had been saving in the basement could resurrect this corpse of a meal. It was bad, and everyone knew it.

"Or does anybody want seconds?" Maria asks. "Jim, can I get you seconds?" With the exception of Ruthie, all have eaten their servings perfectly and then demanded not a single noodle more. But Ruthie has just consumed her second plate and considers a third before deciding against it.

"This is great, Mom."

"I'm glad you like it," Maria says, confused. "Are you getting a sore throat? Your voice sounds hoarse."

"I'm good."

"What do you mean you're 'good?'" her mother asks.

"I'm fine."

"She's fine," Carmela says to her daughter.

"You want some more clams?" Maria asks.

"It's hot, you know?" the grandmother says, fanning her face. "Too hot to eat too much."

Maria turns to her husband. "Can't we get that unit in the window?"

"I was going to a month ago," Jim says, "but now it's August, and soon it'll be getting cooler."

"I'll take a limoncello," Angelo says, steadying his glass as Maria pours. "Let me bring some steaks next time. We'll grill them outside. Less heat."

"So how's life in the world of doctoring?" Carmela asks her son-in-law.

"This summer," he says, "it's picked up. I've taken some cases that are almost ten hours a week altogether. You combine that with the VA, and pretty soon you're talking real money."

"It's too bad you can't talk about your patients," his father-in-law says, sipping his limoncello. "I bet they're pretty interesting."

"They're not boring," Jim says, looking at Maria and then at Ruthie, who smirks.

"So tell me about one," Angelo says. "You don't have to use any names." It's the perennial dinner party request and one that Jim always rejects, but isn't this different? He's dining with his wife, daughter, and the Sedaras, who have played the role of parents better than his own. They won't condemn him for revealing anything, nor judge him for his lack of perspicacity, and didn't Freud reveal the stories of hundreds of patients without their consent?

"I better not," he says.

"We won't tell," Angelo replies. "We know how to keep secrets."

"Well, okay," Jim says, thinking more about another glass of Amarone than ethics. "There was one I found at the river, and he was just about to drown himself."

"What were you doing down there?" Carmela asks.

"It'd take too long to explain. Anyway, I talked to him, and he's alive." The words stop there.

"That's it?" Angelo asks.

"That's the story," Jim says.

After blessing herself, Carmela pronounces, "Jewel in your crown in heaven."

"I doubt it," Jim says, trying to remember whether lies of omission or commission are worse. "Actually, the story doesn't quite end there. Ever since I saved him, if you want to call it that, he's wanted to spend a lot of time with me. He's a great guy, but you wonder if he's becoming dependent."

"Of course he's dependent," Angelo says. "You saved his life. Have you had him over for dinner?"

"No. I'm not sure that would be a good idea."

"Maybe he wants you to."

Jim laughs. "You probably understand people a lot better than I do, Angelo, but in psychiatry, inviting a patient over for dinner is, well—"

"But if you think he's too dependent, you have to understand why, and so you have to get closer in to find that out. There's no other way."

Jim pauses. Is there a psychiatric television series that Angelo's been watching along with *Mannix*?

"So what am I supposed to do?" Jim asks. "Invite him over right now?"

"Sure."

"That's crazy."

Ruthie pushes away her empty bowl of linguine. "This guy sounds groovy."

"But what if I invite him over, and he becomes more dependent?" Jim asks, gazing at Maria, who turns away. "What if he wants to come over every night?"

Angelo says, "Keep your friends close. Keep your enemies closer."

"Right," Jim says, wondering if Angelo regrets not shooting his future son-in-law when he impregnated Maria not six months after she graduated number one from Hallahan. But maybe Dave is an enemy; maybe Angelo's right. It seems unfair, though, to even think that, and since the afternoon on the Schuylkill, Jim has assumed that everything will turn out all right. But what about Dave's wife? Whatever happened to her? And his kids? They just left and have nothing to do with him? Maybe it was all that anger, but if Jim did something wrong, what's to say that Dave's anger wouldn't come out toward him?

After a time, knowing he has stumbled upon a stupendously bad idea, Jim fetches the black telephone with the cord that until now has always seemed too long. Stepping into the next room, he dials Dave's number, and the patient picks up.

"It's Jim. No emergency, just...." He pauses. "We're having dinner, and I was wondering if, well, you wanted to, well, maybe—"

"Of course. I thought you'd never ask."

Ten minutes later, Jim and his father-in-law sit on the porch smoking cigars, and the Eldorado pulls up to the curb, top down. Dave emerges holding a bottle of Glengoyne fifty-year-old single malt. "You have snifters?"

"Dave, this is my father-in-law, Angelo Sedara." The two shake, and they all sit down, as if the meeting had been inevitable. Inside, Maria and Carmela are clanking dishes, and Ruthie has gone to her room. She has a new record, that Pink Floyd album with the ear on its cover, and music trickles out from her opened window.

"What do you think of Nixon?" Angelo asks.

"He'd beat Jesus Christ if the election was today," Dave says.

And so the conversation goes. When politics no longer interest, the men turn to the Phillies, mostly Steve Carlton, and the unfolding of that magical season. The Cardinals were insane to ever let him go, the three agree, but Jim's mind wanders. He used to listen to baseball all the time on this same porch before he went away. Ruthie used to love it too, but not so much now.

The whiskey flows, redolent of caramel and raisins, and Jim's seniors talk of their youths spent in South Philadelphia. There's no mention of trauma and no sign of irregularity. That Dave could appear so normal with so much suicidality inside hits Jim like a punch to the gut. How many others in the Stroud's car line or at the A&P meat counter are ready to blow their brains out?

"Where'd you live?" Angelo asks.

"2300 Block, Sears Street."

"That was right around the corner from the shop."

"You probably knew my mother. Arlene Black," Dave says.

"She still in the neighborhood?"

"No. She's in a better place."

"Recent?"

"1951."

"Still, I'm sorry, but it's where we're all going, sooner probably than we think. That neighborhood isn't like it used to be, and Rizzo isn't going to turn back the clock."

Dave looks at his watch. "Speaking of the clock, I just wanted to stop by to say hello." With a thwack of the porch's screen door, Maria and Carmela step outside. "And I wanted to meet Mrs. Malory. David Black," he says, standing and extending his hand. "Your husband saved my life."

Maria sizes up her husband's patient and says, "And maybe you'll save his."

With a smile, Dave looks at Jim and Angelo, and then at Carmela. "I hope I'm lucky enough to do that. As I said, I should get back, but thank you." Dave says a few more goodbyes and drives away.

"Nice man," Angelo says. "I remember his mother. She was the real McCoy."

"What do you mean?" Maria asks.

"I think he had a brother who was run over in the neighborhood. She never recovered. She wasn't very nice."

"That's so sad," Maria says.

Jim wants his wife to continue—maybe she could understand everything that's baffled him—but Ruthie emerges from the front door and walks right by her family, down the porch steps into the night.

"And where do you think you are going, young lady?" Maria says.

"For a walk."

"Not tonight. You've been out every night this week. You're staying home. We're all going to watch *Love, American Style*."

Ruthie taps her foot, considers her grandparents, and says, "No."

Angelo turns to Carmela, and Maria says, "Excuse me, missy?"

"I'm leaving. Just relax."

Maria frowns. "You're staying home tonight."

"I came to dinner, and you never said that I couldn't go out afterward."

Maria turns to her husband. "Jim?"

"Ruthie, please listen to your mother."

"I always listen to my mother," she says. "There's never been anyone else to listen to. Certainly not you, and suddenly you want to get all involved. I don't need this shit. Just get out of the way."

"What has gotten into you?" Maria asks.

"Forget it. I'm sorry I opened my mouth. Maybe I should be silent like Eliza until I get the chance to throw up in my best friend's bathroom. She told me all about what a great mom you are."

Maria looks at the others and then back at Ruthie. "Why don't you just go inside? I'll be right in."

"It's no big deal," Ruthie says.

"It most certainly is."

"I'm leaving, and congratulations on your first patient."

"Ruthie," her grandfather says. "I haven't seen you all night. I want to talk. We have to plan the duck hunt for the fall, like we always do."

"I'll see you next week." She kisses Angelo and then runs into the blackness.

"Ruthie," Jim shouts into the air, a useless siren. "You're going to be grounded!"

The slapping of her tennis shoes offers the only reply.

Maria shakes her head and says, "This makes no sense."

Jim feels nausea rising to his teeth; it makes perfect sense. He should do something, but what's there to do? The helicopter's already crashed.

Maria turns to her husband. "Why is she acting like this?" Jim says nothing, but his scar stings, always worse at times like this. "You're not telling me something."

"Maybe we should wipe the counters," Carmela says to Angelo.

"No," their daughter says, "you stay! I want you to hear every word, and please don't pretend like you have for the past seventeen years that everything is going to turn out fine." Maria looks stunned, just like she was at the Wanamaker's lunch when Eisenhower was president and Dien Bien Phu was just another place on a movie newsreel.

"I don't know," Jim says, a ring of fire now engirdling his waist. "I'm telling you the truth."

Maria closes her eyes and grinds her teeth. "You always were a terrible liar."

"Just let me think a second," he says, wanting to ignore what he knows. Then comes the punch of reality, like falling through the rubber trees at Snoul.

He runs into the street and screams, "Ruthie!" There's no answer, save the purring of a motorcycle at the end of Barker's Mill.

8

Sitting alone at the kitchen table, Maria holds a Camel in one hand and *Winesburg, Ohio* in the other. She should be reading anatomy and physiology, brushing up on topics forgotten years ago, or at least making dinner. But she started the book before her interview at Woman's Medical when everything was less definite. She might as well finish it. It'll probably be the last fiction she reads for the next ten years, which is all right with her. There was a time when doctoring intimidated her. Now, it promises diversion from the pathology of her own life.

She stubs the cigarette in the ashtray and takes off her reading glasses. They hardly work anyway. Something about being pregnant has warped her vision. She's thirty-four and feels like sixty. It was different when she had Ruthie. Maria was eighteen and felt like she was ten, how unnatural and improbable it all was. She had scoffed at the girls from Hallahan who became pregnant during high school. From bad families, people whispered. A year later, they were laughing at her. According to Pietrolongo, the barrenness that followed had to do with having too much acid in her vagina. That was hilarious, but it made sense. Through whatever metabolic perturbation, the terror of having Ruthie scared her into infertility, and the resolution of another terror, that her husband would come back in a plastic bag, had set things straight. At least that was what she had thought.

She stands up, and her hamstrings tug with pain, two more body parts pushed by the swelling that comes with making life. She hobbles a few steps and evaluates herself in the corroded, full-length mirror that's rested next to the refrigerator since they moved here, almost as if the previous woman of the house wanted to warn herself each time she reached for food. God, she might as well be having triplets, even though there's just one, a boy in fact, which Jim still doesn't know. He thinks that Pietrolongo has kept the sex from them both, readying a surprise, but she's secreted the truth. When he pisses her off, the hiding makes a warm feeling somewhere in her chest, but that's not it entirely. She's never known how to talk to Jim about anything important, and so why should it be any different with his son? Though the talking is hard, the wounding has been easy, fear always behind the anger.

There's also the problem of what to call the kid. You're supposed to name a boy after his father, but that's been ruined since Honey stole "Jimmy" for her autistic son. If Honey hadn't been so selfish, it would have dawned on her that they might have wanted that name for themselves. Of course, Honey doesn't think like that. She never has. She just does what she wants, consequences be damned.

And anyway, maybe Pietrolongo's wrong about the sex. Maria should call him. She took her blood pressure earlier, and it was 148 over 94. That's not good, but her father always had high blood pressure, and it never hurt him. He's the exact opposite of what people expect from an Italian. He never said much when she was growing up, at least not to Maria. She was a girl after all, and her parents had to have wanted a boy if they were just going to have one child. With that silence, there was little for Maria to say in return. So how could she have been expected to learn how to talk to anyone else, including a husband? Becoming friends with Honey, who always knew what to say, brought that inability into relief, and then, by chance, Maria married a man even worse at talking than herself.

She did have three cups of coffee this morning before ten. That's probably why her blood pressure was so high. She could stop drinking the stuff, but then she'd have to take to her bed. She had a paternal great-aunt like that who didn't even speak English and died around the time the Allies were storming Anzio. Carmela and Angelo, when referring to Aunt Francesca, used that exact phrase: "She took to her bed." Why? Had her husband returned numb from some World War I battle and left her alone for the rest of her life? The problem was that Maria had never learned how to sleep and wasn't about to now, the way things were going. She had three, maybe four hours the night before. With the advance of the pregnancy and all the other crap, each night was worse, always dreaming of Jim. How many ways had he been shot, burned, or had a tree fall on him in the Mustang? He would die before her, she knew that, and it was just a matter of finding out how. Maybe wondering made you old.

She was no longer a young woman, that was clear. Maria was heading the way of Ruth Malory, that strange lady who used to ask Maria if she wanted a "cool drink" regardless of the season. Jim had never told her the details, but their marriage had been resisted, however feebly, by Mrs. Malory. There was some talk that she was not even going to come, but Angelo had made the four trips to bring her down from Lehighton and take her back. She wore a suit twenty years out of date and got so drunk she had to be taken back to Roseberry Street, where she insisted on staying during the wedding weekend. She died not a decade later and wasn't even that old, but how many times in how many dreams did she tell Maria not to let Jim go? No wonder sleep was impossible.

The insomnia wasn't all bad because Maria heard things, like Ruthie leaving when she thought everyone was asleep. When had been the first time? It was only a month ago, but it seems like ten years. She goes to meet that boy, Quinton. They've been dating, Jim's told her, and little more. Jim should hit the kid over the head with a crowbar. That's how this sort of thing was dealt with in the old days at 22nd and Tasker. That was when Aunt Francesca lived with them, a preparation for Maria's being a young wife and meeting her crazy mother-in-law.

Violence would make it worse, Jim says. She knows he's wrong, and every time Ruthie goes out, Maria thinks of the girl's grandmother. Ruth Malory the elder married the wrong guy. That was clear. Well, if Jim won't take out Quinton, then maybe she should. Maria knows that she should, but something holds her back, like she's running underwater. Jim still wants to help the kid. It's naïve, it's stupid, but if Maria really didn't understand, she wouldn't have met with Dean Weinberg.

Her cigarette spent, Maria reaches for the pack of Camels sitting between a banana and green apple in the table's fruit bowl and then decides against it. Everyone's driving her nuts, including Jim's patients, and she's supposed to become a doctor? There's a wall calendar on the other side of the refrigerator, each month with a seasonally appropriate image from Currier & Ives. When she was growing up on Roseberry Street, similar pictures, from a sort of Print of the Month Club, decorated her parents' living room. Pinned against once-modern wallpaper of black, white, and gray resembling nothing so much as TV static, these recollections of Americana made Maria feel like a Martian. How about the time when Honey had come over for dinner, like a tourist with a Pan Am bag, sampling the local culture and cuisine? Woody and Jim had been there too, and it was nothing short of a humiliation.

Maria had wanted to leave that prison more than anything, and how foolish the desire had been. She could have become a spinster like her invalid great-aunt, and maybe she should have because August is flying by, which means she'll be a medical student in a month. In June and even early July, the idea of returning had been nothing more than an acorn, but fertilized by Jim's doubt, the seed became a fully formed oak overnight. The pregnancy should have been enough to fill the holes in her life, the absent husband and the daughter who used to look great, at least on paper. The pregnancy was supposed to fix everything but, in its failure to do so, made everything look worse.

Maybe the reason for her return to the wards is even more basic. Jim isn't making any money. Ten hours a week, he told her parents. She should have corrected him and that fraud, but they probably didn't believe him anyway. She had told them about that winter afternoon in '71 when she visited him in his new office. She hadn't expected a packed waiting room, so she wasn't surprised that it was empty. What was concerning was how comfortable he looked with inactivity, as if it were all right if his first patients never came. But then he wasn't inactive, not exactly. He was somewhere else, and there might have been quite a lot of mental activity wherever that somewhere else was. Maria used to think this remoteness dated from Vietnam, but now she understands. It had always been there because it was in his mother, just like it was in Aunt Francesca. And in Ruthie.

The girl was supposed to be like an aunt to her new brother. She had talked about nothing else throughout the winter and spring, and then she lost interest. It was as if she were jealous. If Ruthie were two years old, you could imagine it, but there would be a sixteen-year age difference between the two children, making them stars in two distant galaxies. There was something embarrassing about such a gap, but when Maria had the baby, she would in an instant be one hundred percent more procreative than either Jim's or her parents, and maybe that was the problem. Hadn't she read somewhere that parents with single children were supposed to be the happiest?

She talked with Jim on that first date about their childhoods, strange the things that you remember. Unlike Jim's parents, Maria's could have no more imagined getting a divorce than they could have conceived of renouncing Jesus Christ. You weren't supposed to leave your husband, plain and simple. The nuns at Hallahan said it too, whatever they knew about marriage, but there was an exception for infidelity. Which one of the Gospels was that in? She could pull out the Bible hidden behind those paperbacks she's been reading and find out. You could be unfaithful by cheating, but what if your husband had never been there to begin with?

The phone rings. "Hello?"

"Hi," Jim says. "Where's Ruthie?"

"Do you think I know? Probably with your patient."

"What's for dinner?"

"What's for dinner? Nothing. She's with that boy. Do you care?"

"I'm just asking."

"I can't make a feast every night," Maria says, still remembering the rubbery clams.

"We could go into the city."

"I'm too tired." There's no going back to Roseberry Street. Her parents sold the house years ago, and someone carved it up into apartments. "We should eat the leftovers. It's not like we're millionaires."

"Freeze 'em and meet me in the park in twenty minutes, at the tables near the swings."

"What?"

"I'll get a pizza, and I already have a bottle of chianti from the State Store. We'll have a picnic."

When was the last time they did that? Maybe when they were undergraduates, and they used to drink Champale. The picnic idea is so random that Maria misses the chance to say no. It's hot outside but not unbearable, and the kitchen seems even smaller than normal. You're not supposed to go into the park at night, but the sun will be up for another two hours, and as far as the public consumption of alcohol, it seems a minor offense in comparison to all of their other mistakes.

Forty minutes later, in a white dress that she knows makes her look fat, Maria hurries into the park where she hasn't been for years. This was Ruthie's place, where she learned to ride a bicycle and hit a tennis ball. Then there were the swings. Ruthie loved those. A decade ago, when Maria was a Philadelphia expatriate experienced only with cement lots behind steel fences, the place had seemed like a magical pleasure garden.

Having found the picnic tables, Jim calls to her, "Hey!" Still in his suit, he has loosened his tie. A pizza box, paper plates, napkins, and a thermos sit around him.

"I thought you weren't coming," he says, getting up, trying to embrace her, and hitting his thigh on the table's corner. "You look beautiful."

"Except I'll never lose this weight after the baby." She sees the thermos.

"I haven't had anything," he says.

Maria peers into the cup. Does he drink during sessions? "What'd you do with the bottle?"

"Threw it in the can," he says, pointing to a nearby receptacle. Jim offers her the cup, but she shakes her head. So he swigs it himself and says, "I think we should move." He looks serious.

"Move?"

"To Lehighton. Or maybe Cape Cod. I don't know."

"I guess it was another great day at the office." He seems tired, even more than normal.

"I don't know. I'm trying to avoid the whole thing. I shouldn't have been a doctor."

"There you go again," she says. "What's gotten into you? You never used to be like this." But he did. Doubt has joined them together since the days that they rode the Woodland Avenue trolley. If there had then been none of the malignant questioning surrounding him now, why would he have accepted such an unfair situation in 1955? When she decided that she was not going to the abortionist in New York, and when she told her parents, the three of them expected that he was going to fight. It was all planned out. Jim was expected to deny everything, and she would go with her chemistry books to the St. Felicity's Home for Unwed Mothers in Groveville, New Jersey. After having and giving up the baby, she would return to school in the fall of '56. But he didn't say no. This surrender made Maria almost pity him, then and now, her sympathy always teetering between loyalty and loathing.

Lost in their thoughts, the two of them eat and talk of dry cleaning and water bills. For some reason, Maria can't stop thinking about Honey and the semester they spent in the sorority. When everything happened, Honey, somehow aware of such things, suggested the New York doctor and came along for the consultation. Maria had expected something dirty in a terrible neighborhood, but the man, dressed in Brooks Brothers and wearing a gold pocket watch, kept an office with mahogany furniture and Ivy League diplomas. He only took cash. Maria had been ready to come back a week later and finish everything off, but for whatever reason, Honey talked her out of it. The reversal gave Honey power, and maybe that had been the point from the beginning.

"Everything used to be easier," he says.

"And when was that?"

"When we met."

"You're joking, right? We had a flat tire on our first date."

"I should have never gone over there," he says.

Maria takes his hand and presses. "Finally, some honesty. You made it back. It's done."

"But it's not. It's like, I don't know. My sleep's getting worse."

"I noticed," she says. "Tell me."

"You don't want to know."

"But I do, because I feel I was there too. Sometimes—" She stops. "Forget it."

"What?"

"When you were away, I thought every night that you must have died."

He smiles and stretches. "Well, you got me back."

"Yeah. I guess so."

"I told you," he says, "you wouldn't understand."

"You always say that," Maria replies, throwing his hand aside. "It's so annoying. You assume that I couldn't handle it."

"No, that's not it at all. You're stronger than me. But if I told you—"

"Yeah?"

"You'd never forgive me. I did something so wrong."

"Then ask God for forgiveness."

Jim pauses. "God never came to Cambodia. I strangled you."

Maria shakes her head. "I've been reading about this. It's very common, especially when you drink too much. Your mother drank too much, and what do you expect when you spend so much time with Santoni? He's a bad influence."

"But I've been so stupid."

Maria says nothing, then, "We all have."

A light turns on in his eyes. "We'll drop the Dixons," he says, "and we'll make a fresh start around here. If I'm going to treat Eliza, there's no way to socialize with her parents, and Ruthie can't be her friend."

"But we can't very well tell Ruthie whom she can and can't be friends with."

He's puzzled. "That's exactly what we can tell her. Everything bad has come from the Dixons."

A cool electric shock arcs from Maria's neck to her behind. What's the word? Paresthesia. She learned that term in medical school before she dropped out.

"Why are so you against the Dixons?" she asks. "You had a perfectly fine time chatting courtside with Honey a few weeks ago."

"It's Eliza."

"Not Honey? You sure?"

"Of course, but if you're friends with Honey, then I'm stuck with Eliza, and she was the one who introduced Ruthie to Quinton and the other bad things that she's suddenly discovered."

"I know all about Eliza," Maria says.

"Then maybe we should move." Jim stops and groans.

"What's the matter?"

"Same old, same old. Sometimes it's like an army of fire ants."

Maria tries to touch his abdomen, but he says, "Don't."

"Let me take care of you," she says. "You've never let me."

He looks up, every bit as sad as when he was changing the tire on that crappy car, not even his.

"I think maybe you should be the doctor," he says, wincing.

"And so should you, and we're not moving."

"But how about we go to Swedesboro?"

"Will you stop?" He wasn't even like this when he had to take the ferry and meet her parents before he hurt all the time. "Listen," she says. "We just need a plan. First you're going to fire Quinton."

"But—"

"But what? Is it the money? We'll have enough."

"Yes and no. He's not all bad. It's like there's something that will fix him, and I just can't grab hold of it."

"You can't fix everyone," she says, "and even if you could have once, you can't anymore. He wants our daughter."

"Okay, but what if firing him makes him want her more?"

"I'll chain her to her bed."

"And what about Dave Black; what about Eliza?"

"They're getting better, right?"

"I guess."

"Well, then."

"And Ruthie?"

"I'm sure she'll be fine," Maria says, not at all sure, and sees her husband sweating. "What are you not telling me?"

"Nothing," he says. "You saw it all."

"I don't believe you."

"Eliza's better," he says, pouring himself more wine. "I'll fire her too."

"Okay," says Maria, filled with a sudden, unexpected desire to punch him in the face.

After more silence, he says, "You're angry."

How obvious. "Me? No."

"When we have the baby, everything's going to be easier," he says, smiling, all happy and relieved.

"Yeah? You think so? Just like in 1956? Great. Now I get to have three children in the house instead of two."

Jim's eyes narrow. "I don't know what you mean."

"I mean, you have to grow up, and whatever you've had to deal with in your life, get over it. I have my own problems."

"I know," he says.

"No, you don't. You're so wrapped up in your own damned head!"

"I know I am."

Hearing something in the answer far from satisfactory, she says, "Here's a fact. Our entire life has been because of a ripped condom." He falls back, stunned. "You never loved me," she says. "Admit it."

"That's not true."

"You wouldn't have married me if it weren't for our, ahem, little accident. Be honest, for once! That's why you went over there. You didn't want to come back. You can talk about napalming babies and whatever else, fine, but there's no excuse why you can't be honest about how you feel about me. It's our only chance. Admit it. You married me out of fear."

"No."

"Yes." He doesn't argue. "I'm going," she says, getting up and shaking her head. "Our daughter's probably back from God-knows-where, probably stoned in her bedroom listening to Pink whatever. But at least one of us has to raise her. You know, there's a reason why she's with him."

"It's not our fault."

"Yes, it is. We've failed her. She doesn't even want to spend her birthday with us."

"Maria—"

"What?" He says nothing. When, after more waiting, he again finds no words, she hurls the open pizza box across the table, and the remaining slices fall into dry dirt.

"It's a boy!" She curses, storming off. But it's a whisper, not loud enough for her husband, his eardrums blown out in the war, to hear.

Ruthie hears the question, aloud, that she has wanted to ask Quinton but never will.

"Was that you? In the bushes?"

She waits alone at Sycamore Lodge on a threadbare alcove window seat. Faded, tasseled curtains form an upside-down V above her head. She jostles them, and dust dances against the sun. It's her birthday.

She hasn't told anyone, but her thoughts now ring and buzz. They lack the clarity of a bell, and when spoken, they're not exactly in her own voice. Sometimes her thoughts are just static in the background, like a radio station not quite tuning in. Hearing yourself thinking is not possible, she knows this, but nevertheless, her mind has assumed a certain exteriority, like her thoughts have been laid out for all to see, like goods at a yard sale. The change doesn't bother her, at least, not usually. That she can hear herself think seems almost natural, like it's always been meant to be. If she's not careful, though, Quinton will know what she's thinking, and she's not ready for that. Eliza has been clear: Let a boy know that you want what he wants, and you'll never get it.

Six twenty-seven. It's the butler's day off, and so Quinton invited her over. He was supposed to be here by now, but he's never been punctual. Maybe he wants her to be here alone, as she has been now for almost a half-hour. As strange as everything has been since her parents came back from Cape Cod, it seems stranger that Quinton and his parents could be the only people living in such a house.

He told her to enter through the front door—it would be open, and it was—and meet him in the room immediately to the right. She figured he'd be there, playing the piano or something, maybe a dozen roses on top, but he wasn't. So she walked for a time throughout the large room, sofas and seats hugging its walls, heavy curtains touching the floor, emptiness at its center. How odd to have such a large room with thirteen-foot ceilings and near-vacancy below. Her thoughts expand into this space and then swirl, an atmospheric disturbance. You could play field hockey or soccer in here and maybe set up twenty beds for a Girl Scout camping trip. Why had she stopped doing Girl Scouts? She loved the green, form-fitting dress, the diagonal sash with its patches, and the yellow bowtie. 71202. That was her troop number, and the memory stings. She stopped doing it when her father went away.

She stands, walks to the room's center, and sits on the parquet floor. The grain is worn, as if a hundred soldiers have marched in place. Then she gets it. This was a ballroom, and look how she's dressed, in ripped denim bell bottoms and another stupid T-shirt. *Keep on Truckin'.* What does that even mean? She's dishonoring this place meant for tuxedos and gowns, champagne and dancing. It's like *The Great Gatsby* from ninth-grade English come to life. She studies the oil portrait dominating the room. A mustachioed man in a bright red jacket sits holding a riding crop and with not the slightest interest in what Ruthie or anyone else might think of him. Maidens in muslin, military officers, boys at sport, and girls with spaniels comprise the painting's other subjects. They are like characters from *The Nutcracker*, the ballet that always makes her feel good, even now when she doesn't feel good anymore.

She closes her eyes and sees herself in a white cotton gown. She is tall and beautiful, her hair done up in improbable curls. Her body has filled in all the right places and none of the wrong, and her brilliance completes the attraction. Young men surround her, some awaiting her, some walking away in despair. They are so boring, so average, although all of them are beautiful. They are also rich and from the great colleges, although she's nothing more than a student at Miss Stroud's. It doesn't matter. They want her, white lace and promises. If she told her teachers all of that, they'd think her fantasy was surrendering to safety, that she was preparing herself to become just another Glenwyth housewife. So be it.

"Boo!" Quinton says. When she jumps, he adds, "I did mean to scare you."

She reddens and, catching herself, says, "You should ask me to dance."

"So you like the ballroom?" He's wearing a tweed blazer, a few months too early.

"It's cool," she says, even though it really makes her want to cry.

"There were a lot of parties here. Not recently, of course, and probably not since Franklin D. Roosevelt took away all the fun. Now it's just ghosts." Quinton goes to the Victrola at one of the room's corners. "What should we play?"

"How about *We've Only Just Begun?*" Ruthie says earnestly.

"You think they'll have that here? What do you know from the twenties?"

Ruthie shakes her head. "We don't need a record player. C'mere."

He comes to her, and they dance to her singing, Ruthie, Quinton, and Karen Carpenter.

"I may be odd," he says, "but I'm a regular Joe compared to you."

She doesn't argue. You think you're one person, and like that, you realize you're another. Maybe you're not what others hoped. Maybe you're not what you hoped.

"So what do you think of the place, I mean, the whole place?" he asks.

"It reminds me of the White House. I keep waiting for Mrs. Nixon to pop out of a door."

"You are going to love your birthday present," he says. "But it's very delicate, and you can't just unwrap it anywhere."

He turns and walks from the ballroom, Ruthie following. They soon sit across from each other at a banker's desk in a nearby study, Quinton the loan officer and Ruthie a meek applicant for credit.

"Here," he says, producing a mad tussle of thin, pink paper. "Here. But be careful. Don't grab it. You have to—" He stops.

"What?"

"I'll give it away if I say more."

She stares at the gift, unsure what to do next.

"I'll put it on the desk and be careful. Just touch the wrapping, not what's inside, okay?"

Nodding, she studies the paper and finds an edge. Pulling it away, she sees more wrapping.

"Keep going," he says.

And she does, until she finds a sprig of rosemary, green and white needles with tiny purple flowers.

"It's the herb of remembrance," he says, "and fidelity. I want you to have it, sweet sixteen."

She picks it up and presses it between her fingers.

"No!" he blasts, pulling it from her and cutting himself. Blood on the flowers.

"What happened?"

"It's glass," he says, licking his fingers.

Quinton drops it on the desk, and Ruthie moves her face to it, afraid to touch. She has seen wild rosemary before, and what rests before her is a luxuriant example of the very same herb. But examining it, her eyes not six inches away, she spots its translucency. Painted, sharp, eternal glass has replaced the soft, delicate tissue of life.

"It lasts forever," Quinton says. "God, this hurts."

"Where did you get it?"

"What does that matter?"

"It's just that I've never seen anything like it," she says.

"I've never seen anything like you."

"That's not true. Don't even say it."

"Look at my hand. Look at what I'll do to make you happy."

She feels the sweat collecting beneath the waist of her bell bottoms. "We should get a bandage."

"It'll be fine. Life is painful."

She doesn't argue. She would have two months ago, but no longer. "Maybe we should be just like everyone else and just date," she finally says.

"But you don't want that." He's right. She doesn't because there's a very good chance that he may be the only thing that might—with an emphasis on might—give her life any meaning. It's just that she didn't know that until now, any more than a lock can know about its previously hidden key.

"You're going back in less than a month," she says.

"You're coming with me."

"I'm in high school. I can't just move to a different state." But imagine if she did.

"I'm going to support you," he says. "You're going to finish high school up there and then do whatever you want with your life."

"What about my parents?"

"Leaving them may be exactly what you need. Anyway, after I graduate, we'll come back."

"How are you going to support me?"

"I have my trust, but I don't intend to live off of that. I'm going to be a businessman. I've decided. You don't understand. I'm not going to be like some guy who punches a clock and gets a gold watch at sixty-five." He beams. "I'm going to be a capitalist."

Ruthie thinks of the man in the top hat on the Monopoly board. "But you wanted to be an archeologist, or an anthropologist, or—"

"I'm done with all that stuff," he says.

"But what about the Indians and South America?"

"I don't want to study history. I want to make it."

She stares at his wide eyes, twitching almost, and then at the rosemary. It's so sad that he's willing to give up everything for someone as worthless as her.

He takes her hand. "I would kill for you." He pulls a .357 magnum from his blazer. "Really. Here, touch it, just not the trigger. You couldn't feel it under my jacket, could you?"

She pulls her hand back. "Where did you get it?

"The flower or the gun?"

She can't even say the word.

"I bought it," he says, "if you want to know, in South Philadelphia, not far from Roseberry Street. The flower, I stole."

"Why?"

"The flower or the gun?"

"Why? I just want to understand."

"A glass flower doesn't change," he says, putting the pistol back into his blazer. "It never dies, and it never rots. If you treat it right, you have it forever."

"But it's not alive," she says. "It's not real."

"Who says?"

"Real things die. We're all going to die."

"So you don't like it."

"I do, but we don't need something that lasts forever. We don't need a gun."

Quinton slides away.

"What?" she asks.

"Nothing."

"What."

"It's just that you sound like someone I don't like very much, and his name is Dr. James Ashe Malory. I love the irony of that. I mean, you couldn't make that middle name up, could you? He doesn't understand either. You should see him talk. Well, he's my psychiatrist, in case you don't know."

"He wouldn't have told me, and he hasn't. He knows it's confidential." But Ruthie says nothing about her reading Quinton's file and all the others.

"Don't kid yourself. There's nothing confidential about that guy."

"He doesn't matter," Ruthie says. "When I graduate college—"

"I'll be dead by then."

"Don't say that."

"It's true. I want you to come with me now."

"Where?"

"To Cambridge, Boston, or anywhere where I can at least get to enough classes so I don't flunk. You'll have your own apartment, all prim and proper. We'll go at the end of the month and then right back here to Philadelphia when I graduate. We can even live in Glenwyth if you want. I'm going to do everything right from here on out, and I'm going to make a million dollars!"

"How?"

"I'm going to get my family business back. I'm going to make saws, shovels, whatever."

"But you hate it here."

"I hated it here because I didn't know who I was meant to be."

"But don't you want to travel?" she asks. "You don't even have to work. We can go to London or Paris."

"I've been there."

"I haven't."

"Fine, I'll take you wherever you want for a vacation," he says, "but I just need two places, here and the Cape. You want to go there now? We'll be there by midnight. We can shoot ducks with my .357."

"Cape Cod?"

"No, Cape May. Of course Cape Cod."

"Well, I guess we could, but I just want to be with you. We don't have to drive anywhere."

Quinton gets up from the desk chair and walks to Ruthie. "You're right, as usual. Come on. I'm going to show you my memory palace."

The two of them rise, and she takes his hand. They walk through the forlorn house, two tourists in a haunted castle.

"It was so lonely here," he says. "You'd think all this would make someone happy, and maybe I should have been. I might have had an excuse if I'd been farmed off to nannies and governesses, but it was just them and me. They were old for as long as I can remember. My father never worked beyond reading bank statements, and my mother never had any of the habits that you'd expect. She didn't ride horses, and she even didn't believe in beagling."

"What's that?"

"When a bunch of octogenarians wobble around on some farm and watch a bunch of dogs chase a rabbit. They never did any of that stuff. They just walked these halls, day after day, night after night."

"That's what any parents do," she says. "My father goes to the office, and my mother goes to the A&P. Then they come back and walk around."

"At least they pretend like they're doing something," he says. The two come to a large oil painting of a thin, gray-haired man dressed in the garb of a World War I Army officer. "That's my grandfather. They called him the Brigadier."

"He was in the Army?"

"He was a quartermaster for a time. He was supposed to take saws and everything else to the Western Front in 1917."

"He didn't?"

"He did, but only after the war was over." They walk back to the ballroom and the portrait of the mustachioed man in the red hunting jacket. "My great-grandfather was the last one with any balls," Quinton says. "I want to be like him."

"But you don't have to be the president of the universe."

"I have to mean something. Otherwise, I'm just like my parents and all the other stupid fucks in the world."

She looks at her boyfriend or her savior. Which is it? For all his anger, Quinton just wants to do something and be something that stands a chance of not being forgotten in a sea of nothingness. Her grandfather never cared when he got money, and so why should it be any different with Quinton? Sure, if you're living under a bridge and someone gives you five dollars for a fleabag hotel, that might make you happy, but what does it matter if you live in a two-bedroom house or a mansion? Everyone's dead in the end, anyway.

"You want to go upstairs?" she asks.

They go to a guest room. She's long been an avid reader of her mother's *Cosmopolitans*, but despite all the rehearsed scenarios, Ruthie is unprepared for the actual event. Paneled with mahogany, its windows leaded, the room looks like a set from the Vincent Price movies that her father used to watch, a creepy but auspicious place to change her body. They kiss and undress, her skin dancing. From the moment she saw him atop the Dixons' hill, she's loved him, even though she shouldn't. Her fingers run and, tingling, try everything that Helen Gurley Brown taught her and every other woman in 1972. Most of all, Ruthie thinks of the man in the bushes.

She waits for him to join her and for the pain, but there's no pain and no joining. He tries, but finding her resistant to even the slightest entry, he awakens as a modern-day Adam. She remembers the words from Sunday School: *And the eyes of them both were opened, and they knew that they were naked.* Unaware of how to respond to the limp disappointment that fills the room, she says nothing. In short order, his initial anxiety fructifies with frustration, humiliation, and then anger, and she wonders if, just like that, it's all over. Is it her fault? Maybe she didn't move in the right way, too slow or too fast. He eventually calms, and they give up, deciding to get high instead. When they try again an hour later, the same thing happens, and instead of shrugging it off and getting more stoned, they stare at the ceiling. Again, after a final perfunctory attempt, he gives up. She doesn't care, this isn't about bodies, but he does, and she knows he's gone.

In the end, Quinton deposits her at the end of Barker's Mill and drives away. She drifts home, hides, and all she can think of is that gun.

9

"Do you mind if we listen to music while we talk?" Santoni asks Jim, who looks like a buoy lost in the vast room where furniture floats like islands. "It gets my thoughts flowing."

"Why not?"

"Wonderful." Santoni rises from his mohair velvet chair and walks to the bookcase atop which a turntable, receiver, and speakers sit between two phalanxes of vinyl. "Should we listen to Verdi?"

"Do you have *Carmen*?" Jim asks. He's been thinking a lot about the opera recently. When he went with Woody, Honey, and Maria this spring to the Academy of Music to see Domingo and Berganza perform the work, orchestra tickets middle of the third row, it had been so boring. Now he wants to hear it curtain to curtain.

"Of course," Santoni says, "and I love the fourth act. It's the shortest and the best. You know, Nietzsche thought it was the greatest opera ever written."

He positions the needle on the disk, and so begins the buildup to the final bullfight. It occurs off stage, better that way, more realistic. The horns and the strings come first, pounding staccato, and then the chorus, anything you want for two quarters. The music brims with optimism, despite the imminence of Carmen's death. Don Jose slinks behind an amphitheater pillar, still unseen, waiting to pounce.

The mentor settles in his chair and lights his pipe. The two psychiatrists have gathered in the living room of Santoni's house on Oakmont Road. No longer dressed in the garb of the Tuscan countryside, Ed wears a three-piece, gray pinstripe suit, which makes Jim feel shabby in his khakis and fraying blazer. Black oak bookcases line the walls, interrupted by windows, entryways, and a fireplace, somber and grandiose. Outside, the property's flat backyard stretches unobstructed out of sight.

"How are you, Jim?"

"Honestly?"

"You've looked tired. I figured we should meet." Supervision is the peculiar psychiatric ritual in which one clinician presents a case to another more senior colleague. At least, that's how it's supposed to work, but Jim's meetings with Santoni transpire more as psychotherapy. The master has long told his student that he needs weekly sessions with someone very good—how else can you learn to be a therapist?—but Jim has so far avoided any treatment, even as he endorses the concept. Things have been very busy, and besides, who could understand the past three years?

"How much are you sleeping?" Santoni asks.

"Maybe two or three hours."

"That's not enough. We did experiments at Fort Sam on sleep deprivation, and with enough of it, people get manic." In recent days Jim's thoughts have accelerated, not to the point of racing, but the world has brightened and not in a pleasant way. He can touch more, and more is coming into his grasp, but strangeness seeps over everything, even the banal. The most marked change has come in his understanding of Ruthie. Once like a foreign continent, she's now been revealed to him, and he has the overwhelming desire to whisk her away and tell her everything that he's never been able to share. She would understand. She wasn't planned, and it was hard, but he would never have done anything differently.

"I'll try to sleep tonight," Jim says.

"Can't you?"

"Not really. I mean, I can, but I don't always want to."

"Why?"

"I need time to think."

"About what?"

Jim needs time to think about the secret sauce which flavors every part of his experience. It's been there all along, but he's never noticed. He's been in a dream, not only since the crash but for as long as he can remember, maybe since his father died. Maybe that's the problem. He remembers those summer nights with his mother at the Lehighton bandshell, always wanting to be somewhere else, and Jim was somewhere else. He just didn't know it at the time. Now, there's the sense that he can taste the meaning of life if he just tries hard enough.

"It's like," Jim explains, "it's like I've figured out how to make people better."

"Well, that's good. You'll be a millionaire in no time. How's Black doing?"

"He's practically cured." Jim recounts the backstory, from the cramped conference room to the present, omitting the more malpractical details like the scotch on the porch. Following Jim's hunch that desensitization could cure traumatic neurosis, Dave recited his traumas, working from the easiest to the hardest, and Jim interpreted. Dave's reactions ebbed, and improvement flowed. This past week, for example, he's been talking about his experiences with no more emotion than he might display describing a sad movie.

"So what have you learned?" Santoni asks.

"I don't know. Well, that's not true. I know he's getting better, but I don't know if the exposure is the active ingredient. He doesn't want to kill himself anymore—or at least he says that he won't—and I believe him. If nothing else, he's not going to shoot me in the back of the head, but his problem is more than what happened in Vietnam. He had a brother."

"You didn't tell me that." Catching the opera's tune, Ed says. "Wait. Listen to this part." No longer about selling programs and oranges to the spectators, the music has darkened. His morality destroyed, Don Jose now blames Carmen for their mutual debauchery, but she has been made whole by Escamillo, and she no longer needs the military deserter whom she herself corrupted.

"I didn't know it until this week," Jim says. "He was abused."

"Physically?"

"No, and not sexually."

"Then how?"

"Emotionally, for what he was, or what he wasn't."

Santoni stares at the smoke sailing from his pipe. "Good. You're getting to the heart of it. You want a drink?"

"I have three more this afternoon, including him."

"I didn't say we had to get drunk. I'd offer you a pipe, but you don't smoke, as well you shouldn't." Santoni rises and goes into the butler's pantry, returning with a bottle of Balvenie.

"Just two fingers and neat," Jim insists. His mother used to drink Monongahela rye, like when she stiffened herself to wait in line at Borough Hall each Christmas Eve. Hours later, she would return home with toys that, a week earlier, he had seen lined up in the hallway at his school.

"The good stuff will make the session smoother," Ed says.

"Right."

"So. Black."

"He had an older brother who was killed when he was a toddler, and I think it destroyed the mother, who had already been abandoned by the husband."

Santoni sips his whiskey. "It's not uncommon. The loss of a child is the worst stressor one can face. Some parents crack, and the people around them suffer, especially any remaining children. The husband was gone, which left only the milkman and your patient. The child, of course, has no idea that his mother is the problem and proceeds to see the world as a fearsome place full of abandonment and pain, where abuse is deserved. That's when the fun begins. The anger turns inward. What do you think?" Jim says nothing, and Santoni studies his student. "This one's different, huh? It's got a hold of you."

"Sometimes it happens," Jim says. "You know that."

"No, there's something else. What's on your mind?"

"Nothing."

Santoni shakes his head. "You flex your masticatory muscles in a peculiar way when you're somewhere else. You better not do that in session. People will know."

Jim has been told the same thing by Maria. Since he was a boy, sitting through those free concerts at the bandshell, he's displayed the same facial contracture while thinking. It's not a tic but rather an involuntary tightening, a screwdriver fastening his skin to his skull. The right circumstances, fear, confusion, or boredom bring it on.

He wonders if it makes him look like Mary Pryzbzewski, her name as easy to remember as it was difficult to pronounce. They say that every intern has an unforgettable patient, and Mary P. was Jim's. She had been a radiant freshman at Penn when she began to feel tired and have unexplained fevers. Her mouth dried to a gulch, and she turned red as a beet. A cardiac arrest followed, and by the time she came to Jim's service, her face had hardened to human glass, her expression an implacable mask. Consulting his textbook of rheumatology after one forty-hour shift, so tired he looked drunk, he made the diagnosis of systemic sclerosis and realized that she would not be cured.

He should have moved on, but he couldn't. Despite his earnest efforts, he gawked at the poor girl on rounds and was sure that the slightest tap would crack her into a million shards of female. Mary P. was not, as Jim had been, a scholarship student, but she came from Wellsboro, which made Lehighton look bustling. She seemed oblivious to her future and also to boundaries. She wanted to be his friend. With the prognosis so grim, what could he say in disagreement? *It's not in my job description?* Her parents, hundreds of miles away, were infrequent visitors, and her former friends also stayed away, repulsed by her new, bizarre face.

The patient's flattery drew Jim's solicitude and then his annoyance. Mary P. demanded one bedside consultation after another. *Please get me Dr. Malory. Please.* Although her situation was dire, there was never anything urgent. She was declining with the regularity of an elevator, its arrow tracing a leftward arc in a brass semicircle. Sometimes, Mary P. wanted to provide a bit of history that she thought might have helped with the treatment. *I was bit by a skunk when I was four. I forgot to mention that.* Sometimes she wanted just to talk or to ask Jim about his own life. *You're going into psychiatry? That must be interesting! You have a wife? You're so young to be married.* Her condition made speaking difficult, and the slowness of her words lengthened every interaction. She appeared happiest, like an obedient schoolgirl, when Jim told her of his life, Maria, their girl Ruthie, his mother.

From their white perches, the nurses mocked her and then him. Soon it was: *Your girlfriend wants you. Aren't you married? What would Mrs. Malory say?* He tried to ease away but to no avail. So it went for months, other patients coming and going, cures and deaths, Mary P. the only constant, subject to one failed medical intervention after another. She was also housed in the ward's one single room, perhaps because she was still a student but more likely because of her disfigurement.

In that solitary room, one resplendent October Sunday morning, Jim found himself worrying over Mary P.'s ebbing vital signs. He'd been working a special forty-eight-hour shift and could barely think. Another intern had collapsed from nervous exhaustion and been hospitalized, requiring Jim to take up the slack. Mary P. knew about this, along with all the other intrigues of the interns. Perhaps angry because of his fatigue, Jim sat down on her bed and decided to have a heart-to-heart. He was going to find out just how much she understood, no matter the consequences.

It turned out that Mary P. knew everything. She wasn't stupid. She had, after all, been admitted to Penn, even if she would never graduate. She was ready for the end. She wasn't even unhappy because she had accepted what was coming. There was just one more thing that she wanted, and then she could give in. Would he help her get that thing? Her face was even redder than normal, and when her oblivious intern failed to understand, she made the formal request and added with emphasis: *Then I can die in peace.*

Jim's pulse quickened, but not enough to make him fight or take flight.

When the nurses changed shifts, he locked the door, drew the curtains, and lay on the bed next to her, not underneath and not naked. She crawled out over the sheets, maintaining her bundle of bedclothes. They kissed, they hugged, and that was it. Her dry bone of a body couldn't have done much more, even if she wanted to, but she had a boyfriend now, if only for an hour until the end of a shift.

The next day, Mary P. refused all care and returned home to die a week later. A month after that, Jim was summoned to the dean's office. He expected to be dressed down and dismissed. Instead, the dean handed him a letter of commendation from Mary's father, who as it turned out was no hick but a lawyer and a state senator from Tioga County. The content of the letter, postmarked from Harrisburg and embossed in gold on the senator's letterhead, was clear. Dr. Malory's care had been exemplary and had allowed Mary to spend her final months in relative contentment. Although forever mourning her loss, the senator and his wife would always be grateful to the University Hospital and its caring staff.

Then I can die in peace. The words live with the girl's name. *The secret of the care of the patient is caring for the patient.* Where did he read that? If the truth had been known, he would have been attacked and accused of blundering across a line, but the girl died in peace.

"Are you listening to me?" Santoni says.

"Yes, yes, I am."

"I thought for a second you were having an absence seizure."

"It's fine."

"Like I said, I've known you for a long time, and anything I say is meant to help."

"Fine," Jim says, "what?"

"Despite all the good work you're doing with Black, I'm concerned about your lack of judgment. Maybe it's inexperience. I don't know."

Jim says nothing. He has the almost undeniable sense that Ed knows all about Mary P. and has been waiting all these years to do what the dean did not. Jim looks to the windows, all of them closed tight. Like the Sedaras, his *paisans,* Santoni finds air conditioning unnecessary and prefers to roast like a pistachio. In the shrinking confines of the living room, Jim sweats and feels the welling desire to interrogate Ed and know what he knows. Or maybe Jim's certainty of being detected is a mirage, a shiny flood on a distant stretch of hot highway.

Carmen now taunts Don Jose, backing him into a corner with one only option for escape. The cheery accompaniment darkens to a hurricane, even as the satisfied spectators leave the bullfight unaware. Most people never know what's truly going on. When Jim was an undergraduate, before the Wanamaker's lunch and the ferry to New Jersey, he tried to listen to the Metropolitan Opera on Saturday afternoons, courtesy of ABC and Texaco. It seemed a very collegiate thing to do.

"They're talking about you," Santoni says. So he knows, and maybe the dean too. Maybe they'll retrospectively rescind his internship.

"So it's come out then? Well, they say you never get over your internship."

"What? This isn't about your internship. It's about Black. People have seen you driving around Glenwyth with him in his Eldorado."

"He likes to do sessions in his car," Jim says, scratching his head in mock thoughtfulness.

"And to meet his psychiatrist at Glenwyth Cricket?"

"Purely by chance."

"And what about having him over to dinner with your in-laws and your wife and daughter?"

"How do you know about that?" Jim remembers when his mother walked in on her thirteen-year-old son in the frenzy of masturbation.

"People talk," Santoni says.

"Who?"

"What does it matter?"

"It matters," Jim says.

"Well, if you had to guess?"

The student stares at the ceiling and wonders if now might be the moment it falls in. "Of course I can guess. It's Honey. I know it's Honey Dixon."

Santoni says nothing except, "You have a reputation. There are rules."

Jim holds up the glass, now empty. More! Refilled and reanimated, the junior psychiatrist says, "Ed, Dave's mother abused him, his wife left him, and his brother's dead. Yeah, and he never knew his father."

"Just like you," Ed says.

"Black needs somebody," Jim says.

"Of course. He needs a psychiatrist."

"He needs more than that. Like, like—"

"Like who?"

"I'll tell you a story. When I was an intern—" Jim stops. "Forget it. Ancient history."

"Jimmy, Black needs his brother back from the grave, but now you'll have to do the impossible and play that role."

"Come on!" Jim shouts, feeling an impulse to throw the glass at his supervisor.

"Don't 'come on' me! He needs you to be his brother, but you'll never be able to replace that kid lying dead at some shitty street corner in South Philadelphia. Don't you see? He wants you to be his brother, and then he wants to be you. It won't stop until he can become you, but that only happens if one of you ceases to exist."

Jim stands up and moves toward the fireplace, an actor in a drawing room comedy gone bad. "Do I get any credit here? He tried to kill himself right after your interview, and in many ways because of your interview."

"That all may be true," Santoni says, "but I didn't come to you for supervision. Maybe I should."

"It's not like I'm getting something out of Black that I

shouldn't."

"Are you sure? You never had a brother, and you lost a lot when that Huey went down. Of course, that's not all. Your life, at least your marriage, didn't turn out like you planned."

"So now you're a marriage counselor."

"I do it all the time, with some of the richest couples around, if you want to know. And they're still married. You were going to leave Maria. Ruthie was the only reason you didn't."

"I have to breathe," Jim says, the pain around his gut returning, always coming back.

Santoni opens the door to the screen porch, and the two men walk through it into the backyard, dominated by two towering swamp oaks. A swing hangs from one, and Jim sits on it. Ed stands nearby at a slight distance, like a psychiatric orderly who will avoid getting too close.

"Okay," Jim says. "He's a friend. Maybe I thought I could help him if I was his friend. That's what he wanted, and I gave it to him."

The supervisor takes off his suit jacket and lays it on the back of the swing, next to Jim. "And what do you do when he wants more? Can you give him that?"

Give him what? Dave has never asked for the key to the safe deposit box, little good that would do, or to join the Malorys in their bedroom. Although admitting that the exposure therapy has been helpful, the patient wants companionship more than anything else. Since the invitation to dinner, he has become increasingly familiar, sometimes sitting in the waiting room at session times other than his own and often asking Jim out for drinks at the Legion Post. The psychiatrist has been oblique with Maria about his absences, and she has become suspicious, although just mildly. Ruthie's problems have diverted her attention.

"I can give him what he wants and then get out," Jim says.

"Can you? I guess we'll see. Though where does it end? He's lost everything—comrades, his wife, his father, his brother, and even his mother—that is, the loving one whom he thought he should have had. Is he going to lose you as well? If he does, it won't be pretty."

"He doesn't have to lose me."

"And he won't," Ed says, "because he'll never let it happen. Don't you see how you've lost perspective? You're in way too deep."

That's what Quinton said, and they were both right. When Jim signed the lease two Decembers ago, he anticipated bored housewives and philandering husbands, but he now spends most of his time with Dave, Quinton, and Eliza, cuts on her gut, acid in her throat. If only he could drop it all and do pension examinations at Fort Dix. Or maybe become Nilso's protégé, picking colors for the ER break room.

"So how do I get out of it?" Jim asks.

Santoni deliberates for a moment and then closes his eyes. "I don't know."

"You don't know? I thought this was supervision."

"You can't just drop him. He's too dangerous." It's true; the doctor and his patient have crossed a psychiatric Rubicon. Then again, Jim's done that before and was praised by a state senator. Jim likes Dave, that's the truth of it, and wishes the man were his brother. No one else—not Ed with his tennis-court war—understands what it's like to find yourself upside down, half-deaf, and quarter-dead on a jungle floor and have to kill your way out. The truth is that Dave is the crewmember who lived.

"He's getting better," Jim says. "Soon, the treatment will end, and we'll be friends."

"You're joking, right?"

"No. Freud went on vacations with patients. Remember the four-hour walk with Schoenberg?"

"It was Mahler, and don't forget Jung with Sabina Spielrein while his wife looked after the children. You don't get it. You're never going to be done with him. The best you can hope for is equilibrium. The worst—"

"What?"

"The worst would be a total regression."

"I don't understand."

"Suicide. Or murder."

Jim considers the teacher's house bedecked in baronial grandeur. Ed lives here, and Jim in a peeling bungalow.

"He's not going to hurt me," Jim says.

"Not you, no, but anyone who gets between the two of you."

Jim eyes his mentor and says, "There's a much bigger problem. Ruthie's been seeing Quinton Graves. I figured it would end when he left in the fall, but now maybe he's not leaving. Maria found out a week ago, and she's demanding I do something to break it off. She wants Ruthie to go to Swedesboro until school starts, and she insists that I order Quinton to stay away, as if I'm a judge issuing restraining orders. If I don't, she says she's moving out."

Santoni gazes at the sky. "It might be possible to solve this if there was just you and Black, but Ruthie and Quinton make the situation impossible. You have to terminate them both, immediately."

"But I can't, and even with everything, I still want to help Quinton."

"There will be other patients. Black is bad enough, but Quinton—"

"He's just a poor kid with manic depression."

"Manic-depressive yes," Santoni says, "but he also hates the world for some slight that only he can understand."

Jim walks to one of the two swamp oaks and runs his hand along a large crack in its middle.

"Lightning. We're going to have to take it down," Santoni explains, "before it falls and takes the other one with it."

"Ed, I don't need your advice."

"This is supervision, and I intend to supervise," Santoni says, ignoring his disputatious pupil. "You're drawn to Black because he needs you, and you want to be needed. You also share your losses. Then there's the crisis with Maria."

"There's no crisis," Jim says.

"Like there was no crisis when you got yourself drunk for a month before Vietnam."

"Did you get that from Honey Dixon as well?"

"It doesn't matter, as if I needed corroboration. I was there, and three years later, things aren't much better. You and Maria looked beside yourselves that last morning at the Cape."

"It was an argument. That's it."

"That's it? You're having traumatic nightmares, and sometimes when a patient is asleep, sometimes even with his wife—"

So he knows, just like everyone else, from the cashiers at the A&P to the cafeteria workers at the VA. Did Maria tell Santoni, or did she tell Honey, who then passed the particulars of Jim's murderous rage to her beloved Dr. Santoni? It doesn't matter. There's at least one more person who knows that Captain Jim is insane. Just like Ruthie.

"I don't want to talk about this," Jim says.

"Maria came to me," Ed explains. "She's upset."

"She's pregnant. That's how women get, if you remember." Santoni has two sons—one a bond king in New York and the other a neurologist in California. Maybe if he were a better father, one of the two might have stayed around.

"My real problem is Quinton," Jim says. "He's hunting me down, and he knows I won't run."

"How often does he see Ruthie?"

"I think she's been with him every night, and every morning she's more depressed. If she told me she was suicidal, I wouldn't be surprised. She was a happy kid at the beginning of the summer, and now she spends half of every day in bed. She's also smoking a lot of marijuana, acting like we don't know, like we can't smell it. She's supposed to start school in two weeks, but I don't think she'll go back."

Santoni walks around Jim and the swing. "You seem awfully calm about the whole thing."

"What should I do? Kill Quinton?"

"You don't need to go that far," Santoni says, smiling and taken aback at the same time. "Start with terminating him and sending Ruthie to Swedesboro. That boy won't dare go there, and if he does, her grandfather will set him straight."

"And give up? You think I'd do that?" Of all the directions Santoni could have suggested, this one proves what Jim has long suspected. Despite the mentoring, guidance, and friendship, Ed has always, deep down, thought his junior a quitter. "I'm not giving up!"

"It's too late," Santoni says. "You've already lost. Your patient has seduced your daughter, and he's not going to stop there. He's angry, and the anger has turned to you and your family."

Jim picks up a fallen branch and hurls it across the yard. "What have I done to him?"

"Nothing, but it doesn't matter. He's mad. He's one of the richest kids in Pennsylvania and one of the angriest."

"You always have the answer."

"It comes with time." Santoni gazes across his field toward Oakmont Road. "You'd have that insight too if you had seen him before."

"What are you talking about?"

"I treated him before. I saw him off and on when he was at

White's and then the summer before he went to Harvard."

Jim wonders if the cracked swamp oak might tumble down upon them both. Is *Carmen* still playing inside? She's probably dead by now.

"And you neglected to tell me this?" Jim screams.

"Now, hear me out."

"I'm listening."

"When he snapped this summer, I figured it was just garden-variety manic depression or schizophrenia. You put him on chlorpromazine or lithium, and he's cured."

"But what about when he was at White's?"

"It was just bullying, as far as I can remember. In any case, he fired me."

"You?"

"It has happened," Santoni says, "and I figured you might do better. You have what it takes to understand anyone if you can just understand yourself. Also, you're always talking about how you can't make ends meet, and I figured his fees would last you a lifetime. He could be a permanent patient. Thirty-nine more a week, and you're good until you retire."

"And this is help?" Jim asks. "You should have told me. We should have talked before things got to this. We were sitting on your patio."

"He wouldn't let me."

"What?"

"I asked permission to share my records with you. He refused."

"And that wasn't a red flag? What about all that mentorship crap? Ever heard of off the record?"

"I was going to tell you that afternoon at VA, but I thought you could figure it out on your own."

"Well, I guess I can't," Jim yells. "It's a complete and total FUBAR, and I'm the FNG, the sucker who gets shot between the eyes a week in-country."

"Don't panic," Santoni says. "There's a way out of every maze."

In the ten minutes outside, the temperature has fallen twenty degrees. Without rain or thunder, a cold front has stolen through, fracturing another vertebra of summer.

"All right," Jim says. "I'm waiting."

"You're seeing Eliza Dixon."

"Yes, and next you'll tell me you've been peeping into the bedroom from the Althouses'."

"Okay. Don't have ventricular tachycardia. Honey asked me for a consult."

"For Eliza?"

"Yes."

"Are you kidding me? Don't you think it's a bit unethical to see both a mother and her daughter when they get along like that? What does the Quaalude rep have to say about it?"

"Eliza was a second opinion, and since they both gave informed consent, what was the problem? Besides, how could I not meet the daughter of Honey Dixon? It's a multigenerational case report."

Jim wants to run, go underground before the B-52s glint in the sky, never know what hits you, muscle and bone up through the skin, secondary burn.

Santoni says, "The girl's not well. I did a physical examination, which, when appropriate, you must never forget to do. Do you know that she carved words into her abdomen?"

"What can I say? You win again."

"But why are you taking the risk? She needs to be hospitalized."

"At Byberry, with the catatonics? The Institute isn't much better," Jim says. "I wanted her to finish school if she could."

"And invite her over for dinner too? What would the medical board say? Why did you even take her case? A rescue fantasy? You know her history, or maybe you don't. You don't know, do you?"

Santoni stands over his junior, like a toreador ready to deliver the final blow, and says, "So she didn't tell you? Damn. She was in love with Quinton, but he broke it off with her before he returned for the spring semester, and then she went off the edge, or, I should say, more off the edge. Of course, if I had known that you were seeing her, I would never have referred Quinton."

"Do I have to run every case by you? I ran the Coast Guard by you and found myself in a Snoul rubber plantation."

"You just can't let that go. You have your limbs, and your mind is intact. Quinton consumes women," Ed says, "and Ruthie's next. You have to get her out of there."

Jim tries to catch his breath. "I trusted you, and you betrayed me."

"How's that?"

"You sent me Quinton after just happening not to mention that you saw him for ten years—"

"Three—"

"All the while knowing he'd come after my daughter."

"That's absurd, even paranoid."

"And now you've taken over Eliza and her mother, making clear that I'm not up to the job!"

"Eliza was a consultation. I said that. As far as Honey, she's not your patient, and you're starting to sound like you own her."

"Don't you see? She's trying to get to me through you!"

"What does Honey Dixon have to do with you?" Jim should stop here, studied as he is by this supervisor who has dissected his supervisee hundreds of times since Penn Med. The chemical process of induction has commenced in Santoni's brain, and Jim's next step will be onto a Claymore.

"I'm going home," Jim says.

"We still have time in the hour. I don't get what my seeing Honey has to do with you?"

"Not much. Add it to my tab."

"You sure you don't want to stay for dinner?"

"Are you insane?" The idea of amiable Natalie knowing everything makes Jim want to smash the windows of Santoni's Mercedes.

"I think she's making carbonara," Ed says, "although it's a bit hot for it."

"I'm done."

"I know you're upset, but does this time work for next week?"

"Leave me alone!" Jim shouts and walks to the Mustang, parked next to the two support pillars holding up the house's stable-turned-garage. Jim could drive through both, even dislodging part of the building, but it would fall on him. And besides, the Mustang is the only decent vehicle he'll ever have.

When Jim exits the serpentining driveway and pulls onto Oakmont, he sees Santoni staring at him from the swing, an old man out of place. Natalie has joined her husband, arms crossed above her apron.

Santoni has been Jim's mentor for a decade, but everything ends, like Jim's mother ended. She lived in that studio apartment in the county housing near the railroad tracks that no longer ran, fifty-five going on eighty, always exuding the smell of never having been young. She didn't try to starve herself. It just happened until there was nothing left but bone and skin wrapping, sores in her mouth and dentures in a cup. How strange that the women of Glenwyth seek the thing, starvation, that came so easily to his mother.

And to think, Maria insisted that they name their daughter after this woman.

The white comforter covers Ruthie to her neck, her armor against a world without Quinton. Two weeks ago, her grandfather installed a window air conditioner in her room, transforming it from a sauna to a noisy ice hut. She has tied thin red streamers to the vents, and they stand perpendicular to the machine on high fan. The cooling whir silences the rest of the planet, and that's okay. The blinds are lowered, sending her little room and its single bed into dusk. Although the air conditioner may have been running since its installation, the need for it has lessened. The heat of the previous month has been ground away to a smooth stone, no longer able to hurt. Earlier, a cold rain from the ocean covered Glenwyth.

Sleep has been elusive. Ruthie gets a few hours a night, and this is a blessing as her mind races. Hungry from the marijuana that she smokes at night when her parents are unconscious, Ruthie has packed her underwear drawer with plastic-wrapped sweets and consumes them secretly. Neither her mother nor father has said anything, but they must have noticed. These days, Ruthie smells like damp, dirty laundry left overnight in the washing machine.

Maybe that's why Quinton dumped her. A moment ago, she had believed in him. Sure, he could be distant and flash with rage, nasty and kind, rolled up into a prickly ball, but she knew that deep down he loved her. The love came oddly, down cul de sacs, via roundabouts, but there wasn't much to compare it to. Of course, he wasn't going to drop out of college, but he had more than once mentioned transferring to Penn. It was no Harvard, but there was a museum, and he loved that place. With their proximity assured, or at least possible, Ruthie tried her best to give Quinton what he wanted.

What a complete fuck-up that was; makes her want to cut even now. After the catastrophe, he had stopped wanting to make it right with her parents. Despite all the possible explanations for their failure, Ruthie sees the real reason. Her body knew that his didn't want hers, and quite literally, she didn't let him in. Having driven him away, she has no right to have him back, but she's developed an unquenchable thirst. So she has called, called, and called, every ring ignored. She has even stalked his house and been told by Evans, "Mr. Graves is not at home."

As the likelihood of his return decreased, she freaked. Ruthie would try to become unconscious by eleven, but instead, she thought of him. Then, she would give up trying to sleep, get up, and draw him in myriad poses—naked, as a nineteenth-century business tycoon like his great-grandfather, as a superhero, as a farmer. She figured that the drawings might make her feel better, but they fueled her consumption. As the days stretched from the last time they met, and the certainty of their split became undeniable, Ruthie's art turned to specific parts of his body: his nose, his hair, even his feet. She had no photograph of him, and so the reconstruction had been from memory, but with each rendering, her remembrance slid further from actuality. Her drawings came to represent a person who might be his first cousin or not even. She tried to hear his voice in her mind, but even this changed to something else, grotesque and unrelated.

So she took to her bed and the protection of its comforter, its polyester and synthetic filler as impenetrable as stone. She leaves, but mostly at night, after her parents are asleep. Her journey began with that first escape, and how much hope there had been in the following weeks. Ruthie was sure back then for the first time in her life that she could be a happy person, but here she is again at a dead end. Except for her one departure the night of the dinner with her grandparents, she has never been caught leaving their home, but having dispensed with caution, she will, sooner or later, be captured. That she hasn't been makes her think that her parents are ignoring her, preoccupied with something else. Or maybe they know that she's too far gone and have given up.

In the days just before their separation, Quinton gave her a plastic container full of marijuana, a vessel not unlike the ones in which Maria refrigerates leftover *pasta e fagiole*. The seal confines the drug's peculiar smell, and despite her present rate of consumption, the product will last up to graduation, if that ever comes. Ruthie attended Stroud's three months ago, and the school's teachers, secretaries, and lunch ladies with their hairnets expect that she will return not a month from now. Next year's dress blazer sits in Ruthie's closet. Maria purchased it a week ago in preparation for the first day of school, but what a waste of nineteen dollars. It'd be easier to send another person to the moon than for Ruthie to go back to Stroud's.

She could be a dealer, meeting kids beneath the cherry trees behind the tennis courts. What would the headmistress think of that? From the first time she tried it, Ruthie has loved marijuana, and with Quinton gone, she smokes more and more. She goes nightly, with her peace pipe and just a bit of the stash, to Glenwyth Park or behind the pharmacy or even to the A&P parking lot, a risky place. The police cars often park there like two lovers in sixty-nine, Quinton's observation. When she comes back, she eats, a lot. There's an endless hunger for cookies, cakes, and chocolates, giving her new curves and rolls. Quinton said she was too skinny the first time he looked at her. She can change that.

When Eliza described binging, it seemed so bizarre. Why would you do such a thing? Now it makes sense. When she smokes, she has to eat. When she eats, she feels better, for a time and a bit. With each mouthful, though, there's a growing feeling of disgust. So two weeks ago, she wedged her index finger in as far as she could, and after some fiddling and wiggling, her second digit doing a dance, everything came up, and she felt better. Her mother, preparing dinner across a single wall, never noticed. Ruthie has already done it twice today, always easier and with more complete cleansing each time. What if she could purge so much that only clear liquid would come up? Somehow, that seems so right.

Ruthie's also cutting, with her mother's sewing needles, the kitchen's steak knives, and most recently, her father's razor blades. It's cringe-worthy that she would copy Eliza, but these days, originality is less on Ruthie's mind than relief. Besides, it's not like Eliza ever showed her any of this stuff. Sometimes diseases just spread, like Black Death on the Mongol trade routes. And to think, not six months ago, how irrelevant world history had seemed.

The vomiting is just an appetizer to the main course. Ruthie's been born to cut, to break through the numbness that has, like cellophane, wrapped her soul since she slept between her parents in her mother's South Philadelphia bed. There's even gratitude because the cutting shows the bond she shares with her father. Turns out he's no body double after all. The real Captain Malory has returned, as anesthetized as his daughter, which in a way seems worse than if he had actually died and been replaced. If he could cut, he might feel better, or at least feel something.

A moment after she puts on a record, there's a tentative knock on her window. She says nothing.

"Ruthie? Can I come in?" Fucking Eliza. "Your mother's not home, and the door's locked."

"So?"

"It's 11:00 a.m."

Ruthie gets up and opens the blinds, gray flooding in. Lifting the sash of the other, unoccupied window, she feels a breeze and turns off the air conditioner. How long has it been, this heat cooking her brain? Last night, behind the A&P, she got so stoned that she stumbled, passed out, and banged her head, sore even now. It was still hot then.

"Hey," Eliza says when Ruthie finally opens the front door.

"Hey."

"Can I come in?"

No, because you stole Quinton back with your scheming little hands, and by the way, you are fat, just like you carved on your own stomach.

"Sure," Ruthie says, staring at Eliza's thick ankles and her hush puppies. It's like she's gained ten pounds overnight.

"If you're busy—" But Eliza looks down the hall to the closed door of Ruthie's bedroom. "That's so cool. You're playing *The Nutcracker* in August!" In a different season in a forgotten universe, *The Decoration of the Christmas Tree* entrances children without scars on their stomachs and vomit in their throats.

Two Decembers ago, when everything was different, Ruthie and her parents took the train to New York to see the ballet in celebration of her father's discharge. Her mother wasn't yet pregnant, and her father was, if nothing else, alive with all four limbs. The three of them were there, and that was enough for her and, she thought, them. They even went to FAO Schwartz to buy her a special doll. A few weeks later, Ruthie had found Drosselmeyer, Clara, Fritz, the Sugar Plum Fairies, and the Tchaikovsky LP soundtrack wrapped under the tree on the Christmas morning that was supposed to be the best ever. By noon, though, there had been a fight. Having begun Christmas in Glenwyth, she and her mother ended it in Swedesboro, her father floating somewhere else across the Delaware. She took her dolls with her that day, and with the fantasy recreated, everything was all right. Maria thought nothing of it. As a girl, she had pursued a similar pastime, the remainders of which filled multiple bookcases in her parents' living room.

Back in Pennsylvania, Ruthie's collection was a private one, and she hid them whenever friends came over. These days, the figures usually reside in a trunk stowed under her bed. She planned to throw them in the trash one by one but somehow never did.

"I can turn it off," Ruthie says.

"No," Eliza says, staring at her friend. This morning, Ruthie wears a nightgown with a lace collar and vertical rows of tiny strawberries separated by azure lines, another one of those ridiculous outfits purchased by Maria. "Do you want to get dressed?"

There's no point in hiding anything anymore, and so Ruthie walks back to her room, Eliza following.

They enter, greeted by the *dramatis personae* of Tchaikovsky's classic ballet but not only. An infantile girl in a peasant dress stands on Ruthie's dresser next to a farm boy; they appear to be dancing. On her desk, a complete family has been plucked from the prairie, and there are more than twenty other figurines representing types from the key American periods to World War II. They face in from a semicircle, their attention aimed at the head of Ruthie's bed.

"I didn't know you collected dolls," Eliza says, sitting on the covers.

"It's stupid," Ruthie says, ripping the record player's needle across vinyl.

"If it makes you happy." Eliza scans the room. "Sorry. It's just weird with them all staring at me."

"At least I can depend on them."

"What's that supposed to mean?"

"I don't know."

"Is that why you haven't answered my calls?" Eliza asks, looking at one of the AM Top 40 posters on Ruthie's wall. "Do you think Karen Carpenter's too thin?" When Ruthie shrugs her shoulders, Eliza leans forward and studies her friend. "Are you okay?"

"What do you want me to say? I'm dynamite?"

Eliza zeroes in, looking for something easy enough to find. Ruthie turns away, stands, and evaluates herself in her mirror. Puffy and pimply, she too is ten pounds heavier, with an additional chin. There are scratches on Ruthie's wrist below her nightgown's cuff, but these were practice. The real wounds hide.

"You know I've called you like fifteen times," Eliza says. "Long distance!"

"I've been sleeping a lot."

"Aunt Flo?"

"No. I'm on the pill, remember?"

"Have you done your summer reading?"

"You know me."

"I still can't believe they put *Rabbit Redux* on the list. It's like completely X-rated."

All such bullshit, get to the point: Quinton.

"I haven't seen my dad in weeks," Eliza says.

"I know."

"My mother can't live with anybody except Burtie. It was only a question of when. My parents definitely weren't going to live happily ever after. She'll kick me out next, I'm sure. Honey's started to say that I should apply to boarding school. It's probably for the best. I don't want to be her nurse."

"Lawrenceville?" Ruthie asks.

"Yahhh. No. Not with my grades, but I'd sign up at Valley Forge Military if they took girls. I'm so tired of Honey's crap. There are so many lies, you know?" Eliza produces and spins the steel Army cigarette lighter between her thumb and forefinger, the same one from that first night.

"You want to smoke?" Ruthie asks.

"Are you crazy?"

"You brought out the lighter." There it is, the Army lighter of Eliza's Navy father.

"I carry it with me," Eliza says.

"Maybe we shouldn't smoke. I wouldn't want to have to lie if my mother asks what we've been doing. I don't like *liars.*"

"Why do you say it like that, with the *accent aigu*?"

"Because you're a liar," Ruthie says. "You're with Quinton."

"Him? He's a freak. When I got rid of him, my hair stopped falling out."

Ruthie should slap Eliza so hard that the girl collapses. Instead, Ruthie cries, "He broke up with me!"

"You were seeing him?" Eliza's question, served on a platter garnished with disgust, stuns Ruthie.

And like that, Ruthie's lower lip trembles, the force of feeling pressing through, and the dam breaks. She buries her head into Eliza's lap, sobbing through the diaphanous fabric of her friend's peasant skirt.

"I love him," Ruthie says. There's nothing more to say, or at least nothing that wouldn't sound ridiculous. Strange and mean, he's like a desert waiting for rain, so wildflowers can bloom.

"No!" Eliza shouts. "You think he's this guy who has a soft side, someone who can be saved, but there's nothing there."

"You'd don't know him like I do."

"I knew him before you did," Eliza says.

"You're such a bitch!"

"He's your first boyfriend. There'll be others who are better."

Ruthie stares at the stained carpet of her room. "I need to smoke."

"You can't be doing that all the time," Eliza says. "His stuff is not just marijuana. He mixes it with hash oil and other junk. It's like five hundred times stronger than regular grass."

"You smoke it."

"Until I realized that it was making me crazy."

"And since when are you such a goody-two-shoes?"

"I'm not perfect, you know that, but something happened, and I realized my life doesn't have to be all terrible."

"Something fell from the sky and hit you on the head?" Ruthie asks.

"That's really nice. Yeah, and somehow I think you don't really appreciate how good you have it with your mother."

"Well," Ruthie says, "maybe you can take my place."

"Fuck you. Where's the grass?" Ruthie will not give up the secret, no way. "Where is it?" Nothing. "Fine." Eliza grabs her friend's top dresser drawer and throws the contents, twenty-two matched pairs of socks and four boxes of cookies, onto the floor. Eliza foregoes searching the rest of the dresser and moves on to the desk. With nothing there, Eliza opens the closet.

"Just stop," Ruthie says and nods toward the bed. "Underneath."

Eliza pulls out a barely used leather suitcase initialed "RM." In 1956, there hadn't been time to give Ruthie a middle name.

Eliza tries to pop the rectangular latches, but they're locked. "Key?" she asks.

Ruthie hands her the ring, with which she now travels compulsively, and a small suitcase key hides among the rest. Quinton once said that no one ever checks in the luggage.

Eliza inserts the key, and one of the latches rotates open. She tries the other latch, which doesn't budge.

"Where is it?" Eliza asks.

Ruthie huffs and hands over the other key from the bottom of the mug where she stores pencils. It reads "Sicilia," a souvenir brought back by her grandfather from one of his trips to the island. Angelo planned to take her to the place which he had left and which he had not left at all. He said something about the island that Ruthie never forgot. *Nowhere has truth such a short life as in Sicily.*

"Two different keys," Eliza says. "Fancy." She springs that latch, and the plastic container is revealed, cannabis having supplanted Italian soup. "Do you know how much this is worth?" Eliza cracks the door. "Where's your mother anyway?"

"Probably studying for med school."

"Good. We can chuck all this junk." But Eliza's attention switches from the marijuana to something else. Several sheets of blotter paper, their surfaces gridded with tiny clown faces, sit on the mound of marijuana.

"Have you done this?"

Ruthie pauses. "No." Up until now, she's been too afraid, but there's no point in restraint anymore.

"This is stopping. Now," Eliza says, and peeks from Ruthie's bedroom into the hall in both directions. Seeing an unobstructed path, Eliza scurries into the bathroom and shuts its door, the twist of the deadbolt snapping. It's the same bathroom where she once vomited up her soul.

"Let me in," Ruthie says, following.

"Are you going to be cool?"

Admitted, Ruthie sees that her friend stands above the toilet with the container open. She's ready to dump the pot and LSD into the toilet water, still a violent blue from Ruthie's cleaning an hour ago.

Eliza glowers. "You're purging. Why else would it be so damned blue?"

"Ruthie?" It's Maria, shouting from the entryway.

"Oh, my God!" Eliza begins to pour the container into the bowl, but Ruthie grabs her friend's arm in mid-motion. Although the LSD falls into the toilet, the marijuana spews onto the adjacent tiles.

"Think," Eliza whispers, closing her eyes with the intensity of prayer. "Okay. You go out and talk to your mom. If she's like most moms, she probably went to the market, and so she'll be in the kitchen. She won't see you coming out. But right now you say—"

"In here, Mom!" Ruthic shouts.

"Okay," Maria replies. "But you should lock the front door.

Remember the Althouses."

"Now," Eliza whispers, "you go out and talk, and I'll clean this up. Then tell your mother we're working on summer reading and go to your room. Then I'll go talk to Maria, who will have no idea that I just saved her daughter's life. When that's done, we'll meet in the bedroom where you will have numerous books laid out on your bed. Ready? Stay calm."

Whatever. Ruthie opens the bathroom door and walks to the kitchen, where her bespectacled mother unloads groceries from wrinkled paper bags, but it's not going to change that Quinton's gone.

"How's your summer reading going?" Maria asks.

"Oh, really great. I thought you were at the library."

"I tried, but all I could think about was how we didn't have any toilet paper, and so one thing led to another." A pyramid of rolls sits on the Formica table. "I'm going to put some in the bathroom."

"No."

"Why?"

"Let me do it."

"Well, that's unusual—a helpful teenager."

Ruthie looks out her front door and sees the shopping cart her mother has wheeled home from the A&P. With her parents having only one car, Maria sometimes resorts to such borrowing. Especially on hot days, the results are shame, with other mothers speeding by in air-conditioned comfort, and melting ice cream.

"Eliza's over," Ruthie says.

"Hmmm. Did I lock the front door? Why can't I remember?"

"You locked it, Mom."

"How do you know?" Maria asks.

Ruthie walks into the living room, twists the glass knob a single time, unsuccessfully pulls the door, and returns to the kitchen.

"Okay, thanks. So what are you two doing?"

"Summer reading."

"Good. Two weeks left," the mother says, raising her eyebrows. "How's she taking the separation?"

"I don't know. Okay, I guess."

"That's good. Do you girls want some grilled cheese? They had imported provolone, so just this once, no Velveeta. You'd think it'd be a crime to have cheese you can actually eat."

"Maybe in a little bit."

"Is there something wrong with the toilet?" Maria asks. "I think it's running. I'm going to check."

"I got it," Ruthie says. "I'm taking the toilet paper right now."

Inside the bathroom, Eliza has picked up what she believes to be the final flake of marijuana, but that sweet green odor remains. So she's opened the bathroom's metal casement window and, flapping a bath towel, attempts fumigation. The hardest to clean wasn't the spill but the cannabis in the bowl. Reduced only fractionally with each flush, marijuana pieces kept appearing, but now the porcelain glistens.

Eliza reaches into her bra and removes two matching objects. They are the dog tags of Captain James A. Malory. She puts them into her skirt pocket and walks to the kitchen, where Mrs. Malory and Ruthie organize the Fluff, Snack Mate, and Tab.

"Hi," Eliza says.

Maria turns to the girl, who retreats a half step, and asks, "How about a sandwich?"

"Thank you," Eliza says, "but I've already—" Here she stops. "I can't believe I was actually going to say that."

"Well," Maria says, studying her own daughter, "Ruthie, why don't you put away the toilet paper after all?" The girls look at each other, and Eliza nods imperceptibly. "Eliza can help me in here." So Ruthie clamps the toilet rolls to her abdomen and walks down the hall. Looking at the assortment of toppings and condiments arrayed before her, Maria says to Eliza, "Tell me you haven't done it again."

"I haven't."

"And has the world come to an end?"

"No. I'm actually okay. But I miss my dad. I never thought I would say that."

"They may get back together," Maria says.

"I don't think so," Eliza replies, becoming silent. "I have to ask you something."

Maria puts down her frozen onions, tiny pearls of tastelessness, and motions the girl to the Formica table. In a moment, they sit across from each other like chess players, and Eliza shuffles the dog tags in her pocket.

"I'm all ears," Maria says.

"My mother—"

Maria looks away and then back. "Yes?"

"Was Honey always this messed up? I know that's rude. I guess nobody's perfect."

"I'm certainly not," Maria says. "Ask Ruthie. Kids hate their parents for the things they're not—"

"And parents hate themselves for what they are," Eliza says. "I get it. Only Ruthie doesn't hate you."

A shadow slips across Maria's face, and she dabs her eyes. "Maybe not. I think you know her better than me."

"It's like, it's like she's trying to fill a hole in herself the wrong way."

"You sound like you might become a psychiatrist."

"It's crazy," Eliza says, "but she's kind of like my mother." Maria sharpens, waiting to hear just how this might be so. But Eliza stops, mulling her two options: what Honey would do and what should be done. The girl squeezes the dog tags in her hidden fist, the name of Maria's man pressed into flesh. You can draw blood with steel or secreted knowledge, or you can accept and forgive, and you have to decide sooner than you think what kind of person you'll be.

"Yes?" Maria asks.

"It's nothing, just, thank you."

"Are you sure?"

"I'm sure. And I'll have that sandwich if it's okay." Eliza walks from the kitchen toward Ruthie's room. But she makes another stop first, opening the door of the Malorys' bedroom, out of sight. It's crazy coming in here, but part of Eliza wants to be caught. It's small, with only a double bed and ancient furniture chipped and scratched all over. There's barely room for the mattress and no place to hide.

A portrait of Jesus hangs above the headboard's left side, and above the right, Mary. Eliza pulls the relics from her pocket to view one last time. The Army lighter had been the first clue, and Dr. Malory's dog tags, found in a secret compartment of Honey's hope chest, the second.

The girl pulls open the drawer of the left-hand bedstead table, the one with Jesus above it—Dr. Malory's side, must be. She deposits the tags, more stuff to be forgotten. She should shut the drawer immediately and leave, but she doesn't. Instead, she digs deeper, finding coins, shoelaces, a Purple Heart, and letters addressed to Captain James Malory. There's no time to identify the sender and no time not to. Eliza picks them up. They're sealed, with no return address, but the sender's handwriting is unmistakable. It's the same hand that has signed for a thousand narcotics prescriptions at the Glenwyth Pharmacy.

Only a man would be stupid enough to leave these in his marital bedstead. Eliza will burn them, and no one will ever know. Well, almost no one. If only she had never told Quinton way back when about those damned dog tags.

10

"She wasn't a bad woman," Dave says.

"I didn't say she was," Jim says. "She was your mother."

The two men have completed most sessions since the first in the Eldorado, but the searing heat of July has made an August encore, driving them back into the office.

"But how do I get beyond it?" he asks.

"You understand why it was and how it influenced the way you view every relationship in your life. Then you realize that there's no reason to see your mother lurking around every corner."

A week ago, following the silent invasion of an autumnal cold front, the summer looked like a broken old man. Brisk mornings suggested harvest festivals and Halloween, but the high pressure was again ruined by a return of the southeast wind, bringing Jim back to Snoul. Alternating rain and sun squeeze out the sweat from Jim's sponge, making a hairy coating that can never be removed, proof that the summer will never end.

"She never wanted me," Dave says. "She told me that she would never have had me."

"No one should have to hear that." Jim wipes his brow with his handkerchief. The air conditioner controls sit at *max cool* and *hi fan,* but the heat crawls in through the cracks in the building's walls.

"But I did hear it." The Vietnam trauma has given way to the rocket-propelled emotions of Arlene Black's imploding household, and Dave has grown molten. "She was mean, really mean."

"It was the trauma. She couldn't take it," Jim says. "You were the only person around, and so you paid the price. But it never was about you."

"Then why?"

"Why anything? Why did your brother have to die in the first place?" Why did Quinton have to seduce Ruthie? Why did Jim ever listen to Ed about anything? Everything bad in Jim's life flowed from Dr. Santoni, whose words about orthodox objectivity and calm collectedness still ring through the consulting room. But Santoni was wrong! The unorthodox approach has led not to therapeutic disaster but to success: Dave's readiness to resolve his original catastrophe.

In thirty hours of psychotherapy, the patient has said little about his brother. Now, he says, "You ever go to a party, and everyone's talking about this great movie you haven't seen, and you wish you had seen it, but you didn't?"

"Yeah."

"That's how it is with Peter, without the reruns. She wanted him, and she got me. I used to have this dream. Still do sometimes. Instead of Pete being older than me, it's the reverse, and I'm with him down at the corner, and he's drawing with chalk in the street, and the Deuce Coupe comes around the bend. But he's small, and the car passes over him, and he's like a squirrel between the wheels, and then I jump into the car, and there's a VC driving, and I stab him in the eye with a pencil, and the car disappears, and I'm back with Pete. He's small, and so am I, and we keep shrinking, and we float away."

"You wanted to save him," Jim says.

"I knew I could have. I used to pray for the chance every night."

"Did your father leave after Peter died?"

"Of course, and that's when the badness started. At least that's what my grandmother told me. My mother went to college at the Pennsylvania Academy of the Fine Arts on a scholarship. She wanted to be a painter, but she gave all that up when Pete died."

"How'd she support you?" Jim asks.

"A little bit from my grandparents, but mostly cleaning houses, some in Glenwyth. I started working at twelve."

"You can't blame yourself."

"True, but I have to make sure that it never happens again." Jim looks confused. "I have to protect the people around me. That's what I tried to do in Vietnam. Even at my lowest, I knew I was trying to do the right thing. If it didn't work, well at least I tried. I had lost sight of that but never completely. The only time I can't forgive myself is if I have the chance to protect someone, and I don't. Here." From nowhere, Dave hands Jim a scabbarded knife. Its wooden handle has two metal circles that look like eyes.

Jim's heart skips. The knife's not an M7, not the bayonet blade he used in Snoul, but close enough.

"Where'd you get it?"

"Borrowed it from the Department of the Army. Should have returned it, I guess." Then, with his right forefinger instead of the knife, Dave lunges at Jim's startled neck. "Left internal jugular, right internal, then"—motioning across Jim's abdomen—"the blue worm."

Dave doesn't have to explain. You cut through the abdominal wall and peritoneum, and when the intestines spill out, they're blue, an eviscerated thing that used to be inside.

"You remember the rest?" Dave asks.

There were six additional targets on which Jim had received cursory training at Fort Sam, but he can only think of three: the lung, the heart, and the penis.

Then comes a knock, not at all timid, but maybe not a knock, maybe a hallucination.

"I'm going to put this in my desk," Jim says.

Another knock, this time emphatic.

"Carry it with you," Dave says. "Always. You never know when you might need it."

"In Glenwyth, right," Jim says, smiling. He puts the blade away, gets up, and walks to the door. He opens it a crack and is challenged by Quinton's face only inches from his own. Jim slides into the hallway past Quinton and shuts the door.

"I'm in session," Jim says. "I'll be right with you."

"But time's up." Quinton taps his index finger on the face of his watch. "It's 5:05." No longer clothed in the prep-school attire that he had affected a month ago, he again wears a leather vest, no shirt, and ripped jeans, all reeking of curdled marijuana smoke.

It's 5:07, actually, and Jim's running late again. His rhythm has been warped since the meeting last week with Santoni, and so what? Dave has nearly found the holy grail of psychotherapy. He understands his peculiar conflict, and with a few more hours, he could mystically and irrevocably be changed for the better. But here's Quinton, right on schedule.

"I'm just finishing up, okay?" Jim says. "Can you wait a few minutes?"

Quinton harrumphs. Despite the Aquarian attire, he resembles one of his nineteenth-century ancestors scoffing at a request for a nickel raise or a forty-hour work week.

"It's my time," he says.

"All right. Hold on." Jim re-enters the room, and Dave is already standing.

"Everything okay?"

"Yeah. Some people get antsy."

"That's why you have a knife. Same time tomorrow?"

"Four o'clock."

"Good." Dave hands Jim a fifty-dollar bill, walks two steps, opens the door, looks down, and then stops. Quinton faces him, blocking the exit. Dave doesn't look up, and Quinton doesn't look away. For a moment, they repulse each other in magnetic antagonism. Then Quinton yields, stepping aside, and Dave walks by.

"Remember," Dave says, as he edges down the stairs. "Blue worm." And he's gone.

"Who is that guy?" Quinton asks.

"You know I can't talk about other patients."

"You're shitting me, right?"

"Why don't you have a seat?"

"I'll stand." He looms over Jim.

"As you wish." The psychiatrist takes up his yellow legal pad, trying to pretend this is just another session.

"Man, you're a total joke," Quinton says. "You want to be all prim and proper when it suits you, and then do whatever the hell you want when it doesn't."

"What do you mean?"

"I mean, I've seen you riding around with that guy in his Caddie. Everyone's talking about it. Glenwyth is like a small town, only with a lot more money."

Jim wants to force Quinton to define the term everyone but instead says, "I remember that our first session was in your Corvette."

"I didn't say that there was anything wrong with it, Herr Doktor Professor. I just meant that you've never been a stickler for protocol, if you know what I mean. So please don't start with all the hypocritical bullshit. I get what you're all about, and I'm down with it."

"Sorry?"

"I mean that you are the man! How'd you get to be so cool? Cool, or maybe the fool about to duel."

"I don't follow you, Quinton."

The patient, eyelids stretching, places his face inches from Jim's and says, "One hundred percent fucking all-American wonderful."

"We have to talk about something," Jim says, trying to remember the speech he's been planning for days.

"Yes, we do, Mr. Magoo."

"And I've been waiting to address it for a while."

"Uh, huh, yes?"

"Look. I'm not helping you with this treatment, and I've never helped you."

"Are you serious? This has been one of the most fascinating experiences of my life, and we're just getting started."

"I'm glad that I've been entertaining, but I'm not sure that you've done anything I've asked you to do, and you've done a lot that you should have known not to do."

"Such as?" The door is open, and Jim needs only to walk out, but his feet are glued to the floor. "I'm waiting to learn what exactly I did wrong. Speed? Smoke weed and peyote and do acid? You should meet the other freshmen at Harvard College. I'm a wallflower in comparison."

"You know what you did," Jim says, "and it was a major violation of trust."

"I'm still not following you. Say it, or are you afraid your lips are going to fall off?"

"You seduced my daughter."

"Oh, that. Why didn't you mention it earlier?" Quinton asks, like an insouciant but impudent lawn boy whose attention has just been called to a strip of unmowed grass. "That wasn't me. That was all her, you know, and I can prove it."

"She's my daughter."

Quinton makes a corkscrew motion with his finger, crazy, and says, "And now we come to the part of the session where the darkened pot calls the kettle black, all the while ignoring the obsidian color of the pot's daughter."

And to think that Scotty, dead on the jungle floor, blood oozing from his mouth like a strawberry milkshake, was just about Quinton's age. Where's the knife?

"Cat got your tongue?" the patient continues. "I'm thirsty. It's important to stay hydrated in this heat."

"I have to go to the bathroom," Jim says.

"Okay. There'll be an Ortlieb's waiting for you when you get back. We owned the brewery." While Quinton pulls two forties from his bag, Jim leaves the consulting room and enters the hallway bathroom. He splashes water on his face and notices that etched lines have emerged from the corners of his mouth. He's getting older by the day.

He wants to vomit, but there's no chance of feeling better because the illness is not in his stomach but on the other side of the wall.

When Jim returns, his patient hands him a bottle and says, "I opened your beer. I hope it's okay."

"I'm not going to drink a beer in a session."

"I figured that. So I also brought you a bottle of Pepsi, and as far as the beer, I'll drink yours and mine." He guzzles part of Jim's Ortlieb's and then withdraws another thin-necked, caramel-colored bottle, *Pepsi.* Popping the top with his teeth, Quinton takes a small draught. "Do you mind? Um-mmmm. Nothing beats a Pepsi." He hands it to the doctor and insists, but the psychiatrist waves it away.

"You think I hate you, Jim, but the truth is I admire you."

"Get away from my daughter."

"Why? She's half you. I loved her like I loved you."

"You loved her. So it's over?"

"No," Quinton says. "Never will be, at least not for her, but I have other things on my mind right now. I broke through the wall, just like you did." Jim shakes his head in flimsy denial. "You know I'm right. Be honest with yourself. That's why you're so brilliant. You don't follow any rules."

"Of course I do. I have a medical license right on the wall."

"Hah! A license to talk! 'Five Cents Please.' You're like Lucy in Charlie Brown."

"I served my country instead of running."

"I'm talking about something deeper. Black is the tip of the spear and the nexus of fear. Don't look so surprised. You had him over to your house for dinner, remember? Do you think Ruthie might have just happened to tell me? Don't be stupid now and make me lose my respect for you. I did what I did because you did what you did."

"What did I do?" Jim asks.

"You know that I know what you did, but I want you to say it. I want you to celebrate it and tell everybody, especially your wife. I want you to be proud of it because I've only done what you did first. Don't look so confused. You knew that one woman wasn't enough. No fear! And so what if you're married to a Sicilian with a mobster father-in-law?"

"I think we're done, Quinton."

"You're not going to have a drink?"

"I'm not thirsty."

"You drink like a fish, man, and I can't very well drink alone."

Jim grabs the Pepsi and downs more than half. His mother used to give him cola when he was ill, and it made him feel better, although she always bought a sour-tasting local brand, a dozen of those being a quarter cheaper than Pepsi or Coke. He wonders what his mother would say about this situation. It's easy. *You're going to get in trouble, Jimmy, you mark my words.* She had broken the rules, and look what happened to her.

"So this is it?" Quinton asks. "What if I say no? It's not like you're really going to fire me."

"I can fire you. You've broken the terms of the doctor-patient relationship a thousand times over."

"'You've broken the terms,'" Quinton mocks. "You can fire me, but you won't, because this all turns you on. It's another one of your addictions."

Jim rests his forehead in his hand and then stares back at Quinton. "Leave."

"But I want you to help me, doctor."

"I tried to help you, and you perverted the whole thing."

"No way. I revealed you to yourself. You'll see that soon enough, and I'm going to cure you. And by the way, if it was good enough for Cary Grant, why not you? You'll thank me one day, I promise, just like they used to thank Janiger and Grof. But first, let's just sit for a few moments in silence, remembering all of your brothers-in-arms who died for this great nation."

Jim ignores this nonsense but remembers the picture of the Vietnamese Maria, dappled with dirt and blood at the dying feet of her own love. After several moments with neither of them speaking, Jim empties the Pepsi.

"Hah!" Quinton shouts. "I've got you now." Then, like a nervous scientist awaiting the conclusion of a critical experiment, he asks, "Are you all right?"

"Of course," Jim says. But there's the slightest tinge of nausea, something Pepsi is supposed to fix, not cause. If it worsens, the unsettled feeling might be very close to pain.

"I'm sorry," Quinton says. "We can wrap up since you're not feeling good, and I'm heading back to," sounding like his butler, "'The Lodge,' if you want to talk later." Quinton smiles. "Don't worry. You'll feel better soon."

The patient leaves, and Jim sprawls across the loveseat, suddenly needing a rest from all the commotion, and relax he does. For thirty minutes, Jim lies motionless as nausea slowly spreads in him like a sugary poison. Now he wants to be home in bed, drifts of conditioned air flowing over him, but the stairs to the first floor and the two blocks to his house seem an infinite expanse. How could he feel so ill? He closes his eyes, and instead of shimmering blackness, multicolored polygons, squares, and circles dance like a kaleidoscope. He picks up the phone and calls the house. No answer. Disconnected? He paid the bill, but maybe Bell Telephone never got it. He must go home, but trying to stand, he sinks to the ground. A throbbing headache joins the stomach pain like an off-key orchestral player. Maybe he's dying. Or maybe he's dead and has been since the helicopter went down.

He falls to his knees and then onto his elbows. He's safer if he stays close to the ground, just like in the war. He's never observed the room's carpet with such attention, and he can't believe what he's missed. The pattern, a tannish salt and pepper, is like nothing so much as dirt, which explains why it never appears soiled. Because it always is! Never saw this when Honey, Eliza, Quinton, and Dave stepped to and from the loveseat, crushing him with their souls. Such a revelation; how could he have missed it? So many hours spent here, thinking that he was solving psychological riddles when the greatest mystery lay beneath his feet. He should write a book called *The Wonders of Carpetry*. Of course, it's not a word, but it should be. If Harding could create normalcy, Jim will make carpetry. By the second, the piles become ever more wondrous. Thickened and hairy, they bob like whitecaps in an ocean, like rubber trees, always the rubber trees, always sweetness, always Honey.

The stomach pain's fading, the headache overshadowed by a sense of understanding. But what does he get that he couldn't before? Focusing his eyes seems like a struggle, everything dissolving into two. Soon, without announcement, he stands outside himself looking back in at the pieces of his soul disassembled. He's supposed to be the doctor, but what does he know? Why does anyone listen to him? He's a psychiatrist, but deep down hasn't he always wanted to be a meatpacker? Who is this Malory, with his captain's bars and his air of authenticity? Let them all see the many parts, let him be subdivided to maximize value, helping many at a time instead of one. Easier that way to be eaten alive, one bite at a time. *The Wonders of Carpetry*—it is so right—but he can't move with the waves rushing across the floor. There's water on the carpet, which will ruin his schedule for the rest of the week. Still, the flowing river is beautiful, and he can swim. He will paddle downstairs, and he does.

Outside, the good people of Glenwyth have deserted Athens. Philadelphia was the Athens of America, right? He stands alone, but a million minds crowd the road in front of him. A Mercedes passes. Even after crossing the intersection with Barker's Mill, the SL lingers in his near sight, the car's tobacco brown burned into the cones of his retinas, moving and yet not. Very odd. That goddamned Quinton gave him a mickey, and Jim doesn't even care, not that he's ever cared about much of anything. So passive, that's what he's always been, and yet driving the world forward with a single finger on the power steering wheel of life. Everything goes as it was meant to go, curiously curvy but right for a change.

The London plane tree across Athens bursts into purple flame, just like the burning bush, but bigger. Strange, it was green an hour ago, not burning, and Jim's no Moses. No firemen arrive, and so be it in this new way of being. He wants to climb atop this spectacle, but that would be death, the real thing, incineration. He could jump into the Mustang to search for more purple trees, but Maria has it. Damn. She's always stopping him, pulling him back to earth, ever since that flat tire.

He turns around and takes in his small building. The house at 949 Athens has become glorious. It bends and stretches, and its white stucco reddens. It had always appeared a pathetic excuse for an office, over-painted and poorly mortared, matching his own forced frontage, but tonight it has grandeur. Why not buy it this minute so that he can have it forever? He must! Jim knows the owner, a humped spinster somehow related to Honey. If he can own this building, if he can be this building, he will succeed, and better late than never. This all may look bad, but his patients must feel the energy that he feels now, psyche flowing from his hand into the air. Jim touched the building two years ago when he signed the lease. His soul entered the structure, and there it remains. Where's Maria? He has to explain this secret knowledge, but she's never there, not when he was born, not on that ferry even though they stood next to each other, not in Snoul, and not now. What is with this town? Where is everybody? Have the passersby been abducted? *Everyone's Gone To The Moon!* Jim's watch melts like everything else. He makes out 5:55, which means five more minutes until closing time, like in *It's a Wonderful Life* when George Bailey watches the clock and avoids a bank run. Only, this is a mind run.

Jim circles the building and then sprints around it three times. Maybe he'll do this all night until he catches the tiger by the toe. He's been waiting for this, to be poisoned and to like it. He must have been poisoned because this is no ordinary evening in Glenwyth. If he can catch the firefly and hold it, everything will be okay, but suppose it gets away? He has to stop. The women across Barker's Mill in the A&P parking lot are reading his mind. He can't actually see them, but they're there. They know something too, but they won't say it. Let him find one and see inside her. Better yet, let him see inside Maria and Honey, the most legendary of all roommates, two faces of the same coin. He will run to Honey, and she will make everything better in the way that she makes everything worse. Or maybe he goes to Quinton and jumps into the pool at Sycamore Lodge, offering the heartiest of thanks.

Is that the sound of rotors chopping the air? But where's the helicopter? Looking back to the earth, Jim studies the pavement, and upon it appears a giant bull-man, blue with electricity, human below the neck, horned animal above. Izdubar? The thing stands not even a car length away, glowing, snorting, rubbing its foot. But Jim can think only of that damned opera, the one he never liked, with Carmen, the crazy woman, and the bull. That's when Izdubar lunges, horns first. The doctor is to be gored, thrown into the air, and ripped apart like a *piñata.*

"Jim?" Honey asks, actualized, no dream, no hallucination. She stands two feet from his own legs, which have returned to the front step on Athens and feel disconnected from his torso. Never before has he had such a keen perception of his legs.

And he looks at hers, exposed from above the knee, for the first time in years. She wears that same brown leather miniskirt. What are the chances? He wants to look closer, to find the scar, and beneath it, the muscle, vessel, nerve, and bone, torn and sewn back together, just like him. Her wound predicted his.

"Is everything all right?" she asks.

"Getting the mail." Good thinking, but he did that earlier, all junk like everything before this moment, appropriate for disposal.

"You're sweating."

"It's August in Philadelphia," he says.

"Well, I suppose. Anyway, Eliza's not coming tonight. She's firing you. She says she's all better and doesn't need therapy anymore. I said that's absurd, I mean, really, but of course she won't listen."

"We're scheduled?" he asks, amazed at the reality of appointments intruding into this much finer world.

"Six p.m. Did you forget to write it down?"

"I guess I did. Sorry. No charge. See you later."

Honey wags her finger, the white digit leaving a chalky streak across the sky. "I'll use her time, and I even have a check right here for all the outstanding sessions." She holds up a windowed envelope and smiles. "I'm sorry that I've been absentminded." Her eyes squint. "Are you all right?"

Do you mean other than all this? She's just like him, ripping up the road, looking at the burning magma underneath. Maybe that's their connection, a truth always too much for Maria. *It was just too bright.*

"You look ill," she says.

"Not at all," he answers. "I mean—"

"Can we go upstairs?"

"We can cancel the appointment." He sucks in the fetid damp of a Philadelphia summer evening mixed with the dark wonder of the universe. "Can't we just cancel the appointment? I won't charge you."

"I'd rather we didn't, if it's all right with you." Honey doesn't wait for his answer. Instead, she marches upward, and her mind pulls him along the waterfall that used to be the stairs. They are soon in his room.

"Having a party?" she asks. After inspecting the empty bottles sitting on the wondrous carpet, she dumps them in the trash, a mother visiting her dissipate son. "You know, Jim, you're not an undergraduate anymore. You should have stayed in St. A's and sowed your wild oats before everything got complicated."

"How's Woody?" Damn. What's he thinking?

"Same old story. He's taken an apartment that has two exits. That way, he can let one woman in while another's leaving."

"Hmmm." The murmuring inside him erupts through his lips. Honey ululates, and he wants to hold her just to make it stop. It's getting less pleasant to see the bending picture show of his psychic wind, and where's Maria? She's drifted away, just like she did when she learned he'd been ordered to Vietnam. Yes, he had told her that a DC appointment was certain, and after he had received his orders, she fled in angry horror with Ruthie. So there he was on a Saturday afternoon, sitting alone on the bungalow porch, drunk. His wife and daughter had been away, and Honey had come a-calling.

"I'm going to bring Jimmy home," she says. "I've decided. There's no reason to have him locked up in that place like a criminal."

Of course! The Jimmys, Dixon and Malory, see the same weird world, and that's why neither of them can talk.

"Where will he live?" Jim manages.

"At Wingohocking, of course." Wingohocking. She talks about it like the house owns the road.

"But I thought you were selling."

"I've changed my mind. I'll hire a live-in nurse."

She's all grown up about it now, like it's no big deal, but three years ago there was only desperation, a philandering husband, a depressed daughter, and a silenced son. There was no point to anything and therefore no shame. For Jim, there was possible death, its own sort of snuff, and on that particular eve of his departure, blinding intoxication. What had been the poison then? It was scotch, a going-away present from Ed, the man responsible for everything.

With all the shore traffic of that summer Saturday three years ago, Maria and Ruthie must have still been in Pennsylvania when he spied Honey and her leather miniskirt limping along the cracked Barker's Mill sidewalk. The woman who had foresworn all forms of exercise was out for a stroll. Soon, they sat together inside, blinds drawn in the hundred-degree living room from which Maria had run sobbing hours earlier. Honey might have been caught, maybe that was the point, and soon the aphrodisiacal scar smiled at him from patella to hip. She was right to save her leg, knowing how years later it would come in handy.

"So what's with you and Eliza? She used to like you." The words excite Honey, like she's come to the penultimate chapter in a titillating novel.

"Nothing I can think of," he says, or maybe something he almost understands. During the last sessions, the girl had been observing him, trying to find the last missing piece of some grand puzzle.

"Well, she doesn't want to see you anymore, I'm sure of that. As I said, she's fired you. It pains me to say it, knowing that you're not exactly full."

"Maybe it's for the best."

"But she's not better, and she'll never be better. Trust me. That girl will need years of therapy."

"Has she been cutting herself or throwing up?"

Honey eyes Jim with suspicion. "Well, I didn't know that she was doing all of those things to begin with, thank you very much, but she came right out last night and said all of that's over. Then she sat down, ate the entire Welsh rarebit that I brought home from the club, and didn't even try to lock herself in the bathroom."

"Well, I suppose she's better," Jim says.

"Just like that?"

"People change."

"In bad novels maybe, but you can't just quit being her doctor. She needs therapy. We all need therapy."

"So take her to Santoni. I'm through."

"That's ridiculous," Honey says, staring at the trash can and beer bottles.

"I can't stand the heat, and so I'm getting out of the kitchen. Did you know—?"

"What?"

He's embarrassed to tell her what he finds so satisfying, that the letters of Santoni's name anagrammatize to spell Saint No. If he could have such insight every day, he could continue practicing, but his therapeutic success, limited as it has been, has come from trickery and showmanship, prestidigitation and legerdemain. Without the car rides and traumatic exposures, he is nothing but a bartender without booze.

Instead, he says, "You came."

"I don't know what you're talking about."

"That afternoon."

Instantly, with the torque of a lurching locomotive, she says, "I was retrieving a mixing bowl that Maria borrowed. That's the truth. I thought she was at home." He laughs. "I didn't know that she was in Swedesboro."

"Just out for a walk?"

"I was getting service at the Arco. I had nothing to do but wait."

The idea of Honey collecting a mixing bowl or getting an oil change makes burning trees and electric bulls seem normal. She says nothing more, but she doesn't need to. With every sentence, her mind flowers.

"I was not in a good place," he says.

"True." She writes her thoughts on the blackboard of his brain. *You were drunk as a skunk.*

"I'm a bit off now. I'm not sure why."

"If you stopped drinking the cheap stuff," she says, "you'd drink less. You don't look so good." And her thoughts again explode. *You never look good. We should have been married, and I would have given you what you needed. It wouldn't have been easy, but you wouldn't be in the sorry state you are in today.*

"I keep thinking about that afternoon," says Jim, like the boy who has lost his Halloween candy through a ripped bag.

"Nothing happened," she says. *But something happened. You remember my scar.*

"You're lying," he says.

"I'm not." *I am.* "There was nothing terrible." *At least nothing terrible for me.*

"I never read the letters, and now they're gone."

She smiles. *Now you're the liar.*

"Someone stole them," he says, "within the last month."

"No one stole them. I'm sure you misplaced them, not that keeping them was the smartest thing." *Maria took them, and it's about time that she knows the truth. It's over with her, and the sooner you both realize it, the better. She was going to flush Ruthie down a New York toilet, and I stopped her.*

"What did they say?" he asks.

"Never read one, but kept them nevertheless? Such a man. They said that you hadn't done anything." *Even though you had.*

And there it is, that same leather skirt once unfairly draped across Maria's dressing table. What had it been like? He can't remember, but it wasn't for kicks. She wanted something, just like Mary P. But why him? Why not another sucker?

"You gave me a book that afternoon. Do you remember it? It was *Modern Man in Search of a Soul.* I actually read it. It was very good. The writer is a very strange fellow."

"You're making all this up," he says.

"No. I was there, and you weren't, in a manner of speaking. You vomited in the hallway bathroom."

"And then."

"No."

"You're lying."

"You're drunk," she says.

"The dog tags, night table, the letters—" His syntax is cracking, like he might give up speaking altogether.

"Why are you doing this?" Honey asks. Her hair is the burner on an electric oven, and she lights a cigarette.

"I can't not." Jim stands. He takes in this woman in his loveseat and again sees her on his marital bed, hunched over, naked and sad, a woman growing old even then. Today, here and now, she smokes Virginia Slims, just like in '69, menthol in the air.

"You'd better forget everything." He sits next to her, and she doesn't move away. "It all worked out. So stop."

"I can't."

Honey throws her head against the top of the cushion. "I'm not going to let you do this. I'm going before it's too late."

"I've never been right since," he says.

"You were never completely right before."

"I can't take it anymore. Every night I have nightmares, and every day flashbacks, falling through trees in that helicopter, killing, strangling that boy, seventeen years old, his girl still wondering where he went. I'm supposed to be a doctor, and I crushed his larynx with my own hands. He was alive, and then there was nothing. What do I do?"

"You go on," she says, taken aback like he's never quite seen her. "You never told Maria, did you?"

"No."

Honey sighs. "You go on like I go on. No one has a guarantee."

"And what's the point of all that? I burned my uniform, but I can't get rid of my mind."

"Life is loss. When it's not, then you have something to write home about."

Jim's head falls into her leather lap. She recoils and then relaxes. Her hands fall to her sides, and then touch him, tentatively at first, then rubbing his temple gently.

"You're so sad," she says. "You've always been that way. I think you were sad the first time I saw you. Do you remember?"

"On Woodland Avenue, in the part that doesn't exist anymore."

"You were riding that ridiculous bicycle."

Explosions of light still emblazon his mind, but Jim feels dead. After a time, a single word remains in his mouth. "Why?"

"Why what?"

"Why me?" he asks.

"Because I've always wanted what I can't have."

"So you waited until I was drunk."

"You would never do it sober," she says. "And at least there was something to show for it."

He lurches forward, a million volts of electricity traveling through his spine.

"What?" he says. Of course. "Burtie?"

Honey looks away through the window at the dimming evening, the days getting shorter. "Don't act all surprised," she says. "He looks just like you, and there was never a need for you to know. This kind of thing happens all the time, even in the Radnor Hunt crowd. It's not such a big deal."

Jim tries to walk and collapses into the loveseat. He can see Maria's face hovering in the room with them, with the same sad coloring she had when they took that first ferry ride to Swedesboro.

"I'm going to have to go away," he says.

"No one has ever known, and no one will."

"Including Burtie?"

Honey looks down at her sandals. "People are adopted all the time. It's better than not being born." Here she stops and laughs. "It's life, and besides, did you really think I wanted to have number three with Woody?" There had been a time when Jim wanted so much to resemble Honey's former husband, to cease being the stranger from Lehighton with the mother who worked in a garment factory by day and repaired clothes by night. Not even knowing his own desire, he had dreamed of acceptance by the White Anglo-Saxon Protestants who possessed Lehighton through their Philadelphia lawyers and who owned his dying mother, his dead father, and everyone he had ever met before he left Carbon County.

"You know that you wanted it," Honey says.

"But why did you take me like that?"

"Because it's something I know how to do, and I do it."

He's been cleaved into not just two but four: the madman ready to inject himself with potassium chloride, the dispassionate analyst, a boy sitting in Courthouse Square waiting for something to change his dried-brick existence, and Black waiting for his brother to be mowed down on a South Philadelphia street.

"I'm finished," he says, feeling the dry socket of his missing mind. "I thought I could listen. I thought I could fix people. Maybe I thought in my drunken stupor that I could fix you, but it's too much. I'm no match for it, and I should have never been a father."

She grabs his hands between her own. "Having a part of you saved my life." She rubs his fingers, kneading a loaf. "Burtie's just like you. You look at him, and he already has the same mannerisms. Like when you grip your right side between your thumb and index finger. Burtie does that. You'd never know it unless you were looking, but I'm looking. There are fifty other things, and he's sharp as a tack."

"He'll know."

"No."

"But he's my son."

"Our son." She stops. "Or maybe your son. I don't feel very good these days. I'm tired all the time, and for the first time in my life, I don't actually have an appetite."

"What do you mean?" he asks.

"I mean, the pain is worse, but in different places, and to think that I always assumed that you would be the first one to go."

Green and red flames engulf her, even as her skirt remains, a strange funeral pyre, but the woman's indestructible, less human than spirit, existing before and after time. And what would his life be without her, anyway? He could re-enlist, but the psychiatrist's chances of dying in Southeast Asia decline by the week. Nixon, the man who was finished ten years ago, is bringing the boys back home, but there'll be no reinvention for Jim. He can die. He tried to do the right thing, and he failed. He's the FNG who gets his legs blown off the first week of his tour. No one will say it, and some will even praise his heroism, at least every Memorial Day, but he failed, and he will soon be forgotten, like all failures.

"Do I get to talk to Burtie?" Jim asks.

"Of course. He's been in this very office."

"But he'll never know."

"No."

"And Woody?"

"That jackass? He wouldn't care one way or the other. He hasn't visited his real son in a year, and he treats Eliza like a niece, if that. All he cares about are his golf trips to Pebble Beach. I never even had a single orgasm with him, if you didn't know."

But Jim can only think of Maria, a semester removed from Hallahan, with that sinking look as the two of them sat in

Pietrolongo's parlor.

"My father always loved Woody," Honey adds. "Oh, he was the man for me, and I always listened." She punches the arm of the loveseat. "I knew he was wrong from the second date, but Daddy told me he was right. I trusted him, like with everything else. Of course, Woody loved it when my father came to stay with us. They would drink their days away at the Philadelphia Club."

The sky has darkened to a greenish hue, and she says, "I think of Jimmy as advance punishment for everything I would do wrong. So you're not the only one. I love that boy so much, but it's hard when you get nothing back. I suppose I'm being superstitious, and the problem was my dying bloodline, or too much gin, or whatever else I did wrong when I was pregnant, but Eliza was different. She would have been fine if it weren't for my mothering."

But Jim has crossed the Delaware and returned seventeen years to that December night in the farmhouse when he sat with Carmela and Angelo to explain how he had impregnated their only child. He expected to be knifed at the table, but they showed him equanimity. Perhaps they could see that he wasn't going to run. Maybe they knew they could catch him if he tried. But they weren't even disappointed, and Angelo was already in the position to guarantee him lifetime work and all the Eldorados he could ever want. *She loves you,* Angelo had said. *What can I say?*

Those words are all that remain from that snow-covered evening, the Sedaras' younger selves preserved like flies in the amber of Jim's mind. Angelo and Carmela must have seen what would happen to him now, three years ago, and in the future. They must have known he would betray Maria. They had offered their kind of life to him, and they weren't trying to void his potential or ruin his medical career. They were protecting him from what they knew was coming. *Live a simple life, Jim.* Yes, that evening they said that too, didn't they?

That spring, after the wedding but before Ruthie was born, Jim and Maria returned to Swedesboro for the Feast of St. Alfeo, commemorating an early Christian and his two brothers being boiled in oil in third-century Sicily. The four of them walked through the town, Carmela and Maria bare-footed, and at that point, he could have listened. He could have been safe.

"I wish you had never come here," Jim says.

"I told you, I don't feel good. You're a doctor, aren't you?"

"I was."

"I told you to stop. Everything would have been fine."

"But something wasn't."

"No one has to know."

"But I know," says Jim.

"You'll forget it. I promise. Not literally, but the memory of your former self, the person you thought you were, even if it never truly was, will fade. It's like with my leg. I knew I was going to lose it. No one said it, but I knew it, and I had already accepted that everything in the past—running, riding, looking whole—was gone. It was almost harder when I didn't lose it, and everything had to change again. Instead of a cripple, I was the survivor, thanks to my wonderful doctors. You see, I've always loved doctors."

Jim studies Honey's leg, the leg. It melts away like other parts of his office, like the recollection of his mother and the memory of his father, James C. Malory, the man so forgotten that Jim never needed to be called Junior. The man is usually unimaginable, but today, for some reason, the Mauch Chunk saloonkeeper and bookie with the swollen liver stands bold and jaunty, as if his son were staring straight at him on a 1939 spring day in Courthouse Square.

"I've failed," Jim says, wondering just how yellow his father was at the end.

Honey shakes her head. "You gave me Burtie, who is more than

I could have ever dreamed of. He makes all the pain worth it, and maybe you've fixed Eliza. Jimmy and I need Burtie and Eliza. They're the future."

"I doubt I've fixed her. How am I supposed to fix anyone?"

"You care," she says. "That's what you do. There's nothing else that you can do, and everything else is extra." But who cares for him, the bearer of the caring? He may have slept in Maria's girlhood bed, but if Honey had been honest, everything would have been different. Still, stubborn Maria remains, the girl with the glasses studying them both.

He says, "What do I say when I tell her I'm leaving?" Everything bends, and the ground still tilts. The medical literature said that sometimes the effects of lysergic acid diethylamide-25 were permanent.

"You're not leaving."

"Why not?"

They pause, and Glenwyth sways.

"Because—" Honey chokes, unable to get out the words. "Because I want to do something goddamned right for a change." When he says nothing, she says, "Thank you. You want a ride home? You don't look like you could walk the block."

"That would be good. I'm, I don't know. I feel like I'm inside-out," he says, while she gathers her handbag and steps down into the waiting room.

"And to think I almost forgot," she says, removing the check from its envelope and laying it on the magenta table.

Jim turns off the air conditioning and follows her out onto the porch, then to the side driveway where the Lincoln is parked. Although storm clouds cover the sky, the heat remains in this endless summer. He opens the driver's door for her, and they are blasted with hot air. There's no sun, but there had been. Maybe this is the best use of a psychiatrist, to observe what had been and what could have been. What if he had never taken that chemistry class in '55?

"There's just one thing, Jimmy." Why does she always call him that? Just like the nuns and his mother. "When you're riding a horse and your seat—"

"What?"

"How you sit on the horse. When your seat isn't very good, you get thrown." Honey glances at her leg, and somewhere Quinton Graves grins sarcastically.

They say nothing the rest of the minute to his house. When they pull to the curb, Jim sees that the Mustang is absent but misses the Corvette parked at the elbow of Barker's Mill near Wingohocking.

She takes his hand, kisses it, and then rubs it. "Someday," she says, putting her finger to her lips.

"You'd want that?"

"Shhh," she says, and leans over him to open his door.

Jim gets out, she pounds the gas, and the Continental is gone. Dizzied, he struggles to walk the concrete path to his front door. It stands ajar, something almost normal in this topsy-turvy world. He throws himself onto the couch, ready to sleep, but something's not right. His bedroom, ten feet from his eyes, hums with energy.

He looks down the hallway and then rises, running. He has faced the NVA and VC, and he can open his bedroom door. Before he has the chance, a window breaks, its glass crinkling, and a naked man runs by the living room bay. It's Quinton, no longer quite so cocksure. Jim wants to burst into the bedroom and see Ruthie pull the sheets to her neck, but what's the point? Grounded? Lose TV privileges for a week?

He wheels around and sees a demon running by his front porch, turning north onto Barker's Mill. Jim pushes open the front door and looks toward the bend in the street, just catching his quarry jumping into the topless Corvette.

"Quinton!" he screams, but the engine's thunder silences the shouting. Jim is ten feet from the vehicle when the rear wheels come to life, spitting stone and leaving an empty parking space. The Corvette careens to the end of Barker's Mill and then squeals right onto Wingohocking, bursting into a cloud of psychedelic flame.

Jim seethes, ready for murder, but he also longs for his bed, where he should have been two hours ago. He can rest, think things over, but how can he let this all be? Maybe Ruthie's dead in the bedroom, murdered by Quinton. He should check on her, or he could kill Quinton. But what if she tells him that it was her idea all along? Can't deal with that now.

He hurls open the garage door, Ruthie's bicycle leaning against another peeling wall. Even a girl's Schwinn catches a Corvette if you pedal fast enough. But how to send the right message? Grabbing orange spray paint from the unruly nightmare of the garage, Jim throws the can in the basket, hops on the bike, and starts down Barker's Mill, the tragicomic clown that everyone has always known him to be.

Then the rain comes, and within seconds, it is sheeting. He can't ride the machine on the wet hills, legs already too big for the girlish frame. So he abandons the Schwinn. He runs wild down Wingohocking, paint can sticking out of his jacket pocket, the searing pain of his burn ripping through his body. An almost simultaneous flash of light and thunder make a proximal explosion, but Jim is spared. Passing drivers watch this soaking man in a suit running along a state highway, but no one slows or stops. Wingohocking waves like a ribbon, and Jim sprints up the driveway toward Sycamore Lodge.

Maybe a reasonable conversation should come first.

"Quinton!" Jim howls, smashing the brass door knocker into Republican wood. "Come down here!" No answer. "I know you're in there." He must be. Top now up, the Corvette sits on the gravel next to the door. "I just want to talk with you—like men!"

Silence.

"I've been stressed, and after you left my office, I was thinking how people can make mistakes. I'm not mad. Whatever has happened with Ruthie, I'm still in control! I'm keeping it together, no matter what." He tries to force the door, but the handle gives up nothing. "I'm un-firing you!"

Then the door opens, just a crack, revealing a chain and Evans noting the paint can. "Dr. Malory—"

"Yes, Evans, I'm so glad. Quinton—"

"He says that you will meet tomorrow at the regularly scheduled time. He is presently attending to other affairs."

"What? I have to talk to him now."

"I'm afraid he's indisposed."

"My ass. He was just having sex in my bedroom with my daughter."

Is there the slightest nod? Evans continues, "I'm sure he will be present on the morrow."

"There is no 'on the morrow.'"

"Dr. Malory, as you know, sleep may at times allow for better decisions."

"You really think so? I want to talk to him now."

"Please do think this over," Evans says. Firmness with a smile, like talking to the estate's butcher about the declining quality of the lamb chops. Jim stares. Where does the loyalty come from? Money? Or maybe Evans sees the man before him as the drowned dog that he is.

"Okay," Jim says. "Give my regards to the Court of St. James's." Then, walking to the Corvette without a care in the world, he pops off the spray can top and shakes it, an unseen ball rattling inside. Starting at the front bumper and then moving backward, he writes

OVER MY DEAD BODY.

Not a minute later, the words already blur in the rain. He wants to continue this orange diatribe, but the paint peters out into an oily mist. How many times has he told Maria and Ruthie to replace what's empty? Throwing the can against the side of the house, Jim scans the grounds, looking for something, anything to add an exclamation point. He runs to the pool, that place where his drowning began. Although a few of the freed gargoyles have been reinstalled, most sit idly by. He grabs one, a big one, and returns to the driveway. Like the ape in Kubrick's masterpiece, Jim raises the gargoyle and slams it down onto the Corvette's hood. Once, three times, ten. The previously black, even glistening metal becomes a cracked, deranged, pell-mell copy of Jim's cockeyed mind.

He wants to continue, to show what he really thinks, but instead he looks up at Sycamore Lodge and wonders how many saws were sold to build it. In a billion years, he'll never live in a place like this, not even in a poorer cousin like Oakmont. Jim can already see the moving trucks pulling up to the bungalow on Barker's Mill. He'll go to Swedesboro, where he'll treat farmer's wives and tomato tycoons, that is if Maria lets him come along.

Jim anticipates a few moments to walk around the grounds one last time, but when the three police cars arrive, he doesn't argue. Resourceful Evans must have called the cops at the first bellow, maybe even as Jim was running up Wingohocking. When he sees the batons, though, Jim resists, despite knowing better. He's never been cuffed before, and his wrists soon hurt, like everything else in his body these days. But he also feels secure, knowing it's all over.

When the police car pulls away from the main house, Jim stares back at it through the car's rear window. Evans and Quinton stand on the stone front steps, viewing the retreating cruiser with something between regret and pity.

11

Jim wanted to go to any other hospital and begged to be brought to the Glenwyth Clinic, but the VA was what he got. Officer Lord was one of the three responding. When he recognized the suspect, Lord relieved his comrades and removed the cuffs. During the hour it took to travel the twelve miles to the VA, rush-hour traffic on the flooded expressway, Jim sat curled in the shape of an egg. There were no pleasantries. There were almost no words at all. Afraid to address his prisoner, unsure that he even wanted the man to speak, the officer just drove, embarrassed for them both.

Deposited in the ER waiting room, Jim was then whisked to a nurse's office in occupational health. There he sat unattended for an hour, needles and scalpels within his glance. But he could no more hurt himself than he could high jump to the moon. All action was now impossible. If Jim felt anything, it was that he had become pure perception, and thus he would always be.

Sometime later, he was questioned by an unrecognized medical student who seemed interested in all things psychiatric, or at least in getting an A. The student dutifully questioned Jim for an hour and was followed by his attending. Jim figured he would have to repeat the saga, but the physician, having spoken to Officer Lord, had all that he needed. And so it was that Jim signed himself in. He didn't even have to be committed, which he would have been.

Within another hour, he found himself on the seventh floor in a single room. He knew Number 719 well, having rounded there many times. It was reserved for would-be presidential assassins and collectors of body parts. There was no furniture, only a mattress on the floor, and the walls were indeed padded, which always struck him as odd. Never in his career had he seen a patient hurl himself against a wall, but then he hadn't practiced in the years before Thorazine. The nurse who completed his admission was new and also unknown to him, making him half-wonder if his friends and colleagues had suffered their own reversals and been admitted to other hospitals across the city. Then he observed the name Nilso written on the chalkboard above the nurse's station.

The chief rarely lowered himself to cover the inpatient unit but was sometimes forced to do so when others took their vacations. Despite his usual absence, Nilso had decreed a pharmacological regimen for all newly admitted patients to receive intramuscularly: five milligrams of Haldol, two milligrams of Ativan, and fifty milligrams of Benadryl, or in the dialect of the floor, "five, two, and fifty."

Jim had thought the cocktail appropriate only for highly agitated patients and raised this point to Nilso in the previous months, but his superior brushed off the objection. Police calls to the unit were down thirty-seven percent since the new protocol was implemented, and both the nursing supervisor and police chief were pleased.

At the end of Jim's nursing assessment—no, he had no allergies to medication or food; no, he had no previous psychiatric treatment history; yes, he had had surgery, tonsillectomy at age twelve, and yeah, extensive debridement and skin grafting of his abdomen—he obediently rolled up the sleeve of the shit-colored pajamas in which he was now clothed and received the injection in his left deltoid. This had been Nilso's one policy concession. Originally, he had wanted to inject all inpatients at the buttocks, claiming that the location would provide an easier stick, but he relented when Santoni, who sat on the Restraints Committee, suggested that such an approach might recall traumatic experiences that some of the veterans had suffered, both during their tours and before.

As the needle goes in, Jim sees Ed sitting on his tree swing, sipping a glass of thirty-year-old scotch, shaking his head. The hallucinations are nearly gone now, and so the senior psychiatrist seems more of a shadow. Like a dog returning to his daybed, Jim is walked back to 719 and falls down onto the mattress. The nurse swings shut the iron door, and he hears the sound of the deadbolt. Looking to his side, he sees a sink, open shower, and seat-free toilet in his adjoining, doorless bathroom. He spreads his legs out across the mattress and feels cool metal and then something softer, grittier. Looking up, he sees that the mattress has leather restraints with buckles at all four corners, waiting at the ready, just in case.

When in the past he hypothesized himself in such a situation, as all psychiatrists do, he had been filled with horror and dismay. Now he wanders, lost in a cloud of acceptance. People develop problems, sometimes violent ones. Even that doesn't make them bad, even when they fail spectacularly. Like him. He tried and failed, but he always had the best intentions. It was true that destruction would be his wake, in and out of his family, but it happened. It was over. Maria had tried to become a physician but had failed because it was all too bright. What had she meant by that anyway? He once knew, probably, maybe twelve hours ago. His thoughts have normalized, the polychromatic shapes collapsed into points. He will sleep on the off chance that it has all been a dream.

But it hasn't been, and they're already talking at the A&P deli counter and the Glenwyth Cricket bar. No one is surprised. He knows what they're saying: *You have to be a bit off to be a psychiatrist.*

With Nilso's pharmacotherapy, Jim should be falling into black sleep, but perhaps because of the lingering effects of the hallucinogen, he soon wanders to a Glenwyth of the mind where the sun has risen high into the sky. The air, no longer humid, bites his skin. The summer is over, and the inexorable march to frost and blizzards has begun. The trees, though, maintain a perfect green, if only for another day. Neither automobiles nor people line Glenwyth's streets, and the town has assumed the depopulated look of its rural Pennsylvania cousins, true villages in remote locations whose commercial significance and reason for existence have passed into memory. While growing up in Lehighton, he drove with his mother through these Kleinfeltervilles and New Philadelphias, and imagined them to be ravaged by a plague. The population of the world heaps into taller piles, and these towns shrink.

This Glenwyth is also silent, but instead of being flat in its center like the real town, it has become San Franciscan, so that the walk from the A&P to his office involves an exponential grade. Before he went to Vietnam, he spent a weekend in the City by the Bay and passed through a neighborhood so mountainous that its end-parked cars seemed ready to roll over each other down into the Golden Gate. At the Glenwyth playground, which now extends to the limit of Jim's vision, the terrain is even craggier, with deep green pits and spiking elevations dominating the landscape. Unlike the rest of the town, it is littered with children, from crawling babies to fully formed adolescents, throwing balls and playing other games. He turns away from the pleasure park to a cave that he knows will take him to Barker's Mill Road, and it does. Emerging at its other end after only a few yards, he stands on the concrete walkway between the two postage stamps of his front lawn, and he sees similar cave entrances near the other houses along the street, which are now pink, purple, teal, and aqua. The neighborhood is a Bermudan village, with only his house remaining as it was.

He enters the front door, and Maria presses clothes in the living room, the ironing board wedged in front of their small black-and-white television. He notices that he's clad in his full-dress uniform, worn maybe five times during his tour and burned upon his return. He passes by her unacknowledged and enters their darkened bedroom. From memory he finds their bed. After undressing and laying his clothes carefully on the floor, he enters it. Ready to sleep, he extends his legs across the mattress and realizes that he has a guest. He touches the other's leg, hesitatingly and then boldly, measuring its circumference with his hand. It is not Maria's. He grabs it now, searching for the extended divot of a scar. It's not even Honey's. He feels the outlines of cultivated muscles, and knows that he's in bed with another man, asleep and not roused despite the tactile explorations. Jim jumps on top, fixes his two hands to the man's neck, and squeezes. The motion is not violent but gentle, unending, and almost loving.

There was and is more, but Jim doesn't remember it and never will. The rest of the evening is penumbra. When he wakes the next morning, he thinks for an instant that he has fallen asleep on an overnight shift, and powerless to reach the call room, has been given a bed by the nurses. Then he sees the restraints.

There's a knock on the door, and he's greeted by the starched white form of Nurse Tucker.

"And how are you today, Dr. Malory?" The sane often employ

unnecessary, introductory conjunctions when speaking to the berserk or imbecilic.

He tries to speak, but his larynx may have been removed. He tries again and manages, "What time is it?"

"Three-thirty." There's a slight pause. "In the afternoon."

It's remarkable that he has been allowed to sleep, and in fact, a violation of Nilso's protocol. Although pounded by a headache, his mouth dried and cracked, Jim feels calmer, almost happy. He looks around the room, and its lack of furniture and decorations pleases him. With nothing crammed into the space, so unlike the bungalow on Barker's Mill, his thoughts can expand to their proper size. Maybe that was his previous problem—no room to think.

She holds a tray, VA issue. "Are you hungry?"

He can't say for sure. He feels a twinge of nausea, but this may be an aftereffect of the poison, or maybe because he has not eaten in more than a day.

"I could try."

"You should," she says, laying it on the floor next to his mattress and looking sad. Maybe she doesn't think him insane, or maybe she does and has all along. He takes the cover off the plate and sees the puree. Jim wants to remind her that his teeth—if not his brain—still function, but the words would be wasted. Sometimes the entire unit gets puree.

"Where's Nilso?"

"Came by on morning rounds," she says. "He tried to wake you, even though I asked him not to. Anyway, he couldn't. You were out."

"Was he alone?"

"No."

"Who was with him?"

"You know, those three med students. They're back."

"He brought them in?" Jim asks. "I'm an attending."

Tucker shrugs. It's not like she's the dean of the medical school.

Jim could try to explain that he was saving his daughter from a psychopath, but he hasn't told the truth so far, and so why should he start now? Better: he will sleep through the admission. He's seen other patients pursue this strategy, a hunger strike of the tongue and mind. Most attending psychiatrists detect it quickly, though, and devise their own corrective responses, which never work. Distracted by other patients, boredom, and the desire to make rounds as brief as possible, psychiatrists end up ignoring the inmates who won't talk, ascribing their muteness to personality disorders and "organic" pathologies. Barring agitation, violence, or any other noteworthy behavior, the silent patients are soon discharged, with a plan more or less to do nothing.

"Is Nilso coming back?" Jim asks.

"Should be for afternoon rounds, but without the students. They'll be in ECT."

Jim should ask Tucker why she doesn't call it shock therapy like everyone else, but he understands. Nilso has decreed that "shock therapy" should not be used in place of the acceptable "electroconvulsive therapy" or the preferred "ECT." Abbreviations are always better because of what they hide. Just last month, four new machines were installed, which means there will be an open slot for Jim.

"Thing is," Tucker says, avoiding Jim's eyes, "I need to give you your a.m. meds."

"What?"

"Haloperidol five and Cogentin point five. Nilso's orders."

"But he hasn't interviewed me yet."

She looks down at the floor, her embarrassment joined with the slightest annoyance. When one of your own is on the inside, you may feel sad about it, but Malory's still a patient.

"You know, if it were up to me," she says.

"Right. You want me to take them now?"

"Here." She produces a tiny, flanged paper cup. He could cheek the pills, but if he's discovered, Tucker will be reprimanded by the nursing supervisor, who makes a point of telling everyone that black nurses are lazy. He swallows the tablets and chases them with the cranberry juice cocktail on his tray.

There's a knock on the metal door.

"Dr. Malory," Nilso says, "glad to see you up."

"I'm going to leave you boys to yourselves," Tucker says. "I have medications to count and reports to file." And she's gone.

"So what happened?" This is how Nilso begins his interrogations, *just the facts ma'am.* When Jim started at the VA, he was obliged to attend training sessions in which the chief expounded on the art of the psychiatric interview. A neutral, dispassionate stance was best to snatch the truth from the patient, Nilso said. In certain cases, the interviewer should even avoid eye contact, placing one's sightline perpendicular to the subject's. The goal was to exude a calculated mildness with just the suggestion of force.

"I was poisoned," Jim says.

"Poisoned? That's positively Schneiderian," Nilso says. "Did you swallow your medication?"

"I was really poisoned. It was a patient in my private practice."

"The one whose car you vandalized."

"That's right," Jim says.

"How did he poison you?"

"I'm not quite sure, but I think it was a hallucinogen in a Pepsi. We were in a session. He offered me a beer, and of course I didn't want that."

"But why would he have even offered you a beer?"

"It's a long story. He offered me a Pepsi, and I drank it."

The chief laughs, and the cellulitic ring around his abdomen jiggles. Nilso tends toward obesity, which he tries to address with anorectic eating habits at lunch meetings. He says, "As practitioners, we must never accept gifts from our patients."

"Sometimes it's rude not to."

"And yet we get ourselves into trouble when we do. Don't you think?"

"Depends."

"I want to tell you a story, if I may." Jim prefers that Nilso doesn't, but resistance is futile. The chief is the one with the key. "In '51, I was in Korea as a general medical officer, before my residency, and there was a young man who was brought in with severe battlefield trauma. They fixed most of him up pretty well, but his right arm, his writing arm, was in bad shape, major nerve damage, and the arteries too. The surgeons, you know." Here Nilso makes a slashing movement with the edge of his hand. "'Not worth it,' they said, to do anything else. So, in the team meeting, I offered to change the dressings every hour if I had to, wet-to-dry, remember those? I worked extra for a month, hourly saline irrigations. I was like a goddamned nurse, really. I spent hours keeping the arm so clean you could eat off of it, and it never became infected. The surgeons were so impressed they put in their own overtime, spent weeks on reconstruction, even brought in a colleague from Tokyo, and the kid got better. When it was done, he had pretty good function and no pain, a complete miracle.

"So he's sent back to the States, and I forget about him. A few years later, I'm sitting in my apartment on Woodland Terrace. You can see it from here. It's a rare day off from residency, and a truck pulls up, and out pops the young man whose arm I saved. He sought me out, and from the back of the truck, he emerges with a television. I didn't have one of course, and I wanted one badly. Remember all the great shows, like *The Colgate Variety Hour* and *The General Electric Theater?* Turns out the fellow had started a TV shop, which today has seven locations. If you've bought a TV recently, you probably purchased it at one of his stores. Now, here's the question. Did I accept the television?"

Jim's feeling the Haldol, everything slowing.

"No," Nilso says. "Of course not. You might think that I should have, he was grateful for me preserving his arm, but we are the physicians, and they are the patients. We must never forget that." Jim wants to follow the story, to learn from it. Instead, he's transfixed by the remaining island of hair just above the center of Nilso's forehead, long enough to create a partial comb-over.

"It was a Pepsi," Jim says. "It wasn't a big deal."

"But indeed it was."

"He poisoned me."

"If even true, that proves my point, but I'm not here to lecture you. Let's talk about this quote-unquote poisoning." Nilso draws the quotation marks in the air with his fingers. "What was the substance?"

"I left my gas chromatograph at the office."

"There's no need to be sarcastic."

"I don't know."

"You were poisoned," Nilso says. "You, if anyone, should know. Did you study the signs and symptoms? Remember your toxicology."

"There were colors, shapes. Things were bending, exploding. It was visual. It was probably LSD."

"Ah-hah!" Nilso says and produces a paper from his suit jacket pocket. "There's a signed statement from your patient Quinton Graves, the owner of the Corvette, as you know. He says that it was, in fact, you who quote-unquote administered lysergic acid diethylamide-25 to him as part of the clinical study quote-unquote that you had designed and were carrying out at your office in Glenwyth without sanction from the university or any other governing authority. Haven't you heard of the Tuskegee experiments? They were just in the news!"

"He's lying. Obviously."

"Obviously? Obviously?" Nilso had been looming above his patient. Now he sits down on the floor next to the mattress, placing his hands on his knees. "It's a shame. A few years ago, this would have been inappropriate and strange. Now it's a federal crime."

"I don't do drugs. I've smoked marijuana twice in my life." It was everywhere in Vietnam, but when Jim tried it, he thought the world was even more against him than normal. They called it paranoia, and for the past month, Jim hasn't needed marijuana for that.

"Your daughter certainly has taken to it."

"She's having a tough time," Jim says, wondering if one punch could take Nilso down. "That's also due to Quinton Graves."

"And so you blame the patient, now dating your daughter? Is this really what it comes to?"

"I'm not following you."

"Don't you see? Do I have to explain it? I've been speaking with Dr. Santoni." So Ed's in on it too. "We've both had concerns about you for some time. Your behavior has become erratic, your methods reckless. I suppose it started with your chasing that patient from the hospital."

"He was going to kill himself."

"But there are protocols, procedures."

"And if he wound up dead?"

"We have a system of care," Nilso says, "and the system must be maintained."

This is the system in which psychotic veterans wait months for appointments and suicidal patients are discharged from the ER so they can jump off the Market Street Bridge. Jim could say all of this, but slowness drags him, as much physical as mental. He has become stiff, and moving his limbs is difficult. The rigidity also controls his mouth, making even single words a chore. The nausea grows stronger, and he notices that hives cover his arms. He's never had asthma, but his breathing becomes effortful.

"So tell me," Jim says, "what else did I do wrong?"

"We could discuss your car sessions with Mr. Black. I'm sure you know that I could fire you for even seeing that patient outside of VA. He was my case, but more importantly, it's like you're stealing government property."

"He didn't want to go to the VA."

"Again, we have a system, and our policies and procedures must be followed. I'm trying to save your career, and this is how you act. I know you don't believe it, but I've always liked you. Your work hasn't been very good, that's true, but I kept you on because you're a veteran, and I know what you've been through. I've read all the reports, the crash in Cambodia, et cetera, et cetera."

Jim responds to this monologue by vomiting onto the man's shoe. With almost nothing consumed in the past day, little comes up. The chief, rolling his eyes, wipes his shoe with a hankie, exits to dispose of the soiled cloth, and returns. Trash cans, which double as weapons, are never found in isolation rooms.

"Now," Nilso says, "let's talk ECT."

"For whom?" Jim replies.

"Well, of course. For you. You know that no medication, no talking even comes close." The chief was right. When all else failed, ECT could restore the patient to sanity in twenty sessions. Jim's memory might be erased, and his bones might crack, but at least he would be happy.

"I don't feel well," he says, sinking into the mattress. "I'm having an allergic reaction."

Nilso ignores the complaint and continues his discourse, now imagining voltage, amperage, and unilateral versus bilateral electrode placement. "It's what you need. You won't regret it. Without it, your prognosis is poor."

"I'm fine," Jim slurs.

"No. You have malignant mania of the catatonic type. Unless we intervene aggressively, you're finished." Staring out of the cell's window, the chief waxes for another minute or two before remembering his patient. Then, like he's back in Korea, Nilso rolls up one of Jim's pajama sleeves and sees the hives rising on the man's arm like red smiley faces.

"Tucker!" the chief cries and jumps up to the door. Within a minute, he returns with the nurse and a syringe of adrenaline.

"All right," the major says. "Where do you want it?" Jim points to his left deltoid, and Nilso pushes the needle in with as much pain as medication. The guy can't even give a shot. Jim closes his eyes but not completely. After a time, he sees Nilso and Tucker observing him and conferring at the door. Nilso knows that more antipsychotic therapy is needed, but Haldol has now been pushed off-limits by the allergic reaction. Another neuroleptic could be tried, but none has the same efficacy. There remains, of course, an alternative that also happens to be Nilso's favorite: ECT.

The physician and his nurse converse, observing their rat immobilized in his maze. Nilso gestures toward his own temples, the same hollows where the electrodes will be placed on Jim. If ECT was good enough for Thomas Eagleton, McGovern's VP now kicked off the ticket, why not James Malory? Jim wants to scream that he'll never have it, he'll rip the water fountain from the floor like in that book, but his eyes close, and he sleeps.

~

Daylight again. The morning sun casts the shadow of a window frame on his wall. For two days, Jim has not left his cell. He has, however, eaten. A tray with crusty remains sits next to his mattress. The hives are gone, and he can breathe. Rested and calm, he sits up on the mattress, and for the first time since his admission, understands. Twenty years of preparation, study, service, and practice have been incinerated in a single night. He has made the unanticipated journey from doctor to patient and will now forever be known as a nut job. Even if people again unimaginably trust him with their lives, they will still say, *Now wasn't he the guy who lost it, maybe back in the seventies?* Knowing that he has to explain all of this to Maria and Ruthie, he stands and walks to the door. Locked of course. He tries it again and lurches forward into Tucker.

"Dr. Malory, you look bright-eyed and bushy-tailed." The wide pronunciation makes him think of a porch in South Carolina. Maybe he can still count on Tucker, versed as she is in the ways of getting screwed. It was just a blink ago when the system was locking her out of the Lincoln Memorial and Woolworth lunch counters.

"I need to see my chart, Aldyce."

"Dr. Malory, you know I can't do that, but don't worry. Mrs. Malory's here, and I don't think she's one to be told what to do."

"And Ruthie?"

"No," Tucker says, staring at him like he's just made an off-color comment.

His dread of Maria's appearance and having to explain everything made her previous absence not only acceptable but desirable. But here she is, maybe less angry or maybe just as angry or angrier and even more eager to wrap up the whole unfortunate mess of the last seventeen years.

"She's talking to the major in the family meeting room," Tucker explains. "She's my kind of woman." The psychiatrist remembers the nurse and his wife talking up a storm at last year's VA Fourth of July party.

"Am I allowed to join in?"

Tucker tilts her head toward the meeting room. "Which is why I was coming to get you." She leads him there, and for the first time, Jim walks by the patients for whom he has cared as recently as the previous Wednesday and Thursday. Many of them are still present, and seeing their psychiatrist now dressed in his own pajamas, some accost him, others whisper, and still others seem unimpressed, like this was meant to happen.

"Hey Doc!" one says. "Your hands shaking yet?"

Another, "He don't drink."

The first, "Yeah, not much."

Whisking her patient by the gawkers, Tucker opens the door marked 730A. Where's 730B? In two years at the VA, Jim has never been able to find it. He has conducted multiple family meetings in this space, and the absence irks him each time. Why not just call the place 730? An engineer on duty told him why not: *Because that's the VA Way.*

Inside the room, Maria and Nilso sit on two adjacent sides of a square table. Bolt upright, she wears her pregnant interview suit, and she clutches a black, rigid handbag, one of Carmela's probably. Swollen with pregnancy, Maria also wears her reading glasses, and altogether, the image of severity makes her look ready for a funeral. Maybe she's already spoken to Honey.

Nilso, with his right arm spread across an adjacent chair, appears relaxed, like he's ready for a nightcap. Stapled papers array in front of him, along with a binder with three large metal rings for the inevitable notes from the coming decades of Jim's treatment.

"Hello, James," Nilso says. "Maria's been telling me that she'll be going back to medical school."

"That's what she tells me too."

"That's excellent. It's nice to have two breadwinners in the family. Can come in handy if one of you falls ill."

"I'm not ill."

"Anyway, I was discussing our plan with Maria." Waving away any objection from his patient, Nilso continues, "We can't give you haloperidol because of the allergy, and fluphenazine and trifluoperazine are on back-requisition from the Central Office. We could try to get them from one of the other Integrated Service Networks, but that would require an 8816, and I don't have the time, not to mention approval from the Deputy Undersecretary."

"I want to leave."

"Jim," Maria says. "Listen to him. Please. I told him."

"About what?"

She doesn't answer.

"You know, you could have killed her and your unborn child," Nilso says, the awkward moment drawing him in.

"Okay," Jim says. "I'll file for a writ of habeas corpus. I've helped other veterans do it, and I can do it for myself. I can sue in federal court, be my own lawyer if I have to."

"That's the problem with you, James," says Nilso. "You're always bucking the system."

"It's my right to go."

"Not necessarily."

"Remember that I'm discharged, honorably? You want my DD-214? You can't court-martial me."

"Court-martial? Don't be absurd. We're trying to give you a second chance and going above and beyond, I might add, because of your service. Like when we hired you."

Maria stares at the chief for a moment and then looks down in despair.

Nilso says, "This is complicated. If you were just a traveling salesman, I'd release you right away, but you're not, and the bottom line is that we can't have you treating other veterans or any patients for that matter unless you've received the appropriate treatment yourself. It's a question of public safety."

"Appropriate treatment?"

"Of course. ECT. It's been shown to eliminate mania—"

"And memory."

"I was speaking, thank you. It's been shown to eliminate mania even in the most malignant cases and much more quickly than medication, which we can't use anyway because of the allergy and the back order. You know all this."

"I'm not manic."

"Whatever you say," Nilso remarks.

"And what if I refuse? You fire me, and what else?"

"We follow the rules, which means that Dr. Santoni and I will examine you, and then, assuming we agree, petition the court to convert your voluntary commitment to an involuntary. Then we can complete your treatment, by whatever means necessary." Jim imagines spending Christmas on the unit with its plastic tree, the inmates' families allowed to visit for an extra thirty minutes once a year. Despite the chief's penchant for swiftly discharging drug addicts and those with personality disorders, he has defined a psychiatric subset for which he favors long-term commitment. Of the forty patients on the ward, ten have been there longer than a year. Maria is trembling.

"Fine," Jim says. "Summon the inquisitors."

Nilso shakes his head. "How did you ever make it in the Army?"

"I didn't."

"No, you didn't," Nilso says.

"Or maybe I did."

"How's that?"

"By knowing when to tell people like you to go fuck themselves!"

The chief turns to Maria. "Now that's what I was telling you about. Superficially, it appears that his thoughts are linear and logical, the defense of counterphobic humor being used to create the illusion of normality. Yet the paranoia bubbles below the surface, as when he uses the term inquisitors, and then it flashes into rage. He can lash out at any time, emotionally or physically. He nearly killed you. I know you want to talk with him privately, but it may not be safe. In any case, here's the panic button," Nilso says, pointing to a red circle underneath the tabletop.

"Jim," she says, turning to him, tears messing her makeup, just as they have since she was seventeen. "Please."

"We can call the VA police if you like," Nilso says. "You know they're right downstairs."

"Can I please just talk with my wife?"

Nilso gets up and rubs his hands, washing away the whole affair. "Don't forget the panic button."

He leaves, but Maria says nothing. She's been struck dumb, her face a chaos of misspent mascara. Her hands are hidden, and he's unsure where they've gone. When he moves to her side of the table, he sees that Maria's fingers, swollen and scabbed at their ends, nails chewed to small crescents, polish a silver cross and its white beads. It's the same rosary that hung over the edge of her girlhood vanity mirror on Roseberry Street. Jim has not seen her use it since the days when she walked barefoot with her mother through the streets of Swedesboro for the Feast of St. Alfeo, the martyr's tongue torn from his mouth before he was boiled in oil.

"Where's Ruthie?" he asks.

"With my parents, in Swedesboro."

"Is she okay?"

"She's a little better, I think."

"Thank God," Jim says.

"I'm scared."

He stares at the rosary. "That scared?"

"We should have been going to church all these years."

"There's nothing to be afraid of."

"Oh, yeah? I'm with my parents picking out baby furniture, and when I get back, a policeman tells me you've been committed."

"It was voluntary!" he says to Maria's stony coldness. "It's not that bad."

"Okay, then. Let's walk right out of here right now."

"You know that I can't do that."

"Because you're committed."

"Technically."

"Not technically. Be honest! Nilso told me the whole thing."

"About Honey?"

"Honey? What does she have to do with anything?" Maria hasn't wiped her face, and her flowing cosmetics make her look like she's been beaten, black bruises streaked across her cheeks.

"She came by right after it happened and brought me home, which is when I saw Quinton. Then I went to Sycamore Lodge. I was trying to talk to him."

"Trying to talk? By wrecking his car?"

"Don't believe Nilso," Jim says.

"What's not to believe? He showed me the police report and the pictures. You went crazy, hunted your patient down at his house, and then destroyed his ten-thousand-dollar car."

"But look at what he's done to Ruthie!"

"And so, because of that, you make Quinton the victim and push her in even closer? I can't cry anymore."

"He poisoned me," Jim says

"Right. Nilso mentioned that one." He tries to hold her hand, but she reels it back. "Don't touch me!"

"He did."

"With what?"

"LSD."

She wipes her eyes with a handkerchief from her purse. "Okay. I'm trying to process this. For kicks, he drugs you so that you have a hallucinogenic experience."

"Right."

"A bad trip?"

"You can call it that."

"And then you stalk him, trespass, and damage his property. Why?"

"Because of Ruthie." This silences her. "He's been bullied and/or ignored for most of his life. For some people, that becomes all that they know and all that seems real. And so they recreate it in other relationships. It's how they live. They don't know any other way."

"Why didn't you help him?"

"I tried, but he didn't want help. Then he went after Ruthie. He knew I would react. That's why he did what he did."

"You have to make it right," she says.

"It's too late."

"How do you know it isn't?"

How do you know it isn't? People change so little.

When Jim has nothing to say in reply, she looks at him in that same forlorn way she did when he nearly flunked physics. Back then, it was up to her to save him, and they both knew it. He has bungled things over the years, from his absurd assurances that she wouldn't get pregnant, to physics, to enlisting in the Army, and now this. It could have all been predicted on that date with the flat tire.

Clanging sounds from the hallway, and Jim jumps from his seat. He looks through the six-by-six steel-reinforced glass in the door and sees two VA policemen subduing an agitated patient as Tucker tries to deliver an injection.

"I have to get out of here," the screaming man says. "If I stay here, I'll go crazy!"

Trying to recognize the patient, Jim misses that his wife is crying again. She has taken off her glasses and put them in her purse. In her tears, she resembles the destroyed and pregnant teenager who delivered the news to him at Wanamaker's. The store has a branch near Glenwyth. When he goes there on occasion, he re-experiences the doom that came with Maria's news in 1955. There was nausea and sweating, and time stopped. With everyone else in the restaurant, including Maria, frozen, he looked to the ceiling and saw his freedom ascending to the heavens like a cloud of gas. How did she feel about that moment? He's never even asked her.

"You're never there," she says, "and it's the only thing I've ever wanted."

"What?" he says. "There's been a lot of stress. We're having another baby."

"Right, and you never wanted the first one."

"That's not fair. It's just not what we were expecting back then. We were kids."

"You wouldn't have married me if I hadn't gotten pregnant," she says.

"Why do you say that?"

"Because you wouldn't have. It's true."

"Of course I would've." Would he? It's been the question of his life, and he can no more answer it now than he could have on his way to Swedesboro that early winter afternoon. Honey, always Honey. He ignored her as a sideshow at first, and then actively denied her, but even back then, there was a glint in Maria's eye that said: *Watch out.*

"Be honest," she says. "You don't love me."

"I am being honest, and I do. I don't know why you're doing this." Maybe she's doing it because Honey's told her everything. Maybe there's been a *tête-a-tête* near the canned vegetables at the A&P.

"Let's start with you strangling me in Cape Cod," Maria says, smiling now, gaining her rhythm.

"It was a nightmare. A lot of guys have it. You said so yourself."

"And Freud said dreams are wishes."

"He was wrong, okay?" Jim says, a sour taste in his mouth, remembering how implausible her forgiveness had seemed at the picnic table. "It wasn't you. I have this recurring dream about when the Huey crashed. There are VC and NVA all around. One of them is about to get me, and the only way I survive is by killing him."

"It's not a dream, is it? You actually did it."

"No."

The whites of her eyes are showing. "You did, and so it's another thing you've never told me. You killed someone."

"I'm a doctor. I'm supposed to keep people alive, not kill them."

"So you did."

"I don't want to talk about it."

"But you're making Black talk about it. Why shouldn't you? You took another person's life, and now you're punishing yourself for it. I understand that, I feel that, and if you could just share that, if you could share something that really mattered, really tell me what happened, you could make that, and us, okay."

"I'm not traumatized."

"That's the problem," Maria says, standing up like an avenging angel. "You're the most traumatized person I've ever met, and you can't see it. But I can see it. In case you haven't noticed, we're sitting in a family meeting room with you heading towards a 302 and our daughter, God knows what. And yes, I know what a 302 is."

"Okay, I did it. It really happened."

"And—"

"It didn't bother me. That's what you'll never understand, and that's why I've never been able to forgive myself."

"Who was it?"

"Some kid with a girlfriend. Some poor Vietnamese version of Quinton Graves."

Maria is crying again.

"See," he says. "This is why I don't say anything."

She mouths, "I'll be all right," but gets up.

"Please, sit down," he says. "You can't understand unless you've been there." This explanation does nothing. "Maybe I should go away."

For a moment, Maria doesn't argue. Then, like someone seeing a mess that needs cleaning sooner or later, she says, "No. You didn't leave me then, and I'm not leaving you now." She puts her forehead in her hand. "I wanted you to leave back then."

"I know," he says.

She glares at him. "You have no idea." Then, releasing, "I had my own crazy ideas."

They say nothing for a time. Then, forcing down whatever memory has come into her mouth, she adjusts her skirt and brightens. "It will get better if you understand what this war has done to you."

War, if it were that simple. Vanished father, decayed mother, girlfriend pregnant after a month going steady. The traumas increased minutely and continuously. Then he had to crash and kill, like the under-counting of the solar day only rectified with a leap year. Black might understand, but Maria?

"It will get better," she repeats.

"Will it?"

"Of course. You're sad, but you're not crazy. I mean, not actually."

He evaluates her, as dark and beautiful as when they met. "When I saw that fucker in our bed—"

"Part of me is glad you smashed up his car," she says. "My

father's friends would have done worse."

He tries to kiss her, and she pushes him away. Then she smiles sadly and gives up. Her lips, cheeks, everything fleshy about her has enlarged, becoming ever more inviting. He runs his hand along her arm, but only for a moment.

"Nilso's going to try and have me indefinitely committed," he says, and her corneas glisten. "Maria. Please."

"I'm sorry. This is hard."

"Don't worry. I'm going to get out of here," he says, even though a year ago, he appeared at the federal building to testify against one of his VA patients in a similar situation. "Nilso's getting Santoni, like he said. I'll explain the situation to Ed. He'll understand, and I walk."

"And you trust Santoni? He was the one who dumped Quinton into our lives."

"I trust him," Jim says, trying to forget his thought of driving right through Santoni's garage.

"Like you trusted you'd get assigned to Walter Reed?" she asks. The plan had been perfect. Dr. Malory was to consult on the most challenging psychiatric cases at Centcom, and his wife and daughter would spend their afternoons strolling the streets of Georgetown.

Having not taken her eyes off him, Maria asks, "Have you been with someone else?"

"Have I been with someone else?"

"Yes."

"No," he says.

"Never?"

"Never."

"If you had and you asked me for my forgiveness, I'd forgive you. It'd be hard, but I'd forgive you."

"But there's no need."

"Of course, but if you lie, then you can't be forgiven because there's no person to forgive because you can't forgive a shadow." Maria grabs his hands and peers inside him. "Are you lying?"

"No."

"Are you sure?" she asks.

"Yes."

"Okay, then," she says, exhaling.

He wants to ask her about that doctor near Penn Station, the guy who almost made Ruthie and all her problems moot points. Jim asks instead, "What has Ruthie said about Quinton?"

"Nothing, but she obviously loves him." A pause, and Maria looks away. "And she knows that I know exactly what she's talking about."

"But why did she agree to go with you, then?"

"It was like something snapped when she heard they took you away," Maria says. "He's tried to call her. He may even have been wandering through the farm at night, but he's smart enough to realize that my father likes guns."

"God," Jim says.

"God is right. I just hope it's not too late for praying."

"What if I dropped this all," he says, "got a job with your father, and we lived in some ranch house in Jersey and never saw Glenwyth or goddamned Pennsylvania again? Would you think any less of me?"

"Of course I wouldn't, if that's who you were. But you're not. You're a psychiatrist."

"If I come out of this with a license," he says.

"I love you. It may sound incredible, but I also trust you." He looks at his wife and can almost believe her. "If worse comes to worst, the medical board will trust in you too. If you want to move, we'll move, but not to Swedesboro, somewhere west, Phoenix maybe, after I graduate. I always wanted to go there. You can practice in Scottsdale. I'll do my residency out there."

Honey used to talk about Scottsdale, Frank Lloyd Wright and Taliesin West. She was obsessed with Wright's place, along with *Carmen*, and said often that his compound inspired the silver box on Wingohocking. But Maria's never said anything about Scottsdale.

"There's more to the world than Glenwyth," she says, "and these people don't rule the world."

"What people?"

"People like Honey and Woody. People like Nilso. You think they do because they owned half the town where you grew up, but they don't. Did you know that an Iranian anesthesiologist moved in four houses down on Barker's Mill? The world is changing. Look at our deed for the house. There's a restriction on it barring sales to 'Jews, Mestizos, Chinamen, and the Colored.'"

"I guess they forgot the Iranians and the Italians."

"And people from Lehighton," Maria says. "People like Honey are what my father calls yesterday's story. They still control the Cricket Club, but someday even that'll change."

There's a knock on the door, which swings open before they have a chance to respond. Nilso has returned and sits down across the table from his patient and his wife.

"So what did you decide?" he asks.

"I'm fine," Jim says. "I've been stressed, but I don't have manic depression. I'm not suicidal, and I'm not psychotic."

"I never said you were suicidal. You're better because of the two doses of haloperidol you received before the allergy developed. You forget that I'm trying to help you. Your mania can be sent into complete remission with ECT. You can be normal again, or maybe I should say more normal than you've ever been."

Jim wants to clock his chief, but Maria intervenes and says, "My father happens to be friends with the congressman from South

Philadelphia. So my father can pick up the phone and tell a very powerful person about your harassment of a decorated veteran."

Nilso slants his eyes and says, "I'm still within my rights to petition for commitment and to jointly examine him with Dr. Santoni. It's for your safety and your baby's."

"If you call Ed," she says, "will you play fair?"

Nilso tightens, perhaps annoyed at a civilian calling a military physician by his first name. "I'll stand by whatever Dr. Santoni says."

"Good, and I'll share with Congressman Green how helpful you've been." Maria turns to Jim and embraces him, kissing him to make a point and staring right into his face. She says, "You are the best man in the world, and I'll always love you no matter what." Then she gets up, walks over to Nilso's side of the table, opens her purse, and plops a wad of makeup-stained tissue onto the chief's lap. "Thanks for throwing this out."

When the three enter the hallway, the formerly agitated patient lies motionless on a gurney, drugged into compliance. After giving Jim one more hug, Maria passes with Nilso through the inner and outer locked doors into the world of freedom.

Jim ambles into the day room with its upright piano. This has always struck him as odd, given the improbability that some virtuosic inmate will entertain the patients and staff with Cole Porter. Someone has strewn coloring books and board games across the floor. A partly filled bookcase displays *A Summer Place, None Dare Call it Treason, Point of No Return,* and *The Report of the President's Commission on the Assassination of President Kennedy.* Jim has read or heard of these books and thinks it strange that Nilso has provided the unit's madmen, criminals, and drug addicts with a reading list of sex, conspiracy, substance use, depression, violence, and depravity. Jim plucks *The Warren Commission Report* and sees the name NILSO written in black marker across the pages' horizontal edge. Politics mostly bore Jim, but there would have been no Vietnam War if not for the Texas Book Depository and Lee Harvey Oswald. With his time in combat, trumped up as it was, JFK would have kept things to advisers, and no one would have called him a pinko. Instead, we got Johnson, a combat evader who spent his war inspecting planes and writing reports. When the shit hit the fan, he had no choice but to go all in.

Jim sits and joins the ward's other patients who have assembled to watch an Auroratone film. Nilso is a big fan of these movies, meant to soothe traumatized veterans with psychedelic colors. That's when Jim sees Dave Black, in the same brown pajamas, sitting and reading a newspaper.

"Captain," he says, laying down the funnies.

"What are you doing here?"

"I'm here for my session." Jim scans his patient's body, wondering if there's a wound.

"I heard you were in," Dave says, "and so I thought I'd keep you company. I hope you left the knife in your office."

"Did you—"

"No, but I told them downstairs that I was going to. I said I was 'SI HI.'" VA psychiatrists, including Jim, have abbreviated the phrases suicidal ideations and homicidal ideations as SI and HI, and observant patients have imitated the practice in their own complaints, thus producing the key to guaranteed admission.

"But were you thinking about it?"

"No, and I wasn't even going to kill anyone else except for Nilso."

"When did you get admitted?"

"Just got brought up."

"Have you seen him?"

"No, but probably later this afternoon. I'm just going to tell him I changed my mind about the SI HI stuff. When you're ready to go,

I mean."

"But he knows that you've been seeing me."

"I thought of that one. I'm going to say you cured me and that I had a bout of hysteria when I heard you were committed. Even if he moves me to Seven South, I'll still see you at the activities."

Knowing that Dave would fake an admission as a show of support makes Jim feel better than he has all day, but only for a moment. If Dave would do this, what else would he do?

"You can make it," Dave says. "Do you remember that first day that you were in-country, and you had 363 days left, assuming they gave you two days for the flyover?"

"Yeah." Captain Malory had expected his unit to be in drill formation when he arrived, but they were sitting in lawn chairs, shirtless, drinking Pabst Blue Ribbons.

"We have to get you out of here," Dave says, "so you can deal with Quinton. You're going to have to take him out, you know."

"Sorry?"

"One way or the other, he has to go. It's you or him."

"But he's my patient. Or was."

"Does that give him the right to abuse you and rape your daughter? Some people don't want to be helped. I knew a guy in the service who liked to sneak into villages at night and murder Vietnamese civilians. He'd kill them and cut off their thumbs. He had a box of them when he was arrested. Oh, yeah, then he would burn the bodies. He liked the smell. Could you have helped him?"

"Quinton will go away," Jim says.

"Sure, like the hooded man goes away after the trapdoor springs, and the prisoner hangs like a piece of laundry. You don't see it, do you?"

"I can fix it."

Dave's jaw extends, and his eyes blacken. "You think you can fix it, and I'll let you have your chance. But I'm not going left when

I should go right, and I'm not leaving the lights on anymore. This time, the crew gets back alive."

Santoni picks up a deck of cards sitting nearby and shuffles them. "So he wants to give you ECT?"

"It's ridiculous," Jim says.

"You have been a little excitable, but even Johnson didn't use the hydrogen bomb after Tet. Nilso's a hack. You and I both know it, but you can't deny that you've shown a major lack of judgment."

"I made some mistakes."

"Some? You're not going to last if you continue like this."

"Here we go again," Jim says.

"Do you want to get out of here?"

"Of course."

"Then give me something to work with. Will you see someone after your discharge? Not Nilso, not me."

"Yes. Anything."

"You promise? You'll be a better psychiatrist for it."

"Will I still be a psychiatrist?"

"Quinton's not filing any charges, but you can't say what he really did. At least for now, he's still your patient. They'll arrest him, and he'll sue you for malpractice, breaking confidentiality, and all that sort of thing."

"But he's made threats," Jim says.

"What evidence do you have that they're credible? Do you have them on tape? Exactly. So let it go. He's won, and now he'll leave you alone."

"He's not like that."

"Now you are sounding paranoid," Ed says.

"I'll be less paranoid when I get out of here, and by the way, when do I get out of here?"

"Now, if you want."

"Just like that?"

"You're not crazy, at least not all the time. Anyway, I should have sent Quinton elsewhere, and getting you out is the least I can do."

"Better late than never, but thanks," Jim says. "What about Black?"

"They know why he's here." Dave's been making his way through the unit like a USO entertainer, doing everything but giving autographs. "But first, we have to meet with Nilso."

"Is he on the floor?"

"I can check." Santoni goes out into the hallway and returns several moments later with his colleague.

"Gentlemen," the chief says.

"I know we don't normally discuss examinations in front of the patient," Santoni says, "but I think he could learn from it. Okay. Dr. Malory has traumatic neurosis but no manic depression. That's it."

"Did you actually evaluate him? You weren't in here long."

"I've known Jim for fifteen years, more or less. I also think that he was poisoned with a hallucinogen. Why or how, I have no idea, but the synesthesia, color abnormalities, and warped perceptions fit the literature."

"Which he may have read. Or he may have taken it himself, to tune in, turn on, and drop out."

"For what motive?" Santoni asks, and Nilso says nothing. "He agrees to outpatient treatment, and I'll guarantee that he gets it."

"Would you consider, Ed, for a moment and just this once, that maybe you're wrong?" A sarcastic smile curls along Nilso's lips. "Of course, I hesitate to say anything given your extensive wartime experience in the English countryside."

Santoni says, "Don, Don. Do you remember when you were my

intern?"

"I'm merely suggesting," Nilso says, "that we keep Malory for a time and observe the fluctuating course of his disorder."

"But he wants to go. That's my recommendation."

"That easy-come, easy-go attitude might work in your Glenwyth private practice where the greatest threat is too many G&Ts, but there's something wrong with him, of that I'm sure." Nilso glares at Jim and then turns back to Santoni. "Are we taking bets about where he'll be in a month?"

"I'll take responsibility," Santoni says, "and by the way, how did you ever get to be chief?"

Ignoring his peer, Nilso turns to Jim. "Then it's settled. The esteemed Dr. Santoni says that you're free to go."

"Thank you," Jim says to Nilso.

"Don't thank me."

"Should I report for this week's shift?" Jim asks.

Nilso stammers. "Who was it who said that history first occurs as tragedy and then as farce?"

"What about the medical board?" Jim asks.

"My, we are paranoid, aren't we? Don't you see it, Ed?"

"One thing at a time," Santoni says to Jim. "Why don't we get you out of this place before we worry about the system?"

"Well," Nilso says, "I'm going to let the great Dr. Santoni take the fall for Dr. Malory's next, more spectacular collapse. Nurse Tucker will process the discharge, and just remember, Captain, the system is the only thing letting you out that door."

~

It's dinner time when the meeting with Nilso concludes. Since Tucker functions as both a food dispenser and a nurse, there's no time to complete the discharge papers. The shift change follows, and she loses herself in distraction. Now that the threat of commitment has been lifted, no one seems to care that the psychiatrist remains locked on the seventh floor. It's like he's making rounds, even though he still wears pajamas. After dinner, Jim wanders into Black's room, and they reminisce about Vietnam: burning feces, military payment certificates, and The Four Tops playing everywhere. All that's missing is mefloquine chased with warm beer.

Dave will be discharged before dawn, another Nilsonian strategy to increase the unit's utilization numbers by extending hospital admissions after midnight. When the charge nurse who replaces Tucker gets to Jim, he convinces her to let him stay the night and leave with Dave, since he doesn't have a ride and doesn't want to disturb Maria with a drive into the city. He returns to his room and, putting his head down, sinks into sleep interrupted only by the sunrise.

It's not even 7:00 a.m. when Jim stands at his front door on Barker's Mill. The deadbolt slides, and he tiptoes in. Maria has shut all the windows, except the one that's smashed and still unrepaired. Why does she do that? After he opens them, the fall air flows into the silent living room. He sits there for several minutes and then decides to join his wife in their bed. He has no hope for intimacy, but if he can again get her reassurance, everything might just work out. Or maybe she's already up, reading in the kitchen. She'll make those muffins and coffee.

Thinking he'll try the bedroom first, he tiptoes to the door and knocks. Nothing. With a bit more firmness, he strikes the door and gets no response. Jim opens it, and she's not there. The bed has been made to perfection, reminding him of how he was instructed at Fort Sam. There's a letter with a single word on its envelope, a calligraphed *Jim*. He pulls open Maria's closet. Everything's gone but a few lonely hangers. Someone has also removed Maria's makeup from her dressing table. In the bathroom, only his toiletries remain. In Ruthie's room, posters of The Carpenters and Moody Blues, Nutcracker figurines, books, and clothes have all vanished. The movers have left only her bed, dresser, and desk, making a vacant dormitory room. And, goddamn it, all he can think of is another song. *Alone Again (Naturally).*

Taking the letter, he runs to the garage. The Mustang hasn't left him. Jumping in, Jim turns the ignition, and the engine leaps to attention. Pulling onto Barker's Mill, he drives down the street of his life. He stops at the corner of Athens, and he notices something odd. Someone has placed a letter-size piece of white cardstock in the center of the stop sign's octagon. It reads only: "Doctor." He continues on the road to the pharmacy and sees another card: "Malory." He turns to the left and spies more cards posted on multiple objects down to the intersection with Wingohocking and then back up the other side of the street in front of the A&P. He parks the car and starts running, reading each sign:

Is
A
Drug
Dealer
Who
Also
Cheated
On
His
Wife
With
The
Mother
Of
His

Patient
And
Poisons
His
Patients
With
L
S
D.

Having run one side of Athens to Wingohocking, and then doubling back to Barker's Mill, Jim crosses the street and soon stands in front of his office. Yet it is changed because similar cards now cover the building, all mimeographed with the purple, monotonic face of a screaming clown, hundreds of jokers welcoming him home.

He pulls Maria's letter from his pocket and opens it. It is written in fountain pen, his wife's habit, the perfect penmanship of thirteen Catholic school years, but the ink blurs in circles. The letter has either been written in the rain or cried upon.

Jim,

When I met with you in the hospital, I meant what I said. I loved you. I trusted you. Everything could have been okay if you had told me everything, but as I now know, you haven't told me anything. Even then, you lied to me, as you have for our entire marriage. I might have been able to forgive you if it had just been sex, but you always wanted her more than me, always wanted something that you and I can never be.

As difficult as it will be for me as a single mother, I will survive, with the help of those who love me and without the man who destroyed me, even as I never stopped trying to rebuild him. I will never stop loving you, okay I said it, and that's what makes it so painful that you've never loved me. I hope that Honey makes you happy.

Goodbye.

Not even a signature, as if she forgot or couldn't expend the emotional energy to affix her name. He crumples the letter, throws it to the ground, and runs to the corner of Barker's Mill and Athens.

In the minutes since he saw the first card, the town has awakened, and Jim has never before seen so many people in the streets. They look at the signs, and they look at him, knowing who he is, who he has always been.

When he was a boy, and his mother still could be remembered as the woman who had been beautiful and who had enjoyed the most expensive wedding Carbon County had ever seen, neighbors, shopkeepers, and even priests looked at her in the same knowing, told-you-so way. When his mother walked around town, the drink of choice was judgment, mixed with the bitters of contempt, but even this faded. In time, she withered to insignificance, unworthy even of scorn. She became a nobody, nothing more than the dried leaves collecting in the blue quarter-sphere of the municipal bandshell.

He could try to tear down all the signs, but what's the point? He sits down on the very same park bench where he once saw Ruthie and Quinton kiss, and the people of Glenwyth, seeing the truth and its ultimate irrelevance, walk on by, their faces down.

12

Jim doesn't have to cancel many appointments. His patients do it for him.

When he returns to his office, the answering machine is already filled with excuses and regrets, consuming the tape. He was ready to see patients the day after his discharge, calling that evening to lure them into the office, but the effort was futile. Word spreads.

The next morning, he sees Black, present for his scheduled session, and then spends the rest of the day staring out his window at Glenwyth, his schedule blown open with blank space. That evening, he places his own sign on the front door—CLOSED UNTIL FURTHER NOTICE—and begins to drink. He starts with beer and then moves to scotch. He has accumulated half a dozen bottles of the latter as gifts. People must have thought that his Vietnam experience made him a juicer. During his year in the hooch, he consumed his share of ten-cent beers and twenty-five-cent mixed drinks. There wasn't much else to do. With his return, he had tried to be sober, not drinking during the week, trying to set a good example for Ruthie. He failed.

Locked in his office, he considers pizza delivery but decides against it. He can survive with the nourishment of alcohol. He tries to read *The Case of George Dedlow*, recommended to him long ago by Santoni, but falls asleep on the loveseat. After a night of frequent urination, he awakens, brushes his teeth, and starts to drink again.

To eliminate the chance that Ruthie or her friends would ever raid his supply, Jim had stored his alcohol in the basement of the office, and so he need not go to the State Store or return to Barker's Mill for additional liquor. Honey was right about him and his taste for the sauce. He just hadn't admitted it, just like he hadn't admitted Honey to Maria.

He calls the house over and over, wondering if they might have returned, and each time, he hears Maria's voice, preserved for the answering machine: *Hello, you've reached the Malorys. We're not here right now, but if you leave a message, we'll be sure to call you right back. Have a great day!*

When was that recorded? She sounds so happy, but that was before their estrangement became apparent, when they could still simulate a marriage. Now Barker's Mill has become no man's land, and Jim weighs the possibility that he might never sleep there again. Maria and Ruthie have departed, and he has the loveseat here in the office. That his office bathroom has a shower, something he once considered a mark of unseemliness, is now welcome.

Finishing a bottle of scotch, he breaks the seal on a fifth of vodka. Its tastelessness is less threatening. Again, he attempts to read but with each try, disappears into sleep. He has adjusted the answering machine so that each time the phone rings, the caller's voice broadcasts from the speaker. There are several calls in the morning, but none from Maria, and so he ignores them. Dave phones, but Jim avoids him too. Around three in the afternoon, Jim contemplates a walk, but the thought of seeing a world beyond this room frightens him. So he drinks more and then falls asleep again. Another night passes.

After a still more irritated and interrupted sleep, he awakens Sunday morning, and Honey sits across from him in his own chair.

Maybe he's hallucinating, another electric blue bull or flaming tree. Sunglasses still on, Honey wears an orange and pink dress, covered with squares instead of elephants.

"Out of the frying pan and into the fire," she says.

"How'd you get in here?"

"The door was open."

He sits up and for a moment tries to organize the bottles that sit on his coffee table before sliding back into the leather.

"Please go," he says.

"No. I'll not have you survive Vietnam only to be killed in your consulting room." There's not much he can say to that, pickled as he is like a martini olive. "I want to help you."

"Like three years ago? Like two days ago?"

"I wasn't the one who told her, and as for three years ago, I wasn't there to help you. I wanted to help *me*. If you remember that afternoon, and I do like it was last week, you wanted to help me too. You even gave me your dog tags and cigarette lighter as mementos, which I thought was cute."

"Okay. Let's recreate the scene for a second," he says, slurring one or more words.

"You're not going to make much sense."

"I'm not that drunk, and don't change the subject. I'm about to be shipped off, no idea if I'm coming back. My wife has decided to divorce me, for the first time." Here, Jim hiccups. "And that's when you strike."

"I told you. I didn't want another baby with Woody."

"I was so drunk I blacked out! I thought we just kissed!"

"No."

He looks at his crotch. "It would have been impossible."

She pats her bum leg. "If you want something bad enough, anything's possible. Besides, I really didn't think you'd come back."

Jim stares at her, knowing she wasn't far off. "You're not even sorry?" he asks.

"Why would I be? I'd do it again. So would you."

"Don't tell me what I would do. And Maria—"

"She'll understand. I can explain everything."

"But you acted like Woody."

Here Honey takes off her sunglasses, revealing dark circles, two black eyes almost. "Now that's rather unfair. Don't you see? I'm no competition for Maria. We both know that. You provided a service, and I just wanted another child, end of story."

"Except when it wasn't, and you sent me letters courtesy of the APO."

"Was it so wrong to dream?" she asks. "You'll forgive me if life hasn't ground the romantic completely out of my soul."

"You could have—"

"Gone to New York for an abortion, like Maria would have done with Ruthie if it weren't for me?"

He pours himself another vodka. What's one more death in a sea of mortality? Suicide would make it all so easy, but he can't quite get himself there. He may have a mission: Because of the ruination he's caused, he has to live on and suffer.

"I suppose you left the kid home with a babysitter," Jim says.

"Actually, he's in the waiting room. He's very well behaved."

"What?"

"It was just for a second, and don't act like I should be reported to Children and Youth. He won't break anything."

"Until he wanders onto Athens and fractures his skull?" Jim jumps from the couch, bounds down to the stairs, trips, recovers, and startles when he sees the toddler sitting calmly in the waiting room, building a tower from blocks that his mother has secured from the toy chest.

Jim stares at the boy and immediately sees the resemblance that had for the past two years hidden before him in plain sight.

Looking up, Burtie says, "Where's Daddy?" When Jim says nothing, the boy returns to the blocks.

Honey stands next to them. "I locked the door, dummy. And I took down that ridiculous sign you put up."

Jim turns to the boy. "Are you okay?"

"I'm fine," he says, a smiling sunrise, and taking in Jim's breath, adds, "What's that smell?"

"Doesn't he have great language for a two-year-old?" Honey asks.

The boy goes to the window, points at the Mustang, and says, "Like that car. Can I have that car?"

"See?" says Honey. "He loves cars just like you, and you tell me that's not genetic? I'm sure he'll want an Aston Martin when he gets his driver's permit. I'm going to bring him upstairs with us because I know you won't want your son to see you drinking. Burtie, get your blocks."

The boy obeys, and the three of them go upstairs, Burtie and his blocks in Honey's arms.

"He's so beautiful," she says. "He's got your brown eyes."

If Jim had been asked in high school whether he wanted to have children, he would have said "sure," but it was the farthest thing from his mind in 1955 when Maria delivered her news. A daughter was one thing, somehow unthreatening, but a son, maybe two, presented Jim with an inescapable reflection of all his vainglorious failures. These were the same failures, modernized, that his own father had made.

"I should keep on drinking," he says, even as he sips nothing. "I wish I still had my forty-five."

"What would that do?"

"I wouldn't have to deal with this mess," Jim says.

"And you'd be making another one for your wife, your son, your daughter, your unborn child, and most of all me."

"Okay. So I stick around. My life is still over, just like that."

"It's not. She'll forgive you. She'll even forgive me."

"You don't know Maria."

"I know her better than you do," Honey says. "There's a reason why she got you, and I didn't. Don't you think I know that? Getting sick does something to you. Maybe it makes you honest."

Jim stares at Honey but thinks of Mary P. In the startling void of illness, one can't help but become more selfish, on the off chance that death might be cheated. In games that involve just one round, rule-following is for suckers.

"I don't suppose you know how she found out," he asks.

"I suspect that terrible boy Quinton Graves."

"How the hell did he know?"

She sighs. "I don't know."

He closes his eyes and shakes his head. "Eliza."

"I never told her," Honey says.

"She must have stolen the letters." These were the letters that Jim never burned and instead left in his bedroom, as if he knew deep down what would happen sooner or later.

"Maria will forgive you. I know it."

"With Burtie as proof for the ladies at the Civic Association?"

"She doesn't know about him. Nobody does. Nobody will. Except you. And me."

"And I'm supposed to carry that around for my whole life?"

There's silence, and then Honey says, "Things happen that you never expect, and you get used to them. In the first moments, you never think you will, but then you do. It's like with Jimmy. It was the end of the world at the time, and now it just is. It's sadness every day, that's true, but it just is."

Somewhere there's a girl whose leg was not crushed, who lived in an estate that wasn't crumbling, with parents who loved each other and didn't drink. There's also a teenage boy who can talk and a twin sister who loves her body instead of mutilating it. There's another boy from South Philadelphia with a brother who didn't die, and an Army doctor who spent his war at Walter Reed and didn't get on the wrong helicopter.

"More blocks," Burtie says. "I want more blocks."

"It's a shame you're not a child psychiatrist with more toys than just these pieces of wood. You might have had an easier time of it." She looks around the room and finds nothing to amuse their son. "I think he's getting hungry."

Burtie waves at Jim. "Come here. I want to show you."

Jim kneels and looks at the tower that the boy has built.

"It's going to go right to the sky," Burtie says.

"But isn't it going to fall?" Jim asks his secret son.

"Never."

"See?" Honey says. "He has all your looks and none of your negativity."

Leaving the boy to his construction, Jim says, "I got a call from Evelyn Graves. She'll be back tomorrow and wants to meet with me."

"What'd you say?"

"Nothing. She left a message. I'm exactly not in the position to reply."

"Don't worry. That kid's been a head case since he was sucking on his pacifier. They know it. Evelyn and I went to Stroud's. She was several years ahead, but we maintained something of a friendship, although she was very odd. People like you think that people like us just associate with each other because we judge the commoners and can't stand them. The truth is, we know that no one can stand us."

"Except those who envy you."

"But you of all people understand that's ridiculous," Honey says. "You've been to the after-party."

"I wonder if Tower, Tilney & Webb does malpractice law."

"Evelyn Graves is not going to sue."

"Yeah?"

"That's not something that people like Evelyn and Hugh do. They may fire you, but they'll probably have you to the Cape for a weekend in the process."

"You should sue me for how badly I did with Eliza."

"Not at all. We're doing family therapy, and it's helping. I've started to see how critical I've been. Eliza's never been smart enough, organized enough, thin enough. That's what I thought, and she heard it every day. When she realized she could never make me happy, she hated me and hated herself for her anger. So she decided she had to suffer and started cutting. If she wasn't good enough for me, how could she be good enough for herself? The truth is that I was never good enough for me."

The problem now seems as obvious as that flat tire in 1955. Jim understood as much about Eliza these many months, but why hadn't he just come out and said it so directly to Honey before everything went to shit? His vodka glass is empty.

"Also, I was always trying to make up for Jimmy with her," Honey says. Another breathtakingly clear observation that Jim missed. "Dr. Santoni figured it out and explained it all. I apologized for that, and I asked her for forgiveness. I also told her more about my own parents and how screwed up they made the world look to me, and that's when Eliza stopped cutting and purging."

With those words, Jim feels like performing his own self-mutilation. Perhaps he should try it to better understand his patients.

In any case, he's lost, and unconditional surrender is now his only option.

"I'm glad Ed's helping," Jim nevertheless says.

"He's very good. Don't get me wrong, you did a great job, and we could have never come to this point without your groundwork. You helped us, and now I can help you. I'm going to call Maria."

"Please don't do that," he says.

"She doesn't know about Burtie, and she never will, which means that the moment becomes just a drunken indiscretion. The dinner parties are over, and everyone will know, they already do, but they'll blame me. It's always the woman's fault, don't you think? It'll pass."

"Like your life before your eyes when it's almost over."

"She'll come back. Remember, she owes you one. You've done a lot wrong but also a lot right, like when you didn't run back in '55."

"I'll try to remember that." Jim tries to look away and ignore this force of nature, but he has never been as fascinated with Honey as he is now. She survived the pulverization of a leg, the alcoholism of her mother, the autism of her son, the philandering of her husband and father, and the self-destructiveness of her daughter. Cured of the illusion of a happy world, she has become impervious. She will do quite well mothering and fathering Burtie herself, thank you very much, and Jim, despite his touching concern, need not apply. Notice how she hasn't asked for his assistance.

Instead, Honey will care for Jim, if only with occasional inquiries and Christmas cards to the PO Box where he will receive mail once he is hounded out of Glenwyth. As he sinks to lower social stations, she will regard him at first with concern and amazement, but then with disgust. Finally, her skin will crawl when she sees him. If Burtie turns out not quite as anticipated, everyone will know the reason: His father was a bum. At his funeral, because Jim will die before them, Honey and Maria will be the lone mourners, each looking at her watch. In the aftermath, the two old ladies may even become friends again, united in their disappointment with him.

"I don't suppose you want a drink." He offers his vodka to her.

"No. I have to take Burtie home for lunch, but how about making this your last one?"

The idea is ridiculous. "I'm just getting started."

She shakes her head. "This isn't the end of the world, and things can always be worse."

"How?"

"Well, there's a pain in my breast that won't go away. I have a mammogram in town after Labor Day."

"Nothing could kill you."

"I hope you're right." Pushed off balance by some invisible force, an empty vodka bottle thuds onto the carpet. "Last one, okay?"

"Maybe," he says, rising and walking toward the consulting room door, which he opens. "Goodbye."

"No, no, no," Burtie says. "Not leaving. I'm climbing to the sky."

Jim says, "I'll see you soon, Burtie."

The boy says, "Really?"

"Really."

Burtie hugs Jim's legs and says, "I'll put the blocks back downstairs."

"Thank you."

After a final this-is-how-bad-goes-to-worse stare, Honey departs with the boy, and Jim begins the rest of his life. There's still much more liquor in his office to be consumed, but maybe not just yet.

He opens the window overlooking the parking area and shouts,

"Louisa! Is that all there is?"

Honey and Burtie look up at him, not sure what to say. She stares at Jim, waiting, thinking that maybe he'll say something, hoping, waiting some more, maybe there's a chance. But in the end, he says nothing, and with the toss of her hair, a horse's tail really, she leaves with their son.

After another hour of vodka shots, he can no longer stand, throws up, and collapses on the loveseat. The psychiatrist awakens hours later and wonders whether his son sleeps, whether Honey and Maria sleep. It's night, and the crickets talk to each other beyond the open windows of his office. A drill bores into his temples, and his mouth has been desiccated with sickly sweetness. Jim surveys the empty glassware and considers the fate of his liver. Combined with the alcohol, ten grams of acetaminophen might do him in, leaving a yellowed parchment on the consulting room floor. In practice here for less than two years, he has spent his share of sessions convincing others not to take their own lives. The counterarguments were several and varied by patient—only God can take a life, your family would be destroyed, it's too easy a turn for someone like you—and with each admonition, he felt hollow. After all, what the hell did he know about why someone crushed by pain should choose life?

Incredible. He has come to understand his patients and their hopelessness at the exact moment that he's no longer able to help them. You navigate life with just the compass of control, however imaginary, and when that's taken away for whatever reason, there are only sea monsters and hurricane winds. Some captains go down with the ship, but the sinking is never the result of weakness. The shipwreck comes from the loss of an illusion.

He picks up the phone and dials the house in Swedesboro.

Angelo answers. "Hello?"

"Hi," is all Jim can manage.

"Hiya. She's asleep."

"I'm—"

"Married," Angelo says. "You're married."

"I'm not so sure."

"The two of them are in the same bed, Maria and Ruthie. Just like on Roseberry Street." Just like when he was in Vietnam.

"How've they been?"

"Ruthie's okay. Maria, well—"

"How's the baby?"

"Pietrolongo says she's okay. Came all the way out from Methodist to do a house call. That's dedication. Or maybe he just likes Carmela's gravy. He thinks it's a boy from all the hair on her belly."

"I'm sorry."

"Listen, nothing's ever one-sided, you know."

"Please ask her to call me tomorrow."

"Maybe not tomorrow, maybe not even the day after, but soon. She's never been able to hold a grudge, even when she should, if you know what I mean."

"I deserve that."

"You should have taken that Coast Guard thing, you know. I didn't want to say anything at the time. Well, most people don't deserve what they get. Try again tomorrow."

Angelo hangs up, and Jim sets down the receiver. Outside the consulting room, Glenwyth sleeps. Although he still wears the clothes from his final attempt at psychiatry, Jim has replaced his wingtips with sneakers. *Most people don't deserve what they get.* But there's less exoneration in Angelo's statement than a repudiation of the very ideas of blame and credit. Things just happen, and the world is a random place.

When he was a senior at Precious Blood in Lehighton and captain of the cross-country team, he had the idea that if one run a day put him in good shape, two would be even better. He would run for the second time each afternoon with the team, but his first jog of the day was solitary—at 0300 each morning, long before the idea of sunrise. Even in Lehighton, where men started at 0600 at Palmerton Zinc or for the Valley, the streets were deserted

In those days of the 0300 runs, there was only possibility and potential. Sprinting down Lebanon Street in the dark, he imagined that his departure from the town would occur in similar blackness, and he felt domination over the bandshell, the BPO Elks, and the town's library, an exalted sandstone building donated by Andrew Carnegie, not that the man had ever been to Lehighton. Carnegie's library was an ironic commentary on the town because in Lehighton there was only impermanence. Six months after those runs, Jim was ninety miles south and a million miles away. At least that's how it had seemed, but maybe Jim's life was itself an ironic commentary on what he now understood: He had left Lehighton not at all.

Locking his front door because there will be no more visitors, probably ever, Jim walks onto Athens and turns toward Soapstone. Although the houses are better maintained and the cars are nicer, Glenwyth is Lehighton. It's just as full of life, death, lust, and pain, playing like a Moebius strip. At the intersection, he jogs, limp and all. Still clad in a days-old dress shirt and suit pants, he takes it slowly. Since the burn, it always hurts when he runs, but the night conveys him down Athens, where someone has removed Quinton's libelous signs, and onto Wingohocking. He follows it down to the creek and then turns up the driveway to Sycamore Lodge, panting.

Unseen, Jim circles the mansion, now brightened by multiple illuminated rooms. The black Corvette has been replaced by a cherry red one, still a '67, and a Rolls-Royce Silver Shadow sits next to the sports car on the gravel driveway. Quinton's parents have returned.

Jim retraces his path down the driveway to Wingohocking and considers running to the silver box atop the hill. Maybe Eliza and Honey will take him in. Maybe Eliza will even call him Dad. Instead, he follows the deserted state highway back into the center of Glenwyth. There, he takes a left onto Athens and continues past his office into the park, running its perimeter. From there he moves back down Athens and takes a left onto Barker's Mill. Jim soon stands panting in front of his house, so different from the night he returned from Cape Cod with Maria. Every window has been blackened, reminding him of his boyhood nights waiting for the Germans to bomb Lebanon Street. He walks up the two steps to the porch and sits on the rocker. When they had moved to Glenwyth a decade ago, the town's center was filled with widows and was ignored by families searching for acre lots, flagstone patios, and barbecues. Now, young couples, a group from which he has become doubly excluded, want the village lifestyle. At least that's what the real estate agent told him when they dreamed of a bigger place earlier this year. What was her name? Maybe Jim should call her. Two houses on Barker's Mill have sold above asking in the past month. Maybe the Malorys' former home, despite the pre-war appliances, will sell quickly. When he and Maria attend the settlement, the buyers, well aware of the owners' schism, will wonder how it happened. After the closing, the divorcees will have the awkward moment in the parking lot when they depart, two separate persons holding two separate checks.

Sometime later, Jim gets up and opens the door, which is unlocked. He doesn't think much of it. The stained bed and compromised furniture might as well be stolen. Maria will never live here again.

He walks down the hallway. Not bothering to turn on a light, Jim enters their former bedroom and falls onto the comforter, unaware of a man sitting silently at their dinner table, separated from him by a single wall. When the intruder is satisfied that Jim has disappeared into sleep, the stranger lights a joint and walks through the chambers of the house, including the bedrooms, visible only as a tiny, orange glow.

The psychiatrist awakens after eleven to find a courier's packet sitting on his porch. He opens it and rubs his fingers across the embossed stationery: Tower, Tilney & Webb. Expecting a subpoena, he instead finds a handwritten note from Tilney himself requesting that Jim meet with Quinton's parents at noon today. The meeting would have made sense a month ago, and Jim should have demanded it, no matter how inconvenient a return from their Bermudan plantation might have been. But now?

He lies on his bed and contemplates the folly of those who talk through their lawyers. After the message from Evelyn Graves, Jim had been ready to explain it all, but instead, they enlisted Tilney perhaps with the goal of intimidation. More likely, Mrs. Graves figured a man as stupid as James Malory needed multiple reminders.

Even now, Mother and Father Graves may be sitting in their paneled living room, despondent and enraged. They trusted this doctor and gave him a check for two thousand dollars, a fortune for most men. Then he failed. No matter how awkward their approach might have been, Jim was the one who blew it, and they deserve an explanation for his ineptitude, no matter how humiliating his words might be.

After showering and shaving, he pulls open his closet and sees the suit that he wore for his first day of private practice. It was a gift from the Sedaras, and Maria photographed him in it with her Polaroid while he departed for his first morning on Athens Road. He puts on the suit with his Penn tie and retrieves a box of new shoes that Maria purchased for him last month. New shoes were meant to be saved, his mother used to say, until their use was absolutely necessary.

Jim slips into them and is shocked by his professional appearance. Despite his recent intoxication, he has reverted to the sober medical man, if only for a moment.

Twenty minutes later, he stares at the oaken door of Sycamore Lodge and is admitted to the living room by the taciturn Evans like nothing ever happened.

There he sees a woman who must be Quinton's mother. Her lack of wrinkles suggests that she's forty-five at most, but her hair sits in a white pile of plumped curls. She wears a green polyester pants suit and impossibly appears pregnant beneath her ruffled knit blouse. If she's spent her millions on anything, it hasn't been on clothes. The room's wood seems rubbed, the walls cracked like his own on Barker's Mill.

"Dr. Malory," Evelyn says, "pleased to meet you."

"And you as well."

"Would you like a drink? Or maybe just a sherry. It's a little early."

The thought of more alcohol excites Jim, but he says, "I'll pass. Thank you." Then, he remembers that he's no longer a doctor. Now he's just a drinker, which means there's little reason to lengthen his journey toward cirrhosis. "Actually, maybe a sherry," he says. "Where's Mr. Graves?"

"Still in Bermuda. He couldn't be bothered coming back if we're being honest," she says, pouring two glasses. "That's part of the problem, I think, but I'm no psychiatrist."

Jim notices that perfectly shaped canines and molars line her mouth without crookedness or stain. They could be false but more likely the product of excellent dentistry. Rich people always have great teeth.

"Quinton is not well," Jim says.

"But he does look remarkably better," Evelyn insists, "don't you think? He's a different boy than the one we left." She raises her glass. "This is a toast to your skill and acumen."

"I'm not sure I follow you," Jim says, nevertheless drinking when she does.

"He's much better," she says.

Jim rubs his chin. "I'm not sure we're talking about the same person."

Evelyn licks the sherry from her thinned lips. "He's going back to Harvard in two days. He would never have considered that in June. Also, he's calm and friendly. In some ways, he seems the best I have ever seen him, even from when he was a little boy."

A golden retriever runs into the room and sits at Evelyn's feet. "I hope you like dogs." She rubs the dog's neck. "Yes, Mallory, yes. Oh, I'm so sorry. This is rather embarrassing, but I assure you that we've always spelled Mallory's name with two Ls."

Jim and his mother had one dog, rescued from the pound, and only in high school when their poverty was a penny less grinding. His mother insisted that Butch sleep outside, not out of cruelty, but because she couldn't conceive that a dog would do otherwise. It was only when Butch started to fall asleep at his food bowl that he was allowed inside. Eventually, after becoming incontinent, the mutt was shot through the head. This, Ruth Malory figured, was kindness.

"I don't think Quinton is any better," Jim says.

"But when did you last see him?"

"A few days ago. He's manic and aggressive. He uses drugs continuously—LSD, peyote, marijuana, who knows what else. If he were clean, he might return to normal, but—"

"No, no, no!" she says, waving her finger. "There must be some mistake. We walked through the garden last night." The term *garden* appears an understated affectation to describe the sculpted yew maze that covers nearly an acre of Sycamore Lodge's twelve. "Quinton read to me from Melville, *Moby Dick* in fact. An extraordinary book and never a better one written about the Cape and the Islands."

"Where is he now?" Jim asks.

"Upstairs."

"Would you mind getting him?"

"Not at all." Evelyn turns to the end table and presses a button on a small wooden box.

Evans peers around the corner and says, "Ma'am."

"Could you fetch Quinton?"

"Of course." A minute later, Quinton enters the room and sits next to his mother. The leather side bag and suede vest are again gone. He wears a blue blazer and khakis, and looks like a young associate at a law firm's summer picnic.

"Hello, Dr. Malory," he says, smiling.

His mother turns toward her son and then to the psychiatrist. "You see? He's the perfect image of respectability." And so he is. Quinton has locked the interruptions and freneticism in the attic and buried the grandiosity in the basement. How has he done it? Jim could mention the abduction that initiated their relationship or blurt out the seduction of his daughter. Kidnapping and corruption of minors might get Mrs. Graves's attention. Jim could follow with the drug dealing, then the poisoning and defamation, to stimulate additional interest.

"You've done a brilliant job," she says. Jim stares at Quinton and sees just the blink of defiance, or not.

"I didn't recognize you with your new look," Jim says to Quinton. "I guess you're voting for Nixon."

"I'm over all that Summer of Love stuff."

"I missed it myself. Had a ten-year-old turning eleven."

Before Quinton can supply a rejoinder, Evelyn says, "My son tells me that you have a wonderful daughter. Maybe we all could have dinner sometime. What's she doing for the summer?"

"Visiting her grandparents in New Jersey."

"Where?"

He pauses. "In New Jersey."

"You mean Swedesboro," Quinton says. "Right?"

"I've never heard of it," his mother says.

"That's because you think tomatoes are only eaten by Italians," Quinton says. "My mother doesn't know that Swedesboro's the nation's capital for tomato canning."

"Oh," she says.

"I've read all about the town," Quinton says. "Now I just need to visit."

"Is it near Far Hills?" Evelyn asks.

"Not exactly," Jim says.

Evelyn shrugs and turns to her son. "How do you feel?"

"Great. Life's too short to be depressed."

"Isn't this wonderful," she says to Jim. "You've helped him. You've made a genuine difference in my boy's life."

"You have," Quinton says. "Now, I'm ready to live in the world, instead of in my own mind."

"And that's why we wanted you to drop by," Evelyn says. "We've wanted to thank you. We've never had any medical men in our families. I'm afraid we're nothing but accountants, lawyers, and people of commerce, but we have the utmost respect for your calling."

Jim turns to Quinton. "Do you think it would make sense to see a psychiatrist in Cambridge?"

"No need," he says. "Things are looking up. I called the museum, and I got my old job back tending the flowers. I'll also get punched at the Fly. We could do long-distance phone sessions,"

Quinton says. "Or you could come up."

"Why, of course," Evelyn says, her eyes widening with enthusiasm. "You and your family could stay at the Point. We own the lighthouse at the end of Sandy Neck." The black-and-white tower had been visible when Jim stayed at the Santonis'. Even then, it was a tiny finger beckoning him.

"I thought those were owned by the government," he says.

"Exactly so, until they're decommissioned as obsolete. It's a pity. With all of these social programs of late and whatnot, there isn't a dollar to spend on places and things of historical interest. It was going to be demolished, so we bought it for perseveration. It's a real money pit, although there's some sort of tax deduction, I don't exactly know. Also, I must say it's less than convenient. You can only get there by boat, or across six miles of sand in, what do they call it Quinton, a 'dune buggy?' Really, we bought it for Quinton."

"I guess it's tough," Jim says.

"But imagine," she says. "There's nothing like a lighthouse."

"Mother," Quinton says, "will you excuse us? I'd like to speak with Dr. Malory privately."

"Of course, darling," Evelyn says. "Oh, and Dr. Malory. Don't worry about the car. Sometimes it requires a louder-than-normal voice to get my son's attention."

When she's left the room, Jim says to Quinton, "Any more of that Pepsi that you gave me?"

"That was good, wasn't it? Much better than the other brands."

"Did you know I was coming?" Jim asks.

"I was the one who invited you."

"To finish me off? Why not just stab me in the chest and get it over with?"

"I don't know what you mean."

"I know you put those signs up."

"No, I don't think so, but perhaps one of your enemies."

"Why'd you do it?"

"I didn't do it."

"And telling my wife about…." Jim can't say it.

"About what? Oh, that. Well, you know what they say: Never do anything in private that you wouldn't want everyone to know about."

"I love your lack of insight and remorse. It's a classic sign of psychosis."

"But I could say the same thing about you."

"Fine," Jim says. "We'll do a urine drug test. I bet you're ten out of ten positive."

"You don't get it, do you? I win, and you lose. It's the way the world works and always has. You're just like my father, never giving a shit, even when it's too late."

Jim could strangle the man right here, and if the psychiatrist spends the rest of his life at Graterford or, even better, experiences two thousand volts heating his tissue to the boiling point, well, that will be all right.

"You think you can get away with this," Jim says.

"With what? Truth is, you're the violent one. Look what you did to my car. You know how hard it is to find a nice L88 in triple black?"

"No. I never could afford one."

"You can have the one you ruined," Quinton says.

"You're still out of your mind."

"Sort of. Not really. Maybe I can control it."

"By hiding it."

"I use it, like propulsion. Like the man who founded Howell-Graves. You can't get anything brilliant done unless you burn a bit too bright."

"And what do you want to get done?"

"I want to take back the company, which we no longer control. I'm ready to settle down. Saws are a useful thing, although the real money today comes from bulldozers and forklifts. We haven't talked about it much, but I spent a lot of time this summer learning about the business, reading financial statements, and so on."

"In between the LSD trips and breaking and entering."

"I'm done with all of that, along with the anthropology crap. Leave it to the professors. I'm interested in money, and I've been studying Howell-Graves. You think you know everything, but you don't. I've even visited the offices as a shareholder. Revenues are strong, but costs are far too high. Do you know that we have people making five ninety-five an hour in the Tacony plant? For making saws? Have you ever heard of something so ridiculous? They're even trying to unionize, as if your mother has come back from the grave to inspire them."

"But what about the deprivations of the workers?" Jim asks.

"I've changed my mind on all that. It's survival of the fittest, and I intend to survive. Screw them. Have you been to Philadelphia recently?"

"Every week."

"Yes, I forgot, you and Major Nilso. Well, you see the undesirables more and more every day. We can move production to Alabama or South Carolina, say goodbye to the union drive, and fill every shift at three fifteen an hour. I'm changing my major to economics and plan to write my thesis on how to achieve greater efficiencies in American industrialism."

"You've got it all figured out," Jim says.

"Even before I graduate, I am going to put together a syndicate to take back control, and when I do, the company's going to the next level, provided I can get what I want."

"Which is?"

"Ruth. She can live in Cambridge with one of my aunts or a

governess or some sort of chaperone if you insist, and she'll complete high school at Winsor or Buckingham until I graduate, at my expense of course, and then we'll return to Glenwyth. Then she'll go to Bryn Mawr. Although the engagement will begin now, I promise that we will not marry until she is eighteen. We'll all be a happy family. We'll even have dinner parties, not like the ones with Honey Dixon, but—"

"You *are* insane," Jim says. Nevertheless, he can see the bride and bridegroom at an Episcopalian abbey, himself and Maria sitting on one side in different pews, and Evelyn and Quinton's father, whatever his name is, next to each other on the other. If Jim does nothing, events could, in theory, take the two lovers down this dreadful path, but he also feels a longing for this outcome. Past sins do not guarantee future transgressions, and complete re-imaginations are intoxicating things. Paul hunted the Christians until he became one. If Quinton can be forgiven, why can't Jim be too? Yet something is missing. Quinton has not asked for forgiveness and has instead denied that a crime was ever committed. In this way, the patient and the psychiatrist have become the same person, neither admitting his sins.

"I recall," Jim says, "that when contemplating such a proposal, a gentleman will ask the girl's father first."

"All right," Quinton says. "I'm asking you. She loves me, and I love her. Of everyone, I figured you'd be the one, you know, given your history, who might show some understanding."

"You've trapped her because she doesn't know any better," Jim says. "It's like heroin."

"She'll finish her education, and I'll marry her. It can't be any other way. She's given herself to me. Not to mention that she'll be a rich woman." He waves his arms across the living room and then points toward the picture window, which overlooks the sloping back side of Sycamore Lodge. "This is all going to be mine."

"You could have a billion dollars, and you still couldn't buy her."

"I don't want to buy her. I love her."

"You'll never have her," Jim says.

And Quinton's smile washes away. "I give your daughter the chance to live in a kingdom, to be my queen, and you tell me to fuck off."

Jim locks Quinton's eyes and says, "Don't ever come near her again."

"And what if I do? You'll try to get me arrested? No one will believe you. You're the madman. Everybody knows it."

Evelyn re-enters the room. "Well, another sherry?"

"No, thank you," Jim says. "Quinton and I had a wonderful talk. I'm going to miss him."

"I'll be back," Quinton says. "It's only a few hours away."

"We don't know how to thank you," she says.

"The thanks are all mine," Jim replies. Thanks for confirming his decision to become a meat packer in South Philadelphia or a vagabond wandering the streets of Lehighton. "I'm going to head back to the office, but if there's anything more I can do, you know where to find me."

"Yes," she says. "Oh. I forgot. How are you feeling?"

"Sorry?"

"With the pneumonia. Quinton told us you were in the hospital."

Jim smiles. "I'm much better. Like a million bucks in fact."

Later, Jim sits on the glider at Barker's Mill and notices how the barest salting of leaves covers his stamps of a lawn. The fall sits in the trees, and the air makes his body feel neither warm nor cold. If the temperature could stay like this, Jim could sit on the porch forever and watch the rest of his life ebb away. With the permanent absence of Maria, Ruthie, and his patients, solitude could be his station until he starved. Even now, though, there's work to be done. Jim holds the knife in his right hand and a sharpening stone in his left.

The Eldorado pulls up to the house. The top is down, and Dave gets out.

"Thanks for returning my phone calls," he says, and notices the blade. "Now you're talking, but I thought you were dead or back at VA. Where's Maria?"

"She left me. For good, I think. Took Ruthie with her."

"Why?"

"No. I'm your doctor. You're supposed to tell me things."

"Not only and not anymore. The treatment's over. Now we're friends."

Maybe it's that easy. What the hell. Jim explains it all to Dave, from the first meeting in College Hall to Honey, always Honey, and ends with Maria's departure.

At the narrative's conclusion, ninety minutes later, Dave says only, "Wow." Then, after a pause, "It's like the guy said on the nightly news. '*It became necessary to destroy the village in order to save it.*'"

"I have to leave," Jim says.

"You told her about the kid you killed over there?"

"Yeah."

"So that's a start, but you can't run away," Dave says. "You taught me that."

But Jim runs. That's what he does, after the Huey went down and now. He's just another hunted animal. Maybe he should try to turn the other cheek, like Sister Michael Frederick told him in school. Forgiveness, along with silence, cunning, and exile, may be desirable, but only after you've stabbed your opponent in the back and squeezed the life out of him.

Dave walks back to the Cadillac, opens his glove compartment, and produces a wrinkled paper bag, handing it to Jim. "Here."

Jim opens it and sees an inky black pistol, a carbon copy of the M1911 that he had in Vietnam. "This is insane," he says.

"Maybe, but there's nothing like a .45 for persuasion."

"I'm not even a good shot," Jim says. "They dry-stamped me in basic. I'm supposed to heal people."

"How are you going to do that if you're a dead man?" Bending down to block it from view, Jim rubs his hands across the steel.

"Jesus," Dave says. "Did you check the chamber before you started making love to the thing? You never know when there's one inside." After Jim jerks the slide and nothing comes out, Dave hands him three loaded magazines. "It's cleaned, oiled, and ready."

"For what?"

Ignoring the question, Dave evaluates the lonely, squat, white bin sitting next to the front door. When was it last used? Maybe 1962, when Maria was newly a housewife and Ruthie smiled at everything. Jim had his career in front of him, and the milkman came every Tuesday.

Placing the firearm into the box, Dave says, "Just don't forget about it when you put in an order for half and half."

"You want me to leave that in there?"

"Who knows when you'll need it?"

"I don't need a pistol, and I don't need a knife," Jim says. "I need my wife, daughter, and baby."

"You think there's a God?"

"I guess so."

"Then there's also a Devil, and his name is Quinton. He wants your soul because that's what the Devil does. You turn the other cheek at your own peril, and God helps those who help themselves."

"So why did he do all this?" Jim asks.

"Why did Vietnamese babies get napalmed? Why did Hitler kill six million Jews and Stalin twenty million Ruskies? Good doesn't exist until it stands against evil."

The phone rings inside. "I'm not getting it," Jim says.

"Why?"

"Because it's over, and I don't need anyone to tell me."

"Just get it," Dave says.

"You get it." And Dave does. Left alone on the porch, Jim cannot make out the words of the conversation, but it's brief, and Dave's back, the phone's long cord in train.

"What?" Jim says, annoyed but also amused that Dave covers the mouthpiece with his hand.

When Dave lifts his fingers, the bird voice of a Bell Telephone operator says, "Long distance, please hold."

A moment later, Maria is back, if in another area code. "It's me."

Contrition, humiliation, and sorrow bursting from his brain, Jim says, "Please come back."

"There's no time. Ruthie's missing. She was out in the field, by Paulsboro Road, and she's gone."

"Maybe she got—"

"She's been coming here her whole life. She didn't get lost. Somebody took her," Maria sobs. "Somebody took my baby."

Like water splashed onto incandescent metal, Jim says only, "Quinton."

"How do you know?"

"It's him. I know."

"Then where did they go?" she asks.

"I'm not sure." But he is sure, seeing the lighthouse and its dead beacon. "Cape Cod."

"Then I'll call the police."

"They won't understand. If he's surprised—"

"What? Tell me!"

"He doesn't want to hurt her, but if somebody crosses him—"

"When are you leaving?"

"Now. What about the baby?" he asks.

"Just go," Maria says and collapses into a paroxysm of coughing, maybe an ashtray stacked with butts by her side. "You're going to find her."

"I love you," he says. "It was always you."

She offers nothing in return but the click of a hang-up.

He turns to Dave. "I'm going to Cape Cod."

"Then I'm coming with you. We can take the Eldorado."

"I have to do this alone." Jim finds the cash that Maria has stowed. He pulls the Mustang parallel to the Eldorado, and the Ford sits growling.

"I'm following you," Dave says.

"Don't."

Dave shakes his head. "So you survive the VC to get shot by Joe College."

"He doesn't have a gun."

"I'll bet you a nickel he does."

Jim pushes the gas, drives about fifty feet down Barker's Mill, brakes, and then reverses back to Dave. Putting the car in park, Jim jumps to the porch, grabs the knife, and opens the milk box. He pulls out the gun and the three loaded magazines, and stows the killing kit in the glove compartment.

Dave says, "At least you're learning."

13

After the nine and a half hours to Cape Cod, Jim stops for gas near Sandy Neck at Nickerson's Garage. It's just shy of midnight, but the globular lights atop the Mobil gas pumps remain on. He drove by the station with Maria less than two months ago and didn't notice it. Despite the darkness, Jim now studies the establishment, a garage with two pumps appended to an antique Cape house. There's a window in the front of the garage, and through it he sees several men playing cards, a whiskey bottle at the table's center. He wants to rap on the glass and ask if anyone has a boat to take him to the lighthouse, might as well get it over with now, but he's interrupted by a teenage boy in jeans and a grease-stained, white T-shirt.

"Fill her up?" he asks.

"Yeah."

"Ethyl?"

"Thanks." The tank fills, and Jim reads the map. Not much farther to go. Sandy Neck Road turns to the beach just a bit farther east, then six miles over sand to the lighthouse and the Point. The car's useless from here. Maybe he should sell it here and now. Or maybe they'll take it in trade for another gun, one for each hand.

The pump clicks off, and Jim hands the boy a five, but he doesn't take it.

Instead, the boy asks, worried, "How's your oil?" A black pool fans out over the pavement, making a wavy reflection of the station's sodium vapor lights.

"Oh, God," Jim says.

"Probably a blown head gasket."

"But it was running fine!"

"Everything's going fine until it isn't," the boy says.

"Can I drive it?"

"Sure, if you want to buy a new engine. I'll get my dad." He walks to the garage, and through the window, Jim sees the boy trying to snare his father's attention. The man waves him away, but the boy persists. Annoyed, the proprietor gets up from the table and walks to the pumps.

"What's the problem here?"

"Thank you," Jim says. "I appreciate you taking a look."

The boss eyes him and then studies the slick of oil beneath the car. "Just leave it," he says. The Mustang's another failure not worth anyone's attention. "And get a pan under that!" the boss barks at his son, losing interest and returning to the warm light of the garage.

"It'll be a week at the earliest," says the boy, writing up an order and shearing off a copy for Jim.

Jim gives him the keys, including those to Barker's Mill and his office, a lot of good they'll do. The psychiatrist expects the boy to offer counsel—*not to worry, she'll be okay, we fix Mustangs all the time*—but he retreats into the garage after his father and turns off the pumps. Then he disappears into the attached house, where a light turns on for a moment and then off. Inside the garage, the card game continues, and Jim can hear the laughter.

There's nothing to unload from the Mustang. Jim's wallet wedges into the back pocket of his jeans, and the knife and paper-wrapped pistol rests in his backpack. Inside of that, he also has the three magazines with their twenty-one bullets and four back issues of the *American Journal of Psychiatry.* Jim hasn't used the backpack since the last time he was on call at the VA, when he used to be a psychiatrist. There's no water and no food in the knapsack, though, and none to be offered or had at Nickerson's. Although Jim didn't even stop on the way up, he's not hungry or thirsty, at least not yet.

He walks onto the vacant, cracked macadam where the station gives way to the road. Then he turns back toward the forgotten Mustang, sad in the spotlight. His flight to California on the way to Vietnam departed from the Willow Grove Naval Air Station at night. The time had been his choice, as if he were trying to get a final full day before leaving. Maria had been allowed to drive the Mustang right onto the tarmac, and she had stood there in front of the car's grille as he walked onto the plane. She wasn't alone. Honey had been there too, and Maria thought nothing of it.

Jim turns away and keeps walking. They call it the King's Highway, but reduced to redundancy by the new one to the south, the road now sprawls with insignificance. He starts walking east. In time he passes a cemetery with six-inch headstones, a partly collapsed barn, an abandoned single-track railroad, a tiny clapboard cottage designated SANDY NECK TOURIST INFORMATION, a chapel without a cross in front, an overgrown agglomeration of one-room vacation shanties, and the funnel of a commenced but forgotten side road. Lined with granite, the improvement terminates after ten feet in a thicket. A peeling, cracked sign proclaims ACRE LOTS—FROM $1,000! A single car passes, illuminating the failed development, and Jim contemplates the owner's financial mishap. Were any of the parcels sold or just too few? Maybe quicksand lurks within or a psychotic neighbor across the property line, another Quinton Graves. That's the thing about failure. So many paths lead toward it. In the sky above, innumerable planets exist barren of life, despite the presence of nitrogen, oxygen, carbon, and hydrogen. They tried to create life, and they failed.

The highway turns sharply and then exits the woods and opens up into a clearing. In the full moon, he can see the marsh extending to either side. The salty gas of the bog reminds him of the Mekong, mud everywhere clogging everything. The Marines had not been deterred by the jungles of Guadalcanal and Okinawa, but Vietnam was different. We were supposed to win, just like he was supposed to be assigned to Walter Reed, dining with Maria at the Tabard Inn, laughing at the psychopathology of generals and their wives. Instead, he flew Dustoff. Jim was only asked to ride along when a loony bird was loose in the field. Like on September 23, 1970. He met George and Scotty that very day. They were a new crew, the last of the FNGs, and he knew them for about an hour. Then they were gone, like his parents, like Maria and Ruthie, just like that. Slow partings are the stuff of movies.

Jim comes to the middle of a bridge and can see a river flowing underneath. Following it to the north under the moonlight, he sees it disappear and knows he has found his path to the beach. From here to Sandy Neck Point, no other inlets interrupt the beach's course to the lighthouse. Seeing his path, he climbs over the edge of the bridge and descends to the right bank. There, the low tide has reduced most of the creek to a mudflat.

By the next sunset, he will have found Quinton and Ruthie, but what can he say to them? There's no cease-and-desist order available, and he has lost all capacity for moral suasion, a philanderer and teen impregnator himself. Quinton spoke about marriage, and Jim mocked him. Yet Jim had done much the same seventeen years earlier, in a similarly unpropitious situation. He met with Angelo in that chilly kitchen in Swedesboro and presented his plan to marry Maria, complete his medical training, and raise a family. Angelo responded not with disgust, outrage, or ridicule, but with acceptance. When it was over, they drank grappa to seal the deal, the actual marriage now an afterthought. True, Jim had not poisoned Angelo, but he had dishonored the Sicilian's daughter, which was worse.

Jim walks, feet sinking into the mud, and he hears something that sounds like the highway but must be the ocean. The newspaper that he read when he last stopped for gas in Buzzards Bay referenced a recent Nor'easter, and waves on the distant but normally placid bay recall the event. The creek takes another turn, and he sees a single orange light, a bonfire. He wants to greet the celebrants, maybe one of them has a boat, but the gathering sits across the creek, which has widened and risen with the tide. Here the river straightens, maybe engineered to meet the beach perpendicularly, and it enters the bay between two jetties.

Life magazines used to litter the Doctors' Lounge at the University Hospital. Now, the publication's going out of business, shrinking like an anorexic with each issue. There was one story that he remembers, "Deeper into the Vietnam War." Oppressed with the seven-day work weeks and forty-hour shifts as a resident, he had felt like a coward reading it and shared his feelings with Santoni in one of their supervisions. That's how it all started. Jim's guilt, though, had less to do with what he hadn't done than what he had.

He lies on the sand and sees the stars. Even with the brightness of the full moon, they crowd the sky with far greater density than he remembers from Glenwyth. Only Lehighton ever produced such a heaven before now. The same sky watches over him, but everything else has changed, expectancy now purified into finality. He will find his daughter to the east. He has been instructed to get her.

It may be true love, but with a madman. Sitting over grappa in Swedesboro, Jim had his sanity. Or did he? Maybe, if told to do so, he would have jumped, but he was instead directed away from the cliff.

Did he want to marry Maria? Jim can't remember. He had to, that was clear, but defining one's life because of a contraceptive error may have seemed unwise at the time or at least unfair. There was Honey, the other girls at the College for Women, and the young nurses smoking outside the University Hospital, but really only Honey. Maria wasn't so anxious back then, at least as far as he could tell. That came later, after Ruthie, starting in the white bed on Roseberry Street.

He's never thought of it, but did she even want to marry him? There was the assumption back then that he was doing the right thing, which implied that he could have done the wrong thing, and therefore was to be thanked for not doing so. He had claimed, with his year of high school biology and his presidency of the 4-H, that she couldn't be ovulating, and she had believed him. Thus came another of his many errors. Ruthie was the product, so wonderful for so many years, but maybe her sudden waywardness hasn't been sudden at all. What if the error of her conception has somehow come to the surface, like a deep abscess erupting through otherwise perfect skin? It seems paranoid. Maybe Nilso was right.

But suppose she loves Quinton, and he her. They then become the reverse of Jim and Maria. The edifice of their marriage appeared intact for so many years, but even a one-story building built on mud soon collapses. Now consider Quinton and Ruthie. If they love each other, that may be all that matters. Jim followed convention, and his daughter and wife fled across the Delaware. In contrast, Ruthie and Quinton may, at this very moment, be living their fantasy in a lighthouse. Having poisoned and now destroyed her father, Quinton has shown the dedication that any man would want for his daughter's groom.

But Maria hasn't ordered him to bless a union. Instead, he's to return with Ruthie and in doing so bring the family back to some previous iteration, maybe back to the day just before he saw that *Life* magazine in the Doctor's Lounge. It was '65 maybe, when Vietnam was just another third-world country to him, but he can no more go back than he can persuade Ruthie. She always got what she wanted, which until now has been leads in school plays and victories at Scrabble games. She won't be dissuaded easily. Suppose Jim returns the favor of a kidnapping with another one. What then? Need to think. Maria harangues him to keep moving, but exhaustion pulls him to the ground. His watch shows ten minutes to two, 2:00 a.m. that is, and the echo of the waves calms him and makes rising impossible. He must rest.

And with that, he's sitting in the remnants of the helicopter hanging upside down. There are surgeons, and they rip the charred skin from his guts, giving him new flesh. Jim awakens, sweating, and remembers what it was like when they did the skin graft. Because the surgeons took care of his abdomen before his eardrums, Jim could barely hear himself scream. He falls asleep again. Soon he's walking down a sunlit Barker's Mill Road, and he comes to his house. Opening the door, he's greeted by Honey and Maria sitting in the living room watching television, and in the tiny backyard, people stage a party to the edge of his vision. There must be ten thousand, more than Glenwyth in its entirety. His parents are there, his mother alive and his father too, and so is everyone he has ever known, from Jeannie Trexler and Nilso to Nurse Tucker and Santoni, and everyone in between. And there are Vietnamese, NVA and Viet Cong, and Buddhist monks not burning, and soldiers and patients, Dave and Quinton, and all is good.

Waking again but wanting to go back, Jim sees a gossamer of red rising in the east. There's no campfire to cover and no bedroll to pack. A twisting thirst enveloped him while he slept, but there's no fresh water in sight. He produces a faltering arc of brown urine. Down the beach, he will find the lifeguard station, and they will give him water and keep him sane. He walks, and the sun rises in front of his path. The Cape Cod Bay laps to his left, and to his right, there are sea cliffs, covered with beach plum and phragmites, punctuated with faded wooden staircases. Boats, rafts, and folding chairs sit near them. Like so many other mislabeled things in life, Sandy Neck is blanketed with beach stones.

As he continues walking, the hills to the right shorten. After a clearing, he sees a silver-shingled house next to a flagpole, surrounded by a small parking lot. A steel-piped tower with several chairs on its top stands in front of the house, the apparent location for the lifeguards. But there are none, and there are no swimmers. He walks up to the house and tries the door—locked. Then he remembers that it's just after dawn.

Jim walks across the deserted bathing beach and continues east. The hills to the right rise again, but the dunes are without houses. The pebbles also dwindle, leaving stretches of virgin sand. To the right, a rectangular, white and brown wooden sign indicates 1, and Jim sees that a path next to it breaks through the dune. He leaves the oceanfront and walks to the path's opening. The soft sand way curves to the left and then disappears behind another hill covered with wiry bushes and tall grass.

He comes to the bay's edge and sees it's a straight shot to the lighthouse. He can get there walking, but quicker if he runs. He puts his shoes and socks inside the backpack, and they tumble with the knife and gun. No longer in even the remnants of a suit, he can run, and after starting slowly, he feels rhythm and strength flowing through him, his limp gone.

At the end of his longer Lehighton runs, he would see the sunrise and the creation of an average day. There was the sense of hidden knowledge bestowed, and as he picks up speed across the beach, he gains a similar, solitary perspective. If he falls down and has a heart attack, he'll be dead before he's spotted. The customary pain returns, the itching, gnawing, burning, and shocking, but furious pain is what life really is. Some people understand that better than others, and that's a privilege. This is what his mother, the most privileged of them all, had been trying to tell him, without having the heart to come out and say it.

Why hadn't he come here with Maria when they stayed in the neighboring town? Santoni mentioned it in passing, aware or not of its special significance, but most of their extended weekend was spent in the one-room museums dotting the King's Highway. Perhaps thinking that she would never return to Cape Cod, Maria felt compelled to learn as much as she could about the local history, from the ancient glassworks to the town grange. Had husband and wife come to this beach instead of taking in such New England nonsense, they could have talked about everything from the lunch at Wanamaker's onward. The beauty of this place makes secrets impossible. For so many years, Jim had considered Maria the model of inaccessibility, but on this sand, she would have told him everything: that entire, passionate life of hers that he had never and would never know.

The water is everywhere and nowhere. His throat cracks, and even the mucus in his mouth has evaporated. Jim sees another rectangular sign—**2**. He's a third of the way to the end if the signage has been placed proportionally. He notices dead horseshoe crabs, seagulls, and jellyfish. Out here, there are no lifeguards to rake the beach, and so the crumbs of life accumulate. As a junior-high schooler, he read about the ten thousand years of guano layering in the Atacama Desert, yielding a surface mine of fertilizer. Something similar has happened here, but the resource is of the mind. Ruthie and Quinton have traversed this same path within the last day, leaving the debris of their thoughts. He can feel it.

Jim runs to the water's edge. He expects icy contraction, but when he dips his hands, the water surprises him with its warmth, the parting gift of a storm. Honey, he never saw her run, but there must have been a time before the accident. When he was doing psychiatric consults at the beginning of his tour, he interviewed a recently paralyzed corporal waiting to be shipped back to the Good Ole USA. The man said that he ran in his sleep every night. What could you say to that? Does Honey run in her dreams? Does Jimmy talk?

The sun has crawled above the dunes and warms the air. He had hoped for a cloudy, cool day, the best weather for running, but he will get neither. Still, he doesn't sweat, not good while his body's remaining water floats away and he's squeezed to dryness. He tries to urinate again, and a few drops bubble out. He feels dizzy, like he might flop to the ground.

Jim slows to a walk, a feeling of doom coming in with the tide, and the beach curves now, beginning its rotation to the Point. He should have hired a boat, but how? Having failed so egregiously, he also should have asked Maria how to proceed, but he followed his instincts—again—and now finds himself disoriented on a deserted beach. Jim could stop, but why does it have to be so hard? Why are there no hikers or birdwatchers who just happen to have an extra canteen? He sees a sign: *No Horses Beyond This Point.* Horses? Storm the lighthouse with a cavalry charge?

Then he sees it, a sign with the number **5**, so much for **3** and **4**. He runs to it and gathers that it marks another path. Unlike **1** and **2**, this one dives through a woodland of gnarled pines and scrub oaks, and tire tracks line the sand. He follows them through a stand of blighted pines, twisted limbs without needles. Beyond them, the grass possesses the most satisfying combination of green and yellow he has ever seen. It is life itself.

He turns to the left on the marsh path and sees three shingled shacks, the biggest no more than fifteen feet square. Flaking, their windows boarded, they give him nothing. He spots another building. As large as the other three combined, this one has been covered in orange-brown shingles yet to be weathered, and the windows, uncovered, have been recently installed. There's also a well-mortared brick chimney, from which wisps of smoke rise. The place is inhabited, and the person inside must have water. He could break down the door and take what he needs, he could even knock, but he sees a nearby cistern meant for rainwater. Jim tries the liquid, and it's good. After drinking his fill, he continues and curses, as if the water has allowed rage to flower within him. After more turns, he comes into a clearing across which he can see an assortment of cottages and beyond them, a black-and-white lighthouse.

Although his legs have deadened, he runs again. The path takes him into a village, with a sandy plaza that forms its own version of a New England town green. Narrow Victorians crowd around the courtyard as if they're watching for something, but there's nothing. Not a soul walks about, and no boats are moored in the part of the harbor that touches the other side of the village. Yet beyond it, next to the lighthouse, a small motorboat bobs in the water.

The lighthouse, consisting of the tower itself and the associated keeper's quarters, sits on the bay as Jim had anticipated. Several NO TRESPASSING signs crowd the front walkway. There's no knocker, and so he bangs on the painted, rusted metal of the front door.

"Quinton?" he says calmly, knocking again. "Quinton." A bit louder. There's no answer. Seeing nothing with which to strike, he kicks the door with his right foot, and the equal and opposite force reflected back into his body makes him wonder if he has broken his leg. This could be the wrong lighthouse, or Quinton could be inside listening to every word.

"Quinton!" Jim screams now, but there's still no response. He walks to the cottage connected to the tower. The front door is locked, but the building has windows.

Jim shatters the one closest to the door and climbs through. He expects to smell hydrocarbons, to see drums of Number 2 Fuel Oil, and to stumble against crates marked ammonium nitrate, all being readied for some final act of insanity to destroy a world that Quinton could never understand.

Instead, Jim finds an undisturbed sitting room of Shaker plainness with furniture from the nineteenth century. He walks down the hallway to the sleeping quarters. There Jim studies a child's room with a single quilted bed and a faded rocking horse. Next door is the keeper's room, with a bed looking only wide enough to hold two sleepers if they embraced throughout the night.

The place is less a bedroom than a laboratory. Stacks of blotter papers sit idly on a lab bench next to alembics, beakers, and Bunsen burners. Then he spots a stoppered Erlenmeyer flask with a clear, colorless liquid, labeled SCREAMING CLOWN. Someone has stripped the bed, and hundreds of freshly cut flowers rest upon the ancient mattress, strange, maybe ingredients of some sort. Expecting to find bombs, Jim has instead found flowers. He steps closer and notes how intact and vital they look, as if the lot must have been clipped this very morning.

Jim grabs one of the cuttings but smells neither lily nor rose. Instead, he smells blood, his own. It streams across what had been his curious, inquiring fingers. He drops the flower to the ground, and it cracks into innumerable pieces of glass.

"You can look," Quinton says, "but you can't touch. That's what you said to me."

"Where's Ruthie?"

"She's in the neighborhood." Quinton stares at Jim's hand and the blood that spurts from it. "We should bandage it, don't you think?"

"So you could smear it with feces like the VC used to do?"

"Ruth is right," Quinton says. "You never left Vietnam."

"Where is she?"

"At the gunning shack. Why don't you ask her if she wants to leave?" The smoke drifted from the chimney. Ruthie was there, and Jim walked right by.

"Okay. I'll see you around."

"But you don't understand. You'll tell the police that I kidnapped her." Quinton makes an X of himself in the doorway. "I didn't. She came on her own. She's been unhappy for a long time, and I mean long before this summer. It's like you looked to the stars and missed what was right in front of your face."

"I'm not going to say anything."

"Yeah, yeah."

"I can't," Jim says, "remember? I'm still your doctor."

"Are you? If you see an imminent risk, you break confidentiality. Everyone knows that, and what do we have here if not an imminent risk?"

"The way I see it," Jim says, "we were having a conversation, and I cut my hand on a broken window."

"Nope. You've seen the flowers."

"Nothing more than cheap knickknacks you stole from a tacky gift shop in Buzzards Bay," Jim says. His hand now throbs, blood in a small pool at the doctor's feet.

Quinton laughs. "I guess you never went to Cambridge for the Harvard-Penn Game, too busy changing diapers. If you had, and say you were looking for something respectable to do on Sunday afternoon before you got your train, you might have gone to see the glass flowers at the museum. I borrowed a few, and Harvard's been investigating for months. There were no news stories because that's not the way that Harvard works, but you'll tell them."

"Goddamn it," Jim says. "Will you get me a towel?"

Quinton leaves and returns with a snow-white washcloth. "Thank you," Jim says, wrapping the fabric around his swelling hand. Not much good to stab a knife or fire a gun. "Okay. We can fix this."

Quinton shakes his head. "I don't think so. I wanted Ruth, and you ruined it."

"She's a teenager."

"Just like you were when you tried to have Ruth aborted."

"I'm leaving."

"To return to what? Honey? Maria? With all you've done, how do you give advice with a straight face?"

"You don't know what I've done."

"But I do! Eliza told me everything long before I even met you, like before you cured her. I mean, Eliza wasn't sure, but after a few sessions with you, it was obvious. I tried to come over once to tell her and found Ruth instead."

Jim closes his eyes. Can't react. Life tips to the left or right from a trapeze wire.

"I've done a lot wrong," Jim says.

"Yes, you have, and now comes the punishment."

"But there has to be forgiveness."

"That's pathetic. You could try it with Maria, but you'd be wasting your time. She'll never have you back."

"Maybe, but if she forgives me, she'll forgive you, too."

Quinton twists in the wind of this new consideration. "But she thinks I kidnapped her one and only daughter."

"You don't know that," Jim says, wondering how his backpack can seem so light, like his weapons must have fallen out on the beach. "And if you want Ruthie this badly, you'll have her in time. I know you love her, and you want to be with her. I can't imagine what it's been like for you to suffer."

"That's right, you can't. I'd give everything I've ever had just to feel normal for ten seconds."

"So what happened with you and Ruthie?" Jim asks.

"I didn't kidnap her, you know. I found her staring at the electrical substation that runs along that piece of shit farm in Swedesboro! I saved her life."

"There you are," Jim says. "You wanted to protect her, and you took her to a safe place."

"Yeah, that's damn right, and I gave you the LSD to free you from the prison of your own mind!" Quinton screams. Then he shrugs and lights a joint. "Everyone expects her to be perfect."

"I know she's not."

"But you've treated her like she is. You weren't even parents to her, and you're surprised it's come to this. Does she have to electrocute herself to get your attention?"

"She loves you," Jim says. "I know that."

"Yeah, like she will after this." Quinton pauses, studies his opponent, and then, after a time, says, "Doesn't matter. You're a fucking liar, lying to me like you lie to the rest of your patients about happy endings and all that shit. Like you lied to your wife. Give me your gun and whatever else you have in there." When Jim does nothing, Quinton produces the .357 and aims it at Jim's heart. "Hollow points; they minimize the clean-up."

"No," Jim says.

"Are you the cat with nine lives? How many did you use up in Cambodia?"

"It's not over. Maria and I—"

"Maria! You cheat on your wife and then have the balls to tell someone else how to be in love?"

"I was wrong."

"You're damned right you were wrong. But do something

that's right for a change. You're going to take out your weapon, I know you have one, and put the muzzle in your mouth."

"There are other ways to be happy," Jim says. "You can create instead of destroy."

"That's not where my talent lies." Quinton exhales, his gun still trained on Jim's left ventricle.

"I can still help you. Why else have I come?"

"To get your daughter."

"I could have done that five minutes ago."

"You know, they'll never find your body, and if there's no body, there's no crime."

"I could have killed myself, Quinton. I've thought about it, but the tougher path is to continue through the pain, to right your wrongs."

Quinton breathes in the thought but only briefly. "It's all pretty easy to say that when you're looking into a barrel. If I pull the trigger, you'll have eternity to see how I feel."

"Why'd you steal the flowers?" Jim says.

"Maybe because I knew I would meet Ruth and wanted something to match her beauty. I sound like a fool, don't I?"

"There's also beauty in forgiveness," Jim says.

"There's no forgiveness. You're a Catholic, you should know. They tell you there is, but there isn't. There's only sin, and original sin is seeing what we're capable of—"

"And not doing it," Jim says. "You poisoned me and destroyed my mind. I forgive you. I'm not going to kill you."

"Hah!" Quinton shouts. "No, you're not, and by the way, one day the psychiatrists will call me a genius!"

Could Quinton be right about his miracle cure? The bones and blood of Cambodia are still there, but they've softened, like they're part of someone else's life now. Jim might even walk away, even if that means dying in the process.

"I love you," Jim says. "If those are my last words, so be it."

"You're more of a fool than I am," Quinton says, "and just like your daughter, you always make things more difficult than they have to be."

Jim inhales and exhales, trying to remember everyone who ever mattered to him, including the Vietnamese kid vomiting blood. What will Jim's transformation look like? In seconds what will he become?

"You can shoot me in the back," he says, "you can stab me in the heart, or you can forgive me."

"Didn't you read the book?" Quinton screams. "There's a wisdom that's woe, but a woe that's madness!"

With that, Jim pushes by Quinton, who yields, his eyes ripped wide at this crazy man ready to die. When the psychiatrist keeps walking and doesn't look back, Quinton shakes himself and massages his gun's trigger, ready to make the psychiatrist explode. But at the moment requiring pure action, Quinton does nothing. Imagining the bullets passing through the back of Jim's heart, Quinton thinks of Ruth standing above her dead father, holes in two hearts.

Jim walks out, and Quinton slams the gun's grip into his own calf, wanting to feel an eternity of punishment for such weakness. Then he understands. Ruth is right. Her father's been dead for a long time. When Jim passes from sight, Quinton runs to the top of the lighthouse, sees that he is himself unseen, and like an outfielder straining his arm for the game's final throw, sends the .357 arcing across the sky and into Barnstable Harbor. If Malory says anything about the flowers and the LSD, no matter; they too will be gone within the hour. And anyway, who would believe such a fool?

Moments later, Jim enters the shack and sees the back of his daughter seated at a plain table. She stares at a dying fire. There's an odd smell in the room, like something living mixed with smoke. Ruthie doesn't turn or move. After a moment, he walks in a semicircle and sits next to her, waiting for her to speak. A sprig of rosemary, glass broken for its task and dappled with blood, rests next to her.

He studies his entranced daughter and the almost imperceptible tremor possessing her.

"You're not who you say you are," she mumbles.

"It's over."

"It's not over. It's like a wheel that never stops spinning."

"We have to go," Jim says. "Now!"

"I can't. You of all people should know that."

Drawing closer, he finds the source of the living smell. Ruthie's arm has become a red piece of beef shedding serum and blood like a wet steak. Someone, something has carved a word into her: ALWAYS.

He should unravel his own skin and wrap it over hers, but when he tries to take her arm, she pulls it away and says only, "Don't."

"Who did this?" he says.

She manages the feeblest of laughs. "You did." Without bandages, Jim takes his own bloody rag and presses it against her. "I know everything about you," Ruthie says.

He looks at her, this girl of sixteen who has lived a millennium. He sees his life playing in her eyes, and he knows that there could never have been another ending. As they sit immobilized, the world passes by. A '59 triple-white Eldorado pulls into Nickerson's, and Maria's blood pressure cracks 220 in an ambulance. Santoni waters his tomato plants, and feeling her own breast for the hundredth time, Honey understands that everything really is over. Somewhere Jimmy sings a tune, and Eliza gives a final look at her razor blades before throwing them from the cliff at Dixon Hill. Even now, like a silent angel of death, Dave Black walks by the gunning shack.

"Is Quinton dead?" asks Ruthie.

"No," Jim says, and only with great effort does he keep his daughter from grabbing the shiny piece of rosemary, herb of remembrance, and pressing it back into her weeping skin.

When it's clear she's lost the struggle to take the glass, Ruthie locks her hands and twists. "I'm going to break my fingers!"

"Stop it!" Jim shouts and pulls her hands apart.

After a weaker fight, the energy draining away, she says, "You can lock me up or bury me alive, but I'll never stop haunting you."

Minutes or hours later, when the single bullet passes straight through the man's brain and blasts away the opposite side of his skull, neither Jim nor Ruthie even hears the shot.

14

"Are you ready?" Carmela asks. She lights the candles, and their flames dance in the kitchen's air-conditioned wind.

"Ready," Jim says. He picks up the cake plate and, propping open the swinging door to the kitchen with his foot, enters the Sedaras' dining room with his mother-in-law behind him.

They all sing, "Happy birthday to you, happy birthday to you, happy birthday dear Maria," and Eliza adds the soprano harmony. "Happy birthday to you! What's the matter with Maria? She's okay!" It's the Fourth of July, not exactly Maria's birthday but close enough.

The former psychiatrist places the cake before his wife. It's a confectionary American flag, Carmela's idea, and Maria's raven hair silvers in the light of the candles. She blows just once, and the flames are out. Before Maria can do it, Eliza takes the knife and cuts the cake into large pieces.

Once assertive, Eliza's cheekbones have disappeared into a new, round expression reminiscent of the happy face that Ruth used to wear on a T-shirt. Jim can no longer see the bones in Eliza's legs, which now resemble thick tubes beneath her stockings. Her ribs, the outlines of which would have been visible two years ago, are today covered with a comfortable drapery of flab, especially in the twin spaces where her back meets her arms. Even cutting a cake, Eliza displays confidence, like she has been waiting her entire life to assume this new, expanded form. Had her eating disorder been another one of Jim's delusions from that strange summer? There's also a new formality to her dress. In a frilly silk blouse like something her mother might have worn for Ivy Day 1956, Eliza resembles a sorority president or head bank teller.

"How does it feel to be thirty-seven?" she asks Maria.

"Just like being seventeen, except now I'll have to fast tomorrow."

Eliza wags her finger at Maria in mock seriousness and says, "Don't ever forget. It's better to be fat and happy than skinny and mean."

Having completed medical school, Maria ignored her husband's warnings and matched into psychiatry. She began her internship four days ago. Jim could wisecrack about how things have changed, about how he would never have been released early on the Fourth of July when he started his training. Instead, he reaches for Maria's hand. In her white doctor's coat, still on, and her glasses, no longer just for reading, she reminds him of Ingrid Bergman in *Spellbound*, including the broadening shoulders and largish hips. It's Ruth's new favorite movie, and they watched it together during visiting hours.

Maria never really lost the weight after Paul's delivery, but it's a relief in a way. With each year and each pound, she becomes more graspable and more knowable. In thirty years, Maria will have taken on the spherical quality of her mother, and their marriage will have assumed its full quality of siblingship. After all, as Maria has told him, Catholics don't get divorced.

"You want a piece?" she asks her husband.

"Sure."

The Malorys take their seats at the opposite ends of the metal table that has sat in the Swedesboro dining room since at least Jim's original visit. When he first saw the house, it seemed cheap, even to a Lehighton boy, with its fake wood paneling, plastic slipcovered furniture, and fluorescent ceiling lights. Now he craves every plank of the home's apple-green aluminum siding. Angelo, dining the same night with Jim's mother in another, otherworldly location, has seeped into every part of the house. When the man died a year ago after a stroke, Carmela insisted that Jim sit at the head of the table, in Angelo's place, and that Maria sit at the opposite end. Jim would have thought this a form of mockery if Carmela wasn't devoid of sarcasm. So he obeyed.

After Angelo's death, Jim again suggested to Maria that they move to Swedesboro. With the new bridge, her drive to the Institute, where she would do her psychiatric residency, would be no longer than from Glenwyth. Also, it would be easier for the days when Jim had to work in South Philadelphia at the meat plant. She refused. Despite everything that had happened, there would be no move to New Jersey, Arizona, or anywhere else. Glenwyth was hers, and she wasn't about to be chased away. Nevertheless, the house on Barker's Mill shrank with each month that Paul grew, and Jim longed for the farm's flat acres. In the end, the Malorys moved into the Dixons' house on Wingohocking, and the bungalow's lack of space became an irrelevance.

"Cake!" Paul says.

Burtie sticks his finger through the icing and takes a big lick. "Umm. What's inside?"

"Wait your turn," Eliza says, and turns to Maria. "He's addicted to sugar, this one."

"Who wants coffee?" Jim asks, looking over at Jimmy. He has

given the drink to the young man at times, and it calms him, even though he still doesn't speak. Jimmy sees the pot and waves toward himself with his hand, making the birdsong he uses to signal his wants.

"I can give him a little bit, right?" Jim asks.

"If you want to be up with him all night," Maria says. "Remember I have to round tomorrow at 7:00 a.m."

He can hardly remember what rounding's like. Had Maria chosen to become a surgeon, which had become a brief interest during her final two years of medical school, they would be having dinner in the lobby of the University Hospital while Maria stood four floors above in an operating room holding a retractor.

"Are you going to visit Ruth tomorrow?" he asks, wondering if Maria's embarrassed to be working at the hospital where their daughter's been admitted as a patient.

"Yes," Maria says.

"I could come over in the afternoon."

"And who'll watch the kids?" Maria has a point, but it's always better when she makes it. Friday's one of the days when Carmela doesn't come to Glenwyth to watch Paul, Burtie, and Jimmy. As a result, Jim has to watch them while working from home on the telephone, taking calls from supermarket managers complaining about how wholesale beef prices just keep going up and up and up. Jim types their orders on the Selectric, and then, with the Magnafax Telecopier installed in Woody's former study, "faxes" them—that's what the Xerox salesman called it—to the main office of Sedara Meats at the Food Distribution Center in South Philadelphia. Renting for a hundred and fifty a month, the machine seems extravagant, but Jim has grown fond of the anonymity it provides. With these new, fantastic devices, he can be an actual businessman and justify his salary to Carmela, while mostly not having to leave the house.

"I can watch them," Eliza says, looking now like an ampler version of Julie Nixon.

"Such a good girl," Carmela says.

Ruth—because she's told everyone never to call her Ruthie anymore—was admitted for her third psychiatric hospitalization the night before Maria began her internship. Jim didn't think it was necessary—there wasn't a suicide attempt, even if there was cutting—but Maria overruled him. Dr. Santoni, reached by long distance and no doubt sitting on his deck overlooking Barnstable Harbor, agreed. This was going to be her last admission because Jim would do whatever was necessary to prevent another. What did they do anyway? Jim never even wanted Ruth to be seen by Santoni in the first place, but Maria made that decision. *He's the best, and he knows our family.* The second part was true, but Santoni, in diagnosing manic depression, was wrong.

There were problems with the Malorys, just like with every family, but Ruth had been so normal before that crazy summer. Or maybe not. To her credit, she hadn't smoked marijuana in a year. At least, that's what the drug tests said. Jim had hoped that the paranoia would fade with abstinence, and it had, somewhat. She hadn't been taking the lithium anyway. She said it made her stupid and fat. Even without it, her mind and body are different than they were.

Jim wants to tell her that it doesn't matter, that he still loves her. Things change. The most important thing is feeling better and being alive, but she's more interested in "cutting gills" for herself so she can breathe. Those were her words a few months ago.

"I'm glad that Loeb's the attending. He's good," Maria says, feeling confident, after four days of training, to opine on her colleagues. "He'll also stay in touch with Ed for discharge planning, although I don't imagine that will be for a while."

"She's not getting shock treatment," Jim says, having taken to speaking like a layman.

"We'll talk about that later," Maria says, leaning in towards his end of the table, settling the matter. Eliza looks nervously at her new parents.

"You don't recover the memory loss," he says. "She's going to need her memory when she starts college."

"Jim, she'll have to be alive to start college."

Carmela turns to her new pseudo-granddaughter. "Eliza, are you ready for your senior year?"

"Almost. I have three college essay drafts, but I'm not sure which to use." Eliza and Maria spent the days between medical school graduation and the start of internship touring the colleges and universities of the Northeast. They must have seen more than a dozen. Like a canny realtor, Maria saved Penn for last and has all but said she hopes Eliza goes there. It would be a reach, but you never know. Who would have imagined Jim being admitted twenty years ago? Ruth had also been invited on the tour, but she refused to go.

"Tell her what you're doing," Maria says.

"I'm working in a lab at Children's this summer," Eliza says, "in the new building in University City."

"Are you a candy striper?" Carmela asks.

"No. I'm working in an oncology lab." When Carmela looks puzzled, Eliza explains, "We inject cells with viruses and see if they turn into cancer."

"When did you learn to do all that?" Carmela asks.

"It's not that hard. You just spray liquid from one tube into another, and the viruses do the rest. The professor who runs the lab says cancer's going to be cured by the year 2000."

Before the summer when everything changed, Eliza had never seemed like a scholar, let alone a molecular biologist, but now she's often found with a stack of mimeographed scientific papers, sitting at Honey's old desk late into the night.

Eliza didn't change immediately. She was still thin and depressed that first fall, but the worse things got for Nixon, the better they got for Eliza. The man had won 520 electoral votes not two years ago, but now he has one foot in the grave and the other on a banana peel. Things had also looked good for Ruth in the spring of '72.

"You can visit me in my lab if you want," Eliza says to Carmela. "It's on the seventh floor. The hospital is beautiful. There are games for children right in the lobby, with bells and whistles, and everywhere, there's light."

"That's not like any hospital I've seen," says Carmela.

"The point is that you don't have to be scared when you're sick."

Maria smiles and says, "It is a beautiful place."

Jim has driven by the new hospital, but his thoughts turn more to the blackened stones of the original campus. That was Honey's hospital and stood among tenements in South Philadelphia, not far from Roseberry Street. This meant that for the year of Honey's childhood illness, she and Maria lived not twenty blocks from each other, more ancient history that nobody but Jim cares about.

"I understand," Carmela says. "It's not a scary place."

At least not on the surface, but how long till Maria finds out that she was right in '62 when she dropped out? Everything really is too bright, like staring into the sun.

"Just don't forget about high school," the grandmother continues. "It'll be gone, and you'll never get it back. Do you go on dates?"

"Nonna," Eliza says, "have you spoken with the average boy these days? All they want to do is smoke marijuana and drive Camaros."

Just like Quinton Graves. But the cars these days are weaker than even a few years ago, Detroit muscle wasting away, and to think that Ruth had seemed like the normal one. When was her last good day? Jim can't remember. She had actually gone back to Stroud's after that summer, but she wouldn't open a book. By October, Jim and Maria were sitting in the headmistress's office completing the withdrawal paperwork. Ruth was next enrolled in an all-girls Catholic boarding school in Massachusetts, but she flunked out in the spring of '73, having done no work there either.

"I think Jimmy's going to sleep tonight," Jim says, and hands the young man his cup. Jimmy may never talk, but he's had less than five tantrums in the fifteen months that he has lived with them. He sits calmly, looking at the trees or watching television, especially the static. He does it for hours. Paul and Burtie have become his older brothers, drawing him into their games, even as he holds faithful to his unknown orbit.

Eliza looks at her watch. "Do you mind if I head back?"

"We're not done yet," Maria says.

"I mean when we're done."

"Yes, but you're going to have to take the boys. And what about the fireworks?"

"I've seen them a million times," Eliza says, "and if I leave now, I can make it to the hospital by seven, which will give me an hour."

"I guess that Paul and Burtie could ride in the Lincoln with Jimmy and us," Maria says.

"Cool. Thanks."

"You have to be home by eleven."

"Eleven? I'm coming right home. I have a lab meeting tomorrow, and so I'm not going to the Steamfitter, okay?"

Jim's told the girl about the Steamy, an isolated roadhouse on 322 on the way into Swedesboro. In the old days, Jim had always wanted to go there, and now it's too late. Without a drink in two years, he has become one of those people who, without saying much, make others who drink feel like felons.

"Can I help you with the dishes before I go?" Eliza asks.

"No. Go see Ruth," Maria says.

"Okay," Eliza says, and hugs Carmela.

"I love you too," the woman says, and the girl leaves. Jim hears the Mustang step to life—weird to have Eliza Dixon in the driver's seat. The car has become old-fashioned-looking, but it still runs. Then there's the top, which now leaks in four places.

The Ford looks modern compared to Honey's Lincoln, which sits nearby. The Continental has "suicide" doors, and shouldn't the marketer who came up with that term have been fired? As far as Jim can tell, the Eldorado is the only car still in production with a soft-top, but word is that the '76s will be Cadillac's last convertible ever. Jim read that no one wants them anymore, but the idea seems preposterous. When Dave Black used to pull up in the '59 triple-white Eldo, Jim wanted nothing more.

"We'll get started on the dishes," Maria says to her mother.

"No. You have a long ride back with the shore traffic."

"You sure?"

"You have to be in the hospital tomorrow. All I have to make sure of is that I get up. I have so many secretaries and assistants, like your husband, that it's a breeze. It was much harder running the shop on Tasker."

Jim rises from the table. "Thank you, Carmela."

"It's like a family from Italy," she says, "everybody living together under one roof." On occasion, the seven of them have even piled into the Lincoln and gone to the A&P like an odd-lot Brady Bunch.

"You have to teach me how to make that gnocchi," Jim says to his mother-in-law, thinking of the meals he will be expected to make this week.

"Never," Carmela says. "The secret dies with me, and don't think you're going to talk it out of me when I come this week to watch the children."

"Do you want me to pick you up?"

"No. Mossie will drive me." Carmela has never gotten her driver's license, and she's running out of time. It wasn't a problem when Angelo was alive. He drove her everywhere, never bothered by it, perhaps remembering when roads were unclogged. Now, she hires her neighbors and friends, a dwindling motor pool, to transport her wherever necessary.

"That sounds good. What time do you think?" Jim asks.

"I'll go to seven-thirty Mass, and so I should be there by ten."

"You want lunch?"

"At ten? No. I want you to leave and come back for dinner. You need to relax." These were not the kind of words that Jim heard from his own mother. She was too poor to feel sorry for anyone, let alone him, the smart kid who would go to college and do all the rest.

"Thanks," Maria says, hugging her mother. Then the husband and wife of eighteen and a half years pack up the paraphernalia required in 1974 to care for two toddlers and a wordless adult. They carry out Paul to the Lincoln, Burtie following, and then returning, lead Jimmy to the car. Carmela comes out next, as she and Angelo used to do at the conclusion of any visit. There was always a farewell in the driveway and waves, as if the QE2 were departing Southampton.

Back then, the grandparents didn't leave until the car passed out of view, which took a few minutes given the size and flatness of the farm and its agricultural neighbors. That must have been Angelo's idea. Since his passing, Carmela has dispensed with the long goodbye and returns to the farmhouse when the Lincoln goes into reverse.

By the time the Continental, top up, crosses into Pennsylvania, Paul and Burtie have fallen asleep, and between them, Jimmy stares out the window, mesmerized by the passing cars. Maria drives. She never used to, but she insists on it now, as if Jim might run off the road. She puts on WIBG, with an unknown DJ blathering about something or other. The station's on the way out, all the good jocks are gone, and no one even listens to AM anymore. Then, after another five minutes of ads, the nameless record spinner plays *One Chain Don't Make No Prison.* How that's in the Top 40 is anyone's guess. The Four Tops have gone disco and lost their rhythm in the process, but they'll always remind Jim of Vietnam.

The Malorys say nothing of note to each other until the Glenwyth exit of the expressway when Maria says, "Damn it. We only have an eighth of a tank."

"I'll take it to the Arco tomorrow," Jim says. "Don't worry."

"We should sell this thing in the fall when convertible season's over," Maria says, as if she ever puts down the top. "Probably get more for it then, and anymore it costs an arm and leg to fill up."

Jim says nothing, remembering the days when gas was cheap and Honey Sharpe Dixon could be seen driving up and down Wingohocking, her blonde hair blowing in the wind. Those were the days when Quinton Graves did a hundred on the expressway.

"Are you okay?" Maria asks.

"Sure," Jim says.

"You were thinking about something."

"Well, I wonder about Quinton sometimes."

"Talk about a golden oldie."

"You know, sometimes Ruth says his name in her sleep."

"No, she doesn't."

"Let's change the subject," he says. "We're going to replace the Lincoln and then replace Santoni."

Maria takes her eyes off the road. "Why don't we start by having Ruth take her medication?"

"It's not about pills."

"That's what you tell her, and so she doesn't take them."

"She'll never be honest with Santoni. He knows too much about me and us."

"Will you leave this to me?" Maria asks, neglecting to add that he had his chance.

"She needs a higher dose of lithium." If only. Maria has been practicing for four days and already sounds Nilsonian.

"I'll stay out of it," he says.

She doesn't argue because they both know that he should stay out of it. Jim gave up psychiatry, but not at the insistence of the Pennsylvania Board of Medicine. After the madness of that summer had ended, there was a lot of explaining to do. Quinton had disappeared, and the FBI had its interviews. In the end, he was a missing person, and that was that. As improbable as it sounded, people eventually accepted what Jim said and what he believed. Having lost his love after driving her insane, Quinton had decided to start a new life. This student of the Mesoamerican World was probably in Peru or Uruguay or Tierra del Fuego. That Dr. Malory lost himself in a situation involving his daughter and a patient, a crisis that drove the patient to go missing, also became understandable.

There was even sympathy at the licensure hearing. Although they had not sued for money, Mr. and Mrs. Graves did try to banish Dr. Malory from medicine with a professional complaint, but the board members, doctors themselves, understood and defended him, offering little of the impartiality they were supposed to display. Captain James Malory was an Army veteran with traumatic neurosis. He had served his country, and the doctors on the board weren't hippies. They were still of the previous generation, having themselves been in Korea, Germany, or France. Maybe they had even met their own Quintons at different times and places.

When it was over, Jim still had his license and the VA job, and in Glenwyth, he in time became an object of fascination. He could have found new patients in the private practice, but he didn't want them. One part of his life had ended, and another had begun.

"She'll get better," he says, himself making one of those baseless, vapid statements about the mentally ill that he used to expect from others. "I know it in my heart."

"How about in your brain?" Maria asks, clearing her throat. "I'm sorry. I'm tired. I don't know how I'm going to make it through all this."

"With what we've been through, it can't help but be smooth sailing from here."

Softening, she smiles. "Look at all this life in our back seat."

"I guess it was meant to be."

"I guess it was."

In the immediate aftermath of that incredible summer, they saw little of Honey. It was in the following winter that she sent a card to Maria, and the two women met, the irony of it, at Wanamaker's. Shortly after that, Maria began driving Honey to doctors' appointments, and then, after the diagnosis of inflammatory breast cancer could no longer be hidden, to chemotherapy. Jim tried to contact Honey, but she never responded, and she never came to Barker's Mill again. With Ruth in Massachusetts, they didn't see much of Eliza, who became a better nurse to her mother in those final months than any of the paid professionals.

When Honey died, having achieved the emaciation that she always wanted, there was a cremation, no funeral, and the Malorys moved into the silver box high above Wingohocking, which Honey's estate had sold to Maria for a dollar. It was understood that she and Jim would care for Jimmy, Eliza, and Burtie, with help from trusts for which Maria but not Jim was a trustee.

That Jimmy couldn't talk might be seen as a burden by some, but to Jim, it was a relief. He had said everything that could ever be said, and being with Jimmy was like living in the trees with the birds. It would have made sense for Woody to step up to the job, but he disappeared. There didn't even appear to be a separation agreement, and he wasn't looking for custody. It was rumored that Woody was living in Turks and Caicos on a houseboat, but not even his parents knew.

Maria and Jim sold Barker's Mill six months later to a Chinese pharmaceutical engineer and his taciturn wife. It was a relief that the buyers had no idea about the backstory. They weren't interested in saying much at the closing. Their English wasn't great, and how could stories of block parties and porch card games hold the interest of two people who, the Malorys' realtor said, had survived the Cultural Revolution?

Jim and Maria never discussed Burtie's paternity and never will. But does Maria know, did Honey tell her everything on one of those trips to the chemotherapy suite? Maybe not. These days, the boy has started to look more like Woody than anybody else, and as time passes, Honey's assertions seem as unbelievable as anything from that deranged summer. Last week, Jim even had a dream where Honey came to him dressed in a top hat like Marlene Dietrich and told him that she had been kidding all along.

"I love you," he says to Maria.

She clears her throat again. She's spent a single night in the overnight call room and already sounds like she might be catching a cold.

When no words follow, Jim continues, "You've forgiven me for a lot."

"People are flawed," she says, "and anger corrodes the vessel that contains it." He's heard that somewhere before, maybe last Sunday. In addition to graduating from medical school, Maria has returned to the orthodox Catholicism of her youth. She says the Rosary every evening and tries whenever possible to attend daily

Mass, just like Carmela. It goes without saying that the seven of them—six when Ruth is away—go every Sunday to hear Father Pirrone at St. John's in Glenwyth. They even attend on Holy Days of Obligation, including solemnities that Sister Michael Frederick never mentioned. When Jim suggests that they take a week off here and there, maybe sleep in, he is ignored like another crazy person. That his mother had no time for religion in Lehighton, Maria has suggested, provides all the more reason that Jim should make time now.

We all should be grateful, Maria often says, but maybe she's happy to be alive. The eclampsia from Paul's birth had been followed by a hemorrhage. She had avoided a hysterectomy, and they could have had more children, but they won't. They both know it.

"I'm proud of you," he says, pulling down their visors to block the red sore of the setting sun. "With medical school and everything."

"We'll see." Maria doesn't mention their practicing together anymore, and she rarely talks about medicine, at least with him. Their conversations now revolve around diaper supply and whether they've run out of Hamburger Helper. For a while after Maria started medical school, Jim made detailed lists of the day's events, first regarding Paul and then for the whole family, but Maria seemed bored by these reviews. He likes when she listens to his feelings and shows interest in his domestic successes, but these days, she's always cutting to the solution, even when there's no specific problem.

"I think I might get a part-time job," he says, adding, "in psychiatry. Maybe I'll go back to the VA." She looks over at him, her face leaning towards laughter. "Sure," he continues. "At the VA, you don't even need malpractice insurance."

"Would they take you back?"

"Of course. All that stuff is ancient history." All that stuff like

Dave Black. It made perfect sense that Honey was dead and that Quinton had disappeared, but the vanishing of Black was incomprehensible. This was the man whom Jim and Angelo drank scotch with on the porch at Barker's Mill, the man whom Jim had saved from drowning. Dave loved Jim, that was obvious, and yet somehow had never been seen again after Jim's jaunt to Cape Cod. With all of his professional failures, Jim had succeeded in making Dave well, and now he was gone.

"But we don't need the money," Maria says.

"What?"

"Are you listening to me? You don't have to work."

"I do work, inside the home and for your mother's company. I sold $10,000 worth of sirloin last month."

"You know what I mean." Maria looks like she might pull over the car and scream at him, but she settles, and calmness flows over her. Maybe there's pity as well and a bit of love, even after everything. "I want you to be happy, and I thought this is what you wanted. You always said that this is what you wanted."

"It is."

"Okay, then. That settles it," she says, and the conversation's over. "Maybe we can trade this thing in for a station wagon? I hate this car."

~

Maria takes off her dress in the bedroom and exposes the creamy silken slip that guards her curves and the permanent pink crescent across her abdomen. Now both of their loins have been scarred. Wearing a rococo golden crucifix so detailed that Jesus is squirming, she nestles against her prayer stool and invokes the blood of the Madonna.

Nearly naked, Jim sits on the bed, searching closer to Earth for

Glenwyth through the floor-to-ceiling windows. Although the Malorys—or rather Maria—own every foot of land on the hill, he feels uncomfortable when they sleep with the curtains open, like someone might be looking in.

He picks up a magazine and flips to an article on Cambodia, something about Sihanouk and the king's deal with the Devil, but wasn't the Khmer Rouge supposed to be America's ally? Cronkite never said it, but everyone knew there was no winning. In 1970, Scotty and George knew. That crazy private in Snoul they'd been trying to rescue on that day, he knew. Maybe that's why he went crazy.

Maria startles. "The mail. Did you get it yesterday when I was on call?"

"No."

"I'm expecting my board scores."

"But the dean said that you scored in the ninety-ninth percentile."

"I want to see the paper," she says, setting the alarm for 4:30 a.m. and returning to her prayer.

"I'll go get it." He puts on his bathrobe and walks out into the house, the scene of so much that's been forgotten. He has a weird desire to check on the children but doesn't because he knows what he'll find. They'll be sleeping, without nightmares.

And he has to get the mail, anyway. They used to have porch delivery on Barker's Mill. Now he has to trudge all the way down the hill to Wingohocking and usually finds nothing but advertisements for baby formula and bills.

He walks out the front door and stands on the patio, looking ten miles in all directions. The fireworks have started somewhere over Philadelphia. What an incredible view. Jim can see the Roman candles, poppers, chrysanthemums, and crosettes without leaving his own home. There's also no sound, which makes the spectacle easier to deal with. You could almost forget what gunpowder and flames were really meant to do.

When he makes it down the hill, there's no letter from the National Board of Medical Examiners, but there's an envelope missing a return address. It's postmarked Glenwyth, Penna, July 1, 1974. A distant voice tells him to throw it into the bushes or hide it unopened, but he rips the seal and reads the page. It's without a watermark and typed in a font of perfect, untraceable Courier.

Dear Jimmy,

I know this letter may come as a shock, but you can't have the Eldorado. Nothing personal, but it's gone to heaven. Better that way. I've been back. Of course I have to be careful, not like I can just walk down Oregon Pike smoking a cigar. If I did, I could get you tangled up in something not very nice. I come for visits, here and there, to see how you're doing. Sorry that I have to stay in the shadows. I'm sure you can understand. But how are you? You did the right thing with Maria, and I heard about Honey Dixon. Maybe there is karma, like with our friend Quinton.

Can you please understand that it had to be this way? You cured me, but it had to be this way. You may think I'm crazy, but you would have done the same for me that I did for you. I know it in my heart. I hope we meet again. You may think you've lost the power to heal, may even think that you never had it, but please don't forget: You saved my life, and I saved yours. I will never forget you, and please remember: Our time is forever.

Love,

P.S. For your own sake, burn this letter after reading it.

An ashen smudge sits next to the space of Dave's non-signature, and Jim knows it's the final, infinitesimal remainder of what had been Quinton Graves.

Jim falls to his knees, shaking. His airway almost seals, and he can only hiss. A death rattle? Of a sort. It had to be this way. It had to be this way.

After ten minutes, all the lights flip on at the top of the hill. When Maria gets to him, he hands her the letter, and she reads it at arms' length under the streetlights.

A few miles away on Wingohocking, not in Glenwyth but in a West Philadelphia psychiatric ward, Ruth awakens with a start to the sound of Quinton's voice, coming not from a bush but from somewhere she doesn't know.

He tells her that he'll never leave her, and she knows that he never will.

ABOUT ATMOSPHERE PRESS

Atmosphere Press is an independent, full-service publisher for excellent books in all genres and for all audiences. Learn more about what we do at atmospherepress.com.

We encourage you to check out some of Atmosphere's latest releases, which are available at Amazon.com and via order from your local bookstore:

Icarus Never Flew 'Round Here, by Matt Edwards
COMFREY, WYOMING: Maiden Voyage, by Daphne Birkmeyer
The Chimera Wolf, by P.A. Power
Umbilical, by Jane Kay
The Two-Blood Lion, by Nick Westfield
Shogun of the Heavens: The Fall of Immortals, by I.D.G. Curry
Hot Air Rising, by Matthew Taylor
30 Summers, by A.S. Randall
Delilah Recovered, by Amelia Estelle Dellos
A Prophecy in Ash, by Julie Zantopoulos
The Killer Half, by JB Blake
Ocean Lessons, by Karen Lethlean
Unrealized Fantasies, by Marilyn Whitehorse
The Mayari Chronicles: Initium, by Karen McClain
Squeeze Plays, by Jeffrey Marshall
JADA: Just Another Dead Animal, by James Morris
Hart Street and Main: Metamorphosis, by Tabitha Sprunger
Karma One, by Colleen Hollis
Ndalla's World, by Beth Franz
Adonai, by Arman Isayan
The Journey, by Khozem Poonawala

ABOUT THE AUTHOR

David Procaccino lives near Philadelphia with his wife and family.

Milton Keynes UK
Ingram Content Group UK Ltd.
UKHW040800131123
432470UK00008B/511

9 781639 889129